"If you burn my castle you are choosing to kill me, Jehan. As surely as if you plunged a dagger into my heart."

He pulled her closer, forcing her to arch her neck in order to meet his gaze. She spread her hands against his chest and felt his heart pounding beneath the layers of chain mail and padding. She felt as if she were standing in the middle of a swift-running river, and she was losing the struggle to maintain her footing. Danger, desire, and desperation raged in her blood.

He is your enemy. The refrain was naught but a whisper now, for no enemy would look at her as Jehan was now looking at her. He looked tormented, as tormented as she felt, as his gaze devoured her. She knew no enemy would stand before her for so long, wanting her, yet refusing to take her. She was defenseless. It was his honor that stayed him.

"Very well." His voice was ragged. "For you, Aliénor, I will do this thing."

Relief washed over her, mingling with astonishment. *For my sake,* she thought. *For my sake alone.*

"Kiss me, Aliénor. Let that be your thanks."

She didn't hesitate. She wound her arms around his neck. His lips met hers, hungrily, and passion exploded in her body. There was no control, no struggle, no hesitation. She clung to him as he lifted her off the ground and whirled her around, only to put her on the ground again and kiss her more deeply. She moaned in pleasure as his hands swept over her back to rest in the hollow at the base of her spine. Passion possessed her body, like a demon, and she never wanted to be exorcised from so wondrous a feeling. . . .

MY LOVING ENEMY

LISA ANN VERGE

POCKET BOOKS

New York   London   Toronto   Sydney   Tokyo   Singapore

This book is a work of fiction. Names, characters, places, and incidents are either products of the author's imagination or are used fictitiously. Any resemblance to actual events or locales or persons, living or dead, is entirely coincidental.

An *Original* Publication of POCKET BOOKS

POCKET BOOKS, a division of Simon & Schuster Inc.
1230 Avenue of the Americas, New York, NY 10020.

ISBN: 0-671-74073-3

First Pocket Books printing April 1993

10 9 8 7 6 5 4 3 2 1

POCKET and colophon are registered trademarks of Simon & Schuster Inc.

Cover art by Alessandro Biffignandi

Printed in the U.S.A.

MY
LOVING
ENEMY

Chapter

1

Gascony, 1355

"I MUST KNOW IF PAPA HAS SUCCEEDED. I MUST KNOW NOW."
Aliénor de Tournan glared at her thirteen-year-old brother
from the height of her mare. "I'm going, Laurent. You can't
stop me, so give me the reins."

Laurent's chin puckered like a dried fruit. His shoulder-
length hair, the same rich honey color as her own, shimmered in the autumn sun. He pulled the reins tighter until
the sleek-coated mare snorted and tossed her head against
the restraint. "You should wait here in the castle with the
rest of us."

"I've already waited two weeks for Papa to come back. I
won't wait another moment."

"Patience is a virtue—"

"A virtue I'm in no mood to cultivate, not now." She
reached down and tried to capture the calfskin reins from
her brother's sure grip. "Besides, if Papa has failed, I'll have
a lifetime to develop patience—in a cold convent cell."

His pale face flushed. "You shouldn't scorn such things."

"I'd rather throw myself off the ramparts than return to
that convent."

"Aliénor!"

"Every single day was exactly alike, full of devotions and
work and little else, with nothing to look forward to but the
coldness of the grave."

"Stop!"

1

"And you know very well that if Papa doesn't recapture my dowry lands, that's *exactly* where I'm going to spend the rest of my life!"

Her brother lifted his folded hands to his lips and murmured a prayer. Aliénor released an exasperated sigh. She was wasting her time telling morbid tales of convent life to her brother, when she should be yanking the reins from him and galloping out of the castle. She tucked a wayward tress of blond hair beneath her silk veil and glanced anxiously at the crenellated ramparts. In the gently sloping valleys of Gascony, beyond these castle walls, her father and all his men-at-arms marched toward Castelnau-sur-Arrats, carrying the news that would determine the course of the rest of her life.

It had been two years since a certain brash, bachelor knight had seized the castle and lands that were her dowry. She had spent all that time anxiously awaiting her father to return from fighting private wars in Italy. When he finally appeared at the castle gates two weeks before, he had set off immediately to recapture her lands. Now he had come back. Her waiting was over. Nothing—and certainly not her pious, protective younger brother—was going to make her stay in this castle one second longer.

"Give them to me, Laurent." She held out her hand. "Don't force me to dismount and take them from you."

"I'll give them to you on one condition," he said as she began rearranging her skirts. "You must vow that you'll ride no faster than a canter."

She lifted one fine, pale brow. Her brother was nine years her junior. Her gaze fell to his twisted, useless foot. She never took advantage of his weakness, but today Laurent was testing the limits of her patience. "If I dismount, you know I could wrestle those reins out of your hands."

"I won't help you remount."

She glanced around the busy courtyard. "I'll find Elie."

"Elie's too busy carrying more wood into the castle."

"Then I'll order one of the pages to help."

"If you try I'll make sure you soil that surcoat." He

gestured to the embroidered, crimson silk tunic. "I know you won't greet Father so dirty."

"You stubborn little wretch." She glared at him. Usually Laurent was the most sweet-tempered of the Tournans. She wondered why he chose this time to show the stubborn streak that flowed in their shared blood. "What's *wrong* with you?"

"I'll tell you." He tilted his puckered chin. "I keep thinking of what happened to that pilgrim. The one who was traveling to Compostela."

"That pilgrim was thrown from his horse because he was racing over the roads during heavy rains—"

"His body shattered upon the rocks, like one of the wooden dolls I make for the village children."

She winced.

"I see the wildness in your eyes," he continued, stepping closer to the mare, "and I don't want to find you lying somewhere along the rocky path."

"If my time has come, God will take me. You or I cannot change that."

"Please, Aliénor."

Her fingers curled over the saddle. He squinted up at her with eyes as dark as midnight—a child's eyes—and for the first time she noticed they were filled with fear and worry. She released a long sigh and spoke to him in their Gascon dialect. "Ah, *frai,* you know I ride well. But if this is all you want, then I'll promise not to race—"

"You must *vow,"* he insisted. "And you must make the vow on the souls of those dead from the plague."

"You are as morbid as Death itself." There were too many souls dead from the great plague, too many souls to count. Their two older brothers had died from the plague, far away in Italy. An uncle had died in Castétis, leaving her that castle for her dowry. The villagers had fallen like sheaves of wheat under Death's lethal scythe, leaving only a few dazed survivors to till the fields. Though the last of the victims had died six years before, the scars from the black plague still remained, visible and sore, on the land and on her heart.

"Will you vow?"

"Yes, yes, if that's what you wish, though by my troth I don't understand why you worry so much!" She held out her open palm. "I vow to ride no faster than a canter today—on the souls of those dead from the plague."

He crossed himself and then held the reins up to her. She yanked them from his grip and kicked her mare. The chestnut-colored horse eagerly surged forward and headed directly for the open, gaping portal of the castle. Aliénor leaned over the mare. A page scurried out of her path as she passed beneath the rounded arch of the castle entrance into the shadow of the tower. As they emerged into the brilliant autumn sunshine, the horse's hooves clattered on the wooden drawbridge, but the sound dulled to a muted thudding as the mare's hooves sank deep in the muddy earth of the open field. The skirts of Aliénor's surcoat flapped against her legs as she kicked the beast into a canter. She held the reins tightly. The horse battled against the restraint, with impatience as palpable and quivering as her own.

The rolling lands of her father's domain stretched in all directions. She glanced to the west, past the churning, gurgling river Arrats, which curved its way around the castle hillock, but saw no sign of her father's contingent in the distance. She scanned the southern horizon, where the faintest outline of the Pyrenees was visible through the crystalline air, then she focused on the eastern hills. Now that the morning fog had burned off, the long, wide valley gleamed a pale ochre, and its hollow was dotted with cows and sheep feeding off the stubble of the harvested fields. Upon the southeastern slopes, the outlines of fig trees shimmered in the light. Through their well-picked branches she could see grapevines, still laden with the last of the plump green grapes that twined around the straight trunks. She knew Papa would be coming through this valley, from the east. Beyond those distant slopes lay Castétis, the castle that would have been her dowry.

She nudged her mare toward the path that led down to the cluster of earth and half-timbered houses that hugged the base of the slope. As she cleared the rocky edge and began the descent, she noticed the crowd of villagers gathered near the muddy road. They stared eastward. She followed the direction of their gazes and sucked in her breath.

Papa! He was so close, just emerging from the small grove of fig trees at the edge of the fields. Unconsciously, she urged her mare into a faster pace. The mare obliged with a gallop down the boggy, crumbling, steep road. Mud splattered on the skirts of her tunic. With a quick, guilty flash of remembrance, she reined the horse to a slower pace, gently cursing her brother for trying to restrain her, especially now, when her fate awaited just beyond the village.

She stared at the contingent. The brilliant blue and green colors of the standard of the Vicomte de Tournan flapped in the southeastern wind. She counted the number of men and wondered why Papa had returned with so few when he had set out with so many. She searched for bloodstains, for wounds, for anything—*anything*—that would tell her whether her father had succeeded.

He must have won. She felt the first quiver of uncertainty. What if Papa brought bad news? What if he had failed to recapture her dowry lands? Perhaps Laurent was right: Wouldn't it have been better to wait inside, to savor the last precious minutes of her freedom? She shook her head as the horse continued its canter down the steep road. She remembered, all too well, the dark year when the plague cast its black shadow over the land. During the months she and Laurent had huddled in the castle, she'd wanted to go out and face Death—dare it—rather than wait inside, ill-protected and uncertain. Now that she had a choice, she would rather face her future than cower and wait for it to find her.

She knew very well what would be her inevitable fate if Papa failed. But if Papa succeeded . . . she would have a dowry. A rich dowry was the only thing that could bring a twenty-two-year-old maiden a worthy husband—a husband who didn't mind that the first bloom of youth had faded from her cheeks. There was a wealth of unmarried knights throughout Gascony, in the kingdoms of the Pyrenees, in the eastern holdings of Toulouse, and in the northern lands belonging to the King of France. Certainly, if Papa had succeeded, she could find another husband. Three times already she had failed to marry. The man to whom she was promised in youth died of a fever before he reached fourteen, the age when a man was permitted to wed. The bridegroom her father had hastily found when she was twelve years of age had subsequently died in the plague. Then, two years before, that *thief* had stolen her lands while her father was abroad in Italy, forcing her third husband-to-be to find another wife—one with a suitable dowry.

It was all because of the war, she thought angrily, the endless, bloody war between the French king and the English king. She had never known a time without strife, either between kings, or between the feuding barons of Gascony. Thibaud, her great-uncle, had tried a hundred times to explain the intricacies of the present war to her. Two hundred years before, Eleanor of Aquitaine had brought her lands as a dowry to the English throne. The English king had thus become the Duke of Aquitaine and, therefore, a vassal of the French king. This had been an intolerable situation for over two centuries. Now, Thibaud told her, it was the English King Edward III's somewhat legitimate claim to the French throne that had caused so much trouble over the past thirty years.

She did not completely understand what caused all the fighting, but she did understand that if it weren't for the continuous warfare between those two kings, that bold, landless knight would never have dared to steal her dowry lands. The knight was Gascon, like her family, but *he* was a loyal vassal of the Prince of Wales. *He* was a vassal of the English, whereas the Tournans were staunch supporters of the French king. If their loyalties had been the same, she could have appealed to their mutual sovereign for the return of the estate; but since their loyalties were different she could appeal only to her champion, Papa. Furthermore, her lands were right in the middle of the beleaguered border between the English holdings in Aquitaine and the French holdings in Toulouse. The constant raids, battles, and confusion over which sovereign controlled what lands made unprotected castles like Castétis ripe for capture by wily knights.

Knights like Jehan de St. Simon.

How she hated that man. She hated the very sound of his name. It curdled on her tongue, for certainly it was blasphemous for a thief and a coward to bear so brashly the name of a saint and an apostle. The thought of this man filled her head with what her brother would call unholy thoughts, if he ever knew them, but she couldn't help herself. Jehan de St. Simon had stolen more from her than land and a castle. He had stolen her future. Christian or not, she could not find charity in her heart for the likes of him.

She started as Papa suddenly glanced up, past the crowd of villagers, to where she descended to greet him. She couldn't see his expression behind the lowered visor of his basinet, and she wondered why he still wore the uncomfortable iron helmet when he was so close to home. Her father's short tunic was torn slightly across the chest, but no blood stained the blue and green fibers, nor the eagle embroidered in gold thread in the center. His warhorse rode briskly, tossing his head as he approached the villagers. She pulled her mare to a stop just beyond the crowd, forcing herself to have *some* patience, when all she wanted to do was push through the peasants and demand answers from her father.

Papa searched in a pouch attached to his jeweled baldric and tossed a few silver coins over his vassals' heads. His horse nosed his way through the scrambling bodies. She noticed that one knight wore a bloodstained tunic. She scanned the rest of the men-at-arms. One held a mangled shield, and another tucked a dented helmet under his arm. Several lengths behind the main contingent, a knight rode with a man slung across his horse. There had been a battle, she thought; a recent battle.

The men were uncharacteristically quiet. Usually the villagers' greeting would be met either with great jubilation

—with the warriors dragging the prettiest peasant women upon their horses—or with anger and curses, depending upon whether the recent quest had been successful. But there were no cries at all, at least not from the men. They plodded stoically, in almost dutiful silence, behind Papa. She waited for someone to call out for wine or meat. As Papa drew closer, her heart sank.

He stopped in front of her. He unhooked the chain-mail aventail attached to his helmet and lifted it off his head. A scarlet slash stained his cheek and nose, discoloring his usually swarthy, hard-planed face. He twisted in his seat and handed his helmet back to his squire, then turned and fixed his black gaze on his daughter's face.

"I should have known you'd be here, impatient to know my news."

The words surged to her tongue. "Well, my lord? Did you succeed in capturing the castle?"

"What? No words of welcome? I should think they'd have taught you better in the convent in which you spent your youth."

"They taught me nothing but useless things, Papa. Reading Latin and playing the lute."

"You didn't even bring me wine." He spurred his charger and headed up the slope. She turned her mare around and rode beside him. "You should have greeted me with wine and meat. We've ridden hard this day, and fought even harder, and you meet me with nothing but impatience." He looked at her. The harsh, weathered lines of his swarthy face crinkled in a humorless smile. "Fear not, Daughter. We'll marry you off yet."

"Papa, please!"

"We didn't capture the castle." He watched her face. "We captured something far better than the castle. We caught a means to get the castle and, at the same time, revenge."

"You speak in riddles."

He jerked his head toward his contingent. "Jehan de St. Simon rides with us."

"What!"

"He is my prisoner." His stiff smile widened, showing his yellowed teeth. "His ransom will be your dowry, my daughter, and our revenge."

She was stunned into silence. Papa had *not* captured her castle, but he had captured the knight—the notorious knight who had stolen her lands. She knew, instinctively, that her father would make him pay dearly for his freedom. He would accept no less than the return of her lands as his ransom.

Her lips spread in a quivering smile.

"Did you think I'd fail you?"

"I didn't know what to think." She gestured to the men who followed. "Half the contingent is gone, and these men are so quiet—"

"They are fools!" He glared over his shoulder to his silent vassals. "They are fools who nearly chose defeat over victory. I swore to regain those lands, and I will do as much, before the rains of winter. Come, my hunger is sharp."

She urged her mare into a canter as her father rode briskly up the hill. She curled her fingers into her palms, trying to contain her growing excitement. *Papa has succeeded. I shall be married!* All her fears faded away like shadows melting beneath the force of a brilliant summer sun.

She rode briskly over the wooden drawbridge, followed by the bulk of her father's contingent. She tossed the reins to a page and dismounted. She raced after Papa as he walked toward *Maman,* who looked thin and regal as she stood with her head bowed and her face almost obscured by the crisp white linen of her veil and wimple. Aliénor stopped dutifully by her mother's side, ignoring her frown of disapproval, and watched the Vicomte's men ride into the castle. She realized that only her father's vassals remained; all the mercenaries were gone. She eagerly sought the growing crowd for a glimpse of Jehan de St. Simon.

"Do you seek proof of my success, Daughter?" Her father lowered the wineskin *Maman* had given him, and droplets of the liquid glistened in his dark beard. "Do you want to see the bold knight who stole your lands?"

"Yes, my lord!" *Oh, yes, yes, Papa!* She wanted to see him—she wanted to lay eyes on the man who had caused her so much grief. Never, in the two years she had cursed the name of Jehan de St. Simon, did she expect to have the opportunity to face the villainous knight. At best, she had hoped her father would retrieve her castle by force, either while Sir Jehan was abroad or by killing him in the process. Only in her dreams had she faced the wretched knight and vented the fullness of her wrath.

What sweet justice! She scoured her memory for French curses. She suspected the knight would speak French, rather than her own *langue d'oc*. She dismissed her convent training, which banned the best and the basest phrases from her lips. She didn't need to be a maiden before this knightly dog; he had caused her too much suffering.

The sound of a single horse's hooves clicked over the courtyard. Her father spread his arm in the direction of the prisoner. "Behold the bold Jehan de St. Simon."

The words that surged to her lips lodged in her throat like a lump of lead. Her smile faded. She stared at the slumped knight. He wore a short tunic, but even at this close range she couldn't see the colors of his heraldry. He was covered, from head to foot, in his own blood.

She frowned. Of course he was wounded. Sir Jehan was known to be a formidable knight, one who would not surrender easily. It must have taken a dozen men to subdue him, a dozen men to wound him badly enough that he could be taken prisoner. But there was no joy in venting her long-standing rage against a wounded man. It would have to wait until he recovered.

"Look at him, slumped like a dog," her father said, interrupting her thoughts. "He dared to fight us all. He knows now that no man can steal from the Vicomte de Tournan without punishment."

Papa's face was dark and crumpled in anger. She felt a short, sharp quiver of fear. She turned and looked at St. Simon more closely. Fresh blood still soaked through his ragged tunic, the chain-mail chausses on his legs, and stained the steel of his shoes. Papa had punished him, indeed. As she counted the ragged slices on his tunic, she slowly realized that St. Simon was more than just wounded.

He was near death.

Her stomach tightened in panic. He could not die—not now, not yet! He couldn't die in her father's house, not until Castétis was securely in her father's hands! What was Papa thinking, to wait so long to bring this dying knight to her attention, while he quaffed wine and parried words with her? She hated the vile knight as much as did her father— perhaps more—but to have such an important prisoner so close to death was folly beyond words. If Sir Jehan died in Castlenau, the name of Tournan would be scorned all over Aquitaine, even as far as the French court in Paris and the English court in Bordeaux. Furthermore, a dead prisoner cannot pay ransom. If the knight died before ransom was arranged, then Castétis would go to his liege lord, the Prince of Wales. Papa would never be able to wrest control of the land from such a powerful prince.

Abruptly, she crossed the distance that separated her from Sir Jehan.

"Away from that vile thief! You'll not touch him, not while I'm your father!"

She stopped in front of Sir Jehan's horse. A cold shiver of fear straightened her spine. She turned and faced him. "His wounds should be tended, my lord. Else he could die."

"Then he'll die, and Hell will have one more thief."

"But my lord—"

"Do you defy me!" He glared at her. "Worthy knights have died for your sake. Is this how you honor their memory?"

The horses in the yard pranced restlessly. The clicking of their hooves was the only sound in the courtyard. She stared at her father, and slowly she began to understand why the Vicomte's men remained so silent, why such a strange pall hung over the victorious army. If Sir Jehan died, they would soon be fighting the forces of England.

Her palms grew cold and damp. Strange, almost reddish

lights burned in her father's black eyes. Once, when he was in a rage like this, she had watched him beat his best hunting dog into a pulp of quivering blood and fur after the hound had failed to corner a ten-point stag. She glanced around the courtyard for Laurent, hoping her brother had the sense to hide from her father's wrath.

She knew what she had to do, duplicitous though it was. Later, Laurent would demand she say penance for this lie, but she would rather pray her way out of the sin than let this knight die. She lowered her eyes and sank to her knees. She bent her head in submission. "I beg your forgiveness, my lord, and I am forever grateful for what you and your knights have done." She spread her hands. "I shall submit to your will, *mon père.*"

The Vicomte grunted. She heard his sabatons clank against the weathered stones as he turned and walked toward the castle. "Put the thief in the northwest tower to rot," he bellowed, "until I find a better punishment for him. I'll kill any man who dares to aid him."

She remained on her knees until she heard the heavy oak door of the castle slam loudly behind her father's footsteps. Then she rose and brushed the soil from her silk surcoat. She knew that when Papa emerged from his rage he would regret his orders. He would do what he could to amend his mistakes. She would make sure her father had that chance. The death of St. Simon would not be the cause of the fall of the house of Tournan.

She would see to it herself.

Aliénor waited late into the night for the muted sounds of drunkenness to die in the great hall. When the last voice had faded into silence, she waited a little longer, then tossed off the squirrel-fur coverlet and pulled open the velvet curtains that surrounded her bed. Her chamber lay at the back of the castle, against the chemise wall; thus only two arrow-slits lit the room, along with the dim glow of burning embers in the small hearth. Margot, her chambermaid, slept soundly on her pallet.

Aliénor struggled into her thin shift, then searched blindly under the squirrel coverlet until she found the fur-lined surcoat she had hidden earlier in the day. She pulled it over her head. The two garments were no match for the cold October drafts, and she was tempted to find a mantle in the carved oak chest that lay at the base of her bed; but she might wake Margot in the process, and no one, not even her chambermaid, must know what she was about to do. She picked up the unlit tallow candle that rested on the floor and took the small sack she had hidden under her pillow. As she slipped barefoot over the dry rushes, she fastened the buttons that ran up the front of her surcoat.

In the hallway formed by the wooden screens that separated her room from her brother's, she heard the snores of the knights rising from the staircase. To her right was the solar, where her mother now slept, and, further, the passageway to the large square tower, the donjon. Briefly, she considered passing through her mother's chamber and going outdoors by way of the donjon, but she knew that even if *Maman* didn't wake at her passing—her mother was a light sleeper—then one of the servants sleeping in the tower would undoubtedly wake as she tried to climb over the prone bodies in the darkness. Though the great hall was filled with drunken knights, she knew that they were unlikely to stir at the sound of her footsteps.

She turned left and followed the dark corridor to the top of the narrow, steep steps. She placed a hand on the stone wall and with the other lifted her skirts as she descended. The stairway was as dark as pitch—the rushlights had sputtered out hours before—but she did not hesitate; she knew the stairs well and had no need of light. At the lower level she paused and listened for sounds in the pantry or the buttery, for often the servants stayed awake long after the feast was over, to clean up the refuse in the hall. When she was sure all was still, she headed through the narrow passage, past the screens, into the vaulted great hall.

The embers of a fire still glowed in the massive fireplace, throwing a red-orange light over the scattered bodies of her father's vassals. One of the mastiffs that slept in the room lifted his head and sniffed the air. Seeing her, the dog thumped his tail against the wooden floorboards. A second hound heard the first and lifted his head in curiosity. As Aliénor crossed the hall to the arched wooden door, she heard the click of the hounds' nails as, one by one, the dogs rose from their slumber and crossed the hall to join her. She pushed open the door and swiftly herded them out into the chill October air. Then, without turning to see if anyone had awakened, she closed the door firmly behind her.

The courtyard was bathed in the pristine light of the stars. No clouds obscured the sky, but the frigid wind from the Pyrenees—the *autan* wind—swept through the courtyard, scattering dried leaves along the beaten earth. *Bent d'autan, Ploujo douman,* she thought, absently repeating the peasant prediction of rain. Hugging her arms, she descended the stairs to the courtyard and headed to the inviting warmth of the kitchens.

She passed through the open portal. The slumbering kitchen servants lay clustered near three enormous hearths. Remnants of the evening's feast covered the work tables: chicken and pork pies, large, half-eaten chunks of boiled beef, rectangular loaves of trencher bread, and earthen jugs of hypocras, the heady spiced wine her father liked so much. The dogs lifted their noses and trotted to the tables, jumped until their front legs rested on the edge, then sampled the food within their reach. Aliénor hissed at them and they fell back to the floor, looking at her sheepishly.

The servants were not disturbed by her entrance; they were accustomed to people entering and leaving the room and slept through any interruption. She noticed one large, curled figure apart from the others. She rounded one of the work tables and bent close to him.

"Elie," she whispered, touching his shoulder. "Wake up, Elie. I need you."

The boy's eyes opened sleepily, then widened as they focused on her. She lifted a finger to her lips.

"I need your help."

Elie nodded without hesitation. His thick lips lolled open and his eyes were still glazed with sleep. As he rose from his makeshift bed of dried hay to a height of over six feet, she started; Elie seemed to grow taller and more muscular with each passing day. When she had first seen him, over a year before, he was no taller than she. He had easily grown a head taller in the past year. If the boys who had once tormented him could see him now, she thought, they wouldn't dare hang the witless, burly orphan from a Maypole and burn him with glowing ends of tinder. In his rage, Elie could now crush them with a single blow.

Wordlessly, she handed Elie a wooden platter and pointed to what she wanted: a large piece of cold meat, a loaf of trencher bread, the shriveled, ashen carcass of a well-cooked duck, a jug of hypocras and one of water. Wrapping her sack around her arm, she dipped the wick of her tallow candle into the embers in one of the fireplaces and removed it as the flame flared. Then, with her dogs and Elie in tow, she left the warm kitchen.

The dogs jumped and whined around Elie, who held the food. Aliénor clicked her tongue at them until they walked obediently, if sullenly, to her side. When they reached the entrance to the northwest tower, she ordered them to stay, then pushed open the door. Below her, at the bottom of the spiral staircase, she saw a faint glow. She shielded her candle from eddies of wind as Elie followed and closed the door behind him. The small tower smelled of moss and earthy rot. She lifted her skirts from the stairs as she descended to the bottom room.

"Who's there?"

She did not stop in her pace. "It's Aliénor de Tournan. I've brought food for the prisoner." She rounded the last curve of the staircase and faced the guard at the doorway to the cell. His sword was unsheathed, but the point lay against the ground.

"The Vicomte said that no one is to see the prisoner."

"I've come to bring him food."

The guard staggered a bit, as if he had drunk too much

wine from the freshly tapped cask at dinner. "But the Vicomte—"

"The Vicomte is not himself today," she interrupted. "In the midst of his victory, he forgot to feed and care for our prisoner."

"He told me the knight is not to be fed."

She feigned surprise. She too had heard her father's orders as he roared them across the trestle tables at dinner when one of his vassals, Sir Rostanh, had requested permission to send Sir Jehan food and wine. Her father had risen in rage, defiled the name of St. Simon, and refused the request. Behind the curtains where she and her mother ate their dinner, Aliénor had burned in shame. He risked enough by forbidding her to care for the knight's wounds, but to treat St. Simon so badly was to disregard all the dictates of chivalry. How could Papa so blatantly flout honor in front of his own vassals?

These rages would be the death of him, she thought. They engulfed him and his common sense for days. As had happened all the other times, the rage would dissipate by the end of the week and her father would do what he could to rectify the damage he had done. Until then she was determined to salvage the name of Tournan—and the fortunes of the family—by saving the knight's life.

"Come, Rudel. You've been my father's vassal for many years." She stepped closer to the guard. "Surely you recognize that he is but angry, and it will pass."

"And, with it, my life, if I defy his orders."

"Do you prefer to be punished by my father's hand, or die by the hand of the Prince of Wales?"

The guard quieted. Sensing her advantage, she placed her free hand on his arm. "The Vicomte will never know I was here," she continued. "If I don't tend this knight, he'll surely die. In a few days, when his rage passes, Papa will be grateful that his faithful servants did not allow this knight to die while he was not himself."

"If St. Simon harms you—"

"Elie is with me." She gestured into the gloom behind her.

The guard instinctively crossed himself as he caught sight of the half-witted boy. "Besides, the knight is too wounded to strike," she continued. "He may already be dead."

The guard thought a moment, then reached inside the pouch attached to the belt around his hips and pulled out an iron key. "I suppose it's the least St. Simon deserves, after all that has happened." He fumbled with the key until it scraped into the lock. He pulled the door wide, then took the tallow candle from Aliénor's hand, thrust it into the small room, glanced about, then gestured. "There's the knight."

She peered into the gloom and saw a body lying motionless against the far wall. "Keep the door open. Elie and I shall enter. You stay outside. We'll be done soon enough."

She took the candle and entered the dank room. Elie followed, placing the wine and food near the entrance. She cautiously approached the knight and knelt not far from his side. He was a large man, larger than she had thought when she'd seen him in the courtyard. His head lolled to one side. He still wore his chain mail and armor plates at his elbows and knees, but his baldric and all its attached weapons had been removed. The blood she had seen streaming over his face was now dark and congealed. She wondered if he were sleeping, unconscious . . . or dead.

She reached out to touch his skin, biting her lip in fear it would be cold and lifeless under her touch.

The knight suddenly came to life. She cried out as he encircled her wrist with his hand. She glanced up and found herself riveted by clear blue eyes. Elie moaned behind her, and the guard rushed in and drew his sword. St. Simon's words rose loud and clear in the room.

"Call off your guards, woman, or I vow I shall crush your bones into powder."

Chapter

2

"DON'T, BOTH OF YOU," ALIÉNOR SAID BREATHLESSLY. "STAY back."

She winced as the knight tightened his grip around her wrist, as if to prove that he had the strength to crush it. She noticed, fleetingly, that he spoke her Gascon dialect, rather than French. His matted, bloody hair hung over his forehead. His eyes, bright and blue and fogged with pain, bored at her from beneath the pitch-black locks. She realized that, despite the iron grip around her wrist, this man was too wounded to rise, too weak to fight Elie and the guard, and in too much pain even to hold her wrist much longer. She waited for his weakness to show.

"What's this?" His feverish gaze swept over her face and down the length of her body. "Is the Vicomte so much a coward that he sends a woman to kill me?" His glare intensified. "Or is this my last night of pleasures 'ere I go before God?"

She jerked away instinctively, but her wrist was locked in his grip. "Release me, knight." She raised and leveled her voice. "I have brought food and wine, by orders of the Vicomte."

"The Vicomte would sooner send his maiden daughter to share my bed."

"The proof is in my guard's hands," she retorted. "And if you don't release me, you'll never taste food or wine again."

He ignored her threat. His eyes narrowed as he tried to

focus on her face. He pulled her off her knees and drew her close, too close, and she felt the sharp, pointed ends of the dry rushes dig into her hip as he dragged her across the floor. She braced herself against his chest. He smelled of earth and blood and heat. He stared at her as no man had ever dared, as only a husband should look upon a wife.

"Is it my fever," he said, his voice dry, raspy, and strangely strangled, "or are you uncommonly fair?"

"It's your fever." She stared straight into his bright eyes, all too conscious of the great width of his chest beneath her palms and how fully his body filled his tunic. In health, such a man could snap her in two. "These men can kill you with a single thrust, and will, upon my orders, if you don't release me."

"The Vicomte will kill me in any case; I'd rather choose my own time." He searched her face, and his gaze dipped to the gape of her surcoat, where she had not finished buttoning it in her haste to leave her room. "Has the Vicomte paid you to kill me, pretty one? Perhaps while in the throes of lovemaking?"

"I bring you food, and you reward me with insults." She glanced scornfully up and down his battered body and struck back in a way she knew would hurt most. "In this condition, knight, you'd not even be strong enough to please me."

"Ah, but there'd be pleasure in the trying."

She saw a flash of teeth and heard the gravelly sound of his laughter. She yanked anew and was surprised to find herself free. She fell back abruptly on her hip.

"Where is this wine?" He licked his dry lips. "It's better to die drinking poisoned wine than suffer through a death of thirst."

"It's not poisoned." She rubbed her wrist and eased herself to her feet. As soon as she had stepped away from Sir Jehan, Elie lunged toward the knight. "No, Elie!" She clutched his arm. "You mustn't harm him." The boy looked at her, confused, his gaze shifting from her to the man who lay tense against the wall. She lowered her voice until it was calm and soft. "Come, Elie. He didn't hurt me. See? I'm unharmed. Now, bring me some wine." She was lying, for her wrist ached from Sir Jehan's grip, and she knew there'd be bruises from his fingers on her skin in the morning. The boy watched her for a moment, then reluctantly walked to the pile of food. She told the guard to return to his post and then took a deep breath to steady herself. She took the jug of wine from Elie's hands and brought it over to the knight.

He took the jug in one hand and lifted it to his lips. She watched as his throat moved with each deep gulp. She clutched the bottom of the pitcher as he lifted it higher. "Stop—I'll need some to bathe your wounds."

Reluctantly, he lowered the jug and held it out to her, then closed his eyes and leaned uneasily against the wall. Droplets of the white wine ran over his stubbled chin. She brought the platter of food to him and wordlessly removed his metal shoes.

At least there'll be no more attacks like that, she thought as she assessed his wounds. His breathing sounded loud in the small room. He ate slowly, as if it took too much energy to lift the food to his lips and chew. Blood soaked through his chausses, where broken links bore witness to deep dagger cuts on his thighs and calves. His left hand lay bruised and motionless by his side. She wondered if it were broken or crushed, but she was more concerned with the wound on his head and the condition of his chest beneath his surcoat. It looked as if he still bled, weakly, and she wondered how he could have been wounded so seriously beneath the protection of his armor. Swords were nearly useless against mail, and if this knight wore a coat-of-plates, as most knights did, the daggers that might break chain mail at close contact could not possibly penetrate the plate defenses on his torso.

She would find out soon enough, she thought, as she removed the round poleyns on his knees. He watched her intently, with the concentration of a wounded man trying valiantly to battle the clouds of unconsciousness. She ignored him and continued her work.

"Hair like honey." As she unfastened the vambraces on his arms, he reached out and touched a strand of her hair that had come free of its ragged plait. "Why have you taken pity on me, lovely one, and dared to defy the Vicomte de Tournan?"

"This food comes from the Vicomte," she lied.

"No. Perhaps someone loyal to the Vicomte—someone with honor—but never the Vicomte. Who is paying for your services?"

"No one is paying me."

He tugged gently on the tress of hair until she looked up into his eyes. "It takes great courage to defy your lord in order to tend his wounded enemy."

She frowned at the softness in his voice. He obviously thought she was some serving girl who took pity on him; but she had no pity for him, not this man who had caused her so much grief. She pulled her hair from his grip. She gathered up the pieces of his armor and tossed them aside, then gestured to his chest. "Help me remove your surcoat."

He hesitated only a moment, then leaned away from the wall. Pain spasmed across his face as he raised his arms and she lifted the bloody, torn surcoat over his head. She noticed, immediately, that he wore no coat-of-plates beneath the tunic, and the links in his chain-mail shirt were broken in many places. The wounds on his abdomen must be from daggers, she thought. She hoped they were not too deep and, at the same time, wondered why the knight wore no plate armor for protection.

"The Vicomte caught us when we were riding swiftly. Neither I nor my men were fully armored."

Ignoring his answer to her unspoken question, she reached for the lacings on his haubergeon. He placed his hand firmly over hers.

"It will not be a pleasant sight for such pretty eyes."

"I've surely seen worse wounds on my father."

"Then your father is a knight?"

"Yes."

21

"He's a brave one, to send his daughter to save my life, in defiance of his lord's orders."

"He has defied no orders—"

"Tell me his name," he interrupted, "so I know who to thank when I meet him."

"My father is the Vicomte de Tournan."

The air in the room seemed to thin. His grip tightened on her hand. She watched in fearful fascination as his lips whitened, as his body stiffened. "The devil's own sire . . ." His feverish gaze focused on her face, and he shook his head in denial. "No one so fair could spring from the seed of the Vicomte de Tournan."

"I *am* my father's daughter."

"Then where's your dagger, daughter of Tournan?"

"Dagger?"

"Or have you poisoned your stitching needle? Or has your father thought of a more treacherous way to have me killed, now that his vassals aren't here to stop him?"

"I'll treat you like *any* knightly prisoner in the house of Tournan."

"Then it's torture you've planned."

"How dare you!"

"I've seen your father on the battlefield. I know his methods well."

"Stop. *Enough!*" She was tempted to vent her rage here, now; but now was not the time. He was in no state to face her accusations. When he was well and strong, she would tell him *exactly* what she thought of him. Still, the words quivered on her tongue. There was nothing dishonorable about a man seeking to reclaim his daughter's stolen dowry. She remembered the years she had spent waiting for her father to return from Italy to win back what was rightfully hers. The words spilled from her lips. "My father had just cause for his anger—just cause for attacking you on the battlefield."

His grip on her hand turned to iron. "There is no cause for battling a knight who has given up his gauntlet, or murdering an unarmed squire."

"How dare you lie so boldly, and in the Vicomte's own castle! You're risking my good will."

"As a Tournan, your good will is suspect."

"Are you afraid of a woman, St. Simon?"

"I am wary of Tournan treachery."

"There is no treachery here." She let the full force of her anger wash over her. "If you don't believe me, then listen to this. If you die, then my father's cause is lost. Since you have no heir, the lands you stole from my father will be given to the Prince of Wales—a far more formidable opponent than you. I don't want to see my lands in the Prince's hands." She glared at him. "Yes, *my* lands, St. Simon. Castétis was my dowry."

"I see."

"If it weren't for you, I'd be long married, with a castle of my own. Nothing would make me show you any kindness."

He had drawn her close to him, close enough for her to see the bristles of his dark beard beneath the blood and dirt that streaked his face; close enough to smell the hypocras on his breath; close enough to see his dilated pupils, the stark pain in his eyes. She heard Elie rise restlessly from his place near the doorway.

"Easy, Elie," she said. "This knight can do me no harm."

"You have more courage than your father." His gaze roamed over her face, intimately. "Your father would have called a dozen knights to his aid if I held him thus. You, instead, call off your guard."

"You are as weak as a new-born colt."

"Even a new-born colt can crush a lovely flower."

"Are you going to parry words with me, Sir Jehan, or are you going to allow me to bind your wounds?"

"Bind my wounds. I'm more important to you alive than dead." He released her. "But start with my head wound. I will test your skill first."

As if you have a choice. She stood up. She was surprised to find her knees shaky from the encounter. The knight was strong, despite his wounds. She returned to him with a pitcher of water and the sack of linens. Kneeling by his side, she searched through his dark locks for the slash that had bled so profusely over his face. She found it at the edge of his forehead, spreading from just above his brow to the tip of his right ear. It looked as if one of her father's knights had slipped his sword under St. Simon's basinet and left the ugly gash. She dipped a linen in the water and carefully wiped away the dried blood. The gash still bled, weakly, and she knew she would have to sew it shut.

She suddenly wished she had brought more wine, for the wound had been left untouched for at least a day and its edges were ragged and tender. Her stitching would be painful. She might not like the man she tended, but she had no desire to watch him cringe in pain beneath her touch. She glanced uncertainly at Elie, who watched the knight with bright, distrustful eyes.

"Elie, go to the kitchens and get more wine." Elie shook his head as she rose and collected the empty pitcher. She handed it to him. "You must. This knight won't harm me. Rudel will watch while you are away."

Elie shook his head like a defiant child.

"Fear not, good man, and do as she bids," Sir Jehan said. "On my honor, I will not harm your mistress."

If it were any other knight who lay so wounded on the floor of the room, she would have laughed and said that he could not hurt her, no matter how hard he tried. But twice she had felt the strength of this man's grip and she knew that, despite his weakness, he could conceivably break one of her bones or strike her senseless. No true knight would break his vow. Still, she hesitated to accept the word of honor of a man who had stolen all she could call her own.

"Go, Elie." She could not keep the scorn from her voice. "You have the word of honor of a knight."

The boy reluctantly took the earthen pitcher from her hands and left the room. She returned to Jehan's side and lifted a damp linen to wipe his face. He watched her through half-closed lids.

She slowly removed the mask of dirt and blood from his

features. His skin was smooth around his eyes and forehead, and as she continued her washing, she realized his face was not pitted with scars like that of an older man. She estimated that Sir Jehan could be no older than twenty-seven or twenty-eight years of age. She had always imagined him older, gnarled, and war-scarred, with a body as weak as his honor. Strange how the forces of Evil always had as much strength as the forces of Good. She tossed the dirty linen aside. "Let me see your hand."

He lifted his arm and she gingerly pressed the swelling. He didn't wince, though she knew her probing was painful. She felt no broken bones but suspected his wrist was sprained. She washed the dirt and grease from his fingers, then wrapped a linen around the swollen joint.

Elie returned moments later, breathing laboriously, as if he had raced from the kitchens to the tower. She took the jug of wine from his hands and knelt by the knight's side. She threaded her silver needle and prepared to stitch up the wound.

He took a deep draught of wine before she made the first stitch. He twitched. Fresh blood dripped from her stitches and she knew from the tautness of his long, strong body that her ministrations were painful. She shouldn't care. She should enjoy every bit of pain she inflicted on this wretched man, but she found herself sewing more quickly to minimize his agony. She couldn't watch a stray dog in pain—she certainly couldn't enjoy the agony of a human, no matter how much anxiety he had caused her. She stitched as swiftly and neatly as possible.

"'Tis done," she said, as she cut the end of the thread with her teeth. She washed the wound thoroughly with water and wrapped a linen around his head.

"You are skilled."

She gestured to the leather lacing of his haubergeon. "Do you still fear that I'll plunge a dagger into your heart?"

He spread his hands in submission. She leaned over and untied the lacings that held the edges of his mail shirt together. She pushed the edges apart, revealing a padded aketon and, below the edge of the tight garment, a stained linen shift. With his help, she pulled the heavy haubergeon off his shoulders, then unbuckled his aketon and pulled it over his head, leaving him in his ragged shift. She dragged the heavy chain mail and the padded garment to the pile with his other armor. When she turned around, he was naked from the waist up.

Her first thought was that the knight didn't need padding and iron plates for protection; surely any sword would deflect off the smooth, swelling hardness of his broad shoulders and the sculptured muscles of his chest. Her gaze fell to his abdomen and the strange thoughts fled. She swallowed an involuntary shudder. The mutilated flesh was ragged, torn and bruised.

"Your father's mercenaries wield their maces and daggers well."

"Stop! I won't listen." She knelt beside him and concentrated on his abdomen. She had seen many war wounds since she'd returned to Castelnau-sur-Arrats from the convent. Caring for wounded knights was a womanly duty. Because her mother, despite her many pregnancies and miscarriages, swooned at the sight of blood, Aliénor had long taken over that duty in the castle. She had grown skilled quickly, because the continuous warring between the English and French, as well as the private wars among local Gascon lords, gave her ample opportunity to practice. Yet despite all her experience, never had she seen wounds as extensive and deliberate as Sir Jehan's. The flesh of his abdomen was pulpy and bright with blood and blue and black bruises. She could not sew the cuts, for they were too close together, overlapping, and ragged. She could do nothing but wash the wounds free of old blood and wrap them in clean linens. As she reached for the pitcher of water, she noticed a large, swollen bruise on his side. She wondered if one of his ribs were broken.

Sir Jehan took another deep draught of wine, then lowered the jug and gestured to his abdomen. "Tell me, daughter of Tournan: Does *this* look like a wound made in a fight between knights?"

She didn't answer. She poured a little water over his abdomen, cringing as the muscles beneath his skin rippled in pain. She cleaned the deeper wounds as swiftly as possible and tried to rationalize the cause of the injury. A blow of a spiked mace atop chain mail could cause some tearing of flesh, if the points of the spikes pierced the mail and the padding beneath. Daggers, too—dozens of them—could cause some of the short, bloody slashes that riddled his abdomen.

But not all of them.

She sensed that there was more to the battle between Sir Jehan and her father than what she knew from listening to the men-at-arms talk across the trestle tables during the night's feast. They had been unnaturally subdued, even in their drunkenness. She had attributed their silence to a fear for Sir Jehan's health, to a fear of having to face the wrath of the Prince of Wales. Could they have been silent because of something that had occurred during the battle? Jehan's words rang in her head: *Your father's mercenaries wield their maces and daggers well.* Father had dismissed his mercenaries soon after the battle. It was an odd thing for him to do, for in order to release them he had to pay their wages in gold; and gold was a precious commodity of which her father had very little. Could Sir Jehan have spoken the truth earlier? Could Papa have battled a knight who had surrendered his sword? If Sir Jehan was unarmed, he would be defenseless against the kind of attack that would cause this injury.

She shook her head. This knight was muddling her thoughts. Papa was an honorable man—the greatest, strongest knight she knew. Sir Jehan must have provoked Father, she thought, as she continued her ministrations. He *must* have. There was no other explanation but that. "Drink the wine," she said sharply, "and remember that the man you blaspheme is my own father."

The knight was not listening, for while she probed the sore

flesh on his abdomen he slipped, quietly, into unconsciousness.

"Laurent, you must at least try."

"Why?" He toyed with a small block of oak on which he was carving the face of a saint. "Why must I play at knights' games when you know my intentions?"

Laurent sat beside her on the bottom stair of the castle steps. He wore his usual dull brown surcoat, the woolen one that fell all the way to his leather-soled feet, the one that looked markedly like a Franciscan's robes but without the corded belt. She had had the same argument with Laurent every morning since Papa had returned from Italy. Where once Laurent had gently resisted his knight's training, performing the skills carelessly while she and Thibaud looked on, lately he resisted it with greater and greater force. She wondered why Thibaud was late this morning. Her great-uncle could shame Laurent into practicing, something she never had the heart to do. "You may want to become a Franciscan friar, *frai,* but Papa may have different ideas."

"Father will willingly send me to a friary."

"I know no such thing." She nudged him with her knee. "You're his heir, his only surviving son. He won't give you up so easily to the Church."

"If Father meant for me to be his heir, he would have sent me off to the court of the Comte d'Armagnac long ago. I'm thirteen years of age and still living in his house."

"And I'm twenty-two, his only daughter, and still unmarried. Papa is away from his lands too much." She reached out and brushed his hair out of his face. "You aren't yet too old to be sent off as a page, and next year you'll be old enough to be a squire. Papa forgets—"

"He wishes he could forget." Laurent pulled away. He placed the block of wood aside and stood up abruptly. "He wishes Bertrand and Gaston were alive. He probably wishes the plague had taken me, and not them."

She started. "Spoken like a boy with a true calling."

He flushed. "I'll say penance for that."

"I'm sure you will."

"I'd rather say penance than practice."

"Oh, no." Her lips curved in a smile. "Sometimes I think you enjoy penance."

"Can I be excused for this, then?" He gathered the length of his scratchy woolen tunic in his hand. Lifting it, he gestured to his twisted, useless foot. "Have you ever known a knight with a leg like this?"

"That leg is only a problem on the ground. You know very well that on a horse there's no difference between you and any page in this castle. Knights fight on horseback, Laurent. Not on foot."

He glanced down at his hand, where a small drop of blood oozed out of a cut he had made while carving. "When Papa comes out of his rage, I intend to tell him that I want to join the Franciscans."

Her heart fluttered. The last time Papa had seen Laurent, after returning from Italy, he had burst into a rage at the sight of his limping son. Laurent had stayed clear of Papa ever since. Her father had always had a strange, frustrated reaction to the sight of Laurent, but the reaction was becoming more violent as her brother grew older. She assumed the anger was due to Papa's disappointment that his only living son was not great, knightly material—although she knew Laurent could be, if he put his mind to it, for he rode as well as any other boy and could handle a sword with some deftness. There were old, vicious rumors that attributed Papa's rage to guilt: It was said that her father had struck *Maman* while she was pregnant with Laurent, and that was the cause of Laurent's twisted leg and her mother's subsequent barrenness. Whatever the cause of his irrational fury, she knew that her father's rage would reach horrible proportions when Laurent dared to tell him he wanted to join the Franciscans.

Once it had been accepted as her brother's fate, as a third son, to join the Church. That fate changed when his two older brothers died in the plague in 1349. Despite his sudden shift in stature from third son to heir, Laurent had remained as single-mindedly determined to serve the Church as she, herself, had remained determined *not* to. Though their goals were different, she understood his frustration at his fate. *"Ai, frai,"* she said, wishing she could wipe the soft ripples of frustration from his brow. "What a pair we are! Our fates have been mismatched."

"Not really. Now that St. Simon is captured, you won't be sent to a convent. Father will dower you and find you a husband."

"First, Papa has to persuade Sir Jehan to give him ransom. And he'd best do it quickly, with all the rumors—"

"Do you think the rumors are true, then?" Laurent's wide black eyes, so like his father's, rounded in horror. "Do you think the Prince of Wales is going to raid through Gascony?"

"Papa is preparing for siege." She glanced at the bags of grain, the huge bundles of wood from the forests on the northern slopes, the piles of stones, the sharpened lances, the oak barrels of new wine, and the sundry foodstuffs that lay scattered in huge piles around the courtyard. In early October, such a clutter was common enough, for the villagers took their time in bringing their *rentes* to the Vicomte, and it took several weeks after Michaelmas, the end of the castle year, before the lower floor of the fortress was filled with the season's harvest. But she had lived in the castle long enough to know that there were too many weapons among the rolls of hay and barrels of milled grain. The fact that one of the Prince's loyal men was now imprisoned in this castle made it all the more likely that, if the rumor were true, the Prince would attack Castelnau-sur-Arrats.

Her brows drew together, and she glanced once again around the courtyard. Where was Thibaud? He was rarely late for Laurent's knight's training, and she had things to discuss with him that could not wait much longer. She glanced at her brother. "You've managed to change the subject, Laurent, but I haven't forgotten why we're in this courtyard." She gestured to his horse. "Go now, before Papa returns. At the very least, ride."

His chin puckered and he crossed his arms. "A friar doesn't need to ride a horse."

Suddenly, booming laughter rang out in the courtyard. She turned and saw her great-uncle approaching from around the corner of the donjon. Thibaud always reminded her of an badly wound spool of white woolen thread: His head, with its great mane of stark white hair, was disproportionally larger than his body, which appeared as thin and dry as an old stick. Despite his sixty years of age, Thibaud was anything but weak. His penetrating black eyes saw as sharply as a man half his age, and despite occasional bouts of stiffness, he was as adroit on a stallion as any newly dubbed knight. "There you are, *oncle*. You're late, and I need you." She gestured to Laurent, whose chin had tilted even higher. "I can't even persuade him to ride today. Tell him that, at the very least, friars need to know how to ride a horse well—"

"True Franciscans travel the world on foot," Laurent interrupted, "and never ride horses."

"Fie!" Thibaud scowled. "I have never seen a friar without at least a stableful of horses!"

"Oncle, that's not true!"

"And listen to you, talking about traveling the world on foot." The older man gestured to Laurent's twisted limb. "With that, it would take a lifetime for you to travel from here to Toulouse. A good friar would ride well, to better help the poor in all places."

"I can ride, *oncle—"*

"But you've never tried the lance."

"A lance is a knight's weapon."

"Any man who travels through the countryside, either to make war or to pray for the souls of men, must protect himself."

"My prayers shall protect me."

"With all respect due to God, I've never seen a prayer stop a sword, boy. And if you don't climb on that horse now, I'll toss you on it myself."

Laurent frowned at his great-uncle, then swung a resigned glance toward his sister. "I'll do it just once—just once—then I'm finished with these knights' games for the day."

She stifled a triumphant smile as her brother walked away. When he reached the horse, Laurent climbed carefully onto a cut-off cask and tried to mount the gelding. He gently waved away the stableboy's offers of aid and continued until finally, awkwardly, he pulled his twisted leg over the horse and sat up in the saddle.

"Your father should have sent him to the Comte d'Armagnac years ago. If he's not a horseman soon," Thibaud said, "then he'll be fit for nothing but the priesthood."

"He's determined to tell Papa that he wants to join the Franciscans."

"If the boy values his life, he'll wait until your father is out of his choler."

"If you were here on time, you could have warned him. Where did you hide after Mass? I've been trying to talk to you since yesterday afternoon."

"You don't think I know that, woman?" He gestured to the eastern wall. "I was up there, directing the strengthening of the fortifications. If the Prince does attack, it's more important that these walls are strong enough to resist him, than for your brother to know how to ride in circles. I wouldn't have come down here at all if I didn't see that your brother was getting the best of you."

"Why were you avoiding me? I just wanted to ask you a few questions."

"You couldn't charm the men-at-arms into telling you, eh?"

"They ran away from me every time I approached, as if I were carrying the plague."

"You're his daughter. They know they'll lose more than their tongues if they dare utter a word."

"Utter a word of what?"

Thibaud didn't answer, as if he were absorbed in watching

Laurent put the horse through his paces. The ends of Thibaud's unfashionably long surcoat flapped in the breeze that blew in from over the toothed edge of the ramparts. In the bright sunlight, she could see every creased, stark line of his face. She waited, wondering why her normally voluble great-uncle was suddenly so quiet.

His bushy brows, as white as summer clouds, lowered over his eyes. "You won't believe a word I say."

"Thibaud! When have I ever doubted you?"

"You never believe ill of your father." He fixed his sober gaze upon her. "You probably know more than I, but you are too ashamed to admit it. What I know, I know only from the drunken babbling of the men-at-arms. You've been tending that knight at the risk of your own skin."

"Oncle!"

"You may be able to set your father's cap, but you can't make a fool of me. I saw you leave the great hall the night your father returned, with a candle and a sack. Old bones don't sleep well, especially when the winter is nigh." He gestured to a wounded dog lying at her feet. She had found the hound that morning with a gash in his side, and she was late for Mass because she had tended him. "I've known you since you were a babe, child. You can't bear to watch a hound suffer. I knew you wouldn't allow a man to die, slowly, of battle wounds, no matter what that man did to you."

"You think too well of me. If Sir Jehan had died, I'd be farther away from my dowry and closer to a convent."

"And it's an earthly husband you want, not a heavenly one."

"There is no sin in that."

"No, there is none, *ma petite nièce*, and the sooner you have a husband to keep you in hand, the better. But what your father has done has driven you farther from marriage, not closer to it."

"But he's captured Sir Jehan—"

"Oui, and it's the manner of the capture that is the cause

of all the trouble." He peered at her. "You've seen Sir Jehan's wounds."

"He wore no coat-of-plates," she said, "so it's not surprising he's so battered—"

"You've seen enough battle wounds to know better. You're blinded by youth and tenderness. I'm not."

She stared at her great-uncle. There was no love lost between her father and Thibaud. Thibaud had, in his time, fought valiantly under three French kings and won a lifelong pension from the last of them, Philip VI. But the pension was paid so irregularly by Phillip's son, King Jean, that Thibaud was forced to live on the charity of his nephew, the Vicomte de Tournan. Yet, despite the strained relationship between her father and her great-uncle, she knew Thibaud would not lie. It was not in his nature. Most of the time he was brutally honest, embarrassingly blunt, and she suddenly feared what he was about to tell her. "If it affects Sir Jehan, and his ransom, then it affects me," she said. "Tell me."

"I don't want to hear your cursing, child, when I'm through. I won't have it." When she nodded curtly, he continued. "I can tell you only what I know, only what has been told to me in confidence by the Vicomte's vassals. Your father trapped Sir Jehan and his men in a valley near the Garonne river. He demanded they either surrender or die. He offered them no terms of ransom, no promise of protection. Sir Jehan chose to fight, as any honorable knight would in the face of such . . ." His colorless lips tightened. "Sir Jehan fought, and when it was obvious that his men were defeated, he tossed his gauntlet to the ground in surrender.

"According to your father's vassals, Sir Jehan then surrendered his sword to your father, spat in the dirt as the mercenaries approached, then scorned your father aloud for offering such dishonorable terms of surrender. The Vicomte was so enraged that he struck Sir Jehan in the face with the knight's own sword."

"No!"

"You wanted to hear the truth, and the truth is rarely pretty, child. Sir Jehan couldn't accept such an affront to chivalry; no knight could. He threw his dagger at the Vicomte and gave him that ugly slash he's wearing on his face. When the Vicomte bellowed for the men to take him, the mercenaries descended upon him with a vengeance." He lifted a hand as she began to protest. "No, don't interrupt me, for I won't speak of it twice. Sir Jehan's squire tried, as a good squire should, to defend his master. He was beaten and killed. He was scarcely older than Laurent."

"I don't believe it." She heard her own stubborn voice, even as her thoughts tumbled over one another. Sir Jehan's words suddenly came back to her: *There is no cause for battling a knight who has given up his gauntlet, or murdering an unarmed squire.* She stared at Thibaud, disbelieving, watching him as he curled his hand angrily over the hilt of his ancient sword. "There must be more to it—Father must have been sorely provoked. There is no other reason."

"It was his damned temper. He's had it since he was a boy, and though it's gotten him into trouble before, never has it been as bad at this. Sir Jehan would have died, too, if your father's vassals hadn't intervened and stopped the slaughter. Your father apparently came to his senses soon after. He dismissed the mercenaries and released all prisoners but one: Sir Jehan himself."

"Then he did show amnesty to the other prisoners—"

"It was the least he could do. You are his only favorite, *ma petite nièce*, but you are not blind to his faults. I see it in your eyes. You know I speak the truth."

She wanted, so badly, to deny it. She had doubted Sir Jehan, even after seeing his wounds, wounds that she knew could only have been caused by the combined, frantic thrusts of many daggers on an unprotected man. Now that Sir Jehan's own hateful words were confirmed by her great-uncle . . . Her cheeks flushed with shame. Her mind acknowledged the truth of Thibaud's words, though her heart still rebelled. She hated Sir Jehan for all he had done to her; there were many times over the past years when she had wished him dead. But for Father to ignore all the rules of chivalry, to attack a man who had surrendered, and kill an unarmed squire . . . That was more cowardly and more heinous an act than stealing a woman's dowry while her champion was abroad.

Oh, Papa! How could you have done this?

"There's a black mark upon the name of Tournan," Thibaud continued. "Keep tending the prisoner, Aliénor. Perhaps you, at least, will be spared the stain." He picked up the long wooden lance that lay on the ground. "Laurent, come here." Her brother rode to his side. "Here, boy. Your father's lance. Let's see if you're worthy to take his place."

She flushed anew, sensing the bitterness beneath the words. Her brother clutched the center of the lance and glanced behind him, to where the stableboys were hanging a sack of grain upon a stake driven into the courtyard. When he turned back, he looked at her. "Are you all right, *ma soeur?* You're pale."

She met his dark eyes, even as she struggled to maintain her calm. Laurent must never know about Father. She must somehow protect him from the mark of dishonor that now stained their names. "You can't use me as an excuse not to joust, *frai.*" She returned to the oak steps and leaned against the rail. "Ride on, now."

She watched numbly as Thibaud instructed her brother how to hold the lance against his side, along the length of his forearm. Laurent settled the weight of the ashwood pole in his grip, then whirled the gelding around. As he kicked the horse into a canter, she frowned and tilted her head. Over the cries of the men-at-arms working along the fortifications, over the snorts of the pigs penned near the kitchens, she heard another sound. It was the muted barking of a dozen hounds—a dozen hunting hounds.

She gripped the oak rail of the stairs just as the tip of Laurent's lance brushed the edge of the sack. She watched as Laurent lost hold of the stiff weapon and it fell, clanking, to the earth.

"Try again, boy," Thibaud said, as a stableboy retrieved the weapon. "This time tighten your grip."

But Laurent wasn't listening, and neither was she. For as the boy handed Laurent the lance, the Vicomte de Tournan galloped into the center of the courtyard with the hounds baying at his feet. His gaze swept the cluttered courtyard, then settled on Laurent with angry intensity.

Chapter
3

"SO MY SON HAS EMERGED FROM HIDING."

The Vicomte extended his arm, and a squire took the
hooded falcon from his master's gloved wrist. The greyhounds trotted toward the water trough near the kitchens.
Aliénor stood in mute horror, watching her father's angry
face, and watching Laurent, who sat stiffly upon his horse,
twisting the painted lance in his hand.

The Vicomte gestured to the sack of grain. "I thought you
were worthless but for pining and praying, yet here you are,
training to be a knight." He pulled the thick falconer's glove
off his hand, finger by finger. "Continue," he ordered. "I will
see whether you are worthy of the name of Tournan."

A thought flashed through her mind, a horrible thought, a
terrible thought of betrayal. *Is there any worth, any more, in
the name of Tournan, my father?* She spread her fingers over
her fluttering stomach. She watched Laurent—the boy
destined to take her father's place in the world—nudge his
gelding toward the beginning of the cleared field. Oh, *why*
couldn't Father arrive while Laurent was in swordplay with
Thibaud? Laurent knew how to hold a sword, and how to
parry Thibaud's thrusts, but he had practiced with a lance
only once—unsuccessfully—moments before. She met her
brother's gaze across the space that separated them. His
close-set eyes shone with a strange light.

The Vicomte dismounted and waited, snapping his heavy
falconer's glove against his red-hosed thigh.

"Hold the lance tighter." Thibaud's voice broke the expectant hush of the courtyard. "Raise the tip a bit, and aim for the center of the sack."

Laurent's horse pranced as if he sensed the tension. Her brother calmed him, then eased him around to face the stake. *Come*, frai. *Show Father that you can be a knight, that you can be the Vicomte de Tournan—perhaps a better, braver Vicomte than he himself.* Suddenly Laurent dug his heels into the horse's sides. The gelding broke into a canter, and Laurent tilted the lance as Thibaud instructed. His arm quivered with the weight of the weapon. Puffs of dust rose from the impact of the horse's hooves against the dry earth. He leaned forward as the tip of the lance approached the sack, as if by moving his weight forward he could better pierce the sack and remove it from its stake. She watched with bated breath as the dulled point of the lance ripped the center of the woven bag and grain spilled out onto the courtyard.

For the space of a heartbeat, she thought, *he has done it,* but Laurent's horse did not slow in its pace. The sack did not fall from its fastening on the stake. The point of the lance pierced the sack on one side but did not emerge from the other, and Laurent refused to ease his grip on the lance. She gasped aloud as the lance jerked to a stop. The impact tossed Laurent clear off the horse. He fell to the stones with a hard, hollow thud.

Instinctively, she lunged forward. She took no more than two steps before Thibaud's fingers clenched her upper arm like a greyhound's jaws.

"Stop, woman! Your brother must face him alone."

Get up, Laurent. Get up. Her brother lay against the stones, stunned, struggling to rise to his elbows. *Get back on the gelding.* Her father's scowl grew. She fought uselessly against Thibaud's grip, wanting to do anything—including thrust her own body between her brother and her father—to prevent the beating Laurent was sure to receive. Laurent had just picked up the lance that day; he had only just begun to learn how to use it. *It is so difficult to teach him, Papa, when he is convinced that you despise the sight of him.* Yet she saw the black rage on her father's face, as visible as rolling thunderclouds on a clear sky. He approached Laurent like a hunter approaching a wounded stag. Laurent rose shakily to his feet. He stumbled backward, still dazed from the impact. The courtyard dust covered his tunic.

"This is the son that remains with me." The Vicomte soaked the words in bitterness. "Flesh of my flesh, blood of my blood—unseated by a bag of grain." He swung the back of his hand across Laurent's face. Laurent fell and skidded on the ground.

"Father!"

Thibaud shook her. "Hush, Aliénor, lest you, too, want to feel the back of his hand."

"You will *never* bear my name." Her father turned and riveted his attention on her. "You're only a woman, daughter, but you're worth a hundred crippled sons. With you I'll buy a man worthy to bear the title of the Vicomte de Tournan."

She shook her head mutely. Her father walked away from his son's motionless body. He brushed by her and ascended the stairs to the castle. When he reached the landing, he raised his voice. "Hear me, all of you. Today, St. Bruno's Day in the year of Our Lord 1355, I hereby announce that my estates, title, and all that I hold shall be bequeathed after my death to my daughter, Aliénor, and the man I give her to in marriage. Let it be known to all."

He turned and marched into the castle.

She pulled free of Thibaud's grip and raced across the length of the courtyard. She ignored the hounds who trotted to greet her and pushed away the page who had bent over her brother. She fell to her knees. She ran her hand over Laurent's head and breathed a sigh of relief as his eyes fluttered open.

"It's all right, *chère soeur.*" He eased himself to a sitting position. "I'm not hurt."

"Don't move yet, not until I've checked for broken bones." She swiftly checked his limbs but found nothing but scratches and faint blue bruises, which would grow dark as the day progressed. Blood dripped from his nose, over his chin, and onto his tunic. Despite the fact that the tippets of her surcoat were trimmed in precious miniver, she lifted the trailing ends of her sleeves to wipe the blood from his face. "Father didn't mean what he said."

"Yes, he did." Laurent blinked, still stunned, as she held his chin firmly and continued to wipe his face. "It's for the best," he said. "You're now Father's heiress."

"For the week, perhaps." She caught a drop of blood before it ran down his neck. "By Sunday, Father will take back what he said."

"I hope not."

"You silly pup! Of *course* you want him to change his mind."

"And have all this go to waste?"

She stopped her ministrations and stared at him. He smiled, despite the blood that stained his crooked front teeth, despite the tight grip she had on his chin. She dropped the tippet of her sleeve as the realization struck her like a bolt of lightning. "You fell off your horse intentionally, didn't you?"

He smiled, a sly and wicked smile.

"Laurent! You could have killed yourself!"

"Knight's training has taught me something: how to fall off a horse without killing myself."

"Papa could have killed you!"

"Don't scold me, Aliénor. I'm not in the nursery anymore." He pulled gently away from her grip and wiped his bleeding nose on the sleeve of his coarse tunic. "Don't you see? It's the perfect solution. Now nothing can stop me from joining the Franciscans. And you no longer need to worry about Jehan de St. Simon."

Jehan paced slowly in the small room. He winced at the sharp pain in his side. His head throbbed with each careful step, and the tight scabs ripped open on his abdomen each time he moved his upper body. He could see nothing in the pitch-black, airless room, for not even arrow slits lit or ventilated the small chamber. The thick walls kept the cell cold and damp, yet he felt as hot as if he were walking in full armor on a sweltering summer afternoon. He was still feverish, and he knew he must fight the sickness if he intended to live.

He intended to live, if for no other reason than to wreak vengeance on the Vicomte de Tournan. He had no idea how many days had passed while he was in this feverish state. His wounds ached him, individually, as if a hundred firebrands had been applied to his belly, his head, and his legs. Anger fueled his fever, making him grind his teeth and flex his good hand into a fist. He painstakingly remembered every detail of his last days of freedom, for the fury of the memories kept him awake and alert, and he rolled them over in his head for the hundredth time since he woke from semiconsciousness.

The Prince of Wales had recently arrived in Bordeaux, sent there by his father, the King of England, to punish the rebels of Gascony—the treacherous lords who had transferred their allegiance to the French king rather than remain faithful to the English king, their true lord for over two hundred years. When Jehan received the Prince's order to join his army, he had answered it eagerly. In all the pillaging and plunder of a campaign, in all the seizing of rebel castles, there would be a wealth of opportunity for a knight cunning and swift of sword. Plus, if he culled the Prince's favor, there was always the prospect of heady rewards, the kind of rewards that came only in war or marriage, the kind of rewards Jehan craved more than gold or plunder: land, castles, and titles.

Nothing, not even miles of rebel-infested countryside, could keep him from Bordeaux. While he and his sixteen knights rode swiftly through the lands of Armagnac, a contingent of rebels appeared, trapping him in a valley between a set of rolling hills and the swollen Garonne river. It was a glittering, colorful army of knights, and their trappings contrasted sharply with the rusted chain mail, faded heraldry, and chipped and battered weapons of his own men. He knew there would be a battle, for no Gascon knight loyal to the Prince of Wales could surrender like a coward to rebel knights. He didn't worry too much about the odds. His men, illegitimate sons of highborn nobles, dispossessed knights, younger sons who, like Jehan, chose a life by the sword rather than a life of God, were each worth a dozen of the enemy knights, hampered by their shining, clumsy iron cocoons.

Then he realized that the leader of the rebels was the Vicomte de Tournan. Suddenly the attack took on new meaning. This rebel wasn't here to crush a contingent of the Prince of Wales's knights. The Vicomte wanted his lands back, the lands Jehan had seized for his own over two years before. Jehan's mood darkened. The tiny, half-ruined castle and its handful of peasants were *his* now. He had fortified it, fed its people, ordered the sowing of its fields, and filled it with the plunder of years of knighthood. He had lived in it, waiting for the Vicomte's attack, always in vain. It was his castle now. Why, after two long years of utter silence, did the Vicomte de Tournan suddenly remember his long-neglected Castétis?

Jehan had no time to ponder the question. He would have to fight—and he would have to win. The third son of an impoverished baron, landless, powerless, and untitled, Jehan had earned his living by the strength of his sword arm and his loyalty to Edward, Prince of Wales. Until two years before, the largesse of the Prince had provided him with little more than food, shelter, and enough *deniers* to buy armor and horses. But the capture of the rebel Vicomte's castle was a stroke of fortune. Possession of Castétis had lifted him above the mass of desperate knights who lived and roamed in Gascony. The retelling of the seizure had captured the Prince's attention and lifted Jehan higher in his esteem. Possession of the fortress had given him hope that he could rebuild the fortunes of the St. Simons, the fortunes lost so long ago, in the endless fighting between the English and the French. He vowed he would not return a single hectare of land to the Vicomte de Tournan.

Jehan closed his eyes tightly. The bellow of battle cries, the clash of steel, and the ringing of harnesses reverberated in his head. He had fought the Vicomte's men with all the blindness and brutality of a cornered beast. But when he saw Guilhem, his fourteen-year-old squire, fall wounded from his horse in the midst of the fray, he knew he could not allow this battle to continue to the bitter end. He rode to the Vicomte and tossed down his gauntlet. The act had left a taste as bitter as the juice of unripe grapes in his mouth. In all his years as a knight, he had never surrendered to any man. By surrendering to this one, he was giving up everything.

Much good it did, he thought, as the anger boiled in his chest. The fighting had stopped temporarily. But when the Vicomte approached, took Jehan's sword by the hilt, then struck him with it, the damned rebel left Jehan no choice but to continue fighting. Blinded by the blood flowing over his face, Jehan pulled his dagger from his baldric and slung it at the Vicomte. The coward, in his rage, called his mercenaries to attack.

His memories blurred in a whirl of blood-red, burning pain. He winced as he touched his abdomen, as if he could feel anew each brutal blow from the mercenaries' daggers and maces. Guilhem, although wounded, had tried to protect him. He gave his life in the process. Unlike Guilhem, Jehan knew he would survive his wounds. Unlike Guilhem, Jehan knew he'd see the day when he would face the Vicomte de Tournan again. By his ignoble actions on the battlefield, the rebel had forfeited all rights for consideration as a knight. Jehan stopped his pacing and squeezed his eyes shut. He swore upon all that was holy that he would avenge Guilhem's death.

He heard a voice outside his chamber. He willed away the dregs of his pain and focused his attention on the portal. A soft light seeped in from the edges of the door. It was faint, but steady, like daylight. He squinted as the door opened, then closed his eyes as the light spilled into the small room. He had been in the dark for so long that even the faintest light blinded him. He lifted his arm as if to ward it off. A swirling draft of fresh air followed, and he breathed it in deeply.

"I see you're feeling better."

Her voice was like spring rain on green fields. Calm, husky, soothing. It made him forget his pain, for a moment. It was *her* voice, the voice of the woman with hair like burnished gold, hands as soft as clouds, and a tongue as sharp as a dagger. The daughter of his enemy, and the woman who saved his life. Curiosity made him rash and he opened his eyes, only to be forced to close them against the light.

"The light is faint—yet I see it pains your eyes." He heard her sigh. "I shall bring you candles next time."

He listened to the sound of her footsteps crackling against the dried, dirty rushes as she moved around the room. Another person entered, blocking the light momentarily, and the man's grunts reminded Jehan that the woman had a large, loyal peasant as a guard. He blinked anew. He lowered his arm and squinted at her silhouette against the open door.

So it wasn't my imaginings, he thought, as his eyes became used to the light. Her hair was as rich as the color of honey, and it glowed around her face as it captured the sunshine. The fresh air moved the long skirts of her tunic around her legs and toyed with the edges of the gossamer veil draped neatly over her hair. The light gleamed on the golden circlet around her brow.

"If the light still pains you, I'll tell Elie to close the upper door."

"I'll get used to it."

She walked deeper into the room and gestured to her guard, who stood in the shadows of the corner. The huge boy, dressed in rough homespun that hung menacingly off the bulk of his broad, rounded shoulders, approached and left a plate full of food on the floor by his feet. The scent of charred meat and mustard sauce teased him. He sank down on his haunches—carefully, so he wouldn't move his torso and cause that sharp, stinging pain in his side. He reached for the pitcher of wine and took a sip. It was new wine—the *vendange* must be over—and he drank deeply of the fresh, golden liquid. As he ate, he watched her untie the opening of her sack and search for something inside.

In his feverish delirium, he had wondered if this woman were one of the fairies that were said to roam the foothills of the Pyrenees. She was glorious, he remembered, like a bright ray of light in the darkness of his cell. His fever had diminished now, and looking at her, he knew this was no fairy. Fine gray fur lined the long, trailing sleeves of her pale blue surcoat, and a golden girdle draped over her rounded hips. The chain of her girdle hung away from her taut abdomen as she leaned over her sack, and its movement drew attention to her narrow waist. She was a very real woman, full grown, with a maiden's subtle curves. He wondered how the Vicomte de Tournan could have sired such a creature. God had a strange sense of humor indeed, to bring such beauty out of wretched ugliness.

Dark thoughts scattered through his mind. She was defenseless in this small room, with nothing but a half-witted peasant and a single man-at-arms as guards. He was in no shape to fight, but desperation often gifted men with inhuman strength. If he were clever and careful, he could overpower her guards and have her at his mercy. What sweet revenge that would be, he mused, to take this woman while he was prisoner in her father's castle. He would die for it, but it would be worth the look on the Vicomte's face when he discovered that Jehan's seed had taken root in his own daughter.

He bit into the tough fibers of a chunk of meat and forced the thought out of his head. It was a dark, evil thought, a thought that didn't belong in a knight's mind. He would never become like the Vicomte de Tournan—a man without honor. This woman risked much to tend him, though he knew her reasons were selfish. He was in her debt, even though she was the daughter of his bitterest enemy. To rape her would be as horrible an act as killing an unarmed squire. He would not have an innocent woman's disgrace on his conscience.

It was difficult to be grateful to a Tournan *and* to hate a Tournan, all at once, even though the two Tournans were as different as an angel and a demon. His emotions were still too muddled, and he too weak. She glanced at him warily, and for a moment he saw himself through her eyes. His long, torn shift and ragged hose, still dirty with the blood of his wounds, hung from his frame. He was crouched by the wall, eating like a beast, and had spent the entire time scowling at her. A smile spread beneath the bristle on his face. The ladies of the court at Bordeaux would swoon if they could see him now—not out of desire, but out of horror. Though this woman looked as ethereal as the mists, he sensed she did not frighten easily.

"It's still daylight," he said, putting down the jug of wine. "Isn't it dangerous for you to be here?"

She drew a roll of linen strips out of the bag. "My father is hunting boar in the northern forests. He won't return until sundown."

So, he thought, the maiden has given up all pretense of feeding and caring for me in the name of her father. He chose a leg of fowl and bit into it. He wondered if she knew the truth of what had happened on the battlefield. If she did know the truth, he wondered if she cared that her father had broken all the rules of chivalry, all the rules that separated knights from villeins, and men from beasts.

"I must look at your wounds," she said abruptly. "You may eat later." She approached him and kneeled by his side. He smelled the scent that clung to her hair and clothes, the scent of spices, of fresh air. He had grown to crave that scent during his fever, for it meant ease and comfort, and now he breathed it in with a strange mixture of desire and suspicion. She unwound the linen that encircled his head. Her fingers probed the soreness on his temple.

She brushed the beads of sweat from his forehead. "You're still feverish."

"It will pass."

She reached for the pitcher of water. He closed his eyes as she poured the cool liquid over his wound. The icy flow stung the raw ends of the slash on his temple. He waited until she began winding a fresh linen around the wound before he spoke.

"How long have I been here?"

Her hands paused a moment in their wrapping. "Six days."

"What of my men?"

"The only prisoner my father took was you."

She offered no other explanation. Had the Vicomte released his men, or had he massacred them on the battlefield as he had massacred Guilhem? He closed his eyes. If the Vicomte had killed all his men . . . He rattled their names off in his mind. Jehan vowed he would find out the truth, sooner or later. The Vicomte would pay for his sins.

She finished the wrapping and gestured to his worn, bloody shift. "You must take this off."

He eased away from the wall and pulled the linen garment over his head. He tossed it to a corner.

"You're still bleeding."

"It's fresh. The scabs broke open as I paced."

"You should lie still until it heals. If you move too much it will never settle."

"I'll soon be healed, whether I move or not. You've stolen me from death, despite your father's wishes." She stiffened slightly but said nothing. He watched her as she searched for something in her sack and then decided to test her one more time. "You are kind, daughter of Tournan, to care for an enemy knight."

"Dead, you are useless to me."

"Ah, yes," he mused. "My lands were once your dowry."

"They are my father's lands, not yours."

He reached for a leg of fowl. "I haven't discussed ransom with your father."

"He'll demand those lands in exchange for your life."

"I'd rather die from starvation than give a man without honor an honorable ransom."

"By the way you're eating, knight, I doubt you'd choose starvation."

"Then you admit your father is without honor." He waited as he chewed the dry fibers of the meat. She pulled an earthenware bowl out of the sack and avoided his eyes. "Well, maiden? Have you discovered the truth?"

She shook her head sharply. "I don't know what the truth is anymore."

"You *do* know."

"My father doesn't regale me with stories of the battle-field, Sir Jehan. I'm his daughter, not his squire. Now lean back so I can change those linens."

She bent over his abdomen and found the ragged end of the linen wrapped around his middle. She unwound it, then carefully removed the lowermost linen, which stuck to his wound in places. He watched her ministrations with fasci-nation, for with each unraveling, a deeper flush worked its way to her cheekbones. *She is ashamed,* he thought. The knowledge pleased him more than he expected. He was tempted to sink his hand into the thickness of her hair, bend her head back, and feast his gaze on her soft, tinted skin. He wanted to devour the sight of her shame, if only to prove to himself that it was real.

He gave in to the temptation. His fingers wove their way through her hair and cupped her head in his palm. Her head jerked up as she felt his caress, and her eyes widened. She pulled away, but he grasped the warm, silky tresses and stilled her. Her eyes were like gilded brown velvet, soft and streaked with gold. Her skin had the dewy texture of a young peach, and now it was flushed a deep rose. "I was right: You are ashamed."

"Did you expect me to be proud?"

"His blood runs in your veins."

"And in my mother's, my brother's, in all my relatives' veins." Her pale brows drew together. "Don't judge me so harshly."

"I didn't think a Tournan was capable of shame."

"Then you, Sir Jehan, have a very simple mind."

His lips twitched at the insult. His gaze wandered over her features. "You still hate me for stealing your dowry lands."

" 'Detest' is a better word." She tilted her chin. "Did you expect me to forgive you so easily after two long years of grief?"

"I suppose not." Looking at her, with her unusual, gold-streaked eyes and long, honey-colored curls, he thought that the last thing he wanted from this woman, Tournan or not, was hatred. *I must be healing,* he mused, *to desire a woman so soon.* Over her head he noticed that the half-wit was already on his feet, pacing like a tethered beast. "Your guard is anxious, yet you don't fear me."

"I've been nursing you for six days. I know your weaknesses."

"You should fear me anyway. You would be the perfect instrument of my vengeance against your father."

"I saved your life."

"You expect much out of me to think I'll consider that, after all your father has done."

"I'm told you're a chivalrous knight, despite your thievery."

"Then what took you so long to accept my account of the battle?"

"I would have believed the Devil first." She tried to jerk away, but he held her head tight in his grip. "Only when I heard the same story from another source did I realize you were telling the truth."

"Then you judge me without knowing me, just as I judged you."

"I had reason to believe you false: You stole my lands."

"I took them fairly, by force of arms."

"Fairly!" Her eyes flashed, like golden daggers. "You

waited until my father went away to Florence, then you struck. Is that fair, Sir Jehan? To wait until the shepherd is sleeping to steal the sheep?"

He lifted a brow. Now he understood why it had taken so long for the Vicomte to strike back. Now he understood why this woman despised him so. He was tempted to tell her that he hadn't known her father was abroad when he set out to capture the castle, but he doubted she would believe him. It hardly mattered. He didn't have to explain his actions to this slip of a woman.

He released her. His fingers combed through the ends of her hair as she pulled away. She faced her guard and crooned to him in a soft voice, in dialect. When the boy was calmer, she gathered the earthenware bowl and some linens and knelt beside Jehan. She dipped her fingers into the bowl and a fetid, mossy smell filled the room as, with feathery strokes, she smoothed an unguent over the raw-edged mass of his wound.

Despite her brave mien, he noticed that her fingers trembled against his abdomen. "Has your father found you a husband yet, with my lands as your dowry?"

She glared at him. "Are you so anxious to know who you'll have to battle the *next* time you try to steal my lands?"

"If there's ever a battle, it'll be your father trying to seize Castétis from me."

"Refuse to pay ransom, and your life will be spent in this room."

His lips curved into a smile. "It's not so bad being a prisoner here—in a castle that shelters a woman as fair as you."

"Flattering me won't help. If it weren't for you, I'd long be married and a *châtelaine* on my own."

"Harsh words from beautiful lips."

She frowned and lifted her hand, glistening with unguent, from his abdomen. "As for being a lifelong prisoner here, I won't be sharing your stay. My father is negotiating a betrothal with the oldest son of the Vicomte de Baste, Guy de Baste."

Jehan masked his surprise. He knew Guy de Baste. The Prince of Wales knew Guy de Baste. Though the current Vicomte de Baste was loyal to the French king, his eldest son had no qualms about seeking better relations with the English ruler. Jehan wondered if the Vicomte de Tournan was aware of this and realized, just as swiftly, that he wasn't. Not for any reason would the Vicomte risk his entire estate falling into the hands of someone loyal to the English.

"Struck dumb, are you? Is Guy de Baste such a formidable knight?"

Jehan looked at her as she began winding a fresh set of linens around his abdomen. He was tempted for a moment to warn her that she would be caught between her father's loyalties and those of her betrothed. He didn't, of course, for that would be giving too much away, and it would defeat the Prince of Wales's objective: to bring the lands of these rebel vassals under his control. She would have ample time to discover Sir Guy's secret negotiations on her own, after the marriage. "I was thinking, *demoiselle,* that the man will please you. He is young, no more than twenty-three. Handsome, I suppose, for he's popular with the ladies. But he's an indifferent knight." Jehan stopped himself from saying that Guy preferred to bargain rather than fight. He was glib, looked fine on a horse, and had all the slippery charm of a snake. Then another thought struck him. The Baste estates were considerable in size, as extensive as those of the Tournans. He looked at her in puzzlement. Why would Guy de Baste be interested in a woman with no title, with nothing more for dowry but Castétis? "The heir to the viscounty of Baste is a large prize for a woman who has, comparatively, a small dowry."

She looked away suddenly. She finished binding his abdomen, then gestured to his legs. "You'll have to tend to your leg wounds yourself," she said. "I've been gone too long this afternoon."

He reached out and clutched a handful of her fur-lined, tapering sleeve as she rose to her feet. "What are you hiding from me?"

"You're soiling my surcoat."

"I know the castle and lands that I took from your father won't be sufficient for the heir to the Baste estates."

"That is my father's concern, not mine."

"I also know Guy de Baste. He wouldn't marry a woman who didn't have a title." He tugged her sleeve. "You have brothers, don't you?"

"One."

"He's your father's heir, isn't he?"

"What does it matter?"

"It matters very much." He struggled painfully to his feet, never letting go of the sleeve in his hand. His suspicions were growing, and so was his curiosity. She stepped back as he finally straightened to his full height. "I intend to keep you here until you tell me."

Her brown eyes flickered. "If I scream, the entire garrison will be here in a moment."

"Your father will find out that you've been tending me."

"Then *you* no longer will be tended."

Jehan smiled. She was bold, this creature. Brave and fearless. It was too bad she was the daughter of the Vicomte de Tournan.

"If you *must* know," she said, "my brother was my father's heir, until St. Bruno's Day. Then everything changed. But my father is in a rage and he doesn't know what he does. He'll change his mind before the week's end."

"What did he do?"

"He disowned my brother. He made me the heiress to the title and lands of Tournan."

"Heiress?"

She tugged her sleeve away from his slackened grip and began to gather her things. "I've left you some meat, a pitcher of water, and some linens—"

"Then my lands and castle—they don't matter anymore."

"If you wish to have those clothes washed, I'll send my laundress to fetch them."

"You've got a dowry, with or without Castétis."

She said nothing. He looked into her gilded brown eyes

until she looked away. Jehan suddenly realized that this woman no longer tended him in order to ensure that his ransom would be delivered. She no longer needed his lands and castle. She was the heiress to the entire Tournan estate—an estate far greater than his simple Castétis. Yet she came to his room, still, as if nothing was changed, swallowing her hatred of a man who had stolen her dowry lands, feeding him and binding his wounds.

Why was she here? Was it simple compassion? Was it out of a sense of duty? Was she here to try to regain her father's long-lost honor? He couldn't tell by looking at her young, flushed face. He knew one thing: Whatever the reason, it was incredibly, recklessly brave.

"You've continued caring for me," he murmured, "though you will no longer profit from it."

She wrapped her arms protectively around her sack. "I am not so heartless that I can let a man die in my castle."

"Not even a man you detest?"

"Not a man who has been treated so wretchedly."

"No one would blame you."

"I bear the name of Tournan. Someone in the family must show some sense."

He touched her cheek. She flinched but didn't pull away. Her skin was as soft and smooth as the finest silk. He found himself staring at her softly curved lips as they parted. Something moved in him, something that swept away all his earlier evil thoughts about wreaking vengeance on the Vicomte through this lovely creature. He owed her far more than he expected. Further, he admired such noble courage, especially in a woman, especially in the daughter of his enemy. "What you've done for me, *demoiselle,* is a brave and honorable thing."

"There's no joy in defying my father—"

"There is courage in doing what is right, in defiance of all else."

"I must go."

"What would your father do if he knew you were tending my wounds?"

She shrugged, a delicate movement of fragile bones under the silk of her wide neckline. "He won't find out until his rage has passed."

"Send one of your servants with food from now on. I won't have your punishment on my conscience."

"I assure you, Sir Jehan, that you have hurt me far more than my father ever could."

"Ah, but I didn't know you as I know you now. I won't repay your kindness by continuing to put you in danger."

"If you want to repay me," she said, stepping away, "then give my father Castétis."

"No, *demoiselle*—"

"It's the only payment that will suffice." She paused in the portal. "The sooner you are gone and this is settled, Sir Jehan, the sooner I can try to wipe the stain from my name."

"I'll find another way to thank you," he said, managing a slight bow, despite the pain, "a way far greater, far nobler, than giving your father Castétis. You have my word on it."

Chapter

4

ALIÉNOR GENTLY STROKED THE BLOND FEATHERS ON THE BREAST of the sparrowhawk and spoke the soothing words she always used to calm her. The hawk worried with her wings, spreading them unsurely, as Aliénor kicked her mare into a canter. She continued her cooing and tightened her grip on the jesses.

"She's still not used to the horse," Laurent said in a low voice as he nudged his gelding faster. "She should be on a lure by now."

"There'll be time enough to teach her the lure, after she's accustomed to my mare."

The dogs loped in front of the horses, sniffing among the underbrush for rabbits and thrushes as they traveled through the thick woods. The *autan* wind had eased today and the sun shone brightly through the spiny branches of the pines and the bare limbs of the oaks. The cracking of twigs under the horses' hooves was muffled in the thick moss on the forest floor. The chill autumn air stung her cheeks, and the brass bells on the hawk's legs jangled in the breeze.

Aliénor veered toward open ground. The hawk's beak opened in silent threat where it protruded from its feathered leather hood. The Vicomte had returned from Italy with this sparrowhawk and a larger goshawk, and had given her the smaller bird as a gift. The long voyage had disturbed the bird, however, and it was not yet accustomed to Aliénor's touch. She bit incessantly at her jesses, fought each time

Aliénor placed the hood over her head, and though she began to calm down at her words, she tolerated no one else's touch but Aliénor's.

She was a strong, independent, temperamental bird, and Aliénor adored her. She loved the way the hawk puffed out her soft chest, the way the bird stared at her with defiance and intelligence in its light yellow eyes. Even now, as the air rushed over her as they rode, the hawk spread her wings in eagerness to fly. Aliénor had begun to wonder if the bird had been captured too long after she'd left the nest, perhaps the hawk was already too wild to tame. There were times when she was tempted to release the sparrowhawk in the woods, despite her father's inevitable ire. She could claim she lost the bird while training her on the lure: the leash broke from wear, or it slipped from her grasp. She almost preferred to lose the hawk than to see such a wild creature tethered and imprisoned.

Imprisoned. Like the knight. She frowned and shifted uncomfortably on her mare. Her own hawk was treated better than Sir Jehan. In her mews, the hawk had light and air and the companionship of several other hawks and two falcons. The knight, by contrast, spent his time alone, beaten and restless, in the silence of his musty cell.

The situation was unbearable. Father's rage had subsided, somewhat, but he showed no sign of relenting in his behavior toward Sir Jehan. Aliénor tried her best to compensate: She sent tallow candles to his cell so he would not spend his time in utter darkness. She ordered the rushes swept out and relaid with rosemary and marjoram from the castle garden, to flush the stifling room of its noxious, sickly fumes. She ordered Jehan's ragged tunic and hose beaten clean in the Arrats. She was tempted to send his haubergeon to the smith to have the broken iron rings relinked, but she thought the move too bold—she would surely be discovered.

At least Sir Jehan was recovering, she thought. Considering the extent of his wounds, that alone was a miracle. The last time she visited him, he paced the length and breadth of the room like a wild beast. In the small, dim cell he seemed to loom over her as Goliath must have loomed over David. Each time she entered and saw how strong he grew, she wondered if he would strike her or vent his rage at the Vicomte on her. She wondered when the beast would grow too wild to be chained and, in an attempt to win his freedom, attack the one who fed him.

She knew her thoughts were foolish. Jehan had been kind to her since he discovered her father had made her an heiress. Each day she went to his cell, he demanded that she send someone else with his food, rather than put herself in danger. She refused, for if her father found out she was tending the prisoner, she would be punished; but if he found out one of the maidservants helped, the maidservant would be brutalized. Sir Jehan's vivid blue eyes watched her whenever she was with him. Now that the clouds of fever had long passed, she found them disturbingly intense. They were beautiful eyes, of the palest blue—almost gray. Such lucid eyes were wasted on a man. They belonged to a maiden, to a woman who could use them to capture a husband.

She shook her head. She shouldn't be riding in the autumn sunshine and thinking how much her enemy's eyes looked like the clear October sky. She was supposed to despise him. Only two weeks before she had yearned to confront this knight with anger and contempt. Now it was difficult to muster either emotion. It wasn't simply because Father had made her his heiress, thus lessening the need for those lands. Nor was it because Father behaved dishonorably, and she needed to make up for his behavior. It was because Sir Jehan treated her with deference, as any poor landless knight would treat a noblewoman of higher rank, and he did it despite the fact that she was his enemy's daughter. He was acting like a chivalrous knight—in spite of his thievery.

She was coming dangerously close to forgiving him. The thought was strangely disturbing.

She reined in her mare as they reached the top of the slope just east of the castle. She clicked her tongue to capture the dogs' attention so they would not race too far ahead. Laurent lagged behind, at the edge of the forest, for he refused to race, and Aliénor had unintentionally kicked her horse into a fast canter. She soothed her hawk and waited for Laurent to catch up.

"We shouldn't ride out of sight of the castle," he said as he reined in beside her.

"You didn't have to join me, *frai.*"

"I wasn't going to let you ride alone, not when the Prince's knights could be just beyond the next ridge."

"If the Prince arrives we'll be the first to see him," she said, gesturing to the eastern slopes. She turned her mare so the hawk could feel the sunshine on her breast. "Besides, I'm beginning to think the attack may be nothing but a rumor."

"I've prayed to Saint Jude that he won't come."

"Saint Jude!" She glanced at him in surprise. "Isn't it useless to pray to him *before* we're under siege? The Prince might not come, so the cause isn't hopeless."

"If the Prince is coming at all, he'll come to Castelnau."

"You mustn't think that way." She scanned the length of the valley, from the banks of the Arrats to the distant hills. The oaks on the northern slopes glowed in brilliant orange, red, and yellow hues. The harvest was long over, and most of the yield was already milled and stored, either in the cool, lightless bottom floor of the castle, or in the abbey of the nearby fortified *bastide.* "Maybe he won't come at all. It's too late in the season for him to start an attack. The harvest is in, and soon the cold rains will come."

"Father is still preparing."

She followed Laurent's gaze. The village men hovered on the edge of the trench that surrounded the castle walls. Some worked in the deep pit, pulling the weeds and brambles that had grown on the castle side of the slope. If the besiegers decided to rush the walls of the fortress, they'd find it difficult to crawl up out of the trench if the side closest to the wall had no footholds or roots to grip. Armed men paced the wall-walk incessantly.

She shivered, though she was wrapped warmly in a mantle lined with the finest miniver fur. Castelnau-sur-Arrats had never been under siege, but she had heard enough about sieges to fear them. She couldn't bear the thought of months of imprisonment within the walls, with the entire village sleeping in the great hall. She had heard stories about horrifying siege machines that could toss fiery projectiles over the walls into the heart of the castle. She had also heard stories of garrisons that had refused to surrender even though the inhabitants were forced to drink the blood of their horses in order to survive. She wondered if her father would hold out that long.

She wondered what the Prince would do if he succeeded in seizing Castelnau-sur-Arrats.

"Let's talk of something different." She kicked her horse into a walk and turned her toward the castle. "It's too fine a day to think of war."

"Then let me tell you about the friary in Toulouse."

She frowned and looked at her brother from beneath the shade of her pointed hunting cap. "After your antics in the courtyard, I'm not sure I like that subject any better."

"The chaplain told me it's a fine monastery," he began, ignoring his sister's comment. "Many of the older friars teach at the university. He said, too, that some of the friars take pilgrimages together, to Avignon to see the Pope, to shrines all over France, even as far as Rome."

"You'll be spending most of your time within the friary, *frai.* In a cold, lonely little cell." She lifted her face to the weak sunshine. "Is that what you really want? To be hidden away from the world?"

"I want to be closer to God."

"Isn't there enough time to be with Him when He calls you?"

"Aliénor!"

"I *know* what it's like to live in a convent." She lifted her arm higher, and the sparrowhawk spread her wings. "For seven years I watched those holy sisters live and die in that tiny little abbey, while the whole world, their whole life, simply passed them by. I don't want that to happen to you, *frai.*"

"I've long chosen—"

"They wouldn't even let me run in the sunshine. They were so worried I'd soil the black wool of my tunic, or tear my linen kirtle. They scolded me if lagged behind in the garden rather than racing to prayers. They punished me if I dug my fingers into the wet earth, or chewed on a blade of fresh spring grass, or snipped the wall blossoms and buried my face in their fragrance." Aliénor watched a small flock of late-migrating sparrows emerge from a copse of elms; they skimmed down the slope, then turn up again, gliding on a twisting breeze. "The sisters were always thinking, always *thinking,* never once stopping to *feel.*"

"Their minds were on more important things."

"I never realized all I was missing until I left the abbey and came to this castle." She glanced at him. "I found out I had a younger brother. A five-year-old brother with black, frightened eyes. No one told me. All those years, I could have watched you grow from a babe to a child. Instead, the only messages I ever received from the outside world were the sugared almonds that *Maman* sent during Christmas."

"I remember them. We haven't had them for years."

"The sisters took them away from me, as if it were blasphemous to enjoy anything soft or sweet."

"They are comforts of the flesh."

"Exactly! I can't have them after I die." She spread her free arm so her mantle gaped open, showing the rich girdle draped around her hips, beneath the slash of her silk surcoat sleeve. "While I'm on earth, I shall take my joys in earthly pleasures—especially in a husband, and children, and the warmth and comfort of a strong castle."

"I shall pray for your soul, Aliénor."

Her lips twitched. "With all your prayers, I could be the Devil's handmaiden and still be welcomed at Saint Peter's gates."

"Not if your nature leads you into sin."

"Oh, stop! You sound just like Father Dubosc. Both of you have so little faith in me." She closed the folds of her mantle as the wind tugged on its edges. "You know I can live a good life outside the cloisters. And you, my brother, can pray for the souls of men just as well without suffering, begging, and poverty."

"I can't." He glanced at his twisted foot. "I have too many sins to atone for."

She frowned, noticing her brother's glance. He had always blamed himself for his lameness. He treated his twisted, useless leg as if it were a physical manifestation of some dark sin buried in his soul. She had argued with him long and hard about that ridiculous notion, but she had never been able to dislodge it from his head. It didn't help that his father despised him, his mother paid him little attention, and the villagers always made the sign of the cross whenever he limped by, despite the fact that he went to the village only to give alms and gifts to the vassals of the castle. Laurent's soul was as pure and clean as spring waters, he was generous to a fault, and she hated to see him torture himself in this way. "It's difficult carrying the sins of the world upon your shoulders, isn't it, *frai?*"

He shrugged. "The sins of this family are more than enough. Between you and father . . ." He sobered. "There is one small problem with joining the friary."

"I know."

"If I want to be more than a lay brother, father has to make a donation."

"The friary in Toulouse will demand it. After all, you are the only son of the Vicomte de Tournan."

"Do you think he'll refuse?"

"Oh, no. He'll pay."

"How can you be so sure?"

"He'll pay to wipe away his own sin, Laurent, his sin of

dispossessing his only son—if he really does dispossess you." She hesitated, thinking of Sir Jehan. "He may pay to wipe away all his other sins as well."

"And I shall pray for him when I am in the friary, so that he may be forgiven."

She could scarcely believe Laurent would pray for the welfare of the man who scorned him, who beat him, and who had taken away his birthright. She knew she could never be so forgiving. Her brother did have a touch of the saint in him. He had to, she supposed, to want to join the brotherhood of the Franciscans.

Then, as she gazed upon her brother's familiar features, she realized that Laurent really was going to join a monastery. It was no longer a powerless threat. The thought disturbed her. He had been claiming he would for a long time, and until now, the claim was nothing but a young boy's dream. Now that he was dispossessed, he was free to do what he always wanted to do, what he always swore he would do, what he was now destined to do if the Vicomte did not soon change his mind.

The hope that Papa would change his mind was growing more unlikely with each passing day. For a few days after her father's announcement, she had waited, anxiously, hoping he would retract his hasty words in front of the entire household. No retraction ever came. Laurent's name never left his lips. Furthermore, the Vicomte de Baste, the father of Guy, had recently arrived at the castle. Such a visit, through a countryside rife with rumors of the Prince of Wales's imminent attack, could only mean one thing: Her father and de Baste were negotiating a marriage contract, between the heir to the lands of Baste and the heiress to those of Tournan.

Laurent would join a monastery. He was no more than a boy, truly, she thought. He would turn fourteen years of age just before the Christmas feasts. He was thin of face and figure, and pale to the point of sickliness. Yet, despite his outward frailty, he had a brilliant light in his black eyes, and he sat straight in his saddle. He had always wanted to join the Franciscans. He had surprised her that day in the courtyard when he'd intentionally failed with the lance to provoke his father. She had never expected him to be so clever, so willing to risk so much to have his way. Her brother was a Tournan after all, but it was so easy to forget it when she gazed upon his young, pious face.

Her heart lurched a little. If Laurent joined a monastery, she would never see him again—or so infrequently that it amounted to the same. She remembered the day she first laid eyes on her brother. She had just arrived home from the convent. Laurent had skulked in the corners of the castle, following her around in the shadows, but never greeting her. Neglected by *Maman* and the servants, he was dirty and unkempt, a quiet, frightened child with eyes like black coals. She took him in hand. She taught him how to walk straight and tall despite his awkward limb. She watched him smile his first smile—certainly, it seemed like his first—when she presented him with his own pup, a fine greyhound from a litter they had watched being born. She hid Laurent from their father whenever he was in a rage. As the boy grew older, she urged him to wield a sword and ride a horse, like any other boy his age. Now he was planning to leave. She felt a looming sense of loss, as huge and overwhelming as the dark specter of the plague. Laurent was the last of her siblings; if she lost him, she would be alone.

She reined her mare to a halt a few steps before the drawbridge to the castle. Dropping her reins on her lap, she reached out and touched her brother's arm. "Promise me, Laurent, that you won't leave Castelnau until I am wed."

He hesitated. "You shall be married soon, I expect. The Vicomte de Baste has arrived—"

"Just promise me."

"Does it mean so much to you?"

"Yes."

"Then I won't leave, *ma sor.*" He made the sign of the cross. "Not until you are safely wed to the next Vicomte de Tournan."

* * *

Aliénor walked nervously down the stairs of the castle, smoothing the snug red and green *mi-parti* surcoat over her waist and abdomen. She wore a gold chain wound with a rope of pearls around her hips. Her circlet rested on her head, over her veil. She wondered for the hundredth time if the Vicomte had summoned her for good news or for bad.

She entered the great hall and saw her father, alone, close to the huge fireplace cut into the thick rear wall, the wall the castle shared with the fortifications. He looked up as she entered, and to her utter surprise, he held out both hands to her.

"Come, my daughter. Let me look at you."

She lifted her skirts and walked over the crinkling rushes. The heat of the fire warmed her as she neared the hearth. She gave one hand to her father and dipped in a low curtsy.

"Up, child." He tilted her face by the chin and frowned. "I can hardly call you that anymore. How old are you now?"

"I will be twenty-three next Candlemas Day, my lord."

His frown deepened. The slash he'd received in the battle with Sir Jehan glowed angry and pink across his cheek and nose. "I didn't realize how much time had passed." He released her chin. "But it matters no more. I've found a husband for you, Aliénor. A strong, healthy knight."

She blinked. She wasn't surprised. The Vicomte de Baste had left for his own estates only that morning. But this was the fourth time she'd heard those words—*I've found a husband for you, Aliénor*—and she forcefully suppressed her excitement. She could not help but think she was cursed, as the servants often whispered, and this fourth attempt at marriage would also fail.

"He's the heir to great estates. What's this silence? Don't you wish to know his name?"

"Of course, my lord."

"He is the eldest of de Baste." He placed his hands on his hips, at the level of his thick gold baldric. "You'll not only be the Vicomtesse de Tournan, but also the Vicomtesse de Baste. Have I not done well for you?"

"Oh, Father . . ." She lifted her hands to her lips, for her exclamation was not of joy, but of disappointment, for this last act confirmed unequivocally that her father had dispossessed Laurent. "Have you made all the arrangements for the betrothal?"

"The Vicomte agreed before he departed."

"But what of my dowry lands—the lands held by St. Simon?"

Her father's face darkened. "Your dowry, my daughter, is my entire estate. Have you forgotten so soon?"

"No, my lord." She lowered her hands from her face and smoothed her palms against the woolen surcoat. "But isn't Castétis a part of my dowry? It is, after all, a part of your estate."

"It's insignificant compared to all else I've given you."

"I only wished to know its fate." She dared to place a hand on his arm. "It was, for so long, all that I hoped for."

Her father's frown did not soften at her touch, and she let her hand slip from his arm. He turned and walked away from her, clasping his hands behind his back. "St. Simon has refused to give Castétis back to me. He seems to prefer imprisonment."

"You've spoken to Sir—to the prisoner?"

"Of course I have." He looked at her. "He looks surprisingly healthy for a man who, three weeks ago, was all but dead. I expected him to beg for release. Instead, I find him strong, healthy, and defiant."

She hoped her father would blame the color in her cheeks on the glow from the fire in the hearth.

"It's for the best, I suppose. If the thief had died, it would not reflect well on me. But in his healthy condition, St. Simon is in no mood to humor my recent behavior. I've decided to release him from the tower and allow him to roam freely into the courtyard—with guards, of course. Perhaps the fresh air will give him a better disposition."

"I think it would." She lowered her eyes as her father glanced at her sharply. "It's like the hawk you gave me,

Father. She is gentler and tamer since I've removed her from her cage and put her in the mews. She flies to the lure now."

He grunted. "Sir Jehan will fly to my lure, sooner or later. If he doesn't, he'll find himself forever imprisoned in that tower. One way or another, I shall have those lands before the feast of the Epiphany. That will be your wedding day."

And Laurent? she wanted to ask. *What will you do with Laurent?* She knew from her father's expression that she had won one battle—she was forgiven for having tended Sir Jehan's wounds—and she knew better than to start a war by mentioning Laurent. Another day, perhaps after Sir Jehan agreed to give her father her lands as ransom, she would approach him about Laurent. She knew now that her brother would never be the Vicomte de Tournan, but she could at least convince him to bestow something upon the Franciscan monastery Laurent wanted to enter. She could not leave this castle, she could not marry into another family, before making sure Laurent was settled.

Impulsively, she closed the distance between her and her father, raised herself up on her toes, and kissed him lightly on the cheek. "Thank you, Papa." She curtsied quickly, then turned to the door. "I must go and tell *Maman* so I can begin preparations."

She left the great hall by the main door and raced out into the cool, windy day. She would tell *Maman,* eventually, but right now she wanted to find Laurent. Lightly touching the oak rail, she gathered her heavy skirts in one hand and skimmed down the stairs. She glanced around the courtyard but saw no sign of him. Some of the men-at-arms practiced their swordplay, sweating and posing for two young kitchen servants who fed the pigs gathered in a pen near the outdoor kitchens. The steward hovered near the door, collecting the last of the fruit and wine owed to the Vicomte by the men who worked his land. Other armed men paced the wall-walk, their attention half on the horizon, half on the mock battle taking place below.

Three greyhounds and her favorite black and white spotted spaniel trotted to Aliénor's side. She petted their heads as her gaze swept the courtyard and settled on the chapel. Clicking her tongue so the dogs would fall in place around her, she turned in that direction. If Laurent was anywhere this time of day, he was in the cool interior of the church, praying for someone's soul. Probably hers, she mused. The Vicomte de Baste had feasted late into the night with her father, and she had stayed awake still later to bring food to Sir Jehan. She had been too weary to rise for Mass.

"Demoiselle!"

She stopped in the middle of the courtyard. She turned and searched for the man who'd called her. She saw three men walking briskly toward her from the direction of the stables. Two of them she recognized as her father's vassals, but the third . . .

Her breath caught in her throat. It couldn't be him, she told herself, even as she scanned his clothing. He strode too surely for a man who only weeks before was a breath away from death. Yet he wore the surcoat, the surcoat with the huge bloodstain that would not come out of the front, no matter how much tallow and wood-ash soap and hard pounding the laundress used. She recognized the ragged hose, the bandage that still covered his left hand. He should look ridiculous in such worn, tattered clothes. He should look weak, tired, battle-weary, but as he came closer he looked as vibrant and fresh as a newly dubbed knight.

Her heart lost its steady, even rhythm and began to pound awkwardly in her chest. Father had been true to his word: He had released Sir Jehan from his cell, and he had seen fit to allow the knight a bath as well. The scar on his forehead was hidden beneath his dark, shoulder-length hair, which gleamed with chestnut highlights in the sunshine. His lips spread into a smile as he approached, a smile she could see easily now that his face was clean of the dark bristle that had obscured his features for weeks, a smile that produced—of all things on a knight's face—a deep dimple on one lean cheek.

"Demoiselle," he repeated. His shadow reached her be-

fore he did. She stepped back in surprise as he towered over her, his height overwhelming in the bright of day. Instinctively, she lifted her hands in defense. To her utter surprise, Jehan clutched her right hand, lifted it to his lips, and then fell to one knee in front of her.

She stared, speechless, at his bent head, which, because of his height, was no more than a few hands below her chin. Her hounds hesitantly sniffed the knight, and the spaniel dared to nudge Jehan's bandaged hand. She felt the warmth of Sir Jehan's lips on her fingers, and the feeling was frighteningly pleasant. For a moment she stood in utter shock, too overwhelmed to respond, waiting for him to speak.

He lifted his head but did not release her hand. Their eyes caught and locked, and Aliénor wondered how she'd ever thought them gray—they were as blue as the clearest sapphires.

"I have you to thank, daughter of Tournan, for my freedom."

"Freedom?"

"Oui. If I hadn't been released from that tower, I would have torn it apart with my bare hands."

She was having great difficulty thinking when his fingers caressed her own, when his gaze traveled over her face with such intensity. "I . . . I don't know what you mean."

"You intervened with your father, to have me released and set under guard in the courtyard."

Suddenly she remembered what her father had just told her: He had allowed Jehan to leave the tower. "No, I had nothing to do with it. Father's rage has passed. He freed you of his own will."

The knight's smile widened, the dimple deepened. "Humility is a fine virtue in a maiden, but I know your hand was in these doings."

She opened her mouth to protest, then closed it, knowing that Sir Jehan would never believe her father capable of regret. She suddenly became aware of the silence in the courtyard. The men-at-arms had stopped their swordplay and they, along with the servants near the kitchens, were watching. Even the steward had stopped quarrelling with one of her father's yeomen to stare at them in interest. She realized her hand was still lost within Jehan's larger one.

"Please arise, Sir Jehan." She pulled gently on her hand. "The men are staring."

"So am I."

She flushed and glanced at the castle windows. "If my father should see you thus—"

"I shall tell him I was simply overcome by your beauty and could not control myself."

"He'll toss you back in the tower."

He rubbed his thumb across the back of her hand, then reluctantly released it. "I suppose you're right." Petting the hounds around him, he stretched stiffly to his full height and stared down at her. "It's worth the punishment, to see your beauty in the bright of day."

"You're beginning to sound like a troubadour, Sir Jehan, and there are people listening."

"I didn't fall on my knee in order to hide my admiration." He gestured to the width of the courtyard. "I want everyone here to know who among the Tournans is the most worthy of their loyalty."

She held her breath in surprise. She knew, even as he said the words, that they were a blatant insult to her father. Yet they were also meant as a compliment to her. Something woke in her breast, something disturbing and wonderful, something that stirred more forcefully as she met and held Jehan's gaze.

"'Tis true," he continued. "I won't forget how much you risked to come to my aid. I'd pledge my own sword to you, but it seems I've lost it."

She glanced to where his baldric lay, denuded of its sword and dagger, across his lean hips. "That's fortunate for you."

"Demoiselle?"

"It will prevent you from making hasty pledges, Sir Jehan." She stepped back a little, away from the force of his presence. She narrowed her eyes against the glare of the sun.

"After all, I could ask you to use that pledged sword to return my old dowry lands, and then what would you do? Battle with yourself?"

He laughed, suddenly, sharply, and the spaniel barked in response. "You shouldn't have reminded me—it would have made your father's task easier."

"My father will get what he wants. He usually does." She turned away. She needed to get out of the sun, to get away from this man's overwhelming presence. She started walking to the chapel, and Sir Jehan fell into step beside her.

"Shall we make a pledge of our own?"

He touched her arm, lightly, but she felt the heat of his fingers as if her forearm were bare and not covered with the tight linen sleeve of her undertunic. "What sort of pledge?"

"That we shall not talk of Castétis. Leave that discussion, as it should be, to your father and myself."

"Then we have nothing to say to each other."

"Haven't you ever whiled away an afternoon in conversation, *demoiselle?*"

She reached the shade of the walkway, just in front of the chapel. His hand still lay, lightly, on her forearm. He stood so close to her—close enough for her to smell the lingering scent of the harsh soap he had used to strip his body and clothes of blood and dirt. The guards hovered a few steps behind. She wondered why they didn't order the prisoner to take his hand from her, or to move away, and then wondered why she didn't give him the order herself.

"For an hour, then," he urged.

She forgot, completely, what he had asked. "An hour?"

"Yes. Let's not talk of those lands for an hour." His fingers traced the newly sewn seam of her sleeve, lying against her inner wrist. "You might even come to like me."

His smile was slow, sure, and tempting. How had he hidden *that* beneath his beard? She wondered how many innocents had succumbed to that grin and, in the process, lost their virtue. She, of course, would not lose her virtue— that was pledged to her betrothed and the guards would never let this prisoner be so bold—but she could lose some

71

of her nice, safe preconceptions about Jehan. She tilted her head in consideration. She had once hated this man so much that she had cursed him to the very bowels of Hell. Now, despite the fact that he had caused her so much misery, she was beginning to *like* him.

What harm could be in it? She was betrothed now, and the heiress to the lands of Tournan. Sir Jehan could cause her no more harm. Her breath caught a little. She felt a pulse throb unevenly in her throat. He was handsome, in a vibrant, overwhelming sort of way. What harm could there be in flirting with a knight, a handsome knight, a knight who had been shamefully mistreated by a member of her own family?

"Very well, Sir Jehan." She turned toward the mews. "You have until the midday meal. We shall not speak of . . . you know what."

Chapter
5

JEHAN FELL INTO STEP BESIDE HER AS SHE HEADED TOWARD THE
wooden structure of the mews. The hounds trotted happily
around her feet, carefully avoiding her long, trailing skirts.
He wondered where the page was—the one who took care of
these dogs—and why the boy wasn't keeping them kenneled
instead of letting them run free in the courtyard. The spaniel
stared up at the maiden as if she were the only creature in
the courtyard.

He knew he was staring at her in the same way. The red
and green surcoat clung to the sweet curve of her back, then
fell in soft folds below her hips, reminding him in a forceful,
personal way that he had not lain with a woman for weeks.
He had been waiting all morning for the opportunity to
thank her for getting him out of the cell. Over the last few
days, he thought he would lose his senses if he remained in
that stinking, tiny room any longer. But when he saw her at
the top of the castle stairs, and watched her skim down them
as lightly as a leaf on the autumn wind, he forgot his original
purpose for searching for her. He wanted to tear the veil off
her hair and watch the sunlight play among her tresses, then
arch her willowy body over his arm and see whether her lips
were as soft as he imagined. He hadn't, of course. His battle
senses returned, making him conscious of the two guards
who shadowed his every move. Soon after, his wavering
sense of chivalry returned. This woman was a world above
him in rank and wealth. She deserved to be treated as a lady,

73

not a loose-skirted peasant. And he had too great a reason to bow his head before her; he wouldn't dishonor her by showing her his lust.

The fever must have addled him. She was an heiress to a viscounty, and he was nothing but her father's prisoner. Following her around the courtyard, as star-struck as her damned hounds, was foolish torment. He *should* be looking for a way to escape this castle. If all had gone as planned, Prince Edward should have entered Armagnac days ago. But instead of gathering information about the castle's strength and searching for a way to escape, he was spending his time idling in the autumn warmth, flirting with the daughter of his enemy.

"Wait here, Sir Jehan." She passed through the narrow door of the mews. "I'm bringing my hawk out into the air."

The dogs sat obediently by the door. She reemerged minutes later with a heavy, boiled-leather glove on her hand that drooped around her thin forearm. The hawk's talons dug into her covered wrist. She deftly loosened the tie on the back of the hawk's hood with her free hand and her small, sharp teeth, then carefully lifted the hood off her head. The hawk blinked several times, and her round yellow eyes scanned the courtyard.

"She's still not used to me." She tucked the hood into a leather bag slung across her hips. "Father gave her to me only six weeks ago."

"Your father is a generous man—to his daughter."

"I think, Sir Jehan, that my father is a forbidden subject. Come, let's circle the courtyard."

"I'm at a disadvantage, *demoiselle* . . ."

Her lips curved. "My name is Aliénor."

"Qu'em belha."

"My father thought it was lovely, too. It was his mother's name. I forgot you spoke Gascon—you spoke to me in that language when I first tended you. Where did you learn it?"

"I am Gascon. I was born in western Armagnac."

"Oc," she said, switching into the dialect. "But you're English-Gascon. Most English-Gascons speak only French."

"My family has lived in Armagnac since my great-grandfather moved to Gascony, so Gascon is my native tongue." He gestured toward the castle. "Your father speaks French, and he's not English-Gascon."

"He has to—he communicates often with the King of France." She tilted her chin and riveted him with those bold gold-brown eyes. "Not a word about my father's loyalties, Sir Jehan—or I vow this conversation will end."

His lips quirked into a smile. "I know where the battlelines are drawn."

"There's another reason why my father must speak French," she continued. "My mother is from Normandy. After nearly thirty years in this castle, she still hasn't learned our dialect."

"If she's from Normandy, that explains your hair." He stilled the urge to reach out and touch it beneath the silk veil. "There are few Gascons so fair."

"My mother's eyes are more unusual—they're the shade of blue heather."

"Heather is common on the hills. The color of your eyes is more rare." He gestured to her bird. "They're the shade of a hawk's plumage—brown with streaks of pure gold."

She shielded her eyes with a feathery sweep of lashes. She jerked on her skirts as one of the hounds stepped on the hem. "You *should* have been a troubadour, Sir Jehan, not a fighting knight."

"And spend my time singing love songs to wary maidens?"

"You certainly have the tongue for it, and it would have saved me a lot of misery. A lute is far less powerful than a sword."

"That depends on what one wishes to capture. A lute can capture a woman's heart far swifter than a sword."

"But a lute," she said pointedly, "cannot capture a castle or lands."

"It can if the troubadour uses a lute to woo and win a woman who *has* such riches."

"But then the only injury is the lady's broken heart."

"And with a sword the win is bloody, quick, and certain."

"Not so certain," she mused. "In the case of Castétis, you might have done better with a lute."

"I think, *demoiselle,* that even a lute would have been useless." He gestured to her sparrowhawk. "After all, you can't lure a falcon with an empty hand. Before Castétis, all I had to my name was a horse and rusty armor. I must make my fortune by the sword first—then use a lute to augment it."

"I shall warn the ladies of Gascony." She peered at his bandaged hand. "Fortunately, you're powerless for now. The swelling seems to have subsided."

"Then unwind the linens."

"And release you to wield your terrible weapons?"

"Milady, there's not a lute or sword in sight, and I don't think the guards will hand me either."

She smiled, showing a glimpse of teeth as even and white as a string of perfectly matched pearls. "I suppose, then, it can do no harm."

"Good! I am tired of spilling wine on my tunic."

"You'll have to unwind it yourself." She tilted her head toward her hawk. "I, too, have only one hand today."

Jehan searched for the end of the linen, then rapidly unwound the cloth. He flexed his stiff fingers as they were freed.

"Any pain?"

"No."

"You shouldn't raise a shield for a while—or a lute—but it looks healthy."

"Did your mother teach you so much of healing?"

"My mother faints at the sight of blood." She cooed to her sparrowhawk as they passed the tumult at the castle portal, for the noise caused the bird to stretch her wings and open her beak anxiously. "The midwife taught me all she knew after I came home from the convent, so I could take over my mother's duties."

"You'll make a man a fine wife someday."

" 'Someday' is during the feast of the Epiphany."

He curled his stiff fingers until he felt the pain. "Your father didn't take long, did he?"

"He took far too long. I'm nearly twenty-three years of age."

"In the flower of womanhood."

"Scarcely! The girls I knew at the convent are all married, one with eight children, at last count."

"You sound envious."

"I am. They've run castles on their own, they've watched the cycle of a dozen harvests, they've given life to children and watched them grow—"

"Has your father promised you to Guy de Baste?"

"Yes." She looked at him with narrowed eyes. "You told me he was popular with women. I'm still not sure if that's a good quality or a bad one."

"That depends on what you seek in a husband."

"I seek only a husband. I don't care if he's old and fat and pitted with scars." She paused. "Well, maybe I do care. But I can't ask for much—not at my age—and if my husband isn't handsome, well, it's a sacrifice I'll make to stay out of the cloisters."

She moved away from the penned pigs and goats as they neared the kitchens. She kicked her feet against her long, trailing skirts, raising up little puffs of dust in the process. He thought, suddenly, that placing her in a nunnery would be like winding a death sheet around a lively, yearling colt.

"Guy de Baste is the fourth man to whom I've been betrothed," she continued. "Two others died before the wedding, and the third abandoned me after . . . the forbidden subject. Sir Guy could be the Devil's own sire and I wouldn't complain, but it's comforting to know he's young and handsome."

Jehan said nothing. He wondered what she would do when she discovered Guy de Baste's slippery loyalties. Which would be stronger: her loyalty to her father and the French, or her loyalty to her husband? He found the question disturbing. He sensed she would be loyal to what she believed to be right—as she was when she tended him in defiance of her father's orders. His thoughts darkened as he wondered what Guy de Baste would do when he ultimately discovered that his wife was no quiet, subservient woman.

"Why are you looking at me like that? You looked like that before, when I told you that I may be wed to Guy de Baste. What are you hiding from me, Sir Jehan?" She stopped as they passed the northwest tower and faced him. "If there is something I should know about my betrothed, I'd rather know before the wedding ceremony."

He hesitated. He wanted to tell her. Certainly, he reasoned, he had an obligation to tell her, after all she had done to save his life. He knew that the knowledge of Guy's ambivalent loyalties was the one thing that would cause her to reject a husband. She would tell her father. Her father would be suspicious enough to delay the marriage until he determined the truth. Aliénor would be denied another husband. Yet, even as he considered telling her that Guy's loyalties shift with the winds, he knew he couldn't. Jehan's loyalties lay in another direction. He was a vassal of the Prince of Wales. The English prince was determined to reunite these rebel lands. If Guy truly had English loyalties and he married the heiress of Tournan, the lands of Tournan would return to the English. If Jehan warned her, he would thwart the Prince's ultimate goal. Jehan owed the deepest, most sacred loyalty to him, that of a vassal to a liege lord. It overpowered any obligation he had to this woman.

Still, he wanted to tell her. As he stared down into her gold-brown eyes, he wanted to make her reject her husband. Guy de Baste didn't deserve such a woman. Such a woman needed to be protected from the cruelty of the world beyond these walls, she needed to be protected from men like Guy de Baste. In the safety of the cloisters and her father's castle, she had grown to be a bold, fearless creature. She didn't know the outside world. He did. He understood its cruelty, its treachery, its harshness to the innocent. He wanted to protect this brilliant ray of light from that darkness.

He wanted her.

"Sir Jehan . . ."

"Have you guessed, Aliénor?" For a brief moment, he didn't care that his desire was emblazoned across his face; he didn't care that the guards hovered several paces behind them, leaning against the northwest tower. The hawk stretched her wings, sensing the tension. "Guy de Baste doesn't deserve you. Any man would be mad not to want you for his own."

"Sir Jehan—"

"Including, and especially, me."

Her cheeks flushed. She did not step away. He expected her to protest, he expected her to react with shock. Instead, she held his gaze. Desire surged in him. He wanted to taste her skin, to bury his face in the heat and fragrance of her hair, to run his fingertips over her soft, bare shoulder.

"You mustn't say such things." Her voice lowered to a whisper. "You are my father's enemy, and mine."

He touched her arm, gently, but then he tightened his hold so that she knew his grip would turn to iron if she tried to pull away. "I'm your father's enemy. I am not yours."

"Even now, you hold back Castétis."

"Castétis is all that I have. It is what keeps me from becoming a mercenary."

"Those lands belong to me."

"Your father left them untended and badly protected. The walls of Castétis were little more than rubble, the villeins were starving. I took it by strength of arms—"

"By strength of arms?" Her confusion turned to anger. "You stole something from my father when he was away, when I was defenseless—"

"I didn't know he was in Florence. I kept waiting for him to come and try to seize Castétis back."

"Why are you telling me this?"

"I don't want you to despise me anymore, Aliénor."

He was so close to her that one of the guards cleared his throat loudly. Jehan wished they would go away, if only for a moment, only for *this* moment, as Aliénor stared at him expectantly. He wanted, more than anything, to smother her moist, parted lips in a kiss.

Suddenly the watchman in the portal tower released a cry. The sound echoed through the courtyard, breaking the sweet tension that stretched between them. She stepped away abruptly. She peered around him, toward the gate. The watchman gave the order for the portcullis to be raised.

"We have guests." She gathered her skirts in one hand. "I must go. . . . I must prepare to greet them."

He released her. She brushed by and crossed the courtyard to the mews. By the time she emerged moments later, without her hawk, pulling off the huge leather glove, he had gathered his wits. It was probably for the best that this visitor had interrupted them. His blood was running so hot that if she remained he *would* have kissed her—and probably received a sword in his side. But *damn,* she was lovely, and *damn,* it galled him to think of her in Guy de Baste's arms. He must have lost his senses for sure, he thought, to consider making love to the daughter of his captor in the middle of a sun-drenched courtyard.

"Stop gaping after her, knight, and let's see who braved the roads to visit us." The guards urged him forward, toward the portal. As they approached, Jehan heard the anxious clatter of hooves on the wooden drawbridge, then on the paving stones of the portal floor. A rider dressed in unfamiliar colors, little more than a boy, entered and leaned on the neck of his horse.

"It's a messenger from Seissan," one of the guards said.

The people in the courtyard flocked around the messenger. The steward of the castle raised his voice and the people parted to make a path for him. Jehan couldn't hear the boy's words, but the cries that rose among the cluster of villeins suggested the news. Suddenly the steward's voice boomed out above the babble of the crowd. "Call the villagers to the castle! Man the battlements! The Prince of Wales is burning Seissan!"

The courtyard erupted with activity. The villagers fled through the portal in order to gather their possessions and families from the small village and bring them within the

safety of the walls. Jehan watched the men-at-arms run
about, preparing their posts by piling arrows near the
narrow windows. He scanned the battlements, counting the
men-at-arms, noting where the archers took their places. His
two guards shifted restlessly, staring at the top of the eastern
wall, but they did not leave his side. He sensed he would be
thrown in the northwest tower soon, to free these men for
more important duties. He cursed beneath his breath. It was
too late to plan an escape now. The Prince of Wales was at
Seissan, a few hours' ride away. The Vicomte would lock
Jehan away until the danger had passed.

"You two, go and prepare yourself for battle. You are
needed on the wall-walk."

Jehan turned. The voice belonged to an older man, a
knight about the age of the Vicomte de Tournan. He was
armored richly and wearing a heraldry Jehan did not
recognize.

One guard protested. "The Vicomte said we must guard
him—"

"This prisoner can be guarded by my squire," the newcomer insisted. "Your services are needed to defend this
castle. Go."

The guards obeyed him. Jehan eyed the knight, then
glanced over his shoulder to where the knight's squire stood.
Jehan resisted the urge to smile. The squire was little more
than a boy. Suddenly, escape did not seem so impossible.

"I have waited long to talk to you, Sir Jehan. Come into
the shadows where we won't be noticed."

The knight led him to an arched awning against the
chemise wall. His sword clattered against the plate armor on
his calves and thighs. Jehan wondered why the man wanted
such privacy. Once engulfed in shade, he turned to him.

"I must be brief, for if we're seen together all is lost. I am
Sir Rostanh of Bajon, a vassal of the Vicomte de Tournan. I
speak for two more vassals: Sir Geoffroi of Garrigas and Sir
Doat de Bourreu. We witnessed what happened on the
battlefield the day you were captured."

Jehan scowled. This knight witnessed Guilhem's murder, yet did nothing about it. There was as much dishonor in that as if he had pierced Guilhem with a dagger himself.

"We had nothing to do with the Vicomte's actions," the man protested. "But I see you doubt me—it doesn't matter. What he did was heinous to all of us, yet we've sat weeks in our silence and done nothing, for fear of what he'd do if we raised our voices against him."

"Your apology is too late, Sir Rostanh. My squire is dead and I'm still a prisoner." He gestured to the castle, at the door behind which Aliénor had just disappeared. "Yon maiden has more courage than all of you."

"Yon maiden holds the heart of her father in her hand. She has little to lose. But we, his vassals, hold everything by his good graces. Don't judge us so harshly, Sir Jehan, until you hear what I have to say."

"Say it."

"The Vicomte is our liege lord and we cannot defy him openly, lest we lose our land and be branded traitors. But we can no longer allow him to heap injustices on his name and ours."

"Then betray him and open the castle to the Prince's forces."

"*Non.* If the Prince comes, we will fight him, as is our duty." The knight's face darkened. "Instead, we have decided to help you escape. With conditions."

"What conditions?"

The knight scanned the courtyard nervously. "When you find the Prince, tell him what I have told you. Tell him who has helped you escape. Sir Rostanh of Bajon, Sir Geoffroi of Garrigas, and Sir Doat de Bourreu. Ask Prince Edward to spare our lands, our castles, and our families."

Jehan looked at him in surprise. The knight asked for no gold, no promise of title or wealth, no guarantee that he could keep his lands if and when the Prince seized the Vicomte's castle. He narrowed his eyes in speculation. Perhaps there was no more to this than an effort to save honor.

"Make your decision quickly, Sir Jehan, before people become suspicious of us."

"I cannot promise the Prince will listen to me."

"He will, if you argue with intent."

"I can promise you only that I will try." He glanced around the courtyard. "When do we strike?"

Father was furious. Aliénor slipped deeper under the pelts on her bed and pulled a feather pillow over her head to try to block out the sound of his angry voice. His rage had been going on for hours, since Jehan was discovered missing, and the squire who guarded him was found unconscious in the top room of the northwest tower.

Missing. . . . Her father's rage had reached new heights when he received the news. Not only had the prisoner escaped, but he had spent half a day wandering in the courtyard and learning all he could about the castle defenses. Jehan knew how many men paced the wall-walk, how many yeomen and women filled the castle courtyard, how many arrows and stones and how much oil they had prepared to fend off seizure. He knew the layout of the castle. He had a general idea of how long their salted pork, wine, and milled grain would last in a siege. And the Prince of Wales, Sir Jehan's liege lord and the Vicomte's most powerful enemy, burned and pillaged only a handful of leagues away.

Her father had blamed his escape on treachery, and Aliénor had to agree. How else could all the armed men on the wall-walk avoid seeing the prisoner tie a rope around one of the toothed crenellations of the rampart and lower himself down into the trench that surrounded the castle? Where did Jehan get the rope? *Who gave it to him?* When the squire who had guarded Jehan gained consciousness, he denied that he had helped Jehan escape. The Vicomte had beat him until the boy lay bleeding on the rushes. Then Father had turned his rage-filled eyes on her, his own daughter, in front of the men-at-arms, in front of the villagers who had rushed into the great hall for shelter from the sudden rain, and demanded to know if she'd had a hand in Sir Jehan's escape.

No! She was shocked by his accusation. *Would I risk my own fate, Father, for a knight who has done me nothing but harm?* The Vicomte didn't believe her. He knew she had tended Sir Jehan's wounds; he had witnessed Sir Jehan's actions yesterday afternoon, when the knight fell to one knee before her. For the first time in her life, Aliénor truly feared her father. Her mother's pleas were useless, as useless as her own innocent denial. For a breathless moment, she waited for his bloodied hand to fall upon her. Instead, he banished her to her room and vowed to deal with her later.

She wondered if Sir Jehan thought about her when he so slyly escaped from the castle. Did he wonder, after all the attention he paid to her yesterday afternoon, if her father would blame her for his escape? Did he feel any remorse at leaving her in such a situation, after all she had done for him? Confusion filled her. He charmed her yesterday, as no man had ever charmed her. He made her wonder if she were not too old to be considered desirable. He looked at her so fiercely when she told him she was to be married to Guy de Baste. A tremor rippled through her, but this was not fear or cold. This was a different emotion, an echo of the feelings that coursed through her body yesterday afternoon, when he stepped so close to her. His eyes, so blue, so intense, burned her, deep inside.

She shifted restlessly in the bed and removed the pillow from over her head. The fur pelts ruffled against her legs, bare where her shift had risen to her mid-thighs. No man had ever looked at her like that. Certainly it was a sin in itself, to stare at a woman until her insides quivered. It evoked a new, wondrous feeling. She had felt as vibrant as if he had wound his hands in her hair, pulled her head back, and kissed her full on the lips.

The thought brought new heat to her cheeks and she sat up abruptly. Laurent would chide her if he knew what thoughts now wandered through her head. Such fantasies were better reserved for her husband-to-be, Guy de Baste, *if* the wedding ever occurred. Now that Sir Jehan had escaped, the betrothal was in danger, for if the knight directed his prince to this castle, the English would settle in for a siege lasting months. There would be no Epiphany wedding.

Perhaps . . . She closed her eyes and shook her head. She dared not hope, but hope blossomed in her chest nonetheless. She remembered Jehan's words: *I am your father's enemy, not yours.* Had he sought her out in the courtyard simply to while away the morning in conversation, or did his words hold a subtle message? Was he trying to tell her, indirectly, that when he escaped he would veer the Prince's army *away* from Castelnau, for her sake? He promised her, weeks before, that he would find a greater, nobler way to show his gratitude than returning Castétis as his ransom. Was it too much to expect of a knight, to forgo vengeance for the sake of a woman?

She sat up in bed, reached for the center of the velvet hangings, and pulled them apart. A pale, gray light filtered through the two arrow slits in the northern wall of her room. A puddle of water grew among the rushes beneath each window, and the rain pattered as it fought to find a way through the narrow openings in the thick stone wall. A chill draft fluttered around the chamber and the fire withered to its last glowing embers. A semicircle of prone, sleeping bodies littered the area between the hearth and the foot of her bed. During the night, the older women who could not fight for space near the hearth in the great hall had been allowed in her room to take advantage of her fireplace. The shapes, swathed in rough woolen cloaks, moved restlessly on the floor. Her father's voice rose anew in the nearby solar.

Sleep was useless, and she needed to talk to somebody. She needed to know if the Prince's army had veered away from Castelnau. She shivered as she slipped out from beneath the pile of pelts and walked silently to the chest at the foot of her bed. Lifting the heavy, carved oak lid, she reached in and pulled out the first surcoat she could find. She lowered the lid and pulled it over her head.

She stepped over the bodies on the floor and left her

room. Glancing both ways in the narrow aisle, she swiftly passed the hallway between her room and her brother's. Laurent's room was brighter than her own, for the dawn light filtered through the twinned, arched window that faced south, over the courtyard. Shivering, she silently stepped over the older men who slept near the hearth and pulled open the hangings surrounding her brother's bed.

Laurent started and sat up straight in bed. She lifted her finger to her lips. "Shh, Laurent, you'll wake the villagers who sleep nearby." She pulled the linens shut and wrapped herself in a pelt. She sat cross-legged and faced her brother. "Well? What happened last night after I was sent to my room?"

He blinked a few times, still dazed with sleep, then leaned over to open the hangings on the other side of the bed. "It's dawn already?"

"Oc," she answered. "I have not slept at all, waiting for the watchman's cry. Is there any sign of the Prince?"

"None, so far." He dropped the hangings. "Shouldn't you be abed? What if Father sends for you?"

"He's too busy making preparations for siege."

"He could have beaten you last night."

"He didn't, *frai.*" She shrugged. "It would have been unjust, for I'm innocent. I didn't help Sir Jehan escape."

Laurent looked at her skeptically.

"Of course I didn't help him! Why would I? I'm due to be married at the feast of the Epiphany—"

"Married?"

She nodded, remembering that in the confusion of the messenger's arrival yesterday afternoon and Sir Jehan's sudden escape, she had forgotten to tell her brother the news. "Sir Guy de Baste will be my husband. I went to tell you yesterday, but I was delayed."

"Delayed by that knight, I suppose."

"You look just like Father when you scowl."

"If Father saw Sir Jehan and you yesterday, then I am not surprised he suspects you."

"All Sir Jehan did was kneel in front of me."

"He touched your arm, too."

"He just thanked me for caring for his wounds."

"I *knew* you tended him!"

She bit her lip as she realized she had slipped and revealed her secret.

"You'd better say penance for defying Father."

"Listen, Laurent, if Sir Jehan had died, think of what would have happened to all of us."

"Nothing that would not have happened anyway." He gestured toward the east, through the linen hangings at the base of his bed. "Just outside, somewhere east of here, is the Prince of Wales with his men." He paused for a moment. "Is there any chance that Sir Jehan may persuade the Prince not to attack, because of tenderness toward you?"

The word lodged in her mind. *Tenderness.* Somehow it did not seem to describe the look in Jehan's eyes yesterday afternoon.

"You *did* save his life." Laurent's eyes were black and steady, and full of hope. "Do you think he'll intervene for your sake?"

"Don't be foolish." She shook her head, unwilling to voice her own hopes. "He's a knight—I don't know what he's thinking. Is there no more news?"

"Just about Seissan. They say that the Prince's men pillaged the city completely before they burned it. They . . . they killed the men, they dishonored the women, even the women of an abbey." He looked down at his hands. "What if they come here and somehow get into the castle?"

"Ai, frai . . ." She took her brother into her arms. He hugged her, as he had not done in years, not since the plague struck the village. She had heard only snatches of stories about the destruction of Seissan, for the men quieted when she wandered near. She knew Laurent had heard the worst, for the men would not spare a boy, even one as sensitive as Laurent. "Listen to me. Seissan was not well protected. Its only defenses were wooden palisades—they're easy to burn. Castelnau is made of stone and is far stronger than that city. We have enough supplies to survive a siege of many months,

so don't fear. The Prince won't take us. Father will fight to the last man."

Suddenly the Vicomte's voice roared from the solar. She heard the men at the foot of the bed stir from their slumber. The sound of many voices—the voices of the men-at-arms—came from her father's chamber, and she felt the first tremor of fear. Laurent struggled out of her grip and pulled open the linens. Footsteps clattered on the steps. She saw the flash of armor as men ran through the corridor with torches in their hands. A babble of women's voices came from her room, and Father's voice grew louder as he left the solar and headed toward the aisle between her room and Laurent's.

"Hide, Aliénor! Father mustn't see you."

He pushed her behind him and she tumbled atop the covers. She stiffened and remained in the furs when she heard her father's voice just outside the room, calling for all the men to come down to the hall. The villeins rose from the floor and left Laurent's room.

"What is it?"

"I know not." He closed the hangings on one side, crawled over the bed, and opened them on the other side. Dressed only in his shift, he stumbled to the floor and limped to the glass window clouded with silver stain. He struggled with the latch for a moment, then pushed the window out. She shivered as a blast of cold, rainy air entered the room.

She brought him a pelt and wrapped it around his shoulders, then stared out the window. She sucked in her breath as she saw the knights running for the stables and ordering their horses to be saddled. A crowd of armed men gathered on the wall-walk on the eastern side, and they stood pointing toward the horizon.

"They've sighted the Prince's men."

"No!" She ignored the rain that splattered her face. "Father wouldn't ride out to attack such an army—"

"I fear he would."

"You can't mean . . ." Her eyes widened and she stared at her brother, who stood, careless of the cold, with the pelt drooping on his narrow shoulders. All lingering hope that Sir Jehan might steer the Prince's men away for her sake shriveled and died.

"Father was furious, Aliénor. I don't think I've ever seen him in such a rage. His face reddened so much. . . ." Laurent bit his lower lip. "This is what I feared, this is what I prayed against. In his anger, he'd rather fight the Prince's forces than stay and defend the castle."

"That's madness!"

"Oc." Laurent agreed. He crossed himself. "Pray, Aliénor. Pray that his madness won't be our death."

Chapter
6

"HE HAS ATTACKED, MY LORD." JEHAN PULLED HIS DESTRIER TO A halt in front of the Prince of Wales, sending up a spray of mud that stained the blue, red, and gold trapper draped over the Prince's horse. "The Vicomte de Tournan saw your advance guard camped in the valley and couldn't resist. He charged out of the castle with about forty men-at-arms. There are fewer than a score of trained men remaining inside the fortress."

"You were right." The Prince grinned. "The rebel's a fool."

"He's as mad as a wild, wounded boar, and he has no idea that you're so close." Jehan glanced toward the Prince's retinue—four hundred men-at-arms, four hundred mounted archers, and three hundred archers on foot—who waited impatiently in the morning drizzle. "He's charging after the advance guard as if *they* were your entire army."

"He'll soon be faced with a thousand men." The Prince laughed, loudly and fearlessly, as only a twenty-five-year-old reckless youth on his first campaign could laugh. "This will be fine sport. Where is my squire?"

Jehan twisted on his mount and pointed to a young man who crouched behind a boulder on the peak of the ridge. "Your squire will give the signal when the advance guard has engaged the rebels."

The Prince turned and lifted his arm. The men in his contingent immediately prepared for battle. They removed the sodden blankets that had muffled the horses' neighing during the trip from Seissan to Castelnau. They hastily buckled on their baldrics, and their swords clanged against their armor. The sound echoed in the misty valley, but silence no longer mattered, for the fox had already been drawn out of his den.

Jehan's mount pranced beneath him, sensing his restlessness. Jehan could not wait to see the expression on the Vicomte's face when the Prince's retinue surged over the edge of the hill into the valley of Castelnau-sur-Arrats. He tightened his hands on the sodden reins. The Vicomte would soon discover that he was not battling a dozen men of the advance guard, but over a thousand trained, battle-hungry, plunder-crazed men. *Sweet vengeance.* It tasted better than he had expected. He had anticipated a moment like this for three long weeks in the dank darkness of his cell. He could hardly believe his own good fortune.

After escaping Castelnau with the help of Sir Rostanh, Jehan had headed toward the reddish-orange glow of burning Seissan. He had no trouble finding his liege's army, for three thousand drunken men took up a lot of space and made enough noise to wake the dead. He had more trouble finding the Prince's crimson silk pavilion among the tents of Sir Reginald Cobham, the Earl of Warwick, the Captal de Buch, and other high-ranking English and Gascon knights. He finally asked a guard, who recognized Jehan's faded, bloodstained heraldry and led him directly to the Prince.

Jehan found Edward lolling against pillows embroidered with the heraldry of a rebel knight and eating heartily of meat and bread from the cellars of Seissan. He greeted Jehan with stunned surprise. Jehan took a seat among the stolen draperies and, between bites of roasted venison and huge draughts of hypocras, related the details of the battle with Tournan, his imprisonment in Castelnau, and recent escape. When he finished, the Prince said he had thought Jehan was dead. After the Vicomte's attack, two of Jehan's released vassals had raced to Bordeaux to tell him about Tournan's brutal behavior. The men feared Jehan wouldn't survive his wounds. At Jehan's query, the Prince assured him that his sixteen men were well. They lodged in Castétis now, protecting that castle against attack.

The Prince planned to seize Castelnau in the morning. Jehan told him that it was well provisioned, strongly fortified, and full to the ramparts with men-at-arms. The Prince's eagerness waned, for he didn't want his troops bogged down in a lengthy siege, even for a rebel as vile as the Vicomte de Tournan. This campaign was a *chevauchée*—a quick, burning, pillaging raid—not a structured attack. He had come to punish the rebels in the swiftest and most effective way possible, by destroying their source of income. Jehan suggested that they draw the rebel out of his castle by ruse, thus making the fortress ripe for the taking. The Prince laughed gleefully at the prospect, then bestowed upon Jehan a fine black destrier and his pick of the stolen armor.

It would not be long now. Jehan petted the side of his destrier's neck, trying to calm him while Edward's personal retinue mounted as a group and waited for the squire's signal. The trap he had set worked almost too smoothly; for a moment, he wondered if the Vicomte had set a trap of his own. He shook his head. He knew one thing for sure about the rebel: He was governed by emotions, not common sense. His rage would be his undoing, and Jehan's victory.

The squire suddenly stood up and waved his arms. "That's it, my lord," Jehan said. "The advance guard has engaged the Vicomte de Tournan."

"Forward!"

The Prince's command echoed through the valley. Jehan kicked his own horse into a gallop. The living mass of men and horses swarmed around him as the army surged forward, stretching out over the length and breadth of the valley. Cries of *St. George!* rose from the mists. His horse's hooves sank deep in the muddy earth, but it didn't slow his pace. The stallion was as restless and as anxious as he was to join the fighting. The Prince and his front line surged over the top of the ridge and then galloped down the slope.

Jehan pulled his destrier to a halt just at the height of the ridge. He lifted his visor to survey the valley. The tenacious rain bit into his face and seeped through the chain mail that covered his throat and shoulders. The men-at-arms passed him on either side, bumping his huge stallion in the process, but Jehan held him steady. He wanted to take a good look at Castelnau-sur-Arrats before he joined the attack. By the end of this afternoon, the strong fortress that rose on the opposite ridge would be in the hands of the Prince of Wales.

He gazed at the straight, limestone walls, cream-colored in the cloudy dawn. Half-timbered hovels hugged the bottom of the slope, looking soggy and forlorn through the gray haze of rain. He knew that if it weren't for his intervention, those hovels would be ashes by midafternoon and the castle naught but a charred ruin. But Jehan had his own plans for the fortress. Boldly, he had told them to the Prince, who had laughed and said that perhaps it would be done.

Where once he was prisoner, Jehan vowed to be lord.

A mighty prize for an impoverished knight. He scanned the crenelated ramparts, the grove of almond and fig trees on the opposite slopes, and the length of fertile land nestled between the hills. It was a prize greater than any he had ever imagined. If the Prince of Wales thought fit to grant him these conquered lands—if he did, it would be a gesture of ultimate favor—then Jehan would be titled. He would no longer labor in the castles of his liege lord, serving him endlessly, always a vassal and never a lord. He would have his own castle, his own large retinue, and the thought filled him with lust.

He kicked his mount forward, surrendering to the swift current of the charging army. As he descended the slope, he peered over the bobbing heads of his fellow knights toward the heart of the valley. The Vicomte and his men stood, shocked, battling with the advance guard and staring up at the sea of men that poured over the ridge. Jehan laughed loudly but the sound was lost in the rain, the clatter of armor, and the cacophony of battle cries. He watched as his enemy's men retreated from the advance guard in a vain attempt to race toward the safety of the castle. It was too late. The right flank of the Prince's army closed in. The rebels reared back, then rode away *en masse* toward the northern vineyards and beyond, to the woods. Jehan watched in anticipation as several of the Prince's men surged forward in pursuit. He kicked his own horse faster. He would be there when the Vicomte was captured. He would strike his own blow of vengeance.

The pain in his side twinged hard as he bent lower on his horse's neck. He cursed the wounds the Vicomte had inflicted, wounds that had not yet healed. The Prince had suggested that Jehan stay behind in the fighting, for he knew the wounds still pained him, but Jehan refused. He had spent too much time in the dark tower of Castelnau-sur-Arrats, and he was not going to stay away from the fighting like a woman. His nostrils flared as he smelled the rich, fetid earth pummeled by his stallion's hooves. He veered toward the north, to aid in the chase. In the process, he crossed dangerously in front of several knights' mounts. He realized, with a start, that the bulk of the army had ignored the small group of fleeing men and was headed directly for the castle.

Fools! He lifted his sword and yelled for the knights to pay heed to the rebels, but his words were lost in the wind and rain. The pressure of the entire army surged behind him, forcing him on toward the castle. Jehan kicked the destrier into a faster pace, looking for a gap in the flow so he could pursue the Vicomte. Little by little, he eased his way to the edge of the body of the army. But as he broke through the coursing flow of men, Jehan saw that Tournan had already disappeared into the woods. He cursed. The Vicomte and his vassals knew the forests too well—this was their land, and they could cross the treacherous ground swiftly. The Prince's men entered the woods and followed the Vicomte's trail briefly, then gave up the chase.

The men might give up the chase, but Jehan wouldn't. He dug his spurs into his horse's flanks. The Vicomte would *not* escape. The rage sizzled in his blood. He had waited too long to give up so easily. He crossed the remnants of a field of grain, crushing the sodden, short stubble. He was free of the rushing river of knights and nothing slowed his pace as he headed up the hill. He led the destrier into the grove of fruit trees, heedless of the trailing grapevines that snapped beneath his stallion's hooves. He followed the path of the pummeled earth. The pine trees and oaks that formed the edge of the woods protected him somewhat from the rain, and Jehan blinked to clear his vision. He could hear nothing above the roar of the army in the valley behind him, the cries of the Prince's men in the distance, and the constant patter of rain. *Tournan is ahead, somewhere,* he told himself. *He could not have gone far.* He followed the path of overturned leaves and crushed moss deeper into the woods. He searched through the fencing of trees for riders. He soundly cursed the knights who had ignored the fleeing rebels. If they had followed, they would have caught the Vicomte before he could escape. He knew why the men had given up the chase: The rebels would only be worth the effort if they were captured alive and ransomed, but before the day was over they would have nothing left to ransom but the armor on their backs. What good was armor, when gold, tapestries, jewels, and women lay just ahead, in a simple, badly protected Gascon castle?

Jehan brought his destrier to a sudden stop.

Aliénor.

The rage boiling in his blood chilled to ice. *Aliénor.* He twisted hard on his saddle, wincing as the motion caused a sharp pain in his side. He peered through the trees toward the castle. He was too far away; he couldn't see if the Prince's men had yet succeeded in entering the fortress. *Aliénor was within that castle, unprotected, abandoned by her own father and facing an enemy contingent of over a thousand men.* Aliénor was there, perhaps in danger, while he raced after vengeance.

The Prince had promised, he reminded himself: She would not be harmed. Jehan had told him about Aliénor the night before, as they planned the attack of Castelnau, and his liege lord had assured him that the noblewomen of the house would be respected. Yet as Jehan peered behind him, he remembered that the Prince had also ordered that Seissan not be burned, and he could still smell the stinging scent of charred palisades on the westerly wind. There were so many men in the Prince's contingent, too many men to control. If the walls of Castelnau were breached and the castle taken before the Prince could enter and maintain order, Aliénor could be in great danger.

He was torn, suddenly—torn between his desire to capture the Vicomte and kill him with his bare hands, and his desire to return to the castle and protect her from harm. *Aliénor.* How frightened she must be, listening to the war cries of the invading knights just outside the walls. His throat tightened and he resolutely whirled his horse around, back toward the castle.

When he had discussed his plans to capture Castelnau with his liege lord, Jehan had also sworn, on his honor, to protect Aliénor de Tournan. He would make sure she was taken care of after her castle was seized. His protection would be his way of showing gratitude for all she had done for him. But in his eagerness to wreak vengeance on the Vicomte de Tournan, he had almost forgotten his obligation to the man's daughter. He imagined her, suddenly, vividly, crushed under the weight of one of the rampaging men-at-arms. He tightened his grip on the reins. He had to reach the fortress before the most precious of its treasures could be plundered.

He stared at the castle as he reached the edge of the northern woods. Armed men swarmed around the limestone walls, searching for a way to attack the structure. A few arrows flew from the castle's arrow slits and bounced off the boiled-leather jerkins of the foot soldiers. Jehan scanned the battlements and saw only a score of men manning the walls, and among them, only one or two showed the glint of armor. Already, brush and earth filled the trench that surrounded the castle at several points. Despite the rocks being thrown down from the ramparts, the sporadic spray of arrows, and the rivers of boiling oil, the men continued to fill the trenches. The Prince's knights milled around restlessly, waiting for the walls to be scaled by the foot soldiers so they could enter and pillage at will.

As he raced down the hill, he saw the foot soldiers begin leaning several ladders against the wall. He kicked his destrier faster across the treacherous, boggy land. He knew that the defenders of the castle would soon be overwhelmed by the surge of foot soldiers. He heard the first cries of victory as a man surmounted the eastern wall and battled with one of the defenders. He glanced down the slope to the small village, where several knights were trying unsuccessfully to set fire to the damp mud-and-timber houses.

Already they defy the Prince. He hoped Aliénor had had the foresight to hide herself somewhere within the castle. He had a sinking feeling that she was probably one of the people racing along the wall-walk, tossing stones down on the foot soldiers. Suddenly the knights on the southern side of the castle kicked their horses into a run and Jehan knew that someone had made it to the tower atop the portal to lower the drawbridge and raise the portcullis. The stinging scent of smoldering wood rose to greet him as he rounded the corner of the fortress and headed toward the open portal.

He nosed his destrier among the line of knights and clattered over the drawbridge. He pushed through the crowd in the lower courtyard and swore as he saw several knights run out of the castle, carrying a heavy tapestry among them. Dropping the reins, he swung off his stallion and raced across the muddy earth until he reached the wooden stairs.

He pulled out his sword, swung open the door, and entered the great hall. Men-at-arms milled in the vaulted room. Two knights stood near the hearth, drinking out of a barrel of wine they had found nearby and waving joints of lamb. A dozen others pulled down one of the huge bright tapestries that covered the wall, while a handful of servants cowered in a corner. Seeing no sign of Aliénor, Jehan ran across the rushes toward the nearest staircase.

Two rooms flanked the aisle at the top of the stairs. He looked in one and saw a knight hold up a woman's girdle, made of gold links and pearls, and he recognized it as belonging to Aliénor. But there was no sign of Aliénor in the room. Suddenly he heard a woman's cry. He ran into the room that faced him.

His blood ran cold. A woman with golden hair rocked amidst the tangled pelts of her bed, wailing aloud, while one of the Prince's knights stood nearby.

The knight was retying his braces.

Jehan released a cry of fury and lifted his sword. The knight started and stared at him in shock. The woman wailed louder and lifted her head. Jehan froze in surprise. The woman's eyes were pale blue, red-rimmed and unfocused, her skin wan and wrinkled. The hair that tangled in knots over the fine blue wool of her tunic was gold, but threaded liberally with silver. This was not Aliénor. Jehan realized that this could be no one else but Aliénor's mother. "This is a noblewoman, not a servant," he snarled, turning to the knight. "The Prince's orders were to leave the noblewomen alone."

"A rebel's wife is no noblewoman."

He had no time to argue with this swine. "Where is your daughter, Vicomtesse?"

She did not answer. Her crying and rocking continued.

"If you want your daughter to be saved from your fate, then tell me where she is."

Jehan heard the barking of dogs. He ran to the twinned, open windows. His gaze scanned the courtyard, from the tumult at the portal to the knights on foot drinking liberally from a cask of wine. His gaze stopped just outside the chapel. There struggled Aliénor, barefoot, tight within a knight's grip.

Aliénor gasped as the knight's mailed arm dug into her ribs. She kicked, but the soaking skirt of her woolen surcoat dulled her blows. Spots appeared before her eyes as she tried, desperately, to draw some air into her lungs. She slumped against him. He laughed just above her ear and then he roughly grasped her breast. Her cry brought the hounds from all corners of the courtyard. She heard them, barking, snarling, and saw their lithe bodies in a blur of gray fur as they swarmed around her and the knight. He swore and pulled his sword from his baldric. She sucked in deep gulps of air as the knight's grip loosened around her chest.

The moment she saw the Prince's army swarm over the southern ridge, she knew what she had feared all along: that the small group of knights camped in the valley had been sent to lure Father out of Castelnau. Her blood had run cold, for it was the perfect trap. Not only was Father in danger of capture, but so was his castle. She had watched with horror as men dressed in green and white tunics raced down the hill toward her home. Thibaud had bellowed for all the villagers to man the wall-walk. She threw rocks over the ramparts, heedless of her great-uncle's command to hide, until Laurent pointed to a foot soldier who had climbed over the wall. She knew then that it was too late. She and Laurent had to hide from the brutality of the English forces until they could throw themselves upon the Prince's mercy. They raced to the chapel.

The chapel was stormed only moments after they reached the upper floor. Laurent was horrified as he watched the men-at-arms seize the gold trappings on the altar. His gasp brought the men up the spiral staircase to where they hid. She rose and showed herself, in the process hiding Laurent behind her skirts. She knew she was in grave danger, but Laurent, the only son of the rebel Vicomte, would be killed on sight. Fortunately, the leader was too interested in her to look beneath the bench where Laurent lay. He dragged her out of the church and into the courtyard, and she knew by the way he fondled her now that she would not long remain innocent.

She could not believe this was happening. The courtyard was filled with the Prince's men, drinking Tournan wine, eating Tournan bread, brawling with the men who had manned the ramparts, stripping the house and chapel of its drapery and gold. Over the past weeks, she never believed that the Prince of Wales would actually *succeed* in seizing the castle. It was inconceivable. The bottom floor of the main building was filled to the wooden rafters with salted meat, grain, and wine. The stinging, frigid rain that prickled her face was the first sign of the coming winter, and any long-term siege would be doomed in such a cold, dangerous season. Furthermore, Castelnau-sur-Arrats was one of the strongest fortresses on the border, with thick, stone walls, high on a hill overlooking the valley, towers on each corner and a portal guarded by a drawbridge and portcullis. Properly manned, it was invincible.

But it was not properly manned. The castle, despite all the painstaking preparations for siege, had fallen within moments of the Prince's attack.

Papa, Papa, how could you leave us here, open and unguarded?

The knight's grip tightened again. She kicked in vain against his shins, but nothing seemed to take his concentration from the hounds that circled him. She peered over her shoulder and saw her dogs as she had only seen them in the hunt: teeth bared, saliva dripping from their red gums, the ruff on the back of their necks high and stiff as they snapped at her attacker. One greyhound dared to lunge forward. She cried out as the knight swung his sword high, and the hound's growl of fury dissolved into a yelp of pain. Without hesitation, the knight brought his sword down on the dog and quieted his cries.

Undaunted, the others swarmed around the knight, preventing his movement, backing him up against the ancient limestone wall of the donjon. Other men stood away from the ferocity of the beasts, watching the battle with amusement. She writhed and fought to be set free. The knight released her and she stumbled as her feet touched the earth. Through the tangled netting of her wet, unbound hair, she saw him raise his hand against her. Her feet suddenly lost their grip on the earth. Her cheek stung, she whirled around, and her forehead connected with something cold and hard.

Black, heavy clouds of unconsciousness swept over her and she dug her fingers into the earth. From a distant place she heard, still, the battle between the invader and her dogs. She fought to cling to the sound, for the sound meant sanity, it meant consciousness, and despite the pounding of her head she knew she must stay alert if she were to survive. She cringed as she heard the deathly, gurgling cry of a dog and the horrible crunch of steel against bone. Something warm ran down her forehead. She wiped her brow, looked at her fingers, and saw blood.

She shifted her weight and winced as she rolled over. Her vision blurred and she blinked to clear it. The knight's legs ran with blood where the hounds had sunk their teeth into his chain-mail chausses and broken the links and his skin. The knight still fought, but only two hounds remained. She released a strangled gasp of horror as she saw the bloody remains of her dogs scattered on the ground.

Then, suddenly, the two hounds stopped barking and growled in a low, constant pitch. She saw, beyond the shape of the knight, the spread legs of another knight.

"Can you find no better foe, knight, than these hounds and a woman?"

She sucked in her breath. She recognized that voice, even distorted in anger.

"That woman is mine."

"That woman is the daughter of Tournan."

"All the better to bed the daughter of a rebel knight."

"Do you scorn the Prince's orders?"

"Words," her captor said with contempt. "Words meant to save face, but really mean nothing—"

She heard the distinctive sound of a sword being drawn from its sheath. Her captor stepped back and raised his weapon in response.

"Are you a fool, St. Simon? You can have the woman when I'm finished—"

Steel clashed against steel. The two dogs that remained, a mastiff and her best greyhound, staggered away from the battle. They limped over to her as her captor surged forward. The dogs' sides heaved. They licked her face and hands. She carefully touched the mastiff's bloodied fur and nuzzled his wet, musky pelt as she hugged him. Her head ached and darkness beckoned her, but she struggled to stay conscious. She focused on the two men who fought in front of her.

The knights circled and she finally saw Jehan. She started a little, and the clouds of unconsciousness receded. *This* was how she had always envisioned him. He fought bare-headed, his black hair clinging to his forehead and neck. His blue eyes glittered beneath his dark, heavy brows. He was fully armed, from the ridges of his coat-of-plates beneath his tight-fitting surcoat, to his chain-mail chausses. A baldric hung about his narrow hips. He swung his heavy sword as if it were weightless, as if he weren't hampered by unhealed wounds, as if he were sparring rather than fighting the knight with intent. For a moment she lay stunned, watching him move, surprised at the smoothness and grace of his gestures, almost forgetting that the battle that took place before her, was *for* her.

A group of men gathered to watch. Jehan stepped on the body of one of her dogs. He hesitated only a fraction of a second, but long enough for the knight to crash his heavy sword upon Jehan's shoulder. Jehan lurched to the left but stepped back to avoid another blow. The knight surged forward and Jehan uncoiled and released a mighty blow to the warrior's hip. The man cried out in pain and backed away, glaring at Jehan in disbelief. Then he charged anew.

Movement out of the corner of her eye captured her attention. Laurent emerged from the chapel, clutching a heavy wooden stick in his hand. Despite the pain that throbbed in her head, she pressed away from the donjon and motioned for him to hide. He shook his head stubbornly, then turned his attention back to the battle. She realized she shouldn't be sitting here, waiting for this battle to end. She and Laurent should be trying to escape. She scanned the courtyard and knew as she did so that escape was impossible. The Prince's men filled the yard, overflowed the wall-walk, and spilled out of the great hall to hang on the wooden stairs. Even if she and Laurent could escape, they had no place to go.

She had to stay, and wait, until there was a winner in this battle. She began to pray for Jehan to win but stopped herself. It was because of Jehan that the invaders were here. It was because of Jehan that she had nearly been raped—and might still be raped—by the knight who fought him. He had accompanied the Prince's army here—perhaps even led them—rather than veer them away.

I must not trust Jehan.

Black, sooty smoke rose from the wooden stables and stained the gray sky. The rain dampened the men-at-arms' attempts to set it afire. Beyond the clashing of swords, she saw someone tossing clothing and gold plate out of the solar window into a pile just in front of the stairs. To her shock, she watched one of *Maman's* favorite surcoats float slowly to the ground. She wondered where her mother was in this chaos—there had not been enough time to find her and bring her to the chapel earlier. Cries of victory rang through the courtyard as someone raised the Prince of Wales's pennon atop the portal tower. *All is lost, all is lost. Where is Father? Why isn't he here, fighting against these invaders, protecting me from harm? Why is Jehan de St. Simon, his worst enemy, doing what is by blood his duty?*

Jehan was protecting her with every bit of his strength. She winced unconsciously as the knight pushed Jehan away by the shield. Aliénor knew that Jehan's hand was still sore and she wondered how long he could keep his grip before his strength gave way. Yet he kept up his attack. Rain dripped from his nose, his chin, from the sodden hem of his tunic. She noticed that he held his shield tight against his left side, the side with the sore rib. His weapon sang through the air, so smoothly it seemed to slice the fine drizzle.

She began to succumb to a heavy lethargy. She struggled

to keep her eyes open, to concentrate on the battle in front of her. Though her captor attacked with slow, lethal thrusts, Jehan bent and moved to avoid each clumsy stroke. His sword moved like lightning and always found a mark. The other knight's chest heaved in an effort to catch his breath, but Jehan stood as strong and sure as when he had first challenged him.

"Stop!"

She started out of her weariness. A knight, riding the largest, finest destrier she had ever seen, rode between the men. He unhooked his aventail, pulled off his basinet, and tossed it in the mud between them. His thick, drooping mustache fell to beneath his chin and dripped with rain.

"Have my knights so bored of pillage that they fight among themselves?"

She glanced at the newcomer's surcoat and recognized the quartered arms of England and France. With a shock, she realized he was the Prince of Wales. The men who surrounded him fell to one knee, but Jehan and the knight still stood, with their swords tight in their hands, warily looking at one another.

The Prince waved his sword above him. "Speak!"

"This knight sought to take a prize from me." Her attacker gestured to where she sat. "This woman—"

"A woman?" The Prince's eyes flashed at Jehan. "You defy another knight over a woman?"

"She's the Vicomte's daughter."

The Prince looked at her. She suddenly became conscious of her mud-streaked surcoat, the disarray of her hair and her bare feet. She felt vulnerable, sitting helplessly on the ground. She was a Tournan. She would stand before her enemies. Mustering her strength, she leaned against the wall of the donjon for support, lifted herself to both feet, and faced him. She cursed the pain that speared through her head and joints, she cursed the weakness that forced her to lean back against the cold, wet wall. The Prince's gaze encompassed her dishevelment and the rents in her surcoat.

"She tended me despite her father's orders to the contrary," Jehan explained. "I sought only to protect her honor."

"The honor of a Tournan?" The Prince turned his gaze away from her and fixed it on Jehan. "Only yesterday you swore there was no such thing."

"It is her father who has no honor."

"You didn't tell me the maiden was so fair."

"She is fair in more than one way, my liege. This woman fed me when the Vicomte would have me starve. Her skill in healing saved me when I was all but dead. Though I shall kill her father in my own good time, I am bound to protect her."

"What say you, knight?" The Prince turned to her attacker. "Is she worth facing Sir Jehan's challenge?"

"I knew nothing of this." The man lowered his sword. "There are wenches aplenty in this land. I'll not risk my neck for one."

The knight bowed to the Prince and stepped away. Jehan glared at him. The Prince gestured to his squire and dismounted.

She closed her eyes as she felt a sudden weakness in her knees. Her head swam and she lifted her hand to her brow.

"Aliénor?"

She looked up and found Jehan, only a step away, his intense blue gaze fixed on her face. She struggled to focus on his features. With what little strength remained in her body, she lifted her arm and struck him full across the face.

He did not flinch at her blow, but his blue eyes grew hot in fury. "Is this the thanks I get for fighting for your virtue?"

"You expect thanks?" She spoke in Gascon, a language she knew only he and her people would understand. "You sent the attackers *to* me!"

"What's this?" the Prince interrupted. "Doesn't she know a civilized tongue, Sir Jehan?"

An angry muscle moved tightly in Jehan's cheek. "She speaks French, my liege."

"Oui." She turned to the Prince. Her head pounded with

each word, but her anger screamed to be vented. "I told Sir Jehan that Englishmen have no honor."

Jehan snapped, "Don't be a fool—"

"Sir Jehan just saved your virtue," the Prince interrupted. "And in my presence, he has sworn to protect you."

"Protect me!" She winced as Jehan shook her arm in warning, but she ignored caution. "He sent an *army* to my home. Is that the Englishman's idea of protection?"

"*I* sent the army, not Sir Jehan. Your father is my father's vassal, yet he cleaves to the King of France."

"*You* never would have known how to draw my father out." She turned and glared at Jehan, then spoke in Gascon again. "That was *your* idea, wasn't it?"

"Quiet! Have you lost all your senses? The Prince holds your fate in his hands, *nesci—*"

"Yes, I'm a fool. I'm an ignorant fool who believed you were an honorable knight."

"I battled a fellow knight to protect your virtue. I risked my liege lord's displeasure—"

"You made me believe you were my father's enemy, not mine. Yet, within a day of escaping this castle, you prove to me that you *lied!* You *are* my enemy!"

"What babble is this?" the Prince asked angrily. "What is she saying?"

Jehan's lips tightened. "She is saying, my liege, that she is humbled before you and she begs for your mercy."

"Precisely what I thought."

She glared at Jehan, mute with pain, as his fingers dug so deeply into her arm that her hand grew prickly and numb. He was warning her to watch her tongue in front of the Prince, but she was too angry to care. Jehan had betrayed her. He had charmed her into liking him, trusting him, and then had broken that trust completely. Her head pounded and she struggled against the pain. She would not succumb to it—not here, not in front of the Englishman who had conquered her castle and the knight who had made such a fool of her.

"I suppose I could have mercy on her," the Prince mused.

"Since she is only the daughter of Tournan, I can hardly blame her for her father's treachery."

"I have already felt the edge of your vengeance—Ow!"

"I could take you as my prisoner, *demoiselle,* but I will accommodate your request for mercy. That will be your reward for defying your own father and tending my knight."

"I want no gifts from English hands."

"Enough!" Jehan interjected. "This is the firstborn son of the King of England, Aliénor. Guard your tongue before you lose it." He turned to the Prince. "Forgive her, my liege. She has been ill-used."

"She will be ill-used no more. I will send her to a safe place, a place of her choice."

"The place of my choice is here," she said firmly. "I'm not leaving."

"It will be dangerous here," Jehan growled, once again in Gascon. "Heed the Prince's words—don't spurn his offer."

"I shall spurn it, as I shall spurn all your false kindness. You wish to cast me out of this castle, but I won't leave so easily. I'll stay with my people."

"And with the Prince's men-at-arms, then? My liege has claimed this castle as his own, wrenched from the hands of a rebel."

"Since you are claiming Castelnau, then I'm now your prisoner," she told the Prince, in French. "I shall see an English Prince's honor in truth. I will see it in how you treat your noble prisoners."

"Better than your father, *demoiselle,* and that I'll vow." He turned to Jehan. "Are you sure this is the same maiden who tended your wounds? She's got the tongue of a wasp."

"Her tongue outstrips her sense." Jehan released her. "She'll be just as safe here as traveling through these lands. Perhaps her presence will tempt the Vicomte into returning to Castelnau-sur-Arrats."

"This fortress must be left ill-guarded, for I need all my men. The Comte d'Armagnac is near."

"Where?"

"In Toulouse." He glanced around the courtyard. "Once

the baggage wagons catch up to us, we'll strip Tournan's castle and be on our way. I vow I will bring the head of Jean d'Armagnac to my father." The Prince gestured to three men. "You will stay. Choose four men each to secure this castle until I return."

The Prince turned and walked away. Jehan glanced at Aliénor, who glared at him with brilliant, golden eyes. "I'll be back. For your own good, stay where you are." He turned and followed the Prince. When he reached his side, he called, "Sire, I would stay here as well."

The Prince stopped, turned, and lifted one heavy brow. "Is your vengeance for Tournan dimming so soon? He will undoubtedly join the French forces in Toulouse."

"Vengeance can wait." He glanced to where Aliénor leaned against the donjon. "I made a vow last night. I am bound by honor to stay here."

"You are bound to follow me," the Prince retorted. "Any other obligation is secondary."

"As you said only yesterday, my liege, I'm still wounded and will be of little use to you on the battlefield. Here I could guard these walls well."

"You did well enough today. She's my prisoner and she'll be protected."

"She will be alone with fifteen men-at-arms."

"I need my knights on the field of battle, not playing the courtier with my prisoners." He turned to leave. "She will be safe. My men will follow my orders."

"As they did at Seissan?"

Jehan said the words in a low voice, too low for anyone to hear but the Prince, who stopped angrily. It was known to all that he had forbidden his men-at-arms to burn the town of Seissan, yet in the frenzy of pillage and plunder they defied his orders and the city was now nothing but charred wood and smoldering, wet timber. The Prince was enraged but had done nothing, for what other reward did these men have but to rape and steal, and vent their battle-hunger on the towns that defied them?

"I meant no insolence, my lord," Jehan continued. "But

the lady risked much while I was her father's prisoner. I won't risk any less when she is the prisoner of my liege lord."

He glanced angrily behind Jehan, to where Aliénor still stood, soaked from rain, with blood running down the side of her face. "I think the maiden's virtue is in more danger in your presence."

"I've sworn to protect her."

"And who has sworn to protect her from you?"

"Do you doubt my honor, my liege?"

"You've proven your prowess in battle and your loyalty to me. There's one more quality a good knight must have, Sir Jehan, and I've never tested you on it. Can you be chivalrous to a dispossessed noblewoman—even one as fair as the daughter of Tournan?" He lifted his hand as Jehan began to answer. "It's action, not words, that will answer my question. You may stay and protect the woman. But mind—I shall summon you when I need you, and no woman shall keep you from my side."

Jehan bowed and waited until the Prince had turned away and walked deeper into the courtyard. The rain seeped through his surcoat, through his mail, to the raw flesh on his shoulder, but he didn't call a woman to tend it. He had other things on his mind. He turned on his heels and wound his way through the bodies of Aliénor's slain hounds to where she crouched, near the two dogs that remained.

She glared up at him as she heard his step. Her arms tightened around the necks of the hounds. "Let me be, Sir Jehan."

"I can't. I've made you my charge." He looked at her, confused by her angry reaction. "I risked my sword and my honor for you. Why are you so defiant?"

"You brought these English beasts here." She stood up abruptly and glared at him. "What of my father? Did you kill him in the valley?"

"Your father escaped, though if I had seen him I wouldn't have hesitated to kill him." She winced and swayed slightly. He noticed that the cut on her head still bled and a large lump swelled beneath it. She was wounded; perhaps that was why she was so irrational. He would argue with her later, when she was stronger. "Come into the castle, out of this rain."

"What does it matter if I stand in the rain? What does anything matter? I have no more castle, I have no more lands." She struggled weakly as he reached out and clutched her shoulders. "You've taken everything from me: my dowry, and now my family's castle."

"The Prince of Wales took this, not I."

"You led him here."

"He planned to come here, whether I found him or not." He felt her weight as she leaned more and more against him. Her eyelids drooped heavily and her chin dropped to her chest. "Come, Aliénor—"

"Come where?" She lifted her face and her eyes glowed with a golden, furious light. "Come into the castle and view what your *English* have done? Shall I watch while they steal my gowns, my linens, my circlets? Shall I watch while they drink their fill of new wine and eat the grain my father's vassals have spent a year cultivating?" She pointed to the castle as a bright yellow bolt of cloth fell to the ground in front of the steps. "I won't even have a dry tunic to don when they are through."

"Do you think so ill of me, Aliénor, that I would leave you in such dire poverty?"

"You'll give me a crust where once I had the entire pie."

"You speak in riddles."

"You'll retrieve one of my gowns, Sir Jehan, and expect me to grovel in thanks at your feet," she said, struggling out of his grip, "when in fact all the gowns and the chest they were in and the room where it resided—it all was mine, only hours ago, before you and your lord stole—"

"You're raving like a madwoman." Reaching beneath the sodden folds of her woolen surcoat, he swung her up into his arms. She weighed nothing. He felt the swell of her hip against his abdomen, the length of her back against his arm. She felt good in his arms, warm and soft. He felt a strange surge of possessiveness. She was *his,* now. His to protect.

"Don't put me in the castle. They'll destroy it. They'll slaughter all of us—"

"Hush," he murmured. "The Prince has promised to save the castle, and all the inhabitants who submit peacefully."

"Englishmen have no mercy—"

"My lord has plans for this castle."

Her fingers dug defiantly into the chain-mail sleeves of his haubergeon, even as she succumbed to the heavy lethargy of unconsciousness.

Chapter

7

ALIÉNOR WOKE SLOWLY, PLAGUED BY A PERSISTENT, POUNDING headache, wondering why the sun streamed in so brightly over her bedclothes and why Margot hadn't stoked the fire to warm the chilly room. When she heard Margot's step she turned over and realized that the velvet hangings that usually fell from the wooden canopy of her bed were gone. No wonder the sunlight streamed over her bed. Why did Margot decide to clean the draperies today, she wondered, and why didn't she wake her before taking them down? She searched blindly for the mountain of squirrel, hare, and beaver furs that usually covered her bed but found nothing but a single sheepskin and a ragged wolf pelt. What in God's name was happening?

Then she remembered.

Margot stood near the hearth, stoking the fire. She glanced over her shoulder as Aliénor sat up abruptly in bed. "Ah, you're awake, *damaiselo.*"

"The English . . ."

"They're gone. All but fifteen men and that knight."

"Gone?" The lingering gray mists of her groggy sleep dissolved. "How long have I been abed?"

"A full day."

"The English have come, and gone, in only a day?"

"Like a winter storm, *damaiselo.* They loaded their carts, then marched off toward the west."

Aliénor glanced around the room. Her miniver-trimmed

mantle and three surcoats were missing from the pegs near the hearth. The unicorn tapestries that had covered the southern wall were gone, as were the wrought-iron candelabra that once flanked either side of the fireplace. Margot had obviously tidied the room while she slept, but nothing could hide the fact that it had been stripped, from floor to ceiling, of everything of worth. Then she thought of something far more precious than cloth or gold.

"Where's Laurent?"

Margot glanced nervously toward the door. She lowered her voice. "He's sleeping in the kitchens, dirtier than a common villager."

"The English don't know he's here?"

"They don't look far beyond a cask of wine, milady."

Aliénor swung her legs over the side of the bed and rose shakily to her feet. She closed her eyes, then opened them again, as the blood surged to her head, causing the ripened lump on her temple to pound more forcefully. She walked over the crushed rushes, clutching her head, then stood in front of the fire and held her stiff fingers out to the warmth. "What of Thibaud and *Maman?*"

"Sir Thibaud was wounded during the fighting. He's with the other prisoners in the great hall." Margot poked at the flames and then adjusted her torn bodice. *"Dona* is still abed."

Aliénor hardly heard Margot's words, for as she spoke, she noticed the dirt that soiled the seat of Margot's tunic and the ragged rents along its length. She took a deep, shocked breath and looked up into Margot's averted face. Her chambermaid had been used by the English men-at-arms, used in the vilest way a man could use an unwilling woman. Aliénor shivered as she vividly remembered the pawing of the knight who had held her, the knight who had struck her and caused the swelling on her head, who had wanted to violate her in the same way Margot had been violated. Aliénor realized that she was looking into a sort of mirror—a mirror of how she would have looked if she had not been saved.

Aliénor jerked back, away from Margot and the warm hearth. She knew she should say something, but all she wanted to do was run away. Everything was violated: her room, her castle, and even her own defenseless chambermaid. Turning away abruptly, Aliénor walked to one of the narrow windows and stared out at the forest beyond. *All is lost.* Yesterday she was the heiress to this castle and these lands, and now she was nothing but a prisoner, as poor and vulnerable as any villein. She glanced down at her shift. She wondered if she had a tunic to wear to cover her nakedness, or a veil or net for her hair, which now flowed unbound down her back. She wondered if she would be kept locked in this single room, like a falcon forgotten in the darkness of the mews.

Despair pulled and tugged at her heart, threatening to overwhelm her. What fate would the Prince choose for her and for her family? What hope could a dispossessed, impoverished, imprisoned woman possibly have? She struggled to conquer her growing desperation. She scanned the edge of the woods. Suddenly, she remembered something Jehan had told her, before she had succumbed to unconsciousness. He claimed her father had escaped the invader's attack. She gazed at a distant grove of elms. Was it true? Was her father alive? Or was he dead, lying unshriven, deep in the dry autumn leaves? She closed her eyes. He must be alive. He must be free. If he were free, he would return, and take back what was so vilely stolen from him. He was her single tiny spark of hope.

"You're awake."

She opened her eyes. She recognized the voice. She heard Margot's gasp but she did not turn.

"Aliénor? Are you feeling better?"

The muscles in her neck tightened. The despair fled, chased by a stronger emotion. Jehan sounded concerned. Concerned. As if her health meant something to him. This knight had once vowed to show his gratitude toward her by some great, noble gesture. Was this the gesture? Sending a sea of Englishmen pouring over the southern ridge into her home? The day before he escaped, he insisted he was not her enemy, yet he had betrayed her. He was false, as false as all the pretty compliments he paid her when he was a prisoner in this castle, the compliments she was foolish enough to believe.

"Better?" She had a very unladylike desire to snort. "Is that how I'm supposed to feel the day after my home is seized?"

His voice tightened. "I see nothing has changed."

"Everything has changed. The whole world has turned upside down."

"That it has," he agreed angrily. "But this castle still needs to be run. If you're healthy enough to argue, then you're healthy enough to take charge in the great hall. I have enough to do without doing woman's work as well."

"Maman is the lady of the house. Speak to her, and remove your wretched self from my presence."

Silence greeted her words. She turned around. He stood at the end of her bed, his dark hair combed away from his shaven face, a clean tunic stretched tautly across his chest, one hand resting possessively on the pillar of her canopied bed. His presence in the intimate confines of her chamber was looming, dangerous, threatening.

His gaze traveled, with growing intensity, down the full length of her body.

She became suddenly aware of her near nakedness. In her anger, she'd forgotten that she wore nothing but a thin shift. With her back to him, her long hair screened his view, but now she faced him. The midday light seeped in through the window behind her, and she knew he could see through the linen. Her hair, unbound, reached nearly to her hips. The darkness of her nipples pressed against the material. She knew, by the direction of his gaze, that he could see the curve of her waist, and the blurred, soft junction between the length of her thighs.

One part of her screamed for her to cover herself, but another part of her stilled her movements. Defiantly, she tossed her head so the sunlight played in her hair, so her tresses would not obscure his view. Margot cried out and ran for the chest at the end of the bed.

"No, Margot. Let the knight see what he has done to the daughter of a great warrior." She spread her arms. "Do you see, Jehan? You've stripped me naked and left me with less than a common pauper."

"No peasant," he said, his voice husky, "was ever so well formed."

His gaze slipped over her like a physical thing, and wherever it rested she grew warm. She stiffened her spine, aware that the movement made her hardened nipples brush against her shift. His hands curled into fists at his sides. He wanted her, like the other knight had wanted her. His passion seemed to flow from him to her on a swift-moving current.

She felt very strange. She waited for him to move forward, to push her boldness one step further, and she found herself wondering what she would do if he came closer. In truth, she was mad to stand before him like this. Jehan was no longer her father's prisoner. He was no longer trapped in a small cell, dependent on her for food and care. She was *his* prisoner now. The man who stood before her, the man who swore to wreak vengeance on her father, was now powerful, strong, and free.

She tilted her chin. She had started this boldness. No matter how odd she felt, no matter what disturbing thoughts flew like startled birds through her head, she could not stop it now.

"I suggest you cover yourself," he said, "before I forget that I'm a knight."

"What knight with honor would do what you have done to me?"

"I've done nothing, *yet*—but if you don't dress I will, and honor be damned."

Margot thrust a woolen tunic into her arms. "Please, *damaiselo,* before it is too late."

She held the tunic against her midriff, ignoring her maid,

still glaring at Jehan. "I see you saved some of my clothing from the scavengers you call English knights."

"It's the least I've done for you this past day." He nodded toward the tunic. "Will you refuse to wear it?"

"I'm angry," she retorted, "not a fool."

"Good." He walked toward her, and she pressed back against the wall. "You're no longer the princess of this castle, Aliénor. There are men here who would sooner drag you to their pallets than listen to one word of your defiance." He stopped in front of her. "You'd best remember, too, that all that stands between you and them is me."

"So a fox will guard the hen."

He was too close. She smelled the wine on his breath from the midday meal; she saw the individual ridges of his coat-of-plates strain against his surcoat. She pressed the woolen tunic close to her body, hiding her breasts. She had pushed him too far; she could see that now, she could hear it in his ragged breathing.

The prisoner had become the warden, and the warden the prisoner. He stared at her with lust plain on his face. She should be frightened of him, but it was not fear that coursed through her veins. Her senses were honed to sharpness. She was acutely aware of his height, of the luster and thickness of his chestnut-black hair, of the intensity of his blue eyes, of the great width of his shoulders. She smelled the freshness of rain on his tunic. She heard the slight scratch of his armor plates as they moved against one another. Her heart beat erratically in her chest and she wondered why the room, which only moments before was cold, now seemed so hot.

"You must trust me." He took a lock of her hair from her shoulder. It gleamed in the light as he rubbed it between his fingers. "You treated me well while I was a prisoner. I've vowed to do the same for you."

"I was free before I met you."

"The Prince made you his prisoner, not I."

"But *you* were the hound that led the charge—and *you* are the dog he left to watch over me." She jerked her hair out of his grip, taunting him and the fury in his blazing eyes. "What will happen to me when your master calls you back to his side?"

"I shall leave you in good hands."

"I've seen the English men-at-arms. I'd rather be left bleeding in a forest full of wolves."

"You know I could take you now." His eyes lowered, to her chest, to the dress she hugged tightly to her figure. "I could toss you on that bed and make you a woman."

She released a sharp gasp. He grasped her shoulders and pinned her against the wall. The tunic slipped from her grasp, exposing her bosom, and to her utter shame he feasted on the sight.

"You've been cloistered in this castle too long, Aliénor. It's time you learned what you do when you tempt a man and stand so bold and naked in front of him."

He wound his hand in her hair and pulled her head back. His mouth covered hers and pressed so hard that their lips sealed with heat and moisture. Her body throbbed suddenly, violently. No man had ever touched her like this. Had it been only two days since she stood in the castle courtyard, looking up at him, wanting him to drag her into his arms and kiss her, like this? So much had changed. She must protest. She must struggle. His lips crushed the words that had already died in her throat. The bristle on his chin scraped her skin. His arm tightened around her back. His body pressed against hers, completely.

I must push him away. Her limbs refused to answer. She found herself digging her nails into his shoulders, deep into the plates beneath his tunic. He pressed harder against her mouth, compelling her to part her lips. She quivered like the string of a lute as he slipped his strong, warm tongue against her own and began a seductive sort of swordplay. His breath was hot and moist. His throat vibrated beneath her fingers as he released a strangled groan. It was as if she had mounted a wild, unbroken colt and lost the reins. All she could do was cling desperately to the beast as it raced mindlessly, completely out of control.

Margot's cry brought her to her senses. Her eyes flew open. Jehan pulled away. His breath was quick and ragged. His face was so close that she could see the streaks of gray and blue that battled in his irises. She felt his fingers spread, hot and bare, against her back.

Then she remembered. She was his prisoner.

He will not make a fool of me twice.

"This is your honor, then," she said breathlessly. "Faith, I'd say there's little honor in this."

He released her abruptly and stepped back. "Get dressed. You're needed in the great hall."

He turned on his heels and left the room.

Aliénor adjusted the long, trailing sleeves of her fawn-colored surcoat as she left her chamber. She had taken her time dressing. She knew Jehan would be waiting impatiently in the great hall, but she didn't care. Prisoner or not, she was the daughter of a vicomte. He had no right to order her around like one of the men-at-arms.

Besides . . . she needed the time. After he left her chamber, it took forever for her heart to stop pounding. She still felt the lingering pressure of his rough lips on her mouth, as if he had just stopped kissing her. He had no right to kiss her like that. He was nothing but an untitled English sympathizer, an impoverished knight who stole what he wasn't given. When he was a prisoner in this castle, she had risked her own safety for his sake. Now that their positions were reversed, he took advantage of her weakness, of her vulnerability.

She took a deep, trembling breath as darker thoughts ran through her mind. Laurent had always told her that because of Eve's original sin, a woman was more prone to sin than a man. Were they sinful, these feelings that tumbled and burned in her body, still, though Jehan had kissed her for only a matter of moments? She had never felt the like. She shook her head. Even if they were sinful, she refused to feel guilty. She hadn't tempted Jehan into kissing her—he had done it of his own volition. If she found some strange pleasure in it, it was not her fault.

She would have to be careful. Jehan was prone like any other man to mindless lusts, but now he was the man ordered to protect her virtue. She was the Prince's prisoner, not his, and she vowed that if Jehan dishonored her like that again, she would carry the tale to the Prince and watch him vent his rage on Jehan.

Her disturbing thoughts came to an abrupt halt as she stepped into the hallway between her room and Laurent's. The castle was as filthy as a peasant's hovel. The hallway stank of stale wine and rotting meat, the rushes were tangled with dirt and discarded bits of food. She peered into her brother's room and sucked in her breath. It looked violated. It was bereft of all movable items: the draperies that hung from his bed, the wall tapestries, the candelabra. His chest lay open and empty but for a few ragged tunics that hung over the edge of the wood. A man-at-arms snored loudly on the soft bed. She cursed him as she turned toward the steps. Her brother, a boy born of noble parents, slept in the kitchens, while this base-born foot soldier slept on a feather mattress. She had a mind to tell Jehan of Laurent's presence in the castle, if only to force him to treat her brother with honor.

She pushed the thought out of her mind. She couldn't trust Jehan with her own virtue; she certainly wouldn't trust him with something as precious as her brother's life. Laurent would stay in hiding until she knew exactly what the Prince had planned for her and her family.

She lifted her skirts from the debris and descended the stairs to the lower floor. The English army had stolen all her golden girdles, so her surcoat hung loose around her waist and hips. Margot had hastily plaited her hair and wound it about her head, but when her chambermaid searched for a veil, she could find nothing but a worn piece of linen. Aliénor had scorned the garment. She'd rather be seen as bareheaded as the poorest serf before she wore such a veil.

She stiffened as she entered the great hall. She scarcely recognized it without the rows of tapestries. It looked as wantonly naked as a harlot. The huge, hand-hewn stones that formed the walls glistened with dampness, and lines of soot stained the masonry where the tapestries had left long strips of wall exposed to years of smoke. Though a fire roared in the enormous hearth, spewing heat into the vaulted room, without the tapestries confining the warmth the hall was as chilly as the courtyard.

The trestle-tables were still up, though the time for midday meal had passed. The stench of grease, stale wine, and old boiled meat lingered in the air. Her mastiff, her greyhound, and her spaniel, who had escaped the bloody fight the day before, rooted around in the rushes. The wounded and the prisoners lay near the wall. Several armed men in the Prince's colors lounged by the hearth, staring avidly at her. She looked quickly away and saw Jehan. His back was to her, and the reddish light of the fire glowed off the plate armor on his arms. He wore a new, clean tunic, and the material stretched dangerously thin across the width of his shoulders. One of his legs was propped up on a bench and he toyed with a chalice on the table—her father's chalice—as if it were his own.

"There you are, child. I feared you were harmed."

She saw Thibaud lying on a pallet of hay near the wall. A bloody linen encircled his upper thigh. *"Oncle!"* She rushed to his side and fell to her knees. "You are wounded."

"Ay! It's nothing but a scratch." Thibaud stared at her intensely. "I saw Sir Jehan fight that knight who attacked you. No one touched you, child?"

"No."

"Good." He nodded decisively. "'Tis a sorry state we're in. Your father told me to protect the castle, but there were too many English. I battled one, and three took his place."

"Father should never have left the castle. He fell into Sir Jehan's trap too easily."

Thibaud closed his eyes and laid his head back against the straw. His skin was as pale as his hair, and she glanced anxiously at his wounded leg. "Who tended you?"

"Some English man of medicine."

She kneeled beside him and gently pulled at the edge of the linen. She smelled no putrefaction; only the earthy, spiced smell of the remnants of a poultice. She saw the gleam of a fever on her great-uncle's forehead, but otherwise he seemed healthy. She decided against rewinding the linen; Thibaud needed his sleep more than anything.

Jehan's voice came suddenly from behind her: "One moment longer and I would have carried you down here bodily."

She glanced over her shoulder and lifted her gaze up, up, to Jehan's face. It was as unreadable as one of the chaplain's precious Latin texts. She rose to her feet and tried, valiantly, not to blush. "Your English friends left me little." She gestured to her ungirdled tunic and bare head. "My chambermaid and I had to search for what I now wear."

He ignored her explanation and gestured to Thibaud. "Do you know this knight?"

"If I do? What will you do? Punish him for being faithful to his liege lord?"

"This man is already a prisoner for that."

"Then what difference does it make if I know his name?"

"Hush, child," Thibaud said, rising stiffly to a sitting position. "Speak with respect to your betters. The Prince of Wales has won this castle fairly, by force of arms. Sir Jehan is his *châtelain.*" He eyed her. "He saved you from disgrace yesterday—"

"Should I grovel at his feet in thanks when it was by his hand that my attacker entered this castle?"

"You used her given name," Jehan interrupted.

"Oui. As her great-uncle, I have that right."

"Hush, Thibaud!"

"I will not hide my name from this knight like a coward. I am Sir Thibaud de Tournan, uncle to the Vicomte de Tournan." He gestured to her. "My great-niece is only trying to protect her kin, Sir Jehan, so forgive her for her boldness. She knows little of the ways of knights."

"I know enough of foolishness——"

"Heed your great-uncle," Jehan interrupted. "He has the wisdom that you and your father lack."

"Wisdom?" she exclaimed. "Thibaud is wounded and imprisoned, while I am healthy and my father is free. Where's the wisdom in that?"

Thibaud shrugged at Jehan. "As I said, she knows nothing of chivalry."

"The Prince's men scorned the peasants who battled on the ramparts yesterday," Jehan said, peering at the elderly knight, "but they remarked on one knight with a beard like snow, who fought as if he had seen no more than thirty winters."

"I have seen twice that many winters, and worse wounds, yet I still have enough pride to claim that knight was I."

"Pride shall be your undoing then," Aliénor interrupted. "You claim yourself a Tournan before a knight who hates all who bear that name."

"Is this true, Sir Jehan? Will you judge me by my name?"

"I have been known," he said pointedly, "to make exceptions."

"But I have not the golden tresses nor the fair face to entice you."

"Oncle!"

"Oui, that is true, Sir Thibaud." Jehan laughed. "Yet it seems you have the character that your nephew lacks. That's enough for me to overlook the unfortunate circumstances of your birth."

"Then give him a cloak or some pelts to keep him warm," she demanded, unnerved by the conversation and the undercurrents between the two men that she did not understand. "Why do you leave this knight on the coldest side of the great hall with nothing but his armor to keep him warm? Sir Thibaud rode with three French kings in his day."

"I've been waiting for you to bless us with your presence, *demoiselle,* so you can take care of such matters." He gestured to the other wounded men. "I'm a knight of the

Prince of Wales. I'll keep meat on the table and the roof secure over your head, but I won't distribute food and wine and comfort like a woman."

"How kind of you to protect *my* castle and find food from *my* forests to put upon *my* table." She tilted her chin and glared at him. "If your English friends hadn't stolen the food, you'd have nothing to do at all."

"Quiet, woman," Thibaud warned. "Sir Jehan has enough quarrel with the Tournans—"

"And the Tournans now have a quarrel with the St. Simons."

"By my faith, you'll bring the wrath of God upon us!"

"No, Thibaud, let her be," Jehan interrupted. "I prefer a spirited woman to a weeping one."

"I shall never cry in front of you."

"Good. I need you working, not weeping. Tell me while your wits are still about you: Are there other Tournans in this castle?"

"Only Thibaud, my mother, and I."

"No more grandparents, great-uncles, cousins?"

"No."

"What of your brother? The one the Vicomte disinherited while I was prisoner here?"

Her eyes narrowed. Sir Jehan had a memory like a vat of honey—anything that flew into it stuck. "Why do you want to know? Are you planning to kill the son of my father?"

His eyes darkened. "Do you think I would kill without consideration, without mercy?"

"Your vengeance against my father led you here, did it not?"

"I didn't kill you, and you bear his name."

"You are indebted to me. I saved your life."

"That debt, *demoiselle*, has been paid several times over."

"That debt has grown to the size of a king's ransom." She lifted her skirts from the rushes and brushed past the knight. "As for my brother, he's safely ensconced in the monastery at Simorre. He was sent there soon after he was disinherited."

A silence greeted her words. She didn't look at Thibaud, though she felt his gaze upon her. The servants who hovered near the entrance of the great hall stared, but said nothing.

"Then your brother is in danger," Jehan said. "The main body of the Prince's army planned to lodge in that city last night—perhaps in that very monastery."

"God be with him, for he is surely fleeing the English."

"If he comes here, I shall welcome him. Unlike your father, I don't make war on boys."

She flushed, remembering that her father had killed Jehan's young squire when Jehan was taken prisoner. She glanced around the great hall. "This room is a disgrace. Have you slaughtered all the servants?"

"I should have, for they are as useless as sheep." The anger threaded through his voice. "They need the strong hand of a woman to guide them."

"I'm surprised you haven't carried my mother bodily down here and forced her to do her duty."

"I would have." Jehan walked to the trestle-tables, picked up the chalice, and took a long gulp of wine. "But the servants say she isn't herself."

"Strange how that happens," she jeered, "when one's husband is driven away, one's castle is stolen, and one's peasants are beaten and killed."

"You don't seem to have suffered overmuch."

"The deepest wounds, Sir Jehan, are the kind that don't bleed."

"Then since you're not faint from *your* wounds," he argued, "you won't object to taking your mother's duties and making them your own."

She realized she had been outmaneuvered. She also realized that the men-at-arms, the servants, and the wounded men were all watching her and Jehan curiously. All conversation by the hearth had stopped, all movement in the buttery and pantry had ceased. Thibaud had a smile on his face, a wide smile, as he glanced from her to the knight. Jehan looked as he had looked in her bedchamber this morning: angry, intense, and determined. She realized she was taunting him again, and this time in public. The last time she had done that, he had kissed her as no man had ever dared. The way he looked now, he was planning to do it again, and this time there would be an audience.

She had no choice. Flushing, she turned to the servants hovering near the buttery and pointed to the trestle-tables. "Take down these tables," she snapped. "Fetch the chaplain and tell him to gather the food that remains to give to the villagers. I'm sure they need the bread, even if it is only crusts from an *English* table." Two young men rushed into the hall and began disassembling the benches and tabletops. She pointed to one of the women. "Get the kitchen servants in here. These rushes must be gathered and burned. Find more, if you can. If you can't, then cut some wet clover from the valley and sprinkle it around. This place smells as bad as the stables—as the stables once *did,*" she corrected as she glared anew at Jehan. "I suspect we have stables no more."

She whirled away before he could answer and checked the stock of wood by the fire. She ordered what was left of her bedclothes to be brought down to warm the wounded men, and she ordered all the older men who were well enough to go out and gather tinder for the fire.

When she turned anew, she walked straight into Jehan. He gripped her shoulder. "Come."

"Come where? You just ordered me to set this hall to rights."

"I want to show you the stables."

"What stables? I saw them burning yesterday."

"If it weren't for my orders to put out the fire, that and all the other wooden structures in the courtyard would have gone up in flames."

"You loose the crows on the harvest, then expect gratitude when you save one stalk of grain."

He grunted as he pulled her through the hall. He pushed open the door and dragged her out into the bright sunlight. She blinked a few times to adjust her eyes as he pulled her down the stairs to the courtyard. His fingers dug into her upper arm.

"You're hurting me!"

"I should turn you over my knee."

"After this morning, Jehan, I don't doubt that you would."

"I thought you'd have enough sense not to mention that." He released her, then turned and faced her, towering over her like a giant. An echo of the morning's emotions swirled in her body anew. "Since you've mentioned it, I'll say what I have to say: I'm sorry."

"Sorry?"

"I'm here to protect you from attacks like that."

"So you claim!"

"You *did* provoke me."

"I did no such thing!"

"You are a full-grown woman, Aliénor, a fact you made difficult for me to ignore."

"You walked into my chamber without a sound," she protested. "Then you attacked me, like a beast!"

"A beast, is it? A beast wouldn't have risked his life for you yesterday. He wouldn't have stopped at kissing you—"

"How dare—"

"—nor would he have saved this castle." He gestured to the courtyard. "Look around you. Tell me what you see."

She glanced around for no other reason than to look away from him. She couldn't hide her surprise. Though the stables near the front portal were charred by fire, the villagers worked nearby, cutting the branches off the trunk of a small oak tree in preparation for the rebuilding of the wooden stalls. Women gathered the branches, broke them down, and piled them into faggots for firewood. As she watched, an Englishman rode through the portal—on one of her father's favorite Pyrenean steeds—with a brace of hares hanging from his saddle. Other men and women walked in and out of the courtyard, some with dried meat, others with bags of grain. The courtyard had been cleared of debris. No arrows or spears or bloodstains marred the dark earth.

"I could have burned this place to the ground," he said

angrily. "The Prince could have killed you and every one of the villagers. He had the right. You are all, in his eyes, rebel vassals." He clutched her arms again, and she felt the full force of his strength. "Instead, because of my request, he not only spared your people and your family, but he spared this castle and the village below. He gave up fifteen of his own men to garrison the place. I could have left you here, Aliénor. I could have left you at the mercy of the men-at-arms. I chose to stay. I want to protect you."

"It's the least you owe me."

"I have given you more than any knight would give." He shook her once, in exasperation. "I fell to my knees before you. Don't you remember that? I've gone on my knees to only one other person—the Prince of Wales. How does it feel to be honored equally as much as the man who may someday be the King of England?"

"It was a lie—it all was a lie. You convinced me that you weren't my enemy, yet look what you've done! You led our worst enemy here, tricked my father, and took away my dowry."

"The Prince would have done the same. Would you have me defy my own liege lord?

"Yes!"

He looked at her incredulously. "I suppose you expected me to give up vengeance against your father as well?"

"You made me believe you would."

"Sir Thibaud was right! You know nothing of chivalry. I'm a knight, Aliénor, not a saint—"

"That's quite obvious."

"—and I won't betray my vow of fealty to the Prince—not for anything, not for a woman. If it weren't for me, your situation would be much worse."

"How much worse could it get?" She blew off her face a lock of hair that had fallen out of her ragged plait. "The villagers call me *maudit*. Cursed. I'm cursed, Jehan. Not a week passes after my fourth—my *fourth*—betrothal is finally settled, and *you* come with your wretched master and conquer my father's lands! Another wedding lost."

"Count your blessings. Guy de Baste's loyalties are as slippery as wet steel."

"I'd rather be wife to a knight of questionable character than prisoner of a man with none!"

For one tense moment, she feared she had pushed him too far. She waited for him to bend her over his arm and bruise her lips, to kiss her until her body became a stranger to her. Instead, he squeezed her shoulders until they were hunched around her ears.

"You are the most ungrateful wench I know."

"You've taken everything from me."

"I've saved your virtue."

"Virtue!" She spat out the word. "What good will *that* do me now? Do you know what the Prince will do when he returns?"

"He'll probably send you to a convent."

"Yes—where I'll waste away like a withered old fruit, bitter and forgotten. I'd rather be dead!" She pulled away from him and was surprised to find herself free. "Think on that, Jehan, the next time you feel you've done right by me."

Chapter
8

JEHAN KICKED HIS HORSE INTO A GALLOP, REACHING BACK TO secure the lean young buck that lay strapped across his stallion. This was the second time he had hunted today; he spent the early morning tracking a boar with the dogs in the far northern forests. He needed to hunt. The stores of meat in the castle were low, and a frigid wind swept through the valley, a brutal reminder that the cold, tenacious rains of winter were imminent. Hunting was as good an excuse as any for leaving the castle, and certainly a better excuse than the truth.

The truth was that if he spent another moment near Aliénor, he would drag her to his pallet and *honor be damned.*

An image of her entered his mind, unbidden and powerful. Naked but for a length of wispy, transparent linen, she had stood without shame, while the midday light poured through the fabric and caressed her body. The image had haunted him for three weeks, tormenting him in the night, forcing him to rise and seek release in whatever servant girl was willing. Those brief couplings were only a temporary reprieve from his ardor. When he finished, Aliénor's image was still fresh in his mind. Each morning he saw her, in the flesh, as proud and desirable as ever.

He had wanted her when he was a prisoner, but not with the intensity with which he wanted her now. Then, he was nothing but a landless knight, while she was the heiress to a huge estate. He had gazed upon her as a man might gaze upon the stars; they, like Aliénor, were lovely, distant, and untouchable. Yet suddenly, miraculously, the stars were within his reach. She was no longer an heiress, but a prisoner. He was no longer a prisoner. He was the *châtelain* of her castle, holding it for the Prince of Wales, with prospects for greater glory. It was as if someone had told him of great riches, and he desired those riches, and then the riches were before him, and his desire for them multiplied. Aliénor had tumbled from her lofty perch, and he yearned to caress the fallen angel.

He could have her. There were no guards watching him. The prisoners were under his control. She was the daughter of the man who had killed his squire. He could call it vengeance, the vengeance he had forgone when he had turned his horse away from the path of the fleeing Vicomte de Tournan. When he kissed her, he had tasted the innocent desire of a woman who was as incapable of controlling her needs as she was incapable of controlling her emotions. He knew she would be a storm in the bedchamber—the kind of woman whose ardor could wear out the strongest knight—and he wanted to be the man to teach her loving.

He groaned and shifted uncomfortably in his saddle. He could not touch her, no matter how much he wanted her. Where once he was imprisoned by high, stone walls, he was now imprisoned by the shackles of chivalry.

She was the Prince's prisoner. He was bound by duty to treat her honorably. But beyond this obligation was his own oath to protect her, the oath he'd made when he and the Prince planned to take over the castle. He could not forget: She had risked her father's anger to tend his wounds, she had kept him sane when he had teetered on madness in the dark cave of his cell. He owed her his life. He could not repay her with stealing her virtue, no matter how eagerly her pliant body moved against his.

To make it worse, she always seemed to be near, never allowing the fire to burn down to embers. She took over what should have been her mother's duties: tending the wounded men, meting out food to the villagers, ordering the great hall to be cleaned until it smelled as sweet as a church. She defied him constantly. She seemed to shoot sparks, like a thick pelt in the dry winter, snapping and crackling at the touch. Her defiance surprised him, for he had expected gratitude. He had saved the castle and the village from destruction, he had saved the lives of her tenants and protected her own virtue. But she refused to see that he had done more than any knight would do for a woman. Any less honorable knight, he mused, would have kissed the defiance out of her and found pleasure in the taming.

I'm living in a hell of my own making.

He slowed his stallion as they broke through the edge of the forest and rode across the open field to the castle. The beast shook his great black head, and white foam flecked off his mouth. The horse stumbled as one of his hooves fell into the river of ruts that still scarred the clayey earth. Jehan veered the stallion toward firmer, flatter ground. Though Prince Edward's army had left Castlenau three weeks earlier, the rain had not yet washed away the tracks of the army's passing. He scanned the path of the deep ruts, past the fortress, past the swollen Arrats river, to where the uprooted earth spread over the next set of hills as if a giant plow had pushed through the land.

Somewhere to the west, the Prince still raided. Jehan frowned. A few days after Edward left, a peddler had come to Castelnau from the direction of Toulouse. The man told Jehan that the Prince of Wales had audaciously crossed the Garonne river upstream from Toulouse, thus avoiding the Comte d'Armagnac's army in Toulouse itself. Further, the entire raiding army—baggage trains, mounted knights, men-at-arms, and foot soldiers—had boldly crossed a swifter, more dangerous river, the Ariège, on the same day, leaving the French army behind two flooded rivers and the entire rich country of Languedoc spread out, unprotected and unsuspecting, in front of him.

At any other time, Jehan would have been pleased to hear

of his liege lord's success in war. It seemed as if God Himself were leading the young Prince of Wales to victory. The Comte d'Armagnac, the French king's lieutenant in Gascony, had not marched after him, despite all the damage the Englishman had done to his land. According to the rumors filtering back from the states of Languedoc, the Prince had already taken the town of Carcassonne and burned it, along with that of Narbonne. Jehan had never expected him to travel so far west in this raid—far outside of the ancient limits of Aquitaine. But as each day passed, he grew less and less appreciative and more and more impatient.

He wanted his lord to return to Bordeaux and settle the lands and castles he had seized from the rebels. Most of all, he wanted the Prince to give Castelnau-sur-Arrats, and all that was in it, to *him*.

It was too much for a powerless knight to ask, even from a lord as generous as Edward. The only land Jehan had ever owned was Castétis, stolen from the Vicomte de Tournan, and it was meager and poor compared to this estate. He wanted Castelnau more each day he spent directing the rebuilding of the village, meting out petty justice among the tenants and redistributing the land tilled by the men who had died in the siege. He wanted it more each day he spent hunting in the black forests of oak and pine, each time he walked the wall-walk and viewed the verdant, fertile land. If the Prince were to give these lands to him, in gratitude for his service . . . It was a lust in him now, a lust that grew parallel in strength with his passion for Aliénor. So much was wrapped up in this place. If his lord gave it to him, he would have vengeance on the Vicomte de Tournan. He would have a title. He would have this, all this, and all that came with it.

Including Aliénor de Tournan.

She filled his mind as his horse approached the entrance to Castelnau. The stallion's hooves clattered hollowly over the wooden drawbridge. For a moment, Jehan was engulfed in darkness beneath the tower before he entered the courtyard. He noticed several villagers occupied with the slaughter of some pigs they had rounded up from the nearby woods, the pigs the Prince's men had scattered after taking all they could kill and carry. He directed one of them to cut the deer from his saddle. He strode toward the wooden stairs, climbed them, and entered the warmth of the great hall.

The men-at-arms idling around the hearth quickly lowered their wineskins and returned to the work of sharpening their lances and swords and hewing arrows from elm branches. Jehan's gaze passed icily over them, for he knew they chafed at the inactivity in the castle, especially since the Prince of Wales warred and collected booty far west of Toulouse. He turned toward the buttery, intending to fetch some wine to quench his thirst. But as he neared the wooden screens, he stopped. Hushed voices floated in from the aisle between the buttery and the pantry. He approached. One of the voices was unfamiliar, the soft voice of a boy. The other, undeniably, was Aliénor's.

"If you're caught with a sword in your hand he'll know for sure," she said.

"He won't catch me," the boy said. "I'll practice only when he's hunting, and where no men-at-arms will see me."

"And where will you get a sword? Will you steal one from the English and be whipped for the theft?"

"Thibaud has one."

"Thibaud is old but not foolish. He won't lend it to you."

"He sleeps this time of the afternoon. You know that. How else would you be able to sneak out of the castle to collect your weeds?"

"They're not weeds. They're herbs. And if I didn't sneak away for that short hour I'd become as daft as Mother, sitting up in my room and bewailing my fate."

"Thibaud is supposed to be guarding you when Sir Jehan is away."

"You've changed the subject."

"I'll come with you, and practice in the fields, where no one will see us."

"And how will we leave the castle unseen, with you limping, with a sword in your hand?"

"You can hide it beneath your skirts."

"Beneath my skirts!" Jehan heard her frustrated sigh. "I don't understand you! Before the English seized this castle, Thibaud and I had to force you to climb upon a horse. Now, here you are, dressed in rags like any peasant's child, insisting upon practicing swordplay!"

"I have more reason now. After what happened to you—"

"Forget what happened to me," she said sharply. "Jehan saved me from that cur, and he's been keeping those men-at-arms at bay ever since."

"'Tis strange, Aliénor, from a man who can't be trusted."

"He *can't* be trusted, but as much as I despise him, I'm not so blind to know that if it weren't for him I'd be treated no better than poor Margot."

"You'll need a protector when this knight leaves."

"Do you, *frai,* think you can protect me from these men-at-arms?"

Frai. Jehan stiffened. *Brother.* It was just as he had suspected all along.

"I can try. If those greyhounds were brave enough to give their lives for you, then surely I can learn how to wield a sword for the same."

"Oh, Laurent . . ."

Jehan heard the sound of rustling. The boy's voice, when he spoke again, was muffled.

"When I came out of the chapel and saw you, and *him,* I felt so helpless. I wanted to kill him."

"Fine thoughts for a young Franciscan."

"Don't tease me. It was your virtue I wanted to protect."

"Jehan did that for you," she retorted, "though I don't know why he bothered. Now listen to me, you mustn't steal Thibaud's sword. We still have to keep your presence secret from the English. Someday soon, Father will win the castle back. For now, it's best you stay hidden."

Jehan rounded the corner. "I think not, Aliénor."

She released the boy and whirled to face him. She dropped the gathered folds of her surcoat, sending a fragrant spray of dried leaves and autumn flowers over the wooden floor. "You! You're supposed to be hunting!"

"The best prey seems to be within this castle."

She and the boy tensed, like two young deer sensing danger and poised for flight. Jehan lunged for the boy before he could race away. She cried out and stepped swiftly between them, but Jehan thrust her aside and bunched the front of the boy's tunic in his hand. The boy struggled vigorously. Aliénor stepped in, heedless, gripped Laurent's arm and tried to pull him away. In a matter of moments, Jehan had two squirming, fighting Tournans in his hands, each held apart at arm's length.

"Leave him alone!" she cried. "He's done nothing!"

"Quiet!"

"He's not yet fourteen years of age. He's as innocent as a babe. If you touch him, I vow I'll not rest until—"

"Enough!" Jehan tightened his grip on her arm. "Stop your prattling before the entire garrison arrives with their swords drawn."

She quieted and stilled her struggles, but her golden-brown eyes were bright with suspicion. As soon as he loosened his grip on her, she raced to Laurent's side and clutched his arm. Jehan ignored her and pulled off the rest of the boy's hood. His hair, though dirty, was the same distinctive color as his sister's. He was not as young as Jehan expected. He was at that strange, awkward age between childhood and young manhood. He was nearly as tall as Aliénor. He had his father's eyes, close together and as black as midnight. In the dim light of the fire that spilled into the aisle from the great hall, Jehan could tell by the boy's regular features and unusual coloring that he was the spawn of Tournan. "If I had laid eyes on you, I'd have known in a moment."

"The English have seen him and not recognized him," she said. "They've kicked him and scorned him and beaten him as he served them his father's wine and his father's food."

"Blame that on yourself. You never should have hidden him."

"Should I have handed him to his enemies?"

"He'll be treated better as a prisoner of the Prince of Wales than as a kitchen boy."

"Will he? Locked away in the darkness?"

"Locked away?" Jehan glared at her. "Are you locked away? Is Thibaud? Your mother?"

"I'm only a daughter, Thibaud a distant relative. And you keep us imprisoned within this castle."

"Not as well as I should, obviously," he said, gesturing to the debris scattered across the floor. "The hills are full of thieves and stragglers who would slit your pretty throat for the tunic you wear."

"Mother used to tell me such stories. She wanted to scare me into staying within the castle. They didn't work when I was younger, Jehan, and they won't work now."

"Then maybe I should lock *you* away, but I won't treat this boy as your father treated me." He tightened his grip on the boy's crumpled tunic and addressed him. "Why did you hide from me like a coward?"

"He's not a coward."

"Aliénor, please." It was the boy's voice, even and calm. "Let your brother speak."

"My sister feared you would kill me, Sir Jehan, in vengeance for my father's sins."

He glared at her anew. Her chest heaved beneath the mended wool of her surcoat and the stained linen of her tunic. Though her eyes flashed like sparks in golden wine, her face had paled to gray. She edged her brother behind her body. Her gaze fell to the sword hanging from Jehan's baldric, then to the mercy dagger, the *misericorde*, against his right hip, then back to his face. *She truly believes I will kill the boy,* he thought. What would it take to soften her? What would it take to convince her that he would never stain his hands with innocent blood? "You don't seem to understand that I am bound, by oath, to see to your welfare."

"You've turned your vengeance on me and mine," she argued. "I swore my brother would not feel its edge."

The boy lifted his voice. "My sister wishes only to protect me, Sir Jehan."

"She's the one who needs protection."

"I was telling her that before. She tends to be reckless."

"Reckless! I'm the only one with any sense in this castle!"

"You've as much sense as a rabid dog," Jehan interjected, releasing the boy. "You bite and snarl and fight when there is no threat."

"An *Englishman* is always a threat."

"Please, *ma sor.* He's a knight, and bound by his oath. I'm safe here." He paused and lowered his eyes. "I shouldn't have hidden from you, Sir Jehan, but I, too, feared the worst."

"Perhaps you've inherited some of your great-uncle's wisdom."

"That's not a compliment, Laurent. Thibaud has taken to this knight like a puppy to his sire."

Jehan ignored her and gestured to the boy's soiled tunic. "Find yourself better clothes if you can. You shall join me, your sister, and the rest of your family for the midday meal."

Laurent looked up at his sister, who still held his arm in a tight grip. She was frowning, but not at him, at Jehan. Reluctantly, she released her brother and smoothed the bunched wool of his sleeve. "Go, Laurent, before he changes his mind." She wrinkled her nose. "And wash the stink of the pens off your skin."

Laurent limped away. For the first time, Jehan noticed the boy was crippled. His dragging foot made a hideous scraping noise against the rushes in the hall. Now he understood, finally, why the Vicomte de Tournan had disinherited his son. The Vicomte would have no tolerance for imperfections in his children. Jehan waited until his form faded into the shadows, then he faced Aliénor. "How many more Tournans are running around, dressed as servants, hiding themselves from me for fear that I'll torture them because of their name?"

"No more."

"That, Aliénor, is what you said three weeks ago."

"You can't blame me for hiding my brother. You aren't known to love my father."

"The two are not one and the same."

"*I* know that. The question, Jehan, is whether *you* understood. I wasn't willing to risk my brother's life." Seeing the herbs and dried flowers scattered among the rushes, she lifted her skirts and bent down to regather them. After a minute of silence, he crouched down beside her and reached for her chin. He forced her to look at him.

"Promise me you won't do something foolish. Like help your brother escape."

"He has no place to escape to. The English have devastated the countryside."

"Then it doesn't matter if you promise."

"First promise *me* you will do him no harm."

"I vow," he began, without hesitation, clutching the hilt of his sword, "that I will not harm Laurent de Tournan." Her eyes widened. He tightened his grip on her chin. The words surged to his lips: "Will you trust me now, Aliénor? Will you ever trust me? Or must we forever play these games of promises and oaths?"

"My brother is my only sibling. I'd sooner kill than put him in harm's way."

"You think I'm the enemy," he said, "when I'm sworn to be the protector of both you and your brother."

She was so close. Her unruly, soft blond hair sprung from the neat braids she had plaited and wound on either side of her face. His gaze caught hers and clung. Then, like tinder bursting into fire, passion sparked and flared into flame.

He loosened his grip on her chin. He stroked the curve of her cheek. Her skin flushed beneath his hand and he wondered if the rest of her body had this wonderful tendency to blush like the sunrise. The linen tunic she wore beneath her surcoat gaped away from her chest, teasing him with a view of the swell of one ripe breast. She was as alluring and lovely as the fairies that were said to hide in the forests, but she was better: She was real and human, flesh and blood, vibrant and full to the brim with life. Boldly, he traced her lower lip, watching with fascination as her mouth parted and a gasp escaped. *Dieu!* The feel of her moist, hot breath created havoc within his hose.

Suddenly he was only a hand's span away from her face. Her lips beckoned him, half opened, showing the glimmer of her tongue, the wetness of her mouth. The need surged in him, the need to taste her, to rub his lips against hers, to enter her body and make them one.

"It's difficult to think of you as my protector," she said suddenly, not backing away, "when I always feel so unprotected in your presence."

Her quiet words rang out like the loudest of clarions. He froze and looked into her eyes. It was no wonder she felt unprotected around him. *She was.* He was losing this battle with his honor—here, just outside the great hall, crouching amid the rushes with the pungent scent of crushed, dried herbs swirling around them. She wanted him to kiss her, too; he saw it in her eyes. But he had his honor, his damned honor. Summoning a will he did not know he had, he forced himself to lean back on his heels, then to straighten to his full height. He was a knight, not a beast. Before this was over between them, he vowed she would know he was a knight worthy of the name.

She didn't linger. She finished gathering the herbs, then rose to her feet. Carefully clutching the gathered wool of her surcoat to her waist, she walked swiftly, and wordlessly, away.

"Aliénor! Praise God you are here."

Aliénor, carrying her sewing, started as she entered the solar. *Maman,* wild-eyed, clung frantically to the edge of a ragged pelt. She picked at the fur with quick, jerky movements, denuding the thinning pelt of its short brown hairs.

"What is it, *Maman?*"

"I hear fighting! Sword fighting! By Saint Anne, have the English returned?"

"No, *Maman.* They haven't returned." She realized the mistake her mother had made as she heard the distinctive sound of sword crashing against sword coming from the next room. "The noise you hear is only your son and Thibaud, practicing with swords in Laurent's room."

"Laurent?"

"Yes." She walked farther into the chamber. She sat down on a chest near the twinned windows. For the first time since Mass this morning, she was finally off her feet. "For some reason, Laurent has decided he wants to learn swordplay. He's been practicing for the past week with Thibaud. Now that the slaughtering has begun, there is no room in the courtyard, so he practices inside, away from the Prince's men."

"So the English are not here?"

"Rest easy, *Maman.* They're not here."

Her mother settled back on her heels and bent her head in prayer. When she raised her head again, she scanned the chamber, peering at the doors with uncertainty. Her mother had remained in the same constant state of anticipation since the day the English had attacked the castle. Aliénor hoped it would pass, soon, and she would return to her normal self. *Maman* had always been a nervous, fretful woman, but not nearly as bad as since . . . since the attack.

She turned her attention to her sewing, trying to concentrate on the tear near the hem of a surcoat, where she had caught it on a ragged piece of wood. She remembered, all too well, the livid bruises that marred her mother's arms and legs after the invasion. On that horrible day *Maman* had been attacked, as Aliénor had been attacked, but Jehan had arrived too late to save her mother from misuse. Since that day her mother had done little but cry, pray, and sleep, only to wake and cry again. Aliénor didn't like to think about it. She didn't know how to ease her mother's pain. All she could do was take over her mother's duties in the castle and try to lessen her fears by telling her that Father would soon return.

Any day now, she kept telling herself, Father would attack the castle and take it back from the English. Father would release her from this overwhelming responsibility and restore the world to order again. She felt as weary and old as a woman of sixty years. During the long nights, she dreamed of silks and furs, of gold girdles and pearl circlets, of the tenderest lark's tongue pie, of the tartest oranges from the eastern lands. She could almost hear Laurent chiding her for her lust for creature comforts, but she shook his voice out of her head. She hated the way she looked, the way she felt; and the only joy she found these days was in her dream that Father would return, and everything would be as it was before. She would be betrothed again, preparing for a wedding and a new life.

She heard another grunt from the next room and the distinctive sound of a body falling. For the past week, Laurent worked at his daily lessons with Thibaud with the same single-minded eagerness with which he had once prayed. A month before, she would have been thrilled with Laurent's strange change of heart, but now she wondered, and worried. She knew the reason behind his new passion. He wanted to protect her. The thought of Laurent trying to separate her from a lusting man-at-arms filled her with fear.

Furthermore, she was baffled by Jehan's behavior toward her brother. Yesterday, while she combed through her mother's tangled hair and tried to persuade her for the hundredth time in four weeks to come downstairs to eat with the family, she had watched Laurent and Thibaud practicing. Jehan rode into the courtyard and watched them for a while; then, to her utter surprise, he proceeded to take the sword from Laurent's hand and instruct him on how to handle it more deftly. She didn't understand it. Jehan treated him like a younger brother, not the son of his most hated enemy. Jehan told stories at dinner about the Pope's court at Avignon until Laurent was utterly engrossed. And to make it all worse, Laurent had begun to admire the knight—even so far as to chide her for being as stubborn as a Pyrenean mule.

Thibaud, of course, was a terrible example for her brother, and Laurent was an impressionable boy. Thibaud cleaved to Jehan as if he had known him all his days. The two knights drank diluted wine late into the nights. Her great-uncle repeated his war stories, the worn tales that grew more ragged with the years, to a new and willing ear. They discussed the war between the French and English, the relative value of foot soldiers, archers, and mounted knights in a battle, the tournaments that took place frequently in London and around Paris. They even argued about the merits of an English lord compared to a French lord in Gascony, in such heated terms that she feared they would come to blows; but when all the bluster was over, the two of them would raise another wooden tankard of wine and laugh and slap each other on the back. She wondered how Thibaud's fragile bones could take such abuse, and she wondered why he didn't mistrust the man who had caused them so much harm.

Jehan was their *enemy*.

She would never understand men, particularly knights and, even more particularly, Jehan. She admitted, grudgingly, that he had treated the villagers well after the Prince and his army had left the castle. He ordered the damage to their one-room homes fixed. He allowed the peasants to fish in the swollen Arrats river and hunt for hares and deer in the forests, which were once the exclusive privileges of the Vicomte de Tournan. He ordered the English to keep their hands off the servant women, particularly the unwilling ones, much to the anger and frustration of the men, for now that they were not warring along with their liege lord they chafed at the inactivity. Finally, despite all her taunting, not once since the day after the attack did Jehan slip in his promise to her and forget his honor.

She wondered if it was his honor holding him back, or if she had worked herself so hard that she was no longer attractive to him. The thought annoyed her more than she cared to admit. She blew at a curl that hung over her forehead. It floated up, then fell back, stubbornly, over her face. Jehan had ample opportunity to kiss her. He almost kissed her the morning Laurent was caught. What was worse was that she wanted him to kiss her. *Vanity.* Laurent would call it her vanity and tell her it was a sin. She knew her attraction to Jehan was a sin, but she sensed it wasn't the sin of vanity. It was another sin, a darker sin. It was a desire she was finding more and more difficult to restrain, especially in the face of Jehan's baffling behavior.

She was weakening. Whenever he was in the same room, she was conscious of every gesture, every smile, even the way his hands curled around the body of a wooden tankard. She was as mad as *Maman* to be thinking of Jehan in such terms. He was an enemy knight, an English vassal. He was also handsome—breathtakingly so. The women servants never stopped commenting upon him. One morning she had watched him, dressed only in his shift and braies, practicing swordplay with an Englishman. The muscles of his legs, arms, and shoulders bulged and rippled under his skin so powerfully that she found herself as breathless as if *she* were the one engaged in swordplay. What was more devastating were his winning ways; when he wished, he could be as charming as the Devil himself. He was full of stories of the court in Bordeaux, stories that grew so baudy and so hilarious when he told them in front of the fireplace after supper that she found herself laughing aloud.

Aliénor tilted her head as she suddenly heard something through the badly fitted glass of the twinned windows. Excited, manly cries and shouts of welcome rose from the courtyard. Curiosity got the best of her and she placed her sewing aside. She stood up and peered through the columbine flowers and buttercups painted on the glass. The sight that greeted her chilled her skin to ice.

"What is it, Aliénor? What's the noise?"

She took a deep breath and tried to control her features. She turned to her mother. "'Tis nothing, *Maman*. The servants are slaughtering the last of the swine, and they're chasing the pig around the courtyard." She called for her mother's chambermaid. The servant ran in from the donjon. "Watch *Maman,* will you? I'm going outside for a moment."

She walked calmly out of the solar. When she reached the bottom of the stairs, she raced across the empty great hall, heedless of her long skirts, and passed through the oak door. The *autan* wind gusted as she stepped outside, scattering dried leaves over the cluttered courtyard and lifting the edges of her skirts. She stared at the horseman who rode into the center of the courtyard. The horse was heaving and gleaming with sweat. The men-at-arms converged on the rider. Heedless of the cold, she ran down the stairs and joined the crowd as a page took the reins of the lathered horse and the messenger dismounted. There was no doubt. She recognized the blue, red, and gold colors emblazoned on the rider's badge. He was a messenger from the Prince of Wales.

Jehan reached his side first. The *courrier* pulled off his feathered hat and managed a weary bow. He spoke in rapid French. She pushed through the crowd, ignoring the angry comments of the English, until she reached the messenger.

"Forget the formalities," Jehan said. "How does the Prince?"

"The Prince is at Aurade."

"That's less than a day's ride from here."

"Oui, Sir Jehan. He is heading back to Bordeaux. He was planning to pass through here and secure this fortress, but the Comte d'Armagnac's troops guarded the crossing of the river Save near Lombez and Sauveterre, and he was forced to march north to Aurade to cross."

"The French forces have finally come out of hiding."

"In force," the messenger continued. "As of yesterday, the whole French army—five columns—was camped within two leagues of the Prince's rear guard. They were trailing our movements on the other side of the Save. We lost sight of their fires last night, but my lord suspects they will attack soon."

"I must secure this castle then."

"No, the Prince needs his knights to battle the French rebels," he explained. "He wants you to join him on the high road between Auch and Toulouse, near Aurimont, immediately. He believes there'll be a battle at sunrise tomorrow."

She heard her own heart beat hard, heavy, and slow. She looked at Jehan. His lips had tightened in an angry white line.

"What of this castle?"

"It is as always, Sir Jehan. It's to be abandoned in the usual manner."

"What does that mean?" She stepped closer to the messenger. "Tell me: What does that mean?"

"It means to burn it," Jehan said harshly. "To burn it and leave nothing for even the scavengers to take."

Chapter
9

Burn it. The words echoed in Aliénor's head like the clangor of churchbells ringing for a death Mass. She remembered the glow on the horizon, weeks before, when Seissan burned in the distance. Vividly, she imagined the crackle of flames as they consumed the wood vaulting of the great hall, charred the limestone walls, engulfed the wooden beams, and opened the roof to the sky. She stared, speechless, at Jehan, but his attention was riveted on the messenger.

Jehan's hands flexed into tight fists. "It's senseless to destroy one of the strongest fortresses on the border."

"The Prince needs knights now, not castles."

"If you've misinterpreted Prince Edward's commands," he growled, "I vow you won't live to see Bordeaux again."

The messenger bowed. "I don't question the Prince's orders, Sir Jehan."

Burn it. He couldn't—he *mustn't*. She felt the anger in Jehan, tight, taut, like the muscles that now flexed beneath his chain-mail sleeve. She glared at him, willing him to defy his liege lord's order, but he only stared at the messenger in frustration. The men-at-arms cried out in excitement around her. She sensed great movement in the courtyard as they raced to gather their belongings and booty, even as they ordered their horses saddled and loaded.

"The Prince advised haste," the messenger added. "He urged you to depart as soon as I arrived, and to let nothing slow you down."

Jehan's jaw hardened. He turned to one of the men. "Make sure everyone hears the announcement. The Prince's men must be fully armed, provisioned, and ready to ride fast and hard as soon as possible. Tell them to gather outside the walls of the castle. Send someone down to the village to tell all who live there that they must abandon their homes immediately—"

"No!" She clutched his arm and shook it, but it was like trying to shake a mountain. "You mustn't burn the castle!"

"Quiet, Aliénor!"

"I will *not* be silent! It's nearly winter. We'll all die!"

Jehan clutched her arms, hard, so hard that she cried out in pain. His eyes, gray in fury, warned her to be silent. He spoke to the messenger over her shoulder. "There's little food left in the castle, but you can refresh yourself in the kitchens before we leave."

Without another word, he turned and strode angrily toward the castle, towing her like a stubborn filly. She stumbled on the uneven stones of the courtyard as she tried to keep up with his much longer stride. She twisted her arm to free herself from his painful grip, but he held her relentlessly. He pulled her through the mass of racing men-at-arms, up the cluttered stairs of the castle, and into the great hall. Already, only moments after the messenger's arrival, the hall was in chaos: The trestle-tables were tipped over, the rushes crushed into powder, and the wood that once stood piled beside the hearth was now scattered all over the floor. Two men carried full-to-bursting wineskins and joints of meat up from the cellar.

"Where are you taking me?"

He pulled her into the hallway between the donjon and the castle. "To where we can talk—in private."

He pulled her up the crumbling, narrow stairs, which were dug into the thick wall of the tower, until they reached the uppermost floor. He led her into the room where he slept, released her abruptly, and slammed the ancient oak door behind them.

She rubbed her bruised wrist and tried to catch her

breath. She hadn't been to the upper room of the donjon since Jehan had made it his chamber. She noted the oiled skins stretched across the window, the narrow, straw pallet not far from the hearth, and the tangle of armor spread across the floor. It was the sparse, comfortless room of a poor knight, and it surprised her that he hadn't claimed some of the few pelts and linens in the castle for his own.

"Go ahead, Aliénor. You can scream and rant all you want now."

She glared at him and stopped rubbing her wrist. "Is that why you dragged me up here?"

"Yes." He reached for two round, steel poleyns and buckled them over his knees. "I couldn't have you raving like a madwoman in front of the Prince's messenger."

"Tell me you're not going to burn this castle."

He straightened. "I have no choice."

"You can't!"

"Do you think I *want* to burn it?" He paced angrily around the room as he gathered his armor. "I didn't garrison this place only to give it up. I didn't forgo weeks of warring with my lord, weeks of plunder, only to give up the one thing I protected. Damn it, I've spent weeks strengthening it—"

"You may lose a garrison, but I lose my home."

"I lose much more than a garrison, Aliénor. If you knew—"

"You lose nothing," she interrupted, crossing her arms. "You came, you conquered, and now you will destroy and leave. You are no poorer than before. But I will lose everything."

"It is the Prince's order."

"Damn the Prince, and damn your loyalty to him! Don't you realize what will happen to us?"

"Yes!"

"We'll be forced to live in a charred shell, open to English deserters, to thieves, to the frigid winter rain. With no food, we'll starve!"

"You'll be safe—I'll see to it. But I'll also burn this castle. If I left it whole, your father would reconquer it."

"And I might live, with the grace of God!" She stepped closer to him as he buckled his baldric around his hips. "What difference does it make if Father reconquers Castelnau? There is nothing left in it: Our wealth is jingling in English purses, being worn by English women, and decorating English castles. My father will reconquer nothing but an empty shell."

"If your father recaptures Castelnau, no matter how poor, then he'll retain his title and his land. That, Aliénor, is plunder worth a wealth of gold plate and tapestries." He buckled the last of his armor, two tubular steel plates, on his forearms. "I won't allow the Prince's raid to be in vain."

"And if I, and all my people, die, then the Prince's raid will have been successful?" He did not answer. Her body quivered, with fear, with anguish, with the determined need to convince him to save Castelnau. "It's for vengeance, isn't it, Jehan? Vengeance against my father?"

"Your father has a debt to pay. I never denied it. I'll wreak vengeance on him for what he did to my squire, and what he did to me. By my faith and all that is holy, I don't want to burn this castle"—he made a frustrated grunt—"but if I leave it whole I will be doing two things: defying my lord's orders and handing the fortress back, unscathed, to my bitterest enemy." He glared at her. "I *must* burn it, no matter how much the act galls me. I would rather my vengeance be against the Vicomte and not his kin, but now I have no choice."

"You'd rather wreak vengeance on my father than see me and my people live through the winter—"

"I won't abandon you. I've sworn to protect you, and that doesn't stop with the burning of Castelnau. You must leave with me."

"As your prisoner?"

"You'll be defenseless here, without a protector, without the high walls of a castle around you."

"Will I be any safer with you? In the Prince's army, as a

camp follower, I, the daughter of the Vicomte de Tournan? How long do you think it'll take before one of the three thousand *Englishmen* drags me into the bushes—"

"I've sworn to protect you." A muscle moved in his cheek. "I haven't yet broken that oath. If there's trouble, then as soon as I find a safe convent, I'll lodge you there."

"What of my brother? My mother? My people?"

"They can care for themselves."

"They cannot," she protested, "and I won't leave. My father will return to claim his family, even if this castle is a ruin. He'll protect me from harm."

"As he did the day the Prince laid siege to this castle?" His face twisted in scorn. "It could be months before he hears of the fate of Castelnau. Even then, he might not immediately return. He may assume the Prince killed all his prisoners who couldn't pay ransom."

She gasped.

"Fear not. Edward didn't order his prisoners slaughtered. He knows this castle holds only women, boys, peasants, and old men." He faced her squarely. "You must come with me. It's the only way you'll be safe."

"I'm in danger with you, I'm in danger without you. I would rather stay with my family."

"Then I can no longer protect you, Aliénor, and my debt to you is paid."

"The debt is *not* paid, Jehan. I saved your life, and you have given me nothing but anguish."

"What do you want from me, woman?" He ran his hand through his dark hair, rumpling the tresses over his forehead. "I've given you more than any other knight would, I've offered you far more than any knight would—"

"There are ways to defy the Prince's orders."

"Diou de jou!" He whirled on her, a dark, dangerous shadow, as strong as the Pyrenean winds. He clutched her by the shoulders and shook her so hard that her head snapped back. "Don't you think if there was a way, I'd use it? Do you think I want to leave you here like carrion for wolves?"

A loosened curl fell from her plait and brushed her

temple. His hands engulfed her shoulders and held her so tight and so close that she could see every bristle on his cheeks. His nostrils flared, and his gaze fell, suddenly, from her eyes to her lips. As he hovered over her, she could feel his power, his strength, as forcefully as when he had pulled her into his arms, so many weeks before, and kissed her as no man had ever kissed her.

He released a noise that sounded somewhat like a groan. His fingers dug into her arms. "Come with me, Aliénor. I swear, upon all that is holy, that I will care for you."

"No, no, Jehan." She was losing her senses, she was forgetting why she was here, in Jehan's chambers. She must not stare into his eyes and allow him to draw her closer, to wrap his arms around her, and kiss her as he had not dared for four long weeks. She must not allow her own tumbling emotions to obscure the reason why she was here. This man had the power of life and death over her and all her kin. She must use whatever power she had to convince him to choose life. If she didn't, she knew she would never again see the warm days of spring. "Listen to me, please. The Prince ordered that you make haste. The message was urgent. You could leave and claim that you left in such haste that there was no time to burn—"

"There's more to this than those vague orders, Aliénor." His hands flexed over her shoulders. "I won't leave anything for the Vicomte de Tournan to come back to."

"Then you are choosing to kill me, Jehan. As surely as if you plunged a dagger into my heart."

His grip tightened anew. He pulled her closer, forcing her to arch her neck in order to meet his gaze. Her breasts grazed his tunic. She lifted her hands and spread them against his chest, for the strength of his grip had lifted her to her toes. She felt unbalanced in body, and in mind, as she felt his heart pounding beneath the layers of chain mail and padding. She felt as if she were standing in the middle of the Arrats, in spring, with the swift current of melted snow coursing over her body, pushing her downstream, and she was losing the struggle to maintain her slippery footing. Danger, desire, and desperation raged in her blood.

He is your enemy. The refrain was naught but a whisper now, for no enemy would look at her as Jehan was now looking at her. He looked tormented, as tormented as she felt, as his gaze devoured her, from her tangled hair to the valley of her bare throat. He was no enemy; she was sure of it. No matter what had passed between them, she knew no enemy would stand before her for so long, wanting her, yet refusing to take her. She was defenseless. It was his honor that stayed him, his knowledge that he owed her his life and that he had failed to repay that weighty debt. She must muster her scattered senses, suppress these feelings that coursed through her blood, and beg for the lives of her people.

"Jehan . . ." The air seemed thin and scarce, and she struggled to fill her lungs. "I have never begged before, but I am pleading with you now. If there is any shred of sympathy in you, any bit of gratitude for what I have done for you in the past, then for the sake of my life and the life of my people, spare this castle."

"*Ailas,* Aliénor . . ." He shook her gently. "You don't understand what you ask for."

"I'm pleading for my life."

His hands, suddenly, slipped off her shoulders and wound round her body. She didn't have the strength nor the will to protest as he drew her fully against him. Her breasts flattened against his chest. She felt every link in his haubergeon. Her hips were bruised against the buckle of his baldric. He lifted her feet off the cold floor and his hand buried in her tangled, loosened braids. He still didn't kiss her, though his lips hovered so close to her own that she felt his breath brushing her mouth.

"You wanted a great, noble gesture . . ." His voice was ragged. "Very well. For you, Aliénor, I will do this thing."

Her fingers dug into his chest.

"The men-at-arms will be suspicious. I'll have to burn the village. I might have to burn the stables and the mews as well. But I'll save the castle, as you once saved my life. I'll give up my vengeance on your father—for now. We shall be even, you and I."

Relief washed over her, mingling with astonishment. He had no reason to agree; he gained nothing by saving the castle. He could only lose, by incurring the wrath of the Prince if the Prince didn't believe that he left in haste, and by losing a strong fortress to a rebel if her father returned and recaptured it. He had agreed, nonetheless. *For my sake,* she thought. *For my sake alone.*

The realization made her tremble. Perhaps she had not been wrong to accept his word, so long before, that he was a man of honor, a man who might be her father's enemy but swore not to be hers. Perhaps Laurent was right: She had been too stubborn to see that Jehan had done what he had to do when he followed his lord's orders and seized the castle. He had protected her well, over the past weeks, even so far as to restrain himself from doing what she knew he wanted to do right now: kiss her and make her a woman.

"Ay." He tightened his arms around her. "For four long weeks I've wanted you to look at me like this."

"Will you truly do this thing, Jehan?"

"Yes." He hovered a breath above her lips. "Kiss me, Aliénor. Let that be your thanks."

She didn't hesitate. She could think of no better way to show her gratitude, she could think of no better excuse to fulfill the torrid fantasies of weeks of imaginings. She wound her arms around his neck. His lips met hers, hungrily. Passion exploded in her body, like a thousand kernels of grain kept too close to a fire. There was no control, no struggle, no hesitation. She opened her mouth when he nudged her lips, she stroked his tongue as he stroked hers. Her heart fluttered madly in her chest, and she thrilled to feel the hard, heavy pounding of his own against her breast. His fingers loosened the ragged plait until the tresses fell in golden rivers down her back. He pressed against her in a way that left no doubt as to the strength of his desire—but the feeling did not frighten her. She wanted him closer.

He growled, low and deep in his throat. She was drowning in him. She clung to him as he lifted her off the ground and whirled her around, only to put her on the ground again and kiss her more deeply. She returned each embrace with an ardor she had not known she possessed, with a skill she learned as his embrace continued, learned with eager rapidity, with avidity. She wove her fingers in his thick, dark hair. She moaned in pleasure as his hands swept over her back to rest in the hollow at the base of her spine. Passion possessed her body, like a demon, and she never wanted to be exorcised from so wondrous a feeling. *I could give myself to him. He could make me a woman.* The thought didn't frighten her. It didn't shock her with its immorality. It thrilled her, as nothing had ever thrilled her before.

She released his lips to catch her breath. Her neck arched back. His lips touched her throat—ah, his lips were so warm! He murmured her name, breathlessly, raggedly, and she trembled. He found a sensitive pulse at the base of her throat. She felt alive. She felt more alive now than she had ever felt in her life.

His hand cupped her breast over the worn wool of her surcoat. She thought there could be no greater feeling, until the slightest brush of his thumb against her nipple proved her wrong. Her breasts tingled and tightened. Pressing closer to him, she met his lips anew. He took them, eagerly, wrapping his free hand around her neck, nestling her head against the bulge of his upper arm, gently kneading her bosom until she heard herself make a low, gasping cry.

He removed his hand and tore his lips from hers. His blue eyes were as bright as the sky. "You've chosen a bad time, Aliénor, to show me such passion."

She could manage no more than a weak, soft sound.

"No knight has ever been sent off to war with such a kiss." He loosened his grip and urged her to look up at him. She didn't know what to say. She wanted to kiss him again. She wanted him to touch her. She knew, by looking into his eyes, that he wanted the same. "If I'm to fulfill this pledge to you, *couret,* I can tarry no longer, else the castle will burn around us."

Couret. My little heart. Certainly, she thought, the world was already burning around them. Her body was aflame. She smelled the smoky odor of charred wood as she took a deep, trembling breath. She started. The heat in her blood couldn't cause such a scent. She realized that the fires had already begun.

"They're burning the village!"

"*Oc,* and they'll burn more than that if I don't leave you now." His voice lowered. "You can still come with me, Aliénor."

"No." She regained her balance and stepped away from him. The air was chill and damp out of the circle of his arms. "Your duty is to the Prince, mine to my people. I will stay."

He hesitated, as if he wanted to argue with her, but instead he took the jeweled *misericorde* from his baldric and held out the hilt. "Take this. If your father fails to recapture this castle, you'll need it."

She took it and held it against her chest. Two rubies sparkled on the hilt. She watched as he walked around the room, gathering what remained of his armor and belongings. As he heaved his sack over his shoulder, she felt a growing sense of loss. He stopped in the portal and turned around. Across the distance she felt his gaze like a caress. He said three simple words.

"I will return."

Aliénor drew her gelding to a halt as she reached the top of a hillock, one of a chain that edged the valley that held the winding Gers river. The horse tossed his head and flecked the foam gathered around his mouth onto the frosted earth. His sides heaved between Aliénor's hose-covered legs. Laurent and Thibaud reined in beside her.

"The *bastide* of Pavie," she said, pointing to a fortified town in the valley.

"Praise the saints it's still standing," Laurent said in relief.

"Praise those stone walls instead. It must be the only *bastide* in miles that hasn't been burned, pillaged, or garrisoned by the English."

"There's a crowd entering its gates."

"They've come," Thibaud said, "to do what we've come to do: see if there's any food left in Gascony."

Aliénor kicked her gelding into a canter as she descended the forested slope into the valley of the Gers. The iron links of the haubergeon she wore were as cold as ice, and the garment hung heavy on her shoulders. Her lips were stiff and cracked from the pounding of the cold February air. The breeze tugged at the broad point of her hat and filtered icily through the fibers of the man's hose she had donned for the three-hour ride through the dangerous hills. Her fingers had long become numb and stiff, but she didn't stop to warm them in her clothing. Her hunger drove her onward. Her hunger, and the memory of what she had left behind in Castelnau-sur-Arrats.

Three long, hungry months had passed since the Englishmen abandoned Castelnau. The village at the base of the slope existed no more; it was nothing but a black, ugly stain on the banks of the Arrats. The villagers now lived inside the great hall, for, as Jehan promised, the castle had not been burned. The Prince's men, however, had wreaked so much destruction that the fortress was nothing but a cold, empty shell, only good for protecting its inhabitants from the chill of the winter rains.

The English had stolen everything they could carry. What little food they hadn't stolen—joints of rancid, salty meat and mold-ridden bread—ran out by Christmas. Aliénor had no choice but to order the village men to search on foot through the bare forests for what meager game and fowl remained, despite the bite of the incessant Pyrenean winds. The Christmas feasts consisted of old chestnuts and dried mushrooms. When a woodcock was caught on New Year's

Day, they celebrated as if it were a miracle. They sucked the marrow out of every fragile bone in the bird's body.

The celebration didn't last long. On the feast of the Epiphany, Death entered the great hall. The first of the elderly women succumbed to a sudden fever. One young widow, whose husband had been killed during the marauders' attack, became ill soon after. She survived, but her milk dried up and her baby died within days. Death's sinister, invisible shadow roamed through the castle as if it were its lord, empowered to wield his own sort of twisted, indisputable justice. By Candlemas Day—Aliénor's birthday—the chaplain was forced to bless new ground in the graveyard just outside the castle walls, behind the chapel, to make room for the graves dug weekly in the boggy earth. Aliénor was helpless to stop the fevers. *Maman* cowered in the solar. Thibaud and Laurent hunted daily, despite the frigid rains, but never seemed to bring enough hares, partridges, or pheasants to feed the dwindling number of mouths.

The hunger, the sickness and moaning in the castle all reminded her, vividly, of the days of the great plague. She couldn't bear it. Each time another vassal died, she wanted to run to her room and bury her head in the single sheepskin the English had left on her bed. She wanted to pound her ears until she couldn't hear the wails of the mourning women or the cries of the sick. Life was fragile, ephemeral, and she felt that Death's gleaming scythe was constantly poised over her neck. She dreamt restless dreams of roasted venison and mustard sauce; of infidel eggs, hard boiled and stuffed with cheese; of succulent, fat chickens, parboiled, stuffed with bread, saffron, and tart, green spices. Every morning she awoke with the hollow ache of hunger in her stomach and prayed in the small chapel that the men would catch something—anything—during the hunt. Each morning she prayed that her father would return and take control of the castle.

She tightened her grip on the reins. She knew *that* prayer would not soon be answered. A few days before, six men had approached Castelnau bearing the standard of the Vicomte de Tournan. She was so excited that she had raced out of the castle toward the mounted men, only to find that her father was not among them. They were his vassals. Her father was well, they told her. He would be riding with the Comte d'Armagnac to the court of the French king in Paris, to plan a spring campaign against the Prince of Wales. His message to her: hold the castle until his return. These six men, the four oldest of his contingent and two wounded vassals, would help in defending the fortress. She nearly cried out in frustration. *You should be here, Father, protecting your people, feeding them, recovering your lands.* Instead, the work was thrust upon her, a maiden just turned twenty-three years of age.

She had spent her anger in a reckless ride across the hills. During the ride, she discovered the frozen body of her spaniel splayed on the bare, rocky ground. A month earlier she had loosed him and the hounds in the hills because she could no longer feed them. As she covered his small, stiff body with a mound of stones, she realized that she could no longer wait passively in Castelnau, doing nothing but hoping and praying for survival. She must *do* something. She returned to the castle and approached Thibaud. Father had sent some coins, she told him, and the two rubies in her dagger could be pried out and exchanged. They would never survive the winter without more food, and their only hope was to buy it. She knew that the nearest *bastides* had been burned and pillaged by the English. They would not find food there. They would have to travel as far as Pavie.

Pavie was a three-hour ride to the northwest. It was a dangerous ride. Despite the poverty of the area, English marauders and thieves still roamed the war-torn hills, searching for whatever booty the Prince might have left behind in his swift, successful retreat from the French army. Twice over the winter she had had to secure the castle against small bands of thieves. As a result, she decided to dress as a young squire for the trip to Pavie, with her hair pulled up and secured in her riding hat. The dagger Jehan had given her was hidden beneath the voluminous folds of the ragged *jupe* she wore over her chain mail. For further safety, she, Thibaud, and Laurent decided to leave in the morning, before the mists had yet dispersed in the valley, and to ride swiftly and silently through the forests.

As they rode, Aliénor saw the charred ruins of windmills on every hill. A wet, black square of earth on the banks of the Gers river bore witness to where a peasant's hovel once stood. The stripped carcasses of oxen, sheep, and pigs littered the forests. Bare, splintered piles jutted out of the river at intervals, where bridges once spanned the water. In abandoned orchards, fruit trees lay on their sides, cut, like the grapevines that once twined around their trunks. Neither dim morning light nor winter fogs could obscure these scars left on the land by the passing of the English army. The land was raped and destroyed until it was barren.

During the trip, her brother murmured paternosters. Yet while her brother's thoughts turned to Heaven, her own thoughts turned less and less Godly. She had always been aware of her father's loyalty to the French king and had accepted that loyalty as her own without question. Her father had scorned the English for their control over the wine trade, a trade that benefited only those men who lived near Bordeaux. She knew that her father's grandfather had fought against the English in some ancient war, a war that set the loyalties of the Tournans for generations after. As she gazed around her at the scarred remains of her countryside, her loyalties were no longer loyalties inherited from her kin but loyalties she now embraced as wholly her own. She hated the English. She hated them for the suffering they had caused her family, her people, her country. After such destruction, how could any Gascon be so loyal to the English king, whose men caused so much pain, death, and destruction to his homeland?

Unwittingly, she thought of Jehan. His face rose in her memory as vividly as if she had seen him that very morning. Had it been three full months since he had ridden out of Castelnau and out of her life? He had left to join Prince Edward to fight against the French forces. For that reason alone, she should hate him with all her heart. Yet the memory of him brought no hatred. Instead, it brought a warm flush to her chilled cheeks.

She closed her eyes. Her emotions were far too muddled about that Gascon knight. His last act of kindness had touched her so deeply that she could no longer muster anger, defiance, or hatred of the man who had led the Prince to conquer her castle. He proved himself an honorable knight—a knight more honorable than her own father.

And his kiss . . .

She sucked in the cold air and stiffened on the gelding she had borrowed from one of her father's men-at-arms. She had dreamed about his embrace far too often during the restless nights. She spent hours imagining what it might have been like if he had continued to kiss her, if he brazenly pushed away her clothes and touched her, intimately, in all the places where she ached. The thought drove the chill from her body. She wanted him to return, take her in his arms, and make her feel as alive as she had that morning in the warmth of his chambers.

She shook her head. She mustn't wish it. Jehan was an enemy. If he returned, he would return to conquer. Over the past months, she had spent hours upon the wall-walk watching the eastern horizon. She interrogated every traveler who stopped at the castle for shelter and rest, half in dread, half in anticipation, begging for news of the English movements. News came from Bordeaux that the Prince of Wales had sent some of his knights back into the conquered lands to strengthen his garrisons throughout Gascony, but no contingent ever arrived on the eastern hills of Castelnau. The news was good, she told herself. This castle was all she had left, and poor though it was, if she succeeded in keeping it until Father returned she would once again have a chance at a normal life. If Jehan came back to Castelnau, she would have no choice but to hold the castle against him and order her vassals to aim their arrows at his heart.

There was more at stake than her castle and her lands. When and if Jehan returned, it would be on different grounds. He would no longer be her protector. His debt was paid. He would take these lands, and he would take her. He would kiss her again, and as before, she would forget everything—her innocence, their conflicting loyalties, her morals, her immortal soul—and surrender to him willingly.

Aliénor halted abruptly as she neared the edge of the forest. In her absorption, she had almost forgotten that she still wore the garb of a squire. She shook her head free of the disturbing thoughts and concentrated on the work ahead. Awkwardly, she lifted one of her legs over the saddle and slid to the ground. She loosened the sack attached to the saddle's cantle and walked toward the bushes. Laurent pulled his mount to a stop.

"Dismount, Laurent. I'll need you to help me dress."

"It'll be safer if you stay dressed as a squire."

"The daughter of the Vicomte de Tournan will *not* be seen in hose and a doublet!" She burrowed behind the shelter of the bushes. "No matter how poor we are, no matter how desperate our situation, I refuse to be seen in tatters. What if the Comte d'Astarac is here? Or the Comte de Pardiac?"

"Those knights, like most of the Gascon knights, are probably with the King of France now," Laurent argued. "Besides, they'll hardly recognize you dressed as you are."

"They'll recognize Thibaud, and the crest on his shield. They'll greet him knight to knight, and once they draw near, they will know his squire is not a boy." She unlaced the haubergeon, originally made for Laurent, and let it fall heavily to the ground. She pulled her undertunic over her head and trembled in her shift in the frigid cold. She heard Laurent thump to the ground as he dismounted. She peered around the bushes. "Come, Laurent! Either you or Thibaud must help me, and your fingers are far more limber than his."

Thibaud laughed. "There are widows in the village who would argue with you, *ma petite nièce.*"

"Perhaps, *mon oncle,* but methinks you spend more time *un*fastening their clothes rather than fastening them."

Laurent limped toward the bushes. "It's not fitting for the

son of a Vicomte to be buttoning his sister's tunic like a chambermaid."

She lifted a brow as Laurent came around the bushes and began fastening the small wooden buttons. "Have you become so full of swordplay and lances, *frai,* that you will no longer perform a simple favor for your only sister?"

His face flamed. Since the English had left Castelnau, Laurent had continued his knight's training with vigor. His horsemanship had improved to the point where he could lift himself on and off the saddle unaided, and could ride long and hard. Now he could handle a sword and a lance with surprising skill. He had insisted on coming along with her and Thibaud for this long trip, and although she had first objected, she now was glad he had come. Laurent was beginning to act more like the only son of the Vicomte de Tournan, and she wondered if he had given up his dreams of joining the Franciscan monastery.

She stood shivering as Laurent fumbled with the buttons. When he finished, she pulled her best surcoat from the sack. It was one of the two dull woolen surcoats she owned, but this one was lined with gray rabbit fur on the long tippets that hung from the sleeves, a luxury she had painstakingly added over the course of the winter, a luxury that she suspected looked odd among the stains and mends. Hastily she pulled it over her head. It fell in loose folds around her body, verifying what she had suspected: that she was losing weight and probably looked gaunt and completely unattractive. Yet another reason to hope Jehan never returned to Castelnau, she thought. If he saw her now, he would not believe she was the same woman he had kissed so passionately only a few short months before.

Laurent gathered her discarded clothes and armor and put them back into the sack. She fastened the line of buttons up the front. Her hair fell, tangled and knotted, down her back. She ran her fingers through it until most of the tangles were gone.

When she emerged from the bushes, both Thibaud and Laurent were mounted and waiting. Thibaud let out a low whistle and laughed. "Dressed like that, you'll be gathering more than food, Aliénor." He winked at Laurent. "Especially with an old man and a fourteen-year-old boy as escorts."

"I know very well I look like a maidservant dragged through the fields." She struggled to mount. "I can only pray that all knights are out of the *bastide,* off with King Jean to plan vengeance on the English." She heaved herself, ungracefully, upon the steed, then twisted and plunked herself side-saddle. She reached for the reins and arranged her skirts as attractively as she could around her legs. "If *anyone* sees me, without my circlet or my girdle, bare-headed and wearing men's hose beneath my tunic—"

"Only women notice such things," Thibaud interrupted. "The men will notice nothing beyond your hair."

She kicked her horse into a canter and headed down the slope toward the open land in front of the *bastide.* The crowds were thick near the arched entrance to the walled town. When she approached closer to the drawbridge, she was forced to slow her horse to a walk. She scanned the masses. She noticed a merchant in a bright, short, scalloped tunic and pointed-toed shoes, riding a fine horse with a cart full of grain in tow. Aliénor's mouth watered as she saw another cart, closer to the drawbridge, loaded with oak wine barrels. She turned and caught Laurent's eye, then jerked her chin at the carts. Laurent nodded and licked his lips in response. She used the head of her horse to nudge a space among the line of people waiting to enter the town. After a short wait, the crowd carried the three of them through. The watchman at the door looked at the fur on her surcoat and waved them in without comment.

The entrance widened into a square courtyard. An open market filled the center of the square, protected from the elements by a large, thatched awning held up by massive oak tree trunks planted in the middle and on the four corners. The courtyard was surrounded by peaked, half-timbered houses, bright with whitewash in the foggy light of the midmorning. The churchbells suddenly rang from the high, blunt tower on the opposite wall. Aliénor glanced to the church, noticing the arrow slits that slashed the walls and the lack of wide, glass windows. In fortified towns such as this, the church acted as the last refuge from invaders. As she looked around the bustling square, she heaved a great sigh of relief that this particular *bastide* had been spared the ravages of the English.

"Unsaddle, Laurent, then help me," she yelled, trying to make herself heard above the churchbells, the merchant's cries, the squawking of live geese, and the peasants bartering in loud voices. "We must buy what we can and be on our way before dark."

She clutched the purse around her neck, feeling the few precious silver and gold coins that her father had sent her along with his men. She would need to spend them well if she intended to feed the castle and the villagers until the next harvest of grain. Laurent awkwardly pulled his crippled foot over the horse and stumbled to the ground. He wore the same ragged clothes he had worn since he hid from the English. She had insisted he dress as befitting his station after the Prince's men had left, but Laurent stubbornly said he would dress as his people dressed, thus displaying his own version of the Tournan stubbornness. Now, however, she was glad he wore such ragged clothes. He looked no wealthier than a peasant, and thus he wouldn't be cheated in the marketplace.

Thibaud took the reins of Laurent's steed as he limped over to her and helped her unsteadily to the ground. She nearly sighed in relief as her slippered feet hit the hard earth; the long ride had jarred her bones. She was looking forward to stretching her legs as she walked through the market.

"Don't wander far, Aliénor," Thibaud warned as Laurent limped toward the marketplace and she followed, slowly, in his wake. "With two horses, I can't stay too close to you. The crowds are too thick."

"Don't worry." She brushed her wind-blown hair off her shoulders. "I'm going to walk around the outside, while Laurent finds the best bargains."

Thibaud followed her as she made her way through the crowds. Most of the peasants and bourgeois made a path for her, for there were few noblewomen in the town and her presence, even without her gold circlet and jeweled girdle which would announce her station, made quite a stir. She had never been to Pavie, though she had been to a dozen similar *bastides* around Castelnau. This city seemed newer than most. Its stone walls were unscarred and high, and two towers guarded the eastern and the western walls. From what she could see of the narrow streets that shot off the large square, the plan of the city followed the usual criss-cross pattern of streets more faithfully than most. Thibaud pulled his mount beside her to keep a better eye on opportunistic men.

She circled the marketplace. She neared the great, looming bulk of the church. A black cloth covered the cross above the door, announcing the season of Lent. A leper huddled against the wall and rang a small bell to warn her as she came too close. She clutched the purse around her neck. In another time, she wouldn't hesitate to give the leper some silver, but now she needed all the coin she had to feed her own people.

She felt a tug on her sleeve. She turned and looked directly into Laurent's dark eyes. It startled her, sometimes, how quickly Laurent was growing.

"There's a merchant selling grain," he said. "No one is buying it; the English burned all the windmills, so most of the buyers want bread, not grain that needs to be milled and baked. He's accepted five *deniers* a sack."

"Five *deniers!*" The price was more than fair. "Sometimes I think God perches on your shoulder, *frai.*"

"He's taking five *deniers* from me because he thinks I can pay no more. If he saw you, with those furred tippets, he'd charge a dozen."

"Did you see any meat? Pork, mutton?"

"I didn't bother looking."

"Why not?"

"We can't eat meat. It's the Lord's fast."

"We *are* fasting, by default—we're starving. If we can find pork at a good price here, then I'm not going to let Lent come between me and it." She couldn't tell him that she had forgotten about Lent. She had been dreaming of bacon, hot and sizzling with grease, since the day the last pig was slaughtered and eaten.

"I won't help you buy it."

"Yes you will, my brother. You will, and you'll eat it, too, if I have to force it down your throat. When Father returns, I promise the first thing I'll have him do is pay for a papal dispensation." She glanced over her shoulder at Thibaud. "We'll be back, Thi—"

Aliénor stopped in midsentence. A knight, dressed in full armor, was talking to Thibaud. His attendants hovered nearby. She glanced at the heraldry emblazoned on his surcoat and wondered why it looked so familiar. As she stood there, Thibaud pointed in her direction. The knight turned and looked at her.

He dismounted, then unlaced the chain-mail aventail from his basinet and lifted the helmet off his head. His hair, a riotous reddish-gold color, sprang out from the confinement. The contrary winds sweeping into the courtyard toyed with the fine linen of his surcoat. She had never seen him before; she would have remembered such hair. He walked to her, his pale green eyes avid on her face. He reached for her hand. She gave it to him, instinctively, searching her memory for where she had seen that heraldry. As he rose from the kiss, he smiled.

"*Demoiselle* Aliénor de Tournan." He laughed, a light, mocking sound. "I didn't expect to meet you under such circumstances. Yet, I must say . . ." His voice trailed off as his gaze wandered with unabashed appreciation over her hair. "It's a pleasure under any circumstances."

"You have me at a loss, Sir . . ."

He made no effort to tell her his name. He still hadn't released her hand. He continued to look at her, almost appraisingly, and she found her anger growing beneath her confusion. Just as she was about to forcefully pull her hand away from his, he released it, then bowed.

"I am the Vicomte de Baste, *demoiselle,* at your service."

She glanced at his surcoat and realized where she had seen the silver and blue heraldry: on the man who had come to Castelnau to arrange her betrothal, what seemed like centuries before. But that man was much older. "I've met the Vicomte—"

"You've met my father. He has since died, in the battles between the English and the French. I am Guy de Baste, his firstborn son, now taking my father's place in the world." His smile widened as she continued to stare. "If the English hadn't come, *demoiselle,* you and I would now be joined in that most sacred of bonds—marriage."

Chapter
10

ALIÉNOR STARED AT GUY DE BASTE, SEARCHING HER MEMORY FAR back, back before the village was burned, before the castle was attacked, back to the dreamlike days of warmth and leisure. It seemed like years, not months, since Father had arranged a betrothal between her and the knight who now stood before her. So much had happened. Had the English not attacked, she and this knight would have been married on the feast of the Epiphany, a little more than a month ago.

She nervously clasped her callused hands together, then flattened them against her worn woolen surcoat. She noticed the jewels glittering in Sir Guy's low-slung baldric, and the fashionable, dagged edges of his short, close-fitting tunic. She was ashamed that she, the daughter of the Vicomte de Tournan, would be seen with her hair uncovered, without a pearl or a string of gold to decorate her neck, her head, or her waist. She was ashamed to be caught in a *bastide* far away from her castle, protected by a single knight and an untried boy. She knew, simply by looking at her, that Sir Guy could clearly see the fall of the house of Tournan.

She took a deep breath and tilted her chin. "My deepest sympathies for the death of your father, Sir Guy."

"I understand that sympathies are in order for you, *demoiselle.*" His gaze wandered over the length of her ragged tunic, noting all the mends and tears. "Sir Thibaud told me the English seized your father's castle."

"Seized it and then abandoned it."

169

"Ah, it is worse than I thought. Is the damage to the castle irreparable?"

"No." She realized Sir Guy thought her castle had been destroyed. "The English withdrew from the castle last November. They torched the village, but left the fortress untouched."

"I suppose that makes you one of the fortunate ones." He shook his head in sympathy. "Prince Edward has been distributing his conquered castles like tokens of favor among his loyal Gascon knights. Who did the Prince send to garrison your home?"

"No one. My father took advantage of the delay and reclaimed his lands."

Sir Guy's reddish brows shot up in surprise.

"I know, 'tis a stroke of fortune." She spread her hands and shrugged. "The Prince must have heard that my father took Castelnau back and decided not to send anyone to reclaim it. It's a strong fortress, and usually it's not easily seized." She remembered that the Baste lands lay along the path through which the English had raided. Her gaze dipped to Sir Guy's finely embroidered tunic. He didn't dress like a man whose estates were devastated; he looked as prosperous as any English knight. "The Prince also passed through your lands, didn't he, Sir Guy?"

"By the grace of God, my lands were spared."

She wondered, incredulously, how the Baste lands had escaped harm when Castelnau and everything else in the marauders' path was ravaged or destroyed.

"What are you doing in Pavie, *demoiselle?*"

"I came to Pavie to buy provisions," she explained. "The English left us nothing but crumbs. Pavie was the closest town I knew which hadn't been plundered."

"Your father escorted you here?"

"No. He's with King Jean, in Paris."

"Just where I would be," he said smoothly, "if it weren't for the death of my father. But where is the rest of your escort?"

She gestured to Thibaud, and then Laurent.

Sir Guy's eyes widened. "You were escorted by an old knight and a boy?"

"Old, am I?" Thibaud kicked his mount forward. "I'm not so old that I couldn't crush a young head—"

"Oncle!"

"I won't challenge you, Sir Thibaud." Guy turned and bowed before the mounted knight, then spread his arms like a courtier. "It would be folly to challenge a man who has seen so much war under so many august kings. My concern is not in the strength of your arm, but in the number of swords. Surely the heiress of Tournan deserves far more than a single knight to guard her?"

The heiress of Tournan. She felt a strange little thrill. She didn't feel like an heiress, not standing in the middle of a marketplace, dressed in ragged wool, with her hair, unbound and unadorned, flying around her face. It was kind of Sir Guy to soothe her battered vanity, especially when her fortunes were obviously so low. She placed her hand on his arm to draw his attention away from her great-uncle. "Thibaud may wear a tunic from another king's reign, Sir Guy, but I assure you his sword arm is lethal." She glanced at Sir Guy's attendants who stood, fully armed and well-provisioned, near the wall of the church. "I see your men are ready to ride. Are you going to join the king in Paris?"

Suddenly his attention was riveted on her, and on the hand that lay against his forearm. "I am going to Paris, eventually. I have some other matters I must attend to first."

"Then let not it be said that you were delayed from your duties by a woman."

"I have already been detained for so long on my estates, *demoiselle,* that the King of France must wonder where my loyalties lie." He took her hand from his forearm and kissed it. "I can think of no better excuse to delay longer, than to aid a woman of your beauty."

She smiled at his pretty speech, knowing she looked as work-weary as a peasant. "Certainly King Jean would never doubt the loyalty of a Baste. Your father gave his life for the French king's cause."

"Your faith in me is charming, but kings are much more fickle." He smiled thinly. "I cannot in good conscience let you ride through Gascony unprotected. Two of my men-at-arms will escort you back to Castelnau. I shall also order one of the men to return to my castle and send to you as much grain, wine, and pork as my *châtelain* can spare."

Wine. To her shame, her mouth watered and she licked her lips. He noticed her reaction. Gathering her wits, she dipped into a curtsy. "I am indebted to you, Sir Guy."

"Your gratitude alone repays any debt." He lowered his voice so no one would hear them, not even her brother who stood nearby. "Tell me, *demoiselle:* Is your virtue, like your castle, also intact?"

She started.

"Such pretty modesty. Your blush alone tells me it's true." He kneaded the hollow of her palm with his smooth fingers. It was a slow, thoughtful caress, a caress that sent uncomfortable shivers down her spine. "When I return from war, your father and I will talk about this ... delayed betrothal."

She stared at him. He knew, from her dress and lack of an escort, that her lands were devastated. He, too, had ridden through the countryside and had seen what was left of the greatest fiefs of Gascony. Was he toying with her, this silver-tongued knight? Granted, she now held what was left of her estates, but the Vicomte de Baste could find a far richer wife. "It is cruel to tease me." She pulled her hand from his grip. "You know my lands are plundered."

"I have long admired your estate, *demoiselle,* and your lands would extend mine considerably. They shall recover, eventually, from the Englishmen's destruction. My interest right now, however, is more ... basic." His gaze slipped over her body. "When I see your father at the King's court in Paris, by my word, I will ask again for your hand in marriage."

He turned away. She stood speechless in the bustling courtyard as he gave his men their orders. Laurent walked to her side and said something, but she didn't hear his words. She was reeling with Sir Guy's proposal. She was an impoverished old maid who had just received a marriage proposal from a rich young knight. She wondered why she wasn't tingling in joy.

All she could think about was Jehan.

The grain and wine sent by Guy de Baste proved to be the only thing that saved the castle from starvation during the lean months of Lent. Aliénor prayed in thanks as spring came, as fields of wild mustard bloomed on the barren hills and the warm sun conquered the cold rains and the winter fevers. For the first time since the English left, there was hope within the walls of Castelnau. She redistributed the lands of the dead, not caring that she gave more land to each vassal than he could possibly till. As the weather grew warmer, the peasants plowed and sowed their sodden fields. By April, woodcocks, snipes, larks, and quail had returned to the forests from the south. Thibaud and Laurent, along with the other men, hunted well, and for the first time in five months Aliénor and the villagers did not go to bed hungry.

Still, her father did not return to Castelnau.

A long, dry, hot summer followed hard upon the pleasant spring. Aliénor supervised the harvesting of the first of the cereal crops and watched the wheat milled and made into loaves of fresh bread. She and the villagers celebrated the simple taste of new bread as if it were the finest delicacy, but their celebration was brief, for winter lay ahead. They sowed another crop. Despite the stifling heat of the summer, the peasants worked incessantly. They hunted deer and rabbit and fowl and fished daily in the Arrats. They cared for the few vineplants the Prince's men had not uprooted as if they were the last of their children. Aliénor supervised the salting of meat, the milling of grain, the rebuilding of the village and the clearing of land left fallow after all the winter's deaths.

Rumors abounded. She discovered from a band of traveling minstrels that the Prince of Wales had ordered his knights to join him in Bordeaux in June to begin a raid north, through the center of France. It was rumored that the King of England, Edward III, had landed in Normandy and was marching south to meet his son, in order to crush King Jean's forces between them. She was relieved to discover that the thieves who plagued Gascony were going to be put where they belonged: in an army. Now she could send the villagers out to till the land without constantly worrying that a band of brigands would appear on the eastern slope and burn all that the peasants were cultivating. Yet she was worried, too, because she hadn't heard from her father since he'd joined King Jean in Paris, and she knew he would be fighting in the coming battle.

She assumed Jehan would fight on the enemy's side. She tried not to think of him as the months passed. As her father's nemesis and the loyal vassal of an English prince, Jehan was forbidden fruit. If he returned, he would destroy everything she worked for. Wishing for him was like wishing for her own destruction. Yet if he stayed away . . . The thought frightened her. She had discovered something precious the day Jehan left, something fragile and rare, and it had been snatched away before she could taste the full of it. She was cursed indeed. Cursed to desire a knight whose presence was as lethal as hemlock.

As autumn drew near, she threw herself headlong into the running of the castle. She had little choice, for *Maman* had never recovered from the shock of the English attack and remained as fretful and helpless as a babe. She told herself it was good training for when she would be a wife and a *châtelaine*.

Part of the reason for her willingness to direct the running of the estate was Guy de Baste's proposal. If she kept this land in her hands and ran it efficiently, then when Father did return, he might be able to arrange another betrothal with Sir Guy. Not many young noblewomen entered marriage with as much experience in running a castle as she. She had faced war, starvation, sickness, and death. Even if Sir Guy's proposal turned out to be false, the experience might make some other knight overlook her age and take her to wife. A knight who didn't have English loyalties. A knight who wasn't landless and poor and her father's sworn enemy . . .

When the autumn harvest began, Aliénor rode daily through the lands to check its progress. Like any peasant, she took part in the ritualistic game signifying the end of the grain harvest, when the men threw their scythes at the last stalk of standing wheat until it fell under the onslaught. As the month of September progressed, she spent more time in the castle, supervising the steward as he gathered the portions owed to her by the villagers. She arranged for the pressing of the grapes and the building of oak casks to hold new wine. As the first small migration of white geese flew overhead, she sent the men-at-arms into the rustling forests with bows and quivers full of arrows to try their aim on the flocks of birds. When the Arrats river dwindled to little more than a creek, she armed the village children with pikes and led them to the banks of the river to catch the trout that seemed to jump from the shallow creek into their arms. She worked as hard as any of the peasant women. She was determined that this winter would not be like the last—that this winter she would never, *ever,* go to bed hungry.

On the day before Michaelmas, Aliénor spent the morning directing the servants in the preparation for the Michaelmas feast. The air in the hot, smoky kitchen hung heavy with the scent of mustard and herbs. Grease sizzled in the dripping pan poised beneath a haunch of venison. A caldron full of stew bubbled over one of the fires. A young girl turned a spit heavy with the carcass of a goose, basting the bird in its own juices. Aliénor had banned the men-at-arms from the kitchens, for the women had stripped down to their shifts in order to work more comfortably in the stifling heat. She, in her woolen surcoat, could stand no more than a few minutes in the room.

She stepped out of the kitchens to breathe in some fresh,

cool autumn air, wiping her damp forehead with the dirty sleeve of her tunic. A young boy leaned against the kitchen wall, plucking a quail of its feathers. She noticed a crowd of men gathered near the stables and frowned. The men-at-arms were the laziest creatures in the castle. She was hard pressed to keep them occupied, especially when the last thing they wanted to do was work. Her irritation gave way to alarm, however, when she heard the distinctive clash of sword against sword coming from the center of the crowd. The circle broke and two figures scuttled out into the center of the courtyard. She gasped as she saw Laurent, red-faced, waving his sword at an older man.

Not again. She strode purposefully toward the fighters. A firm hand on her arm stopped her in her tracks. She whirled to find her great-uncle. "Let me go, Thibaud."

"It's a mock battle, Aliénor. Let him fight."

"Mock battle or not, there are other things he and these men can be doing." She lifted her hands to her hips. "Didn't I order them to go hart hunting? Must I run this estate by myself?"

"Fie! Your brother's a nobleman and should be doing nothing else but training to be a knight."

"At any other time, Thibaud, I would agree—"

"Look at him," he interrupted. "Look at your brother, Aliénor."

She sullenly glared at the fight. The man circled her brother warily, and Laurent, dragging his bad foot around, watched him. He held the sword firmly in his right arm, raised, poised for the attack. Laurent had grown in the past year, so much that his undertunic clung tightly to his arms and shoulders and ended far up on his calves. She was surprised to see well-formed muscles on his upper arm, straining under the weight of the sword. His opponent lunged. Laurent raised his sword and, to Aliénor's surprise, her brother held his own against the force of the other man's weight. His opponent fell back and a grin spread across his face as he began to circle anew.

Thibaud laughed beside her. "He's as stubborn as a mule. Not much to start with, but he could be a knight, if he put his mind to it."

"He'll be no knight," she interrupted, "if he doesn't do something to keep this estate well guarded and provisioned."

"Woman, it's not the duty of the only son of Tournan to be carrying hay and milling grain like a commoner."

"Oh? Is it the daughter's duty, then? It's the duty of *all* of us, Thibaud, in order to prevent the English from recapturing this castle."

"The Prince of Wales is marching north. He's planning to face the French north of here, not in Gascony."

"You put too much faith in the words of wandering minstrels, *mon oncle*. Half the harvest is still outside these walls. If the Prince arrives, how shall we survive another siege, with no grain, no meat, and no wine?" She bit her lower lip as the man lunged for Laurent again and her brother stumbled back against the assault. "Enough of this. Do men ever tire of these foolish, dangerous games?!"

She pulled away from Thibaud and headed into the center of the fray, but before she could yank the sword from her brother's hand, the cry of the watchman and the sound of pounding hooves brought her attention to the portal. One of the men she had ordered to keep watch on the eastern slopes galloped into the center of the yard. She raced to meet him, clutched the reins, and glared up into his face. "What is it? Why have you run?"

"Damaiselo . . . I was guarding the eastern hills. I saw the glint of armor—"

"How many? How quickly?"

"Twenty, twenty-five."

Thieves. She whirled and pointed to the steward. "Tell the chaplain to ring the churchbell—"

"These aren't English," the man interrupted. "It's the Vicomte, *damaiselo.* Your father has returned!"

Father.

She heard the cries around her as if across a long distance. She stared at the guard. "Are you sure?"

He nodded his head vigorously. "I recognized his pennon: the large silk with the green and blue heraldry, with the eagle embroidered in gold upon it. And he carries his gilded shield." He took a deep breath. "There is no one in all of Gascony with such a shield, *damaiselo*. It's our lord, and he's returned to us."

She stood speechless, stunned, while the courtyard erupted with cries of joy. Could it truly be Father? Could her father finally have returned to his castle, after nearly a year abroad fighting against the English? It seemed too soon, it seemed only a week or two since the wandering minstrel had come to the castle, telling them of the great gathering of armies in the heart of France. Could the battle have already taken place?

She glanced around the courtyard. It was in shambles, with bales of hay and sacks of grain scattered over the uneven paving stones. Why hadn't Father sent a messenger ahead to warn her of his arrival? There was no time to prepare, either the castle, or herself, she thought, as she fingered the chipped, loosened buttons of her surcoat. No one within the fortress seemed to care. The men-at-arms embraced one another and then embraced the half-naked kitchen servants who ran out, despite their state of undress, into the courtyard. Thibaud engulfed Laurent in a hug, then Laurent turned around and lifted one of the kitchen servants off her feet. Aliénor glanced up and saw her mother's pale, sullen face in the window of the solar.

Aliénor took hold of her senses. Whatever the reason for her father's sudden appearance, she still had to prepare for his arrival, and time was short. She looked at the steward. "Send someone out to bring the men in from the fields. They must gather at the village to greet my father." She gestured to one of the women nearby. "The Michaelmas feast will start tonight, so go to the kitchens and see that it's ready. Sweep out the rushes, lay out new ones, and sprinkle them with rosemary. And go to *Maman.* Tell her that her husband is back and make sure she's presentable."

She walked toward the southeast tower. She climbed the spiral staircase until she reached the level of the wall-walk. A crowd of villagers gathered near the few timber and earth buildings that constituted the beginning of the new village. The houses looked strange and new in the bright sunshine. It would take years, she supposed, for the clinging, flowering vines to climb up over the roofs, for the moss to grow and obscure the shiny, flaxen color of the thatch. She was pleased that she had managed to organize the rebuilding of part of the village: It would show Father that she had not been idle this past year.

She saw the knights to the east, closer than she had expected. The contingent spread into single file as they rode near the edge of the stubbled fields. She knew then, for sure, that it must be her father who approached, for no enemy would take such care to avoid the fields. The sun gleamed off their armor. From the distance, Aliénor saw the flying colors of Tournan and the fine tunic and shining chausses on the front rider. The men rode hard, straight, and swiftly. They rode like conquering knights. She sensed that the French must have defeated the English in the great battle.

Father was finally home. She hugged her arms to her chest. Now everything would return to normal. Father would take over the responsibilities of running the estate. He would hunt in the afternoon. He would purchase silks and furs for her, choose falcons and hounds, fill the castle with fine candles and wrought-iron candelabra, with velvet hangings embroidered with the Tournan heraldry, with pewter plate and tankards. He would commission tapestries for the great hall. There would be food and warmth and comfort and ease. *There would be a marriage.*

Yet for some reason, as she stood on the ramparts and watched him approach, she could not muster joy. She glanced over the wall to the graveyard at its base. The swollen earth was riddled with wooden crosses, dried and splintered now, after nearly a year exposed to the sun, wind, and weather. The gravemarkers were a bare testament to the devastation wrought by the English army. She felt odd and detached: relieved that Father had returned, but not happy. There had been too much death and too much pain. She wondered if anything would ever be the same as it had been before the English tore through Gascony.

She wondered if *she* would ever be the same.

Laurent approached her. "It's about time he returned."

"I'm surprised he's here so soon." She peered at the knights. "All we've heard about is the coming battle. It seems too early for the fight to be over and the armies dispersed."

"It's a year too late," Laurent retorted. "Father should never have left you to do what should have been a man's work."

She smiled patiently. Laurent had grown more and more blunt in his criticism of his father over the past year, a trait she attributed to Thibaud's influence. "If there's one thing I've learned, it's that knights tend to war, and peace is women's work."

"And God's."

"Yes, and God's." She wiped some soil from Laurent's chin and felt a downy spray of beard beneath her fingers. "You were fighting again, *frai.*"

"It was my last battle, God willing." He pulled away from her touch and carelessly wiped his face on his sleeve. "Now that *he* is back, all that training will, mercifully, go to waste."

"It doesn't have to go to waste."

"I'd sooner pick up a scythe and tend to the fields than go through life with this wretched weapon in my hands."

"And I thought you were beginning to like those mock battles," she mused. "You certainly got in enough of them."

"Mock battles!" His black eyes widened. "Is that what you thought they were?"

"That's what Thibaud told me."

"I learned to wield a sword for one purpose: to protect

you if you were ever attacked. I found myself, instead, protecting your name."

"My name?"

"The men-at-arms cursed you whenever you sent them out to do a commoner's work."

"They would, the lazy mules!"

"I couldn't sit by while they abused my sister."

"So you *fought* them?" She lifted her hands to her hips. "Men twice your age, three times your strength?"

He grinned, a grin that made him look sly and slightly wicked, a strange expression on her pious brother's face.

"No wonder you had so many bloody noses and split lips. I'm surprised the men didn't cut you into ribbons." She shook her head. "Are you sure, Laurent, that you won't change your mind about the monastery? You've grown as foolish as any knight."

"No, it will be a Franciscan's robes for me. Especially now that Father is here to take over what should have been his duty all along. Look: He's nearly at the village."

The riders had already crossed the fields, and now they galloped past the orchards and headed toward the small collection of hovels, kicking up dust in their wake. She saw the distinctive Tournan pennon—the pennon embroidered by her great-grandmother—and the Vicomte's gilded shield in the grip of the front rider. The villagers cried out in joy as the contingent passed them, swiftly, then began the steep ascent to the castle.

"Come, Laurent. We must wait in the courtyard."

"You'll wait alone. I don't want to send Father into a rage within moments of his return to the castle."

She stopped at the top of the steps. Laurent had grown over a hand's span in height over the past year, and more than that in strength and width of shoulder. Although his foot lay twisted, jutting out beneath his tunic, it no longer dominated his silhouette. "You're not a boy any longer, *frai*. I intend to tell Father what you've done for me over the past year."

"He'll think you've gone daft."

"Are you going to face him, Laurent?" Instinctively, she knew that her humble, pious brother was not immune to the conceit that always accompanied skill in arms among fighting men. "Or are you going to cower in the chapel?"

His black eyes flashed. His lips tightened and he approached her. "You have a tongue like a serpent."

She smiled as she descended the stairs and emerged into the courtyard. Her brother had become a man, after all, with all the foibles and arrogance that came with manhood. If he took the time to look, she thought, Papa would be proud of him.

She crossed the courtyard, which had been cleared of bales of hay and casks of wine in order to make room for the Vicomte and his men. She noticed that her mother still stood, wide-eyed, in the window of her solar, but it was too late to try to persuade her to come down and greet her husband. Father would find out, soon enough, the havoc the past year had wreaked on his wife.

She stopped in front of the wooden stairs and turned to watch the riders approach. First she saw nothing but a cloud of dust rising beyond the ridge, but soon the riders emerged over the edge. The men still rode hard, though they were close to the castle. She wondered, idly, why they didn't slow their pace. She didn't recognize her father's horse—it was not his usual chestnut charger. The great black stallion kicked his legs high as he galloped. Her father's tunic, like the tunics of all his men, seemed abnormally bright in the autumn sun. Father must have done well to commission new *jupes* for his knights, she mused. The sunlight gleamed off the metal of their basinets, and she wondered why they didn't remove the stifling helmets in such heat.

Her heart constricted in her chest, for suddenly she recognized the horse and understood why the men's visors were shut. She cried out and brushed past Laurent. She raced across the courtyard and screamed at the watchman in the tower. "Raise the bridge! Lower the portcullis!" He looked at her as if she were possessed by the Devil. "Listen to me, you fool! It's a trap, a trap! All men to the ramparts!"

She glanced through the gaping portal. The riders were close now. She felt a tearing sense of familiarity, a devastating feeling of impending disaster.

It was not her father who held the standard of the Vicomte de Tournan.

It was Jehan de St. Simon.

Chapter

11

It was too late.

Before the watchman could reach the lever that controlled the lowering of the portcullis, Jehan and more than half his contingent had thundered into the courtyard. The knights spread through the crowd swiftly, challenging every man who held a sword. Within minutes, Aliénor's armed men tossed their weapons upon the paving stones and raised their hands in submission. She stood by the portal in utter shock, watching the dust settle.

Jehan cried, "Raise the portcullis!" The watchman, having no other choice, obeyed the order. The rest of the contingent rode in and circled the courtyard. Jehan, in the center of it all, unlaced his aventail, pulled the basinet off his head, and tossed it to the ground.

The air around her thinned. She couldn't breathe. She gripped the cold limestone wall. Everything was wrong. The sky wasn't the right color. The horizon seemed to have shifted, as if the hills had changed places while she wasn't looking. The honking of the geese above her sounded discordant and out of place. The knight who stood in her courtyard, dressed in the colors of the Vicomte de Tournan, was not her father.

Jehan was back, reentering her life as swiftly and unexpectedly as a summer hail. He engulfed the fortress in his avid gaze as he circled in place, his dark hair tousled by the wind. He had promised he would return, but she hadn't expected him now, not so long after he'd abandoned the castle. She had convinced herself that he was gone for good, that he had decided to stay with the Prince of Wales in the hopes of finding easier quarry. She dug her fingers into the rough wall until the surface scraped her skin raw. She hadn't expected him to return like this. Not dressed in the colors of her family. Not racing into her castle as if *he* were the Vicomte de Tournan, carrying the emblems of her father's lordship in his hands. Such sublime cleverness. She had been duped as easily as a child.

She didn't know what to do. She glanced around the courtyard. Jehan's knights dismounted, climbed the stairs to the wall-walk, and challenged the men-at-arms standing, stunned, on the ramparts. Within a matter of minutes he had paralyzed her people. The villagers who had greeted him at the base of the slope, thinking he was her father, slowly wandered in, staring at Sir Jehan in surprise and wondering what had happened. Not a drop of blood had been shed, not a swordstroke made, and Jehan had captured her castle as firmly as a fish in a net.

"Hear me, vassals of Tournan!" Jehan lifted his shield to the sun and turned his mount about, making sure that everyone saw the heraldry. "I have come from a great battle in Poitiers between the forces of the English and the French. Your late lord, the Vicomte de Tournan, is dead on the field of battle."

Aliénor's blood ran as cold as melted mountain snow.

"The Prince of Wales took these, his emblems, from the battlefield." He lifted up the standard. "By right of arms, I claim this castle and these lands. I, Sir Jehan de St. Simon, am now your lord."

She heard no more. She turned, pushed through the crowd at the portal, and ran recklessly out of the castle.

"Did you find her?"

Jehan shouted the question as he rose from his seat at the head of the trestle-tables. The heavy, carved wooden chair clattered back against the floorboards. The villagers who lined the benches, feasting on the food spread in front of them, suddenly quieted. Jehan stared at Gilles de Larribière, his most faithful knight, as Gilles marched deeper into the great hall followed by a cluster of men-at-arms.

Gilles bowed. "Yes, my lord, we found her . . . in a manner of speaking."

"Out with it."

"We didn't really find her, my lord. She found us." Gilles rushed on as he saw Jehan's scowl darken. "We searched the northern hills again, as you directed, but she's as light-footed as a doe and no one could find her tracks. As night fell, we reassembled just north of the castle. Then, while we were all talking, she walked right out of the forest. As if she were some sort of fairy."

"It's true, my lord," another knight added. "She gave us all a start emerging out of the darkness like that."

"She told us to bring her back to the castle," Gilles continued, "as if half your contingent hadn't just spent the entire day combing the woods for her."

Jehan reached for his chalice on the trestle-table and curled his fingers around the stem. "Where is she now?"

"In the kitchens. She asked, my lord, that you give her some time to make herself presentable."

"You left her *alone?*"

"Sir Thibaud is guarding her."

"You have great faith in the word of one of our conquered knights."

"I would have preferred to watch the lady bathe," Gilles said, "for it would have been a fine sight after so many weeks in the saddle. But I see by your expression that you wouldn't have approved of *that,* either."

Jehan frowned and gestured to his squire. "Go, Esquivat, and wait with Sir Thibaud. Make sure she doesn't escape into the forests again."

Gilles crossed himself. "If the lady gets it in her mind, she'll probably just vanish like some sort of sorceress."

Jehan turned away and walked to the roaring fire. He

lifted his chalice to his lips. Though the golden wine that filled his cup was stolen from one of the finest vineyards near Bordeaux, to him, it tasted like sand. He couldn't enjoy it, any more than he could enjoy the food spread over the trestle-tables for the feast: the trout seasoned with saffron, the pork bathed in bitter hyssop sauce, or the frumenty—a porridge made of hulled wheat berries boiled in milk. Since early afternoon, all his senses focused on one woman, a woman now bathing safely in the warmth of the kitchens.

His fingers tightened around the jeweled cup. He ignored the murmuring of the villagers—*his vassals*— as they returned to their feasting. For hours he had been forced to sit here, in this hall, watching the villagers gorge themselves, waiting for word of Aliénor from the fifteen scouts he'd sent out to find her, when all he wanted to do was mount his destrier and search through the dark, dangerous forests until he found her himself. Instead he was forced to sit idly in the Vicomte's seat and play his role as the new lord—a role tainted by Aliénor's sudden disappearance.

It was his fault that she had escaped and hid in the hills. He had cursed himself a hundred times over for announcing the news of her father's death so openly. Still, he couldn't have helped himself. When he had galloped into this fortress, he was so full of the sweet, heady breath of victory that he could scarcely think, never mind take into consideration the delicate feelings of a woman.

His ruse had succeeded beyond expectations; there was no blood shed in the capture of this castle. He had waited nearly a decade, since he'd been knighted, for a moment like this. Castelnau-sur-Arrats was his. He wanted to shout his ownership to the world.

It had been a long, tormented wait. When the Prince of Wales had called him away from Castelnau the year before, ordering him to abandon and burn the fortress, Jehan had been furious. He saw all his expectations, all he had worked for, slipping away. Since Edward was his liege lord, he had no choice but to answer his summons, but as soon as the Prince's army escaped the French forces and found refuge in

Bordeaux, Jehan asked him if he could return and take Castelnau. It was too late. News came that the fortress was reconquered by the Vicomte de Tournan. The Prince denied Jehan permission; he needed his knights for the campaign the following summer, not bogged down in a winter seige of a single castle. He promised Jehan other lands, another title, a wealthy English widow to wife, and Jehan had no choice but to remain with his liege's court.

But he didn't want other lands—he wanted Castelnau— and he knew he had lost a prize beyond measure. The opportunity for an impoverished knight to capture and hold a viscounty would only come once in a lifetime. His frustration had boiled in his blood to a point where he could scarcely restrain himself in the English court over the long winter. When June came, he eagerly rode north with the Prince of Wales. There was booty aplenty in the fiery *chevauchée* through Berry, Auvergne, and Poitou. Soon they received word that an enormous French army was marching to intercept them. The Prince turned away from the forces of the French king, in order to escape to Bordeaux with the plunder they had collected, but the French king followed them until they were forced to make a stand at a field just outside of Poitiers.

Despite the overwhelming number of French knights, Edward's forces prevailed. The battle was over now, and with it, Jehan suspected, the endless war between the two kings. With a generosity typical of the young prince, Edward presented Jehan with the armor and standard of the Vicomte de Tournan the day after the battle, a gift for his loyalty and prowess. Jehan could not believe his fortune. He took them, and within hours, he gathered his riches and his vassals and headed south. It had been a year, but his lust had not dimmed for the castle on the banks of the Arrats. He wanted to feast his eyes on the land that was now his. *His.* There was no sweeter revenge than this: to take the lands and the castle of his greatest enemy. There was no higher reward for his loyalty than to be awarded a viscounty, one that contained the woman he could not get out of his mind.

Aliénor. She was part of all this, wrapped up as tightly in his feelings for this land as a grapevine, twisted around its vineprop. It was a sort of madness, he supposed, to be so obsessed with a woman, but nothing could erase the memory of her slender, eager body pressed against his on the day he had withdrawn from this castle. He wanted to conquer her now, as surely as he had just conquered her castle—without struggle and without pain.

He wondered how difficult the battle would be. He wondered if she would be angry, defiant, as she was last year after the Prince had seized this castle. He wondered if she remembered their parting as vividly and as strongly as he remembered it. He would have to test her reactions carefully, before he decided exactly how he would conquer the woman he could not forget—the woman he was determined to have.

Esquivat suddenly came to his side.

"My lord, *demoiselle* awaits you."

Jehan turned around but didn't see her within the crowded hall.

"She's not here." Esquivat flushed and lowered his voice. "She insisted on seeing you alone, Sir Jehan. She said she'll be waiting for you . . . in her chamber."

Aliénor stood by the hearth in her room. She wiped her hands on her rough woolen surcoat. Although she had scrubbed them hard with fatty, wood ash soap, her fingers were still sticky from the sap of hundreds of pine needles she had mangled during the long walk through the hills. She rubbed her hands together until the heat between them released a sweet, resinous scent.

Too much had happened in too short a time. She had reacted without thinking this morning when she tore heedlessly out of the castle into the woods. She couldn't help herself. She was shocked by Jehan's sudden appearance, grief-stricken by her father's death, horrified by the loss of Castelnau, frustrated by helplessness, and angry at being so easily duped. All these emotions battled within her, fighting for supremacy, until, finally, she was too exhausted to feel anything at all. She had sunk to her knees in the litter, beneath the elms, oaks, and pines, and hid her face in her hands. Only many hours later, when twilight bathed the bare limbs of the trees in a bluish glow, did she rise and head toward Castelnau. Only then did she feel settled enough to face her fate.

But as time passed and Jehan still did not come to her, she grew more and more anxious. Perhaps he was enjoying the feast too much to join her, she thought. The upper floors were utterly empty—except for *Maman,* who stayed firmly shut up in her solar, and Jehan's squire, who lingered in the hallway just outside her room. No one wanted to leave the great hall and the celebration, which, from the noise rising up from the stairwell, was growing more and more raucous.

She took a deep breath and tried to compose herself. What she wanted to do when Jehan entered was scream in anger, frustration, and defiance—as she did last year, when he and the Prince seized this castle. Once again, Jehan had stripped her of her land and left her defenseless and impoverished. This year, however, there was one fatal difference: Papa lay cold and dead in foreign soil. There was no hope—not even a glimmering, desperate hope—that she would ever again be the heiress of Castelnau.

She was at Jehan's utter mercy. He was Vicomte now. He could do what he wished with the Tournans. He could cast all of her father's loyal vassals out of the fortress, forcing them into a life of brigandry. He could strip the peasants of their holdings and resettle the land with his own people. He could kill all who bore the name of Tournan—and thus eradicate the threat that any Tournan would try in the future to reclaim the lands. All these things were within his rights as the new Vicomte de Tournan.

She must not let him hurt her family. She had returned to Castelnau to wield what little influence she might have with the knight, to argue, to beg, to barter, to do whatever was necessary to save the lives of her family and her people. She feared she had nothing to bargain with. Jehan had long paid back the debt he owed her for saving his life, by protecting her from harm and refusing to burn Castelnau last year. Yet . . . there was something. She trembled, remembering their last moments together, when he set her body ablaze with desire. The feeling gripped her, wild and uncontrolled and powerful. Theirs was a heady passion. It was an ardor she knew she could not control, a power that might be her weakness, not her strength. She had to be very careful, lest she be defeated by the strength of the single weapon she held against him.

She heard footsteps scraping against the rushes in the hall, footsteps far heavier and far more determined than those of the young squire. Jehan entered and paused just inside the doorway. She turned and faced him.

She sucked in a deep, ragged breath.

It was as if no time had elapsed since the last time they'd set eyes upon each other. His gaze burned over her, blue and bold. He took one step forward, then paused, and she felt an urge to yield, to cross the distance that separated them. *Already.* She curled her fingers around the hanging ends of her rope belt as if they were her only anchor. This was too soon, this was too strong. She must not succumb to her own weakness, not yet, not until she was sure everyone was safe. He had the power of life and death over her and all her family. He was her enemy—her *enemy.*

She forced herself to meet his gaze. "I began to think you weren't coming."

"I stayed at the feast until I could leave without notice." His voice was husky, deep, and resonant. "I didn't want us to be interrupted, Aliénor."

She bunched her skirts in her hands and dipped in a short curtsy. "How thoughtful of you, *my lord.*"

"Don't call me that. Not you—never you."

"I must. You are now the Vicomte de Tournan." She straightened from her curtsy. "Though I should congratulate you on your good fortune, you'll forgive me if I don't."

"I expected no congratulations. I expected you to spit fire when you saw me."

"I've spit enough fire in the forest to set all Gascony ablaze."

"My men didn't even see the smoke."

"Your men would scare away a deaf stag."

"I am pleased, *couret*, that you returned here by choice."

She started at the sound of the endearment. *Couret*. My little heart. She swallowed dryly and curled her hands deeper into the skirts of her tunic.

"Aliénor . . ." His fingers clasped and then unclasped the hilt of his sword. "I can't say I'm sorry about your father's death."

"Then don't. Lies would just be salt upon the wound." The words came out more sharply than she intended. "You wanted vengeance, Jehan. You finally got it."

"I wanted vengeance against your father, not you. Yet my announcement sent you flying into the hills."

"It was better that I left," she said, "for my curses were so vile they would have burned the ears of children."

"If it's any comfort, many brave knights died on the field of Poitiers," he said softly. "Your father lay among the flower of French chivalry."

His kindness disarmed her, but she forced herself to stay strong. She must not succumb to his charm, not now, not yet. "If Papa had died in infidel lands and was drawn up to Heaven by a host of angels," she said, "it *still* would have been no comfort to me. Papa was my last hope."

"If he had lived, it would have been no different."

"He would have returned and held this castle against you."

Jehan's brows drew together. "Then you haven't heard the news."

"What news?"

"The battle in Poitiers was a decisive French defeat."

It was the hundredth shock of the day, and as potent as all the others. "How could the bravest knights in all Christendom be defeated by a band of brigands and thieves?"

"I see your tongue hasn't lost its edge."

"And how decisive a defeat could it be that my father's

estates were endangered whether or not he died on the field of battle?"

"King Jean was captured."

She gasped.

"As well as nearly two thousand French knights. Even if your father had lived, Prince Edward would have seized the Vicomte's estates along with a hundred others in the peace treaty to be negotiated." He walked more deeply into the room, lessening the safe distance between them. She stilled the urge to step back and away. "So you see, the English wreaked vengeance against your father—not I. Though I would willingly have struck the final blow."

"Is this supposed to comfort me, Jehan? Do you expect me to be grateful to my Gascon conqueror?"

"Gratitude is too much to ask for." He stopped in front of the fire, at the opposite end of the hearth. "I wanted you to know that these lands would have been taken from your father one way or another. It's far, far better that they are in my hands."

"If Father had survived, he would have held the castle longer than I held it today," she argued. "He wouldn't be so foolish as to leave the gates open to the enemy."

"Not even Sir Thibaud, who has seen forty years of warfare, suspected my ruse."

"I know you better than he."

"Do you, *couret?*"

"I knew the extent of your hatred for my father. I watched it grow before my eyes when I tended you. I never should have underestimated your cleverness." Heedlessly, she let the words of frustration flow. "I should have known as soon as I saw you and your men riding with your visors lowered that something was amiss. I fell into your trap like a blind hare. And I, more than anyone else, knew you would return someday."

"I vowed as much." He leaned against the stone edge of the hearth. "Do you remember that day?"

"Of course I remember." She took a sharp little breath. "I didn't remember soon enough. I should have closed the castle up as you approached, instead of leaving it open and vulnerable."

"That would have been a useless gesture. My men could have lived off the harvest lying in the fields throughout the winter, while you and your people starved. This way, there was no blood shed."

"And no honor, either, nor any opportunity for me to negotiate terms for the fate of my family."

"I see you haven't lost your spirit, despite the hardships of the past year."

"Would you rather I groveled before you?"

"I want you no other way but like this—proud and defiant." He leaned away from the hearth and stepped toward her. "And lovely, Aliénor, incredibly, breathlessly lovely . . ."

"Don't." He was too close. The light glimmered off the gold embroidery on his tunic: the eagle clutching grape leaves in its talons, the symbol of the house of Tournan. He had stolen that from her father. She must remember that, and stop thinking about smothering in his embrace. "You must tell me your plans for my family, for this castle."

"Have you no faith in me?"

"I trusted you once too often."

"You must have some hope, or you would never have returned from the forest."

"Yes." She dared to meet his gaze. "Last year, when you left, you proved that you could be an honorable knight."

"By all the saints . . ."

"You saved this castle," she continued. "We all would have died without the shelter. You abandoned vengeance on my father, at least temporarily. And you risked the wrath of the Prince of Wales in the process."

"What if I told you, *couret,* that the Prince never asked about Castelnau? And when I finally did tell him, he believed without question the excuse that I left in haste?"

"The fact that you risked his anger, for me, is all that matters. I hoped, in this case, you would show as much mercy."

He reached for her hand. She had no choice but to give it to him, to feel the warmth of his grasp. She was rapidly losing her will to fight. He lifted it to his lips and kissed each finger, one by one, and the touch was moist and hot. He looked at her over her bare knuckles. "There is much we must discuss, you and I."

She cursed the tremors that flowed from his lips through her fingers and over her entire body. "Let . . . let's begin with discussing Thibaud's fate."

"That isn't what I had in mind." He massaged the callused pads of her fingers individually. "But if you insist, I'll tell you. Thibaud has paid homage to me. He's my knight now."

"But . . . he was my father's uncle."

"According to Thibaud, he was little more than your father's serf. Your great-uncle wants the lands of his birth to be those of his death, so he swore fealty."

"But what of his loyalty to the French?"

"Thibaud has no love of the English prince, but he also said that his pension from the French crown hasn't been paid in six years. He chose his fate, and I willingly took him as my man."

His hand tightened on her fingers and he stepped one step closer, so close that she could see the individual stitches on his embroidered tunic. She stared at them so she would not have to stare into his eyes.

"What next, Aliénor?"

"What about my mother?"

"I haven't spoken to her. The servants tell me she rarely emerges from the solar, and only then to go to Mass."

"Then you haven't decided her fate?"

"I haven't decided the fate of any woman in the castle, *couret.*"

Her heart jumped and she forced it calm. "My mother knows an abbess in a convent in Auch. She has talked often of joining her there."

"Then I will honor her wish."

She looked up at him. It was a mistake. Looking at Jehan

while so near was like standing too close to a blazing fire during a cold winter night: irresistible and very, very dangerous. "You don't even know what the abbess will ask for taking her in."

"It doesn't matter."

She could feel his breath now. She could see the blue and gray streaks in his eyes.

"Who is next, *couret?* Laurent?"

She paled as he whispered her brother's name. Many knights in Jehan's position would kill Laurent rather than allow the son of a rebel knight to live, or allow a rival heir to his conquered lands and title grow to manhood.

"You'll never trust me, will you?"

"Right now," she said huskily, "I have no choice."

"After all that has passed between us, I would think you'd know me better. You stare at me as if I were about to execute him." His lips tightened. "I offered him a position as a squire—in another knight's household. But he refused."

"Laurent *refused?*"

"He said he wanted to join a friary in Toulouse." Jehan traced the inside of her wrist with his fingers. "I didn't object. A man of God isn't likely to come back and reconquer his father's estates, and your brother has grown nearly to manhood in the past year."

"Perhaps . . . perhaps he's afraid of you, and he chose something he didn't want."

"He told me the only reason he ever picked up a sword was to protect you." One gentle finger slipped up her sleeve and traced a throbbing vein. "I told him it was a worthy reason to learn a sword and lance. He chose his own fate, Aliénor. Are you satisfied?"

Satisfied? No, she wasn't satisfied. Her heart was racing in her chest, her hand was damp, his finger was tracing swirls of fire on her inner wrist. He was too close to her, too potent, and she was losing all capacity to think. "What of my people? What will happen to them?"

He grunted. "Soon you'll be asking about the horses and oxen. Anything to delay the inevitable."

The inevitable?

"Those who wish to leave may leave," he said impatiently. "Those who wish to stay must swear homage to me, two days from today. If they decide to stay, their conditions of vassalage will be the same as before."

"You won't bring your own vassals to till the land?"

"The peasants at Castétis are needed there. The only other vassals I have are my knights. Some shall live here with me and guard this castle. There is room enough for your father's men, and mine—if all your father's men decide to swear an oath of fealty to me." He pushed her sleeve up, and his hand traveled as high as the curve of her elbow. "Have I eased your fears now, *couret?*"

"I hoped you would treat us honorably," she murmured, watching his dark, war-scarred hand trace a fragile bone in her forearm. "It seems that all will be . . . well."

She waited for him to say something. The only fate still unspoken was hers. She prepared herself for the inevitable, but as moments passed and he continued to silently run his callused fingers over the tender skin of her inner arm, she could wait no longer.

"Jehan . . . will you send me off with *Maman?*"

His fingers stopped their endless tracing. "You once told me you'd rather be dead than be sent to a convent."

"What other choice do I have?" Her voice was low and husky. "If I marry a mortal man, I'll have nothing but the care of cows."

"I won't marry you off and I won't send you to a convent." His fingers tightened around her wrist. "If I've been kind to others, *couret,* why would I be so cruel to you?"

She blinked up into his blue eyes, hope burgeoning in her breast.

"Tell me what you want," he demanded. "I see it in your eyes, Aliénor—I need to hear it from your lips."

She knew what she wanted. She wanted him to pull her into his hard embrace. She wanted to feel the ridges and swells of his body, his naked skin hot against hers, she wanted to taste the moistness of his lips. She wanted him to

197

cover her face with kisses, to quench the hunger in her body, to make her feel alive, as he did that day in the donjon.

I want you, Jehan. I want to be your woman. I want to be your wife.

Such a hopeless, futile dream. She was nothing—nothing. The man who stood before her had stripped her of wealth, title, and hope. She could bring nothing to a marriage, nothing but a year of experience in running a castle, certainly nothing worthy of the Vicomte de Tournan. No vicomte would ever marry an impoverished noblewoman when he could lure an heiress of great lands. There was no advantage in it, there was no sense in it, no matter how hot the blood ran between them. Yet her only other honorable option was to join a convent, and he said he wouldn't be so cruel to her.

"*Brèisha!*" Suddenly his control snapped. He released her arm and gripped her shoulders. "My men were right. You're a witch, Aliénor, as surely as I'm a knight. You've cast a spell on me. I can think of no other woman but you."

"Jehan!"

"It's true. I spent a year away from you, a year of warring and plundering—yet I couldn't forget you, or this place, or that afternoon in the donjon. I want you, *brèisha*. I want to finish what we started."

She looked at him, too shocked to speak.

"I see it in your eyes: You want me, too." He pulled her against his body. "Tell me, Aliénor. Tell me that this is what you want. Tell me that tonight—and every day and every night—you will be my woman."

Chapter

12

SHE STARED UP AT HIM, TRANSFIXED BY THE PASSION IN HIS EYES. *He wants me, despite my poverty, despite my lack of dowry or title or land.* He wanted to possess her as thoroughly as he now possessed Castelnau; he wanted to claim her as he had claimed her estate—tonight, now, and forevermore. Suddenly the world was bright and golden, and she felt as light-headed as if she had drunk a cask full of new wine.

She laughed, a breathless, shaky laugh. She was not doomed to a life in a convent; she was not doomed to forever wonder what it would have been like to love this man—she would have him, the man she could not forget, as her husband. This is what she had not dared to hope for as she wandered through the forests pondering her fate. He was offering her life—a life of loving and wonder—and she wanted to reach out and grasp it like a greedy child. Brazenly, she wound her arms around his neck.

"Aliénor . . . I've waited for you for so long."

His voice was strangled, almost unrecognizable. His lips covered hers. His arms wrapped around her, tightly, until she gasped for breath. She welcomed the feel of his hard, uncompromising chest against her body, the nudge of his tongue against her mouth, the moistness of his breath, the musky scent of his skin, the hundreds of mixed, muddled sensations that overwhelmed her as she succumbed to his embrace. He held her close. He was so strong, so much stronger than she was. His shoulders felt as hard as stone. The hunger in her grew with each frantic kiss, with each muffled gasp, with each desperate search for a deeper embrace. She felt no fear. She felt as light and as fragile as a stalk of wheat blown about by the raging Pyrenean winds.

His fingers tangled in the sweep of her damp hair. He pulled her head back and opened her mouth to his caress. He molded her body with one hand, from the nape of her neck to her buttocks. She felt each callus on his fingers as if no wool separated her bare skin from his touch, a touch that grew more intimate as his hand slid over her hip. Her body throbbed. The ridges of his coat-of-plates bit against her sensitive breasts. She wanted his armor to dissolve and her clothes to shred away until there was nothing between them but skin and passion.

He pulled away. He reached up and buried his other hand in her hair, tilting her head until she looked into his eyes. The need showed naked and bold on his face. There was no need for words. He dipped down and wrapped one arm beneath her knees, the other around her back. Her knees buckled as he lifted her up high, in his arms. She tried to whisper his name. Her breath came ragged through her lips. He kissed her as if he were trying to catch it—little teasing kisses. She wove her fingers in his soft, thick hair as he walked toward her bed.

She was living as she had never lived before. Never had she been so conscious of flesh, muscle, bones, blood, every tiny movement of sinew, every stretch of limb. Vaguely, she thought, *Laurent would call this a sin, loving like this before our vows are spoken,* but she let the thought scatter away as soon as it came. They would say their vows soon enough. Right now, all there was in the world, all that mattered, was him and her and this glorious lovemaking. She let the powerful current of passion carry her along.

Her head arched back as he laid her on the bed. He kissed the hollow of her throat. He fumbled with the buttons that ran down the front of her surcoat. She rubbed her face in his hair as he kissed a wet trail down her neck. She felt the heat of his hand on her abdomen, atop the single worn layer of linen she wore beneath her gaping surcoat. He smoothed her taut abdomen and followed the curve of her waist.

Then his fingers closed over her right breast. She arched against his hand. He squeezed her, gently, then rolled his thumb over her nipple. He captured her moan of pleasure with a kiss, then released her breast and lowered his head to her bosom. He dampened the threadbare cloth around her taut nipple with his kisses. His lips drew nearer and nearer to the tip. Her abdomen tightened in anticipation. Blood rushed to the rigid point, making it so engorged and sensitive that the brush of Jehan's breath was enough to make her dizzy. Finally, he captured it between his lips. She gasped aloud, for the gentle pressure of his teeth and the heat of his mouth made her senses scatter like so many loose leaves in the wind.

He raised his head and looked at her. Her breathing was fast and ragged, and she blinked up at him, dazed. She wondered if she had done something wrong, if she were too eager, or if she wasn't doing what she was supposed to do. She knew nothing of this, except, without doubt, she wanted it. *Why does he hesitate? Why doesn't he kiss me, tear these wretched clothes from my body and make me a woman?* She couldn't feel him, for the lines of his body were dulled and distorted by layers of chain mail, plates, and padding. Instinctively, she arched against him.

"Say it." He framed her head with his hands. "Say you'll give yourself to me."

"Yes, yes." She wrapped her fingers around the hard, knotted muscles of his forearms. "Tonight and every night —I'll be yours."

"Brèisha . . ." He kissed the corner of her mouth and let one hand slide down her face, her throat, over her bare collarbone. "I've waited so long to hear such sweet words, to touch you like this. . . ."

"Show me, Jehan."

"I'll teach you everything, everything—you have nothing to fear. Tonight I'll make you mine, and in the nights to come I'll love you, sweet Aliénor, and show you how to love." He kissed her lips, then slowly moved off her and stood up from the bed. He fumbled with the lacings of his tunic. "Take off your clothes, *couret*. I want to see you—all of you."

She glanced anxiously toward the door.

"Esquivat is guarding the stairwell, and your mother is locked in her room. We are alone. There is nothing to fear. Show yourself to me."

Jehan's mind grew cloudy with desire as he freed himself of his coat-of-plates. He could scarcely believe that she gave herself to him so freely—without hesitation—as if she had hoped, all along, that he would ask her to be his. He had been ready to battle for her, to argue with her that she had no other option, to persuade her with caresses that she was made to be loved. But instead, she opened herself like a trusting child, acknowledging this raging passion between them with utter honesty. He would have her tonight—he would have her in all the ways he had imagined during the long nights with the Prince's army—and he struggled to control his own rampant desire.

He watched as she sat up and swept her legs over the side of the bed. With trembling fingers, she unfastened the remaining buttons of her surcoat. Then, with an innocence that made him ache, she shrugged the sleeves off her shoulders and let the ragged wool slide down her curves into a pile at her feet.

His blood heated quickly, sharply, as he gazed on her near-naked body. The shift she wore molded against her, and her flesh glowed through the worn linen. She began to remove the shift, but he approached her and swiftly grasped her wrists. He had changed his mind; he wanted to unwrap this most precious of gifts himself. The sweet scent of marjoram and fennel rose from her skin, teasing him, urging him to kiss all of her naked flesh until he knew every intimate scent of her. He pulled her tight into his embrace, buried his face in her hair, then searched through the golden tresses for her cheek, her jaw, and, finally, her mouth.

He captured her soft, parted lips. Her breath was hot, her tongue moist and eager. She wrapped her arms around his neck. There was no hesitation in her movements, no fear. She was pliant, supple, willing, shifting her weight innocently, seductively against him. He reached down and clutched the end of her shift. His fingers skimmed her thighs as he yanked the shift up, past her hips, past her waist. Wordlessly, without shame, she lifted her arms as he pulled the material over her head and tossed it into the shadows.

She was exposed, naked, open to his gaze. He wanted to touch her all at once. He swept her into his arms, feeling the warmth and softness of her bare flesh. He laid her down on the bed and stretched out beside her. The orange glow of the dying fire poured over the tangled pelts and over her. Her breasts rose and fell rapidly. He looked at the entire length of her, from her crown of honey-gold hair, to the hollow of her abdomen, to the dark blond triangle at the merging of her smooth thighs, to the fragile narrowness of her ankles, and the small, defenseless shape of her highly arched feet. His heart beat painfully in his chest.

He touched her abdomen. She felt as soft as the feathers on a falcon's breast. The muscles gently flexed beneath his fingers. She trembled, as defenseless as the day she was born. He ached to touch her everywhere, to feel her moist need for him, but his heart was pumping too fast, his passion burning too high. No matter how eager her kisses, she was still a virgin.

A virgin, damn you!

He covered her nakedness with his own body. He still wore his hose, his aketon, and his shift. His chain-mail chausses hung by his knees where they were held by leather lacings. All the trappings frustrated his efforts to feel the heat of her. He cursed and thanked the restraint at the same time, for it was the only thing that prevented him from taking her right *now*. His hand swept more boldly over her shoulder, over her swelling breast, past her ribs, the hollow of her abdomen, to where her hip jutted delicately from her side. She arched her back as his hand followed the same route back and rested on her breast. Her dusky nipple hardened against his palm.

He buried his face in the warm nook of her throat as he massaged the firm globe of her breast. Her fingers twined in his hair. The scent of her, the sight of her, the taste of her, the sound of her breath catching in her throat—she was driving him to madness. Passion surged in him, stronger than before. As he rolled his fingers over the pert rise of her breast and suckled on her tender earlobe, she turned her head and tried to kiss him. He couldn't kiss her—not now, not when the fury of a year of pent-up desire boiled in his blood. Too fiercely, he wanted to plunge into her body, to claim it as his own, to feel her nakedness curled around him. He wanted all this energy, all this life, surrounding him, engulfing him, pulsing in rhythm with his own need.

Her fingers wove in his hair. With gentle pressure, she tried to turn his face to hers. Her eager lips brushed his cheek as she drew closer and closer to his mouth. She was tormenting him, for she didn't understand how much he could hurt her, how little she could withstand the full force of his passion. He mustn't touch those soft, pink, trembling lips—not yet—else he would forget she was an innocent, tear off his clothes, and take her with a voracity and power that would leave her hurt and angry.

"Kiss me, Jehan."

His whole body sizzled with fresh flames as he heard her impassioned words. "Aliénor . . ."

"Please."

Aliénor ached for him in a way she had never ached before. Her fingers curled in his hair as his mouth covered hers, forcefully, and she opened her lips to his kiss. Her entire body quivered beneath him. She curled her hands into fists. The kiss she had craved brought her pleasure, but no ease, for the ache grew and deepened, driving her beyond sanity, compelling her to press her naked body against him, to search for some ultimate gratification. She wanted more of him—she wanted all of him. She opened her hands and ran them down his back. He groaned, as if he, too, felt the undeniable need. His weight fell on her. The buckles of his aketon and the mail of his chausses dug into her bare flesh.

She clung to his shoulders. His hands, suddenly, were everywhere, burning over her body and stroking her skillfully in all the hollows and curves that ached the most for his caress. He kissed a path over her jaw, to her throat, and lower, resting briefly on a pulse in her throat before suckling her breast. She pressed her cheek against the pillow and squeezed her eyes shut. Her fingers dug into his shoulders and she wondered why he remained dressed while she was naked beneath him.

As if he read her thoughts, he lifted himself away from her. Impatiently, he unlaced his chausses at the knees and let them clink to the floor. He unbuckled his aketon and unlaced his attached hose, and soon these, too, joined the growing pile. She watched him emerge from the trappings of his clothing. His was a warrior's body, strong and thick of limb, hard of belly. Not since she tended his wounds in the tower had she seen him bare-chested. His abdomen, stained with tight, white scars, rippled with every move. She forgot her own nakedness as she sat up and ran her fingers over the long muscles of his back. He tossed the last of his garments on the floor. He twisted, wrapped his muscular arms around her, and conquered her lips with his own. She felt, for the first time, the wondrous texture of his bare skin as her breasts brushed against the dark spray of hair. She felt *him,* the male part of him, straining hot against her thigh.

He slid down her body, pausing at her breasts. She could not endure this much longer, she had to have him, as a woman has a man, or she would spontaneously burst into flames. She knew about men mating with women—it would be impossible *not* to know, after living in this crowded castle for so many years. She knew there was pain the first time. She knew there could be pleasure if the man were skilled and the woman willing. She had never been told about this ache, this growing need, this burning within her that only increased with every touch of Jehan's lips, with every move of his body on hers, with every stroke of his hand.

She gasped as his fingers wove between her thighs, as he urged them apart until his hand covered her—the heat of her. Her breath caught raggedly in her throat as his fingers moved and he probed the source of her ache. She threw her head back. His lips settled on her throat, wandered up to her jaw, and found her own lips. He kissed her again and there was no hesitancy. It was an untamed, savage kiss, a kiss that plundered and stole and demanded all at once, a kiss that stoked the fires in her blood. It was a knight's kiss—strong and ruthless and conquering—and she was as powerless beneath it as a serf.

She wanted him. He was stroking her into a wildness, into a savagery, that she could not begin to understand. Her body tingled with life. She pressed her hips up to meet his hand. His caresses grew rougher, more uncontrolled. He spread her thighs wider. His fingers left her. She groaned in protest, but only for a moment, for his weight shifted until his body lay between her thighs. He wove his fingers into the tangled hair on either side of her face. He held her still while he kissed her. She felt him probing that secret place between her thighs.

He found her. The world spun and she clung to the width of his shoulders. The roaring in her ears grew louder. He felt hot. She arched in his embrace, urging him to fill her, urging him to take this part of her that no one had ever touched, urging him to brand her *his,* and welcoming him with joy. He groaned, kissed her jaw, and she felt a muscle contract in his cheek. His mountain of shoulders moved again.

Her eyes flew open. Her cry of pain was muffled in the swell of his shoulder. Her fingers dug into his back. She had been warned, she knew there was pain, but she had forgotten it in the heat of her passion. Jehan moved in her, despite the pain, despite the warm wetness that bathed her in that place. Her breathing grew labored and she winced with each powerful thrust of his body, for he seemed to have lost all control as he moved in her, over her, regardless of her sudden stiffness.

She took quick, deep breaths as the pain began to subside. His rocking grew in strength. She ran her hands over the gleaming, hard muscles of his back. He was so powerful, so strong. *I am causing this passion.* The sharp pain eased. She wrapped her arms around his neck. The ache returned as the pain faded into a soreness, and, hesitantly, she relaxed her thighs, then dared to lift them higher against his hips. His movements grew wild, and another shudder, more powerful than before, trembled through his body. He gently bit her neck. He clutched her hip, whispered her name, and stiffened atop her. She gasped aloud as he swelled inside her, causing both soreness and pleasure. She held him close as the last of the shuddering faded away.

And Aliénor smiled, knowing, instinctively, that she had given him a man's pleasure.

Some time later, he lifted himself off her and gathered her into his arms. She pressed her cheek against the dampness of his chest. His breathing settled into a slow rhythm and his fingers toyed in the tousled length of her hair. As the fire in the hearth faded, he reached for a few tangled furs piled on one side of the bed and spread the pelts over them. She looked up at him.

He was frowning.

"What is it?" All her confidence, all her certainty, faded to nothing. Hadn't he found pleasure in her? Hadn't she given him what a wife must give to her husband? "What have I done wrong?"

"You've done nothing wrong, Aliénor—nothing but drive me beyond all reason."

She looked at him, confused.

"When you moved beneath me, my passionate enchantress, I forgot you were innocent. I meant to be more gentle."

"There isn't much pain."

"Liar."

"Truly! It came, and it passed."

"I ravaged you."

"Ah, Jehan . . ." She smiled, her confidence restored. "I wanted you to want me . . . that much."

He smiled a slow, lazy smile, and the outrageous dimple on his cheek deepened. She caught her breath. His rumpled hair hung over his forehead and curled against his neck. He was so breathtakingly handsome, so heart-wrenchingly strong, and he was looking at her—at *her*—with such tenderness, such intensity. Her heart turned in her chest. *Oh, I will make you such a wife, Jehan. I will bear you sons and raise them to be good knights and I will protect Castelnau when you are away. . . .* He lowered his head and kissed her. He pulled away, then kissed her again. She raised her hand to his waist and caressed the long, smooth muscles along his back and sides. He unwound his hand from her hair and traced her cheek.

The ache that had grown in her body during their lovemaking had dulled, but it was still there, growing stronger with each of Jehan's gentle caresses. It was an uncomfortable, frustrated throbbing, a throbbing that increased every time he shifted against her. Every touch of their bare skin, every brush of her nipples against his chest, was sheer pleasure, and continual torment. She ached for him. She wanted him to touch her that way, all over again.

"I still want you, Jehan."

Passion flared in his eyes. He looked at her breasts, her shoulders, and lower, to the shadows between them. *"Couret,* I wanted to spend the night making love to you, but after this . . ."

"Take me again."

His hand slipped between her legs. She flinched as he stroked her, gently. "No, my passionate one. Not tonight. For your sake, we'd best wait for another time."

"No."

She wrapped her arms around his neck and pressed her breasts full against his chest. The ache throbbed in her abdomen, begging release. She kissed him with a boldness that she knew would make her flush with shame later, but now seemed as natural and as necessary as breathing.

Suddenly he crushed her to him, rolling her over until her body lay full beneath his. She felt his arousal against her thigh, and thought, *He wants me, too. Again.*

"You're a greedy wench." He spoke against her throat. "Trust me, Aliénor. I've hurt you enough tonight and we have a thousand tomorrows—"

"Make love to me now."

He growled. "You'll curse me later."

"I'll curse you now if you stop."

She shifted her hips against him, and his words died in a moan. She smiled as he bent and took one nipple into his mouth. He was like a powerful, wild beast, and she thrilled with the knowledge that she could entice the beast beyond all control. Her hands roamed over the huge, swelling muscles of his back, over the mounds of his arms, down his sides to his waist. His kisses burned her lips, her temple, her neck, while his fingers explored the hollows of her body with bold intimacy. He touched her soreness again, but she no longer felt the pain. All she felt was the glorious need for his loving.

She followed the silent urgings of a dark, primitive instinct, an instinct she had discovered sometime during the night. Jehan touched her thigh and she opened her legs without question. He probed her carefully. She arched against his hand. She curled her fingers around that curious part of his body. His breath turned ragged, his touch more forceful. She was losing all control, slipping off the edge of consciousness into a world she had known nothing about before tonight, a world so bright and wondrous she could not speak for the emotions swelling in her chest.

Suddenly he moved off her. She blinked her eyes open. He lay beside her, on his back. He clutched her by the waist and lifted her up into the air, positioning her astride his waist. She brushed away a web of golden-blond hair and stared at him.

"What are you doing?"

"I'm trying to save you some pain." He sat up, wrapped his arms around the swirl of golden hair, and kissed her full on the lips until she was pliant and breathless again.

"Please, Jehan—"

He lifted her and positioned her more directly over his hips.

Suddenly, she understood. "I don't know what to do—"

"You will," he whispered. "It's best this way: If you hurt too much, you can stop."

He throbbed against her. His hands clutched her hips firmly. He kissed the tip of her breast and she threw her head back. He eased his grip on her hips and she felt him, waiting, holding himself still, waiting for her to ease herself onto him.

There was soreness, more than she expected. She winced as she slowly slipped down, as he filled her in this new way. She stopped for a moment, letting the pain pass, then eased down a little more. His fingers dug into her waist and he groaned against her throat.

"By all the saints, Aliénor . . ."

She slipped lower. Her body trembled with this power, the power to affect him so. Recklessly, she lowered herself until he filled her completely.

Jehan gasped aloud.

She rested, speechless, and wrapped her arms around his broad shoulders. She didn't know if she could move, she felt so full, so complete, so much a part of him. *We are one, husband and wife.* His muscles rippled against her, a familiar rippling, and she felt the same trembling begin in her own body. His hands tightened on her waist. He lifted her, slightly, then released her. She moaned at the feeling of him moving in her. He repeated the slight motion, again, again, until she found the strength in her thighs to move higher, to move faster, to break away from the restraint of his grip, to feel the full glory of him impaled deep inside her softness.

Then something happened. Perhaps it was due to the feel of him trembling beneath her, under her control, as wild with passion as she was herself. Perhaps it was the sound of Jehan repeating her name, over and over. But the ache that started so long ago swelled with sudden intensity, swelled until her body was tight with it, until she could no longer control her movements, until she lost all sanity, until she found herself crying his name and moving with a brazen wantonness until, finally, something burst inside her, something so savage and so sublime that she felt as if she were a wild, untamed horse who had just bucked out of its ropes and raced into freedom.

His arms wound tight around her. She was wet with sweat. Her hair clung to her back, her shoulders, her temples. She realized they were both gasping for breath, as if they had just run a long distance together. She leaned limply against him and wove her fingers through his damp, black hair. She sat there, astride his great body, engulfed in his embrace, still, shocked, overwhelmed. He stayed inside her, long, long after she blinked her eyes open.

Slowly, the chill air cooled their sweat-soaked skin. She shivered. Without separating their bodies, he rolled over until she was beneath him, covered with his warmth. He reached for a fur to cover his back.

She closed her eyes, languidly, as the tension seeped out of her. There was no ache now, only the soreness as Jehan shifted his weight and left her. *So this is what it is like to live,* she thought, glorying in the touch of his lips against her hair. In all her imaginings, she had never expected such joy in lovemaking. Somehow, she knew that it was not always like this between a man and a woman. She had always sensed that her mother hated the couplings with her father. The lustier female servants, the ones who willingly gave themselves to the men-at-arms, never hinted at such pleasure. *What glorious fortune,* she thought, *that out of the day's disaster came the fulfillment of all my dreams.* She would not only have a husband, a home, and children, but a man who could make her feel as if she had touched the gates of Heaven.

As she drifted off to sleep, she admitted to herself what she had known since last year, what she had known, perhaps, since the day Jehan had bent on one knee before her in the courtyard.

She was in love with Jehan de St. Simon.

Jehan awoke when the first fingers of dawn slipped through the narrow archer's windows and lit the darkened chamber. He felt the softness of her hair spread over his chest and he looked down at her features, obscured by the golden swirl. A smile spread slow and sure over his face as he remembered the night just passed.

It was as he always suspected, since the first day he kissed her, over a year ago. She was as passionate and giving and wanton as the loosest camp follower—but she was innocent and a virgin. The daughter of the Vicomte de Tournan. The child of his enemy. The one-time heiress to the entire Tournan estates. Now she lay, sated and asleep, as naked as the day she was born, in the circle of his arms.

The fallen angel was *his* now, like Castelnau-sur-Arrats, won by cleverness and strength and swiftness. There was no battle, no struggle. She understood. She gave herself freely to him, and he could hardly believe his fortune. A year ago he was a prisoner in this castle, staring hopelessly at this creature; and now she and all she owned belonged to him. Success had never tasted so sweet, he thought, as he leaned over and kissed her soft, rosy lips.

He watched as her golden-brown eyes blinked open, heavy with sleep. He swept her hair away from her face and watched the corners of her lips tug into a smile as she focused on his bristled face. Then he spread his hand possessively on her bare hip.

"You're mine now, *brèisha.*"

She shifted her weight and winced.

"And there's the proof."

"Mmm."

"I warned you you'd curse me."

"I'm not cursing you, my warrior." She winced again,

then glanced up at him. "But you needn't grin like a friar with the key to the wine cellar."

"I'll be grinning from now until Christmas, *brèisha*. I've won you, finally, after a long and difficult battle." He rolled her into his embrace. "Should I get up and order someone to bring a bath?"

"Not now." She pressed her cheek against his bare chest. "You forget that you're the new lord here. Only serfs, servants, and soldiers rise so early."

"The servants aren't awake—I'd wager they haven't yet recovered from last night. Before I left the feast, I ordered the last two casks of wine we took from Bordeaux to be tapped."

"Ah, so you're a generous lord."

"I didn't want us to be interrupted in the middle of our 'discussion.'"

"How could you be so sure I'd say yes?" she mused sleepily. "After all, you're an *English* knight."

"If you refused, *brèisha*, I would have spent the night persuading you otherwise."

"Mmm . . . Maybe I should have put up more of a fight."

"As it was, it took you a damn long time to come around to discussing what I had in mind for you."

She giggled. He kissed the hollow of her temple. She looked up at him with eyes as soft as tawny velvet, eyes full of emotion and desire. Something tightened in his chest.

"I was always afraid you'd come back and seize Castelnau," she said quietly. "But I think I was more afraid that if you succeeded, you wouldn't claim *me* along with it."

How unusual a woman, he thought, *to take what I offer without grasping for more or demanding what I cannot give.*

"All that time I was with the Prince's army," he murmured, "I could think of nothing but returning."

"I had expected you sooner."

"I would have come back only weeks after I left, but Prince Edward found out that your father had reclaimed his estate. He didn't want me bogged down in a winter siege when he was planning a spring raid through Poitou." He slid one hand down over her shoulder, her waist, to rest again on her hip. "I think the Prince sometimes wondered which I wanted more: Castelnau or you."

She wrinkled her nose. "I wish you weren't loyal to the English."

"Let that be your only regret, *couret.*"

He kissed her, softly, slowly, and her breath was warm and inviting. Her tight nipples brushed against his chest. His hand tightened on her hip. The stirrings of desire began a slow boil in his blood. *Diou!* He'd best stay away from her for the next few days or she'd never let him in her bed again. He released her lips, growled something unintelligible, and rolled off of her. "I'd best go before I do you more damage."

"You'd better go before Thibaud awakens." She clutched a foxfur to her chest as she carefully sat up on the bed. "If he finds you here, and sees this, you'll find his sword in your throat before you can explain."

"I shall probably find it there anyway."

"Not once he understands."

He felt a flash of guilt. *How innocent she is.* Her entire life had changed in the course of a single day and a single night, and she didn't yet comprehend the consequences. She couldn't, for no woman who knew the world as it was would be so happy to face it after this night. He watched as she adjusted her position on the bed. "I didn't even give you a choice, *couret.* I intended to give you one before I made love to you."

Her smile was as brilliant as the morning. "You'd have me choose between a bowl of muddy water and a golden chalice of wine? That, Jehan, is no choice at all."

"I knew that you would never choose a convent." He kissed her again, tormenting himself with her warm, naked nearness. "But I didn't dare hope you'd be so willing to be my mistress."

Chapter
13

ALIÉNOR'S FINGERS DUG DEEP INTO THE FOXFUR SHE CLUTCHED against her chest. She stared into Jehan's eyes, eyes that were misty and bluish gray in the dim light of morning. She shuddered violently, as if rivulets of spring mountain water trickled over her body from her head right down to the soles of her feet.

Last night's conversation roared through her mind. Each word, each gesture, every touch, swirled through her head like contrary winds in a tempest. She remembered that he had treated every member of her family honorably. She remembered hoping and praying that his generosity would extend to her. She recalled her quivering anticipation when Jehan said he wouldn't send her to a convent or marry her off. He had stared at her with such naked passion that she couldn't help but think there was only one other option for her fate—one other *honorable* option—and Jehan was offering it to her. As she searched her memory, she realized with growing horror that Jehan had never used the word "wife," had never called her anything other than his "woman."

Mistress.

Realization struck her like lightning. She choked on the thickening air. She had spent the morning dreaming of the soft length of heather blue satin she intended to purchase for her bridal surcoat. She had spent the night thinking that she

215

was surrendering herself to the man who would be her husband. The beautiful world she had constructed crashed around her like the colorful panes of a stained-glass window shattering under the force of a gale.

"Aliénor? What's wrong?"

She twisted away from him, wincing at the pain between her thighs, the evidence of her foolish, hasty passion. She had been filled with such joy, to think that he found her worthy to be his spouse, worthy to take her place by his side and bear him sons. Sons! She clutched her abdomen, hard, realizing that she might already be filled with child, a child she wanted with all her heart, a child that would now be born into bastardy, a babe that would mark her a whore, a harlot, a woman of the basest sort.

She squeezed back the tears that surged in her eyes and bit her lower lip to keep from crying aloud at her own folly. He loomed behind her. His silence grew ominous, the proof of her terrible, terrible mistake. Suddenly he gripped her shoulders. His ragged nails bit into her tender flesh. He twisted her on the bed until she faced him.

"You expected me to marry you?"

His disbelief was another dagger in her aching heart. She tilted her chin and searched for pride amid her pain. "You said you wanted me," she said defensively, "tonight and every night."

"As my *mistress*, not my wife!"

"A mistress isn't forever."

"*You* will be."

"A mistress can be cast off and driven away as soon as you tire of me."

"You should know me well enough," he said angrily, "to know I offer more than a night's pleasure."

"I *did* expect more." She blinked up at him, trying to clear the tears from her vision, trying to clear the pain and confusion from her heart. "You treated every member of my family honorably. My brother, my mother, my great-uncle. I *assumed* you would treat me the same way."

He cursed and released her shoulders. He rose from the bed and paced around the room.

Aliénor looked away. She was too ashamed to gaze upon his strong, tall, bare body, too ashamed to even *look* at the man who had caressed her so intimately. She heard him pulling on his shift and his hose. She closed her eyes at the horror of what had happened, and the realization of her own wretched foolishness.

He had never said the word "marriage." He never said the word "wife." She had heard only what she wanted to hear, not what he told her. She had welcomed him like the most wanton harlot, *telling* him to take her as only a man can take a woman, all the while thinking they would soon be man and wife. It was all a terrible, terrible mistake, and *she* was the fool. She flushed with the shame of it. She had surrendered to the need to feel him, the need to feel alive, as he had made her feel so long ago in the top room of the donjon. *I am nothing. Nothing.* He already owned her castle, her title, her lands, and all her wealth—he'd taken it by force of arms. Now, through folly, she had given him the one thing that remained: her virtue.

"Aliénor . . ."

His voice was low and full of frustration. The bed dipped as he sat near her. She looked up and met his blue eyes and found them shining with compassion and concern. She swallowed her heart. She could stand anything—disbelief, scorn, even laughter—but she could *not* stand pity.

"It's not the first mistake I've made." She clutched the fur closer to her naked body. "Both yesterday and last night I was foolish enough to give you something precious, without a fight and without negotiating terms of surrender."

"I don't use the same ruses with women as I do in war," he argued. "I tricked you into giving me the castle, but I didn't trick you into my bed."

"Didn't you, Jehan?"

He stiffened. "I never offered you marriage, Aliénor. I thought you understood my terms."

"It doesn't matter anymore." She tilted her chin. "The damage is done."

"Is that what you call what happened between us last night?"

She squeezed her eyes shut. She had feared he would attack from this quarter. "Don't do this, Jehan."

"You can't deny it. You were like a wild creature, warm and responsive beneath me." He leaned closer and whispered, his breath brushing tendrils of her hair against her neck. "I want to taste your passion again. I want to hear you cry out my name—"

"Stop!" She shook her head, trying to dislodge the seductive memories his voice evoked. "Don't you see? The fight is already over and won."

"It's not finished until you understand the terms of surrender."

"I know why a vicomte won't marry a dispossessed noblewoman," she retorted. "I was a fool to even *think* you'd offer me marriage!"

"You were innocent, not a fool."

"I threw myself upon you like a who—"

"Don't." Jehan covered her mouth with his hand, then traced her lips with his fingers. "You were open and passionate. I would have you no other way."

"You're ruthless," she said breathlessly, pulling away from his touch. "How can you use this weapon against me?"

"I'll use any weapon to win this war, *brèisha*. I want you to be fiery and passionate with me again. I want it to be like that between us—always."

"Must you continue until I'm as humble as a serf?"

"I'll continue until you understand." He took her chin in his hand and made her face him. "I will *never* want another woman as much as I want you."

Her response died in her throat. His eyes blazed a brilliant blue-gray. In them she saw determination and intensity, desire and desperation. For a brief moment, she allowed herself to believe his words.

"Marriage is for power and wealth, not for this, *brèisha*. If you had known me better, you would have understood." He traced her jaw with his finger. "There is much I could tell you, much that would make you understand. Will you listen to me now?"

She held the fur to her chest. Emotions rolled and tumbled in her heart. She shouldn't listen to anything this knight had to say; she should push him away and find a dark place where she could hide her shock, her shame, and her grief. Yet, almost unconsciously, she found herself nodding.

He dropped his hand from her jaw and ran his fingers through his rumpled hair. "You might already know part of this story. Your great-uncle knew my grandfather, the Baron of St. Simon. Thibaud battled against his forces during the wars of Edward II." Jehan curled his fingers over the edge of the bed. "Back then, the barony of St. Simon was large and powerful: My family had castles and lands all around Bordeaux, all through Armagnac, and even in England. Now the St. Simons have nothing. My family lost its wealth and power during those wars, and lost the remainder in later wars, until we had nothing left."

"I know what it is like to be dispossessed," she said. "You may have lost your heritage in the course of a generation, but I have lost it in the course of a single day."

"All the more reason why you should understand why I do what I do, *couret.*"

She tilted her chin. She understood why he had conquered Castelnau. Land was tantamount to power, and Castelnau was a large estate. If she had been a man, she would have fought to the death before giving up her castle and her title to an Englishman. But she was a woman, and thus faced different choices.

"When my father died, all he owned went to my eldest brother," Jehan continued. "My second brother joined the Church, and I was left to do whatever I could, for there was no wealth or land for me, not even enough to pay my way into an abbey. All I had was my name and the right to wield a sword. Do you know, Aliénor, what happens to a man without a title or wealth, with nothing but a good sword arm and the willingness of youth to throw himself into a fray?"

"In your case," she said dryly, "he sells his soul and becomes the vassal of the Prince of Wales."

"In my case," he repeated softly, "he loses his soul and becomes a brigand."

Her eyes widened.

"You're familiar with the English brigands who've roamed through Gascony this past year: the ones who've stolen from castles and towns and robbed travelers on the road and destroyed harvests." He opened his hands and looked down upon the calluses that rimmed his palm. "Not so long ago, I was one of them. I stole food from wherever I could take it, be it an abbey's cellar or a peasant's cart; I sold the strength of my arm to whoever would hire me, even if the pay was only a few *deniers.* For three long years I lived like a dog in the hills."

Surprise made her mute. She knew he was a bachelor knight, poor and landless before Castétis, but she never imagined the extent of his poverty. Somehow, she could not envision this strong, tall warrior stealing like a common thief and sleeping, night after night, under the open sky.

"I'm a vassal of the Prince now because of a fortunate mistake: I poached in the royal forests. I was half starved at the time, too hungry to bring the meat to a safer place, so I butchered a stag on the spot. Edward and his men were out on a hunt and they came upon me. I pulled my sword and fought for my life, for I'd rather die in battle than on the royal gallows. The Prince liked what he saw, for he called off his men. When he discovered I was the son of the late Baron of St. Simon, he demanded I become his man. For the first time since I left my father's house, I didn't have to steal or sell my sword to live—or so I thought.

"I was fed for five or six months out of the year on the charity of the Prince. But I was only one of thousands of knights who were released at his whim, without thought of how we were to survive without pay. Between periods of service, I was forced to return to brigandry. I hated it. I wanted the power and security that was once the St. Simons', but that kind of wealth only came with land. Then, during the most wretched year, I found Castétis. The fortress was in rubble and its villeins were starving. I decided to capture it. When Edward found out I had captured a rebel's castle, he no longer treated me like one of thousands of nameless knights in his contingent. Suddenly I had the Prince's ear. I saw a chance, for the first time, to rise above and regain the glory of the name of St. Simon."

He wasn't looking at her anymore. He was staring toward the arrow-slit windows, at the gray light of dawn, and concentration creased his forehead. She noticed a network of tiny white scars that ribbed the back of his hands, the marks of a dozen swordfights, the evidence of his life of warring. She suddenly remembered how stubbornly he had refused to relinquish Castétis to her father when he was a prisoner in this castle. She remembered the wildness in his eyes. For the first time, Aliénor realized she had been looking at a man who had struggled like a savage creature out of the depths of utter poverty, clawing and fighting his way through the world.

"Castétis wasn't enough," he continued. "Over the years, I had gathered sixteen loyal men of my own, and those men needed to be fed and clothed, along with my vassals in Castétis. When the Prince called me to join him in raiding through Gascony, I knew it was an opportunity to gain more lands. If Edward hadn't given me this castle, I might have been forced to steal to survive this winter, just like the hordes of knights who've taken to the roads since the Prince arrived at Bordeaux. I've sworn that I would never be forced into such a life again."

"You have Castelnau now."

He shrugged his mighty shoulders. "I could lose this castle in the blink of an eye and be left with nothing."

"My father is dead, my brother determined to join a friary. There is no one to counter your claim."

"There are other ways to lose a viscounty, Aliénor. My

family lost an estate three times this size in a matter of ten years. I must plan for my future, for the future of my sons, for the future of the St. Simons." He reached out and startled her by covering her abdomen, over the fur, with his spread hand. "*Our* sons, Aliénor. The son who may be growing in your womb even now. He, too, will be provided for. But Castelnau is not enough. I cannot forgo all that I have spent my knighthood fighting for to marry a woman without title and without dowry. I must think of the future."

The future. She could be bearing his son. She was linked to him, even if the sacrament of marriage was never spoken over their heads.

"Do you understand, *couret?*"

His words were gentle, soft, and she felt his fingers over her belly, curling into the pelt, pressing against her. She understood one thing clearly: Her passion had blinded her to the truth. She should never have expected marriage from a man who would have chosen eternal imprisonment rather than give up his only holding—Castétis—in exchange for his freedom. She should never have expected marriage from a man who had once vowed he would win his fortune, first by the sword, then by the lute. He had already conquered Castelnau by might. Now it was time for him to woo and win a woman of title and dowry to wed. She was a fool to expect him to forgo all future prospects for the sake of her, a woman he had utterly dispossessed.

The future. Jehan was thinking of the future. But she, too, must think of *her* future, for the world had taken too sudden a turn.

She placed her hand over his, feeling the tight, white scars ribbing his skin. "How long will it be before you find a wife?"

His eyes flickered, bright and unreadable. "The Prince has made promises, but his promises are often long in coming."

"When you marry," she murmured, "you'll have to put me aside."

"Who will dare to tell me what to do with my mistress?"

"Your wife may be beautiful, and young, and won't like sharing a castle with another woman."

"She'll be rich, and she'll have castles of her own." He took her hand in his and held it tightly. "This will be *your* castle, Aliénor. *You* will be *châtelaine* here. You shall run this fortress as you've run it for the past year, you shall close it against besiegers when I am at war, and you will share my bed every night. I shall drape you in jewels, silks, and furs—not in rags. And I *won't* cast you out—not now, not in two score years." His gaze slipped over her body, scarcely covered by the auburn pelt. "Faith, I wonder if there's enough time left in my life for me to love you as I will."

Love you. A tremor shook her body. *He means make love to me,* she thought.

"Would you rather have poverty, straw pallets, and midnight prayers?" His face darkened. "Or is there another knight?"

"There's no one else who would marry me." Suddenly she remembered her meeting in Pavie. "Not even Guy de Baste."

"Have you developed a softness for that *French* knight in my absence?"

She looked at Jehan's angry face in surprise. "Sir Guy was kind to me during a time of little kindness—"

"Let me tell you something of Guy de Baste." He rose abruptly from the bed. "He negotiated an agreement with the Prince of Wales last winter, so that the Prince would spare his lands during the *chevauchée*. He has no loyalty to any king; he is loyal to no one but himself. I spent the Christmas season with Edward, and Sir Guy was there—supposedly a loyal French knight—feasting on French plunder at an English table."

"So *this* is what you wouldn't tell me last year." She frowned. "It doesn't make sense: When I saw him last winter, he asked to marry me, though he knew my estates were devastated."

"All the traitor ever wanted, despite your loveliness, is these lands, Aliénor. He won't marry you, so don't expect him to save you from *me.*"

"I care not a bean for Guy de Baste." She felt a twinge of anger. "I'm dispossessed, not a fool. I know, beyond doubt, that I have nothing that any man would find worthy in a wife."

"You're wrong, *couret.* You may have no lands, but you have more than any man could want in a woman—wife or mistress."

She looked away. He ran his hand through his tousled hair, ruffling the long dark tresses into utter disarray. Then, suddenly, he stopped his pacing and kneeled in front of her, so his face was level with hers as she sat on the bed. He engulfed her shoulders in his hands.

"This is my fault," he said. "You made a choice, not knowing what your options were."

She stared, mutely, wishing the world were different, and wondering if it really mattered, after all, whether a priest whispered the words of the sacrament over their heads.

"You belong here, and I want you to stay here, by my side, as my woman. But I can't call myself a knight of honor if I don't give you a chance to change your mind. So I will ask you once, Aliénor, but only once, for when the decision is made, it is made for good." He tightened his grip on her shoulders. "You can still leave with your mother and join that abbey in Auch. Or, *couret,* you can stay here as my mistress. You must choose now. I won't wait for an answer."

Choose. She stared at him. Choose between a convent and Jehan, between death and dishonor, between salvation or sin. How simple it all seemed. Being a man's mistress was dishonorable, but life in a convent was no better than a living death. Only warriors were forced by chivalry to choose death over dishonor. But she was a woman, a weak woman, and she knew, without doubt, that she would freely chose dishonor.

There was no other option. She could never go to a convent, not after having tasted the sweetest joy life had to offer. She could never hide away from life, when life might already be growing in her womb. Over the past year, she had never forgotten Jehan's single embrace, despite the despair, the hunger, the sickness, and the constant worry. The memory of his touch strengthened her during the long, cold nights. He was here now. She could not deny herself the glory of his lovemaking. Life was too short, too perilous, too unpredictable. She had always feared one thing—not death, for death would come when it would and no one could prevent it. She had feared she would never have the chance to live.

He was offering her life. She could run this castle, as she had run it for a year. He would give her babes, albeit bastards, and she could raise them and watch them grow to adulthood. She would have everything she always wanted . . . everything but a husband, and something she never realized she craved, because she never dared to think she would lose it: honor.

"Faith, I don't know why you hesitate."

She blinked, struggling out of her thoughts. His eyes were tormented and his lips tight and white in anticipation.

"Have patience," she said softly. "It's not easy for the one-time heiress of Tournan to consider becoming an English knight's mistress."

Something flashed in his eyes.

"But you were right. You knew, even last night, what I would choose. Nothing has changed but my expectations." She lifted her arms. The foxfur slipped off her body, exposing her nakedness to his gaze. "Yes, Jehan. I will be your mistress."

He groaned and pulled her into his embrace. She wrapped her arms around his neck. She felt him, strong, hard, as he pressed her close and buried his lips in her hair, and she closed her eyes against her tears.

"I vow on all that is holy that in this castle, you will be my wife in all but name."

She felt safe in his arms, safe and warm and protected, and for a moment she could believe that it would be like this forever, that he would hold her and love her as fiercely as any man could love a woman. Jehan loved her in his way; she could see it in his eyes. If he didn't, he wouldn't have been so gentle with her, he wouldn't have told her so much of his life. Perhaps after a few months in the castle, he would see that she was worthy of him, that she would be a wife he could be proud of. Perhaps after she bore him a son—the first of many—he would realize that the daughter of the late Vicomte de Tournan deserved more than a leman's bed— she deserved the title and honor of marriage.

She clung to the hope as she clung to Jehan, and his hands grew warm on the bare skin of her back. His lips sought hers. She yielded to him as he pressed her against the tangled pelts on the bed, beneath the weight and heat of his body. She tasted passion on his breath. His hands trembled as they threaded her hair away from her face, as they gently cupped her cheeks and molded her mouth to his. Tears surged to her eyes, for he was so tender, so gentle, as he kissed her thoroughly, as if he hadn't spent the night kissing her, as if he were exploring her lips and tongue and mouth for the very first time.

Then he stopped. His breathing was ragged. He hovered over her, searching her eyes. "We'd best dress, *brèisha*, before I forget your pain."

She had forgotten the pain. He rose from the bed. Reluctantly, she let him go. She knew the hour was late by the brightness of the light streaming in through the window. At any moment, Margot or another servant could enter the room and catch them entwined in lovemaking.

She caught her breath and glanced toward the door. She suddenly realized that she lay naked on the bed, and Jehan was half dressed, roaming around the room, searching for his clothes. The bedlinens were stained with her virgin's blood, and the scattered pelts were hopelessly entangled into knots. The linens still smelled, faintly, of their lovemaking, and suddenly she wanted to hide the linens, or burn them, to cover up the evidence of her shame.

But that was foolishness, utter foolishness. She was his

mistress. She was his woman, to kiss when he wanted, to fondle when he wanted, to keep his bed warm at night. This bed would see more lovemaking, probably before the day was over, and Margot would know soon enough. Surely, Jehan would want to tell the world—surely he'd want to scream it from the ramparts—that the daughter of Tournan, the daughter of his enemy, was now his woman.

For the first time she realized that her decision would have consequences beyond these four walls. She would have to face her great-uncle's anger and shame, she would have to face the scorn on the villagers' faces whenever she attended Mass by Jehan's side. Where once she was the lady of the castle, suddenly she'd be nothing but the new lord's mistress—a precarious, shameful position; and though she might perform the same duties as before, though she might sleep in the same bed and ride over the same fields, no one—*no one*—would ever look at her with respect again.

She flushed hotly. Then she thought of something more frightening, something more painful than the loss of honor and respect.

Laurent.

She clutched her chest. What would he do, her dear brother, the man who had sworn to protect her, when he discovered that his sister had given herself as freely as a harlot of Toulouse to the man who'd conquered their castle? What would he do when he realized she intended to *keep* giving herself to Jehan, over and over, heedless of the consequences? *Your nature,* ma sor, *will lead you into sin.* This was the sin Laurent meant, the glorious sin of loving, of touching, of dishonor, a sin he did not even understand at his tender age.

"What is the matter, *couret?*"

She opened her eyes. Jehan stood above her, clutching her wrinkled shift. "Go!" she exclaimed, waving toward the door. "Go, Jehan, before someone catches you here!"

"Catches me here?" He raised a brow. *"Couret,* I intend to sleep in this bed."

"No! No, you mustn't!"

"It's too late to change your mind."

"We don't have to tell everyone today. We could keep it a secret—"

"Before the sun rises much higher, everyone in this castle will know that you are *mine.*"

She closed her eyes, suddenly envisioning the crowded chapel, envisioning the scorn on the villagers' faces, the condemnation in Father Dubosc's eyes, Thibaud's anger, and Laurent . . . dear Laurent. She wondered if she could ever face him again. She wondered if he would ever speak to her again. She wondered if he would treat her as an excommunicated person, outside of Christian society, a sinner without remorse or conscience.

"Couret . . ." He touched her cheek. "They will all know, sooner or later."

"Then let it be later." She leaned toward him. "Let my mother leave for the abbey—there's no reason she has to know. Let *me* tell my family and my people. Let me tell Laurent. Let me live normally, just a little longer, in my home."

"I'll kill anyone who dares say a word against you."

"Your sword can't protect me from whispers."

"I'll silence the lips through which they pass."

"Shall you kill every one of your own vassals for speaking the truth?"

A muscle moved in Jehan's cheek.

"And what will you do with Laurent?" she continued. "He won't accept this. He'll challenge you first."

"Your brother has much to learn of the world. His education will start today." He drew her up upon her knees. "I've waited a year for you, Aliénor. I won't suffer a night alone."

"I won't deny you—you know I can't. All I ask is that we keep this a secret for a while." She wrapped her arms around his shoulders and pressed close, speaking against his lips. "I have given you everything I have, Jehan—*everything.* Is this truly so much to ask in return?"

* * *

"Treachery! That's the only explanation." Thibaud reached across the table to take a fig out of the bowl between himself and Jehan. "The French knights who fled the field at Poitiers were traitors to their own king."

Jehan shook his head. "If there was any treachery, it was not against the king. The French knights who refused to retreat were traitors to their own common sense. They refused to recognize defeat."

"No French knight could be defeated by thieves, by worthless freemen in boiled leather jerkins."

"The Welsh archers are skilled, and their longbows so lethal that they can fire three arrows to a crossbowman's one. Their arrows can pierce a knight's mail."

Aliénor winced. This was the second midday meal she, Laurent, Jehan, and Thibaud had shared since Jehan took over the castle. Thibaud talked endlessly about the war. He demanded to know how the French knights were defeated at Poitiers, and how the French king was captured. He spent hours discussing the character of Charles, the firstborn son of the French king, who had taken over as regent in Paris while his father was imprisoned. He constantly speculated about whether the French might try to rescue their king in Bordeaux—and thus start another great battle. What was it about knights, she wondered, that they were so captivated by death and war?

Thibaud chewed on a fig. "In my day, no knight of any honor would send the archers ahead of the knights."

"The Prince used his knights; he just used them better than the French."

"Fie! I wouldn't have believed it myself, if pilgrims and peddlers had not returned with the same report. It is beyond belief. King Jean, a prisoner of the Prince of Wales."

"You sound sorrowful, my knight."

Thibaud lifted his great white head. "I fought for King Jean's father. I may be your man now, Sir Jehan, but you cannot change my history."

"It's your experience in war that makes you so valuable to me."

Jehan's gaze strayed, as it had a dozen times during the meal, to where she sat, toying with the rim of a chalice. She looked at him, then quickly looked away, for every time their eyes met she felt as if her body had suddenly burst into flames. Their passion was like a living thing, ever present, purring and brushing against her, making her insides quiver and melt.

For the past two days, Jehan had treated her like a queen. He ordered his men-at-arms to respond to her demands as if they were his own; he insisted that men be sent out to buy cloth to dress her as befitted her position; he consulted her on every decision and often deferred to her judgment; he allowed her to run the castle however she saw fit. The great hall already looked as it had before the English attacked. Jehan's booty now decorated the room. The table was spread with pewter platters and several gold chalices, all over a crisp, white damask cloth. Three of a series of four tapestries depicting a hart hunt graced the walls of the hall, and the fourth, the kill, lay ready on the floor, waiting to be hung. There was new life in the fortress. The men kept the kitchens filled with fresh game. Their singing and laughter echoed off the walls. Jehan meted out petty justice among the tenants, rode over his new lands with her daily, and made every meal a celebration. He eased the burden of her responsibilities, but left her with all the pleasures.

All the pleasures but one, she thought. It had been two days since he made love to her. She had waited for him to sneak into her chamber both nights, for Margot, who normally slept in Aliénor's room, had been conspicuously absent from her pallet and Aliénor had twice seen her giggling with Jehan's squire, Esquivat. She wondered if *Maman*'s presence in the solar—the room that separated the donjon, where Jehan slept, from Aliénor's room—kept Jehan from joining her these past two nights. There were other ways for him to slip into her room, but with each of them he would risk discovery. The castle was crowded before Jehan arrived, because many villagers who were burned out of their homes the previous winter still lived in the great hall, but the addition of Jehan's men-at-arms was making it unbearable. Privacy was as precious and rare as dragon's blood, and privacy was the one thing they needed to keep their new relationship hidden from the world.

Never once did he pressure her to announce her decision aloud, though his gaze flared every time it fell upon her. She, on the other hand, was growing more and more frustrated at this self-imposed denial of their passion. Two days of abstinence was enough to convince her that her decision to become his mistress would never change. Fortunately, *Maman* was leaving Castelnau tomorrow to travel to the abbey at Auch. Then there would be nothing separating her from Jehan's chambers anymore.

She glanced across the trestle-table. Laurent listened intently to Jehan and Thibaud's conversation. Her throat constricted. *Maman*'s departure was only a temporary solution to a much greater problem. She had to tell the world. The first, most important, and most frightening step was to find the heart to face Laurent. She already realized that there was no soft way to inform her pious brother that she had given her virtue outside of marriage to the man who would pay Laurent's way into a Franciscan monastery. The thought of the confrontation made her cringe in shame. She knew Laurent would try to persuade her to join a convent. He would warn her that she risked her immortal soul. He would want to protect her from something from which she no longer wanted to be protected. He would be furious at Jehan—how furious she could not begin to guess. He might refuse Jehan's offer to send him to a friary, thus destroying his own precious dreams.

She must not let that happen. Somehow she would have to convince Laurent of the truth: She *wanted* to be Jehan's mistress. She intended to raise their illegitimate children, openly, in Castelnau. She was not being forced or coerced into sin. She willingly chose dishonor—she grasped it with eagerness. She knew Laurent would be repulsed by her brazenness. But if he realized that he could do nothing to change her mind, then maybe he wouldn't do anything foolish, or dangerous, or anything that would risk his own future.

She hated herself for her own hesitation. Once Laurent knew, the world would know, and her life would be changed irrevocably. She would no longer be treated like a queen in this castle. She was acting like a coward, afraid of the whispers of peasants, afraid of a boy who would turn fifteen years of age near Christmas. She must not hide away any longer, for her frustration was growing to a fever pitch, and the longer she delayed, the more difficult this confrontation would be. When she didn't join *Maman* to go to the abbey tomorrow, then Laurent would know for sure that her fate was not in a convent. The time to tell him was now, before he asked uncomfortable questions—or, worse, before he caught her and Jehan in the midst of lovemaking some dark night.

She stood up abruptly. The men stopped their conversation. "Come, *frai,* let's leave the knights to their talk of warfare." She reached for the bowl of figs before Thibaud could take another. "We'll deliver what remains of this feast to the poor."

She walked to the door, opened it, and leaned against the iron strapwork while the cool autumn wind eddied in the portal. She waited for her brother. His foot dragged against the fresh rushes as he crossed the hall, carrying a platter heaped with the ends of gravy-soaked trencher bread, a few joints of quail, and what was left of the Michaelmas goose. She met Jehan's eyes as Laurent reached her side. *Soon, my love. Soon it will be as you wish.* Once Laurent had passed through, she closed the heavy oak door behind them.

"The villagers will be pleased," Laurent said as he descended the stairs, step by step. "It's been a long time since we've had scraps from the lord's table."

"We'll take them to Father Dubosc to give out as alms."

"So you *did* leave the table to talk to me." He headed toward the chapel. "You must have made your decision."

She nearly choked on the fig she had plucked out of the bowl and popped nervously in her mouth. She stopped in her tracks. She stared at her brother as she struggled with the chewy fig and tears came to her eyes.

"It's no great secret," Laurent said. "You were the only one whose fate wasn't determined on Michaelmas Day. The whole castle is abuzz, waiting for you to make up your mind."

He couldn't know. He couldn't. Jehan had promised to remain silent. She stared at her brother in utter confusion. If Laurent knew of her decision, he wouldn't be smiling at her. With some difficulty, she swallowed the fig. "How . . . how did you know?"

"You're my sister! The day after Michaelmas, I *demanded* to know what Sir Jehan had planned for you." He grinned, and the wind tossled his bluntly cut blond hair. "He said that you had a choice of fates, and when you were ready, you would tell everyone your decision. Thibaud has wagered his sword that you'll choose marriage over a convent."

"Marriage?"

He stared at her incredulously. "You've always told me you'd rather throw yourself off the ramparts than join a convent. Thibaud is going to be furious."

She was struck dumb. No wonder Laurent was so light-hearted. He, Thibaud, and everyone else in the castle had guessed Jehan's intentions incorrectly. *Just as I had.* She stared into her brother's black eyes. They knew only that Jehan had given her a choice, and they assumed that the choice had been between a convent and marriage—when, in truth, Jehan had offered her nothing but a bed. A wonderful, warm, glorious, sinful bed.

So I wasn't such a fool.

"Aliénor, you look so pale."

Tell him, she thought. *Tell him the truth.* Looking into his bright, close-set eyes, she hesitated to destroy his illusions. She remembered, all too well, how her illusions had been shattered the morning after she and Jehan had made love. The truth had devastated her; she feared it would destroy her brother. "You don't understand, Laurent."

"No, I don't! You've railed against convents so much that I've said a hundred Ave Marias for your soul's sake!" He placed the platter of food on the ground, took the figs from her, and placed them beside the platter, then took her hands. She realized, suddenly, just how much taller he was than she. She had to arch her neck to look into his eyes. "How can you think of joining a convent when this knight has made you such a fine offer?"

"It's not such a fine offer."

"You'll be miserable in a convent. They'll imprison you in a little cell, serve you bread and water—"

"Careful, *frai,* you're beginning to sound like me."

"I don't want you to make a mistake," he argued. "Think, Aliénor. If you marry Sir Jehan, then our blood—Tournan blood—will still run in the veins of the lords of this castle. That was what Father wanted all along."

"Father would sooner see me dead than married to an Englishman."

"Perhaps," he continued, realizing the error of his logic, "but he's gone, and we can't hope for his return anymore." He squeezed her hands. "Take what God has given you, *ma sor.*"

Ah, Laurent, if you only knew how eagerly I have taken what God has given me!

"He's a strong knight, and he's wealthy and titled," he continued. "I know how long you've wanted a husband. He'll give you children."

Bastards.

"I'll have nephews and nieces!" His voice broke. "I want to see you happy, Aliénor."

"Oh, Laurent . . ."

He had envisioned such a wonderful life for her—the same life she had once envisioned. But her life would bear no resemblance to the one he had imagined. She would bear children, but they would be born of sin. She would be excommunicated for her adultery, and her brother, whether or not he became a friar, would be forced, by the Church, to ignore her very existence. There could be no reconciliation between them. She wondered if Laurent would ever forgive her for choosing sin over salvation.

"I think he loves you. I see it in his eyes whenever you're in the room."

She started and looked up at him. So Laurent had seen it, too, she thought. She was *not* imagining it. Jehan loved her. *But not enough to give up everything he has worked for. Not enough to make me his bride.*

"It's a rare thing, love between a man and a woman, before marriage." He put his arms around her. "You shouldn't scorn such a gift. Especially for pride."

What about honor, Laurent? Should I scorn it for honor? She laid her head against his shoulder. Her brother rocked her in his arms. She breathed in the lingering scent of frankincense in the woolen fibers of his tunic. This was a strange reversal—her brother comforting her—when, all through their lives, she had been the one to comfort him. He had grown strong in the past year, both in body and in spirit. Strong and determined.

Her courage suddenly flew away, like a flock of sparrows in October.

"Is it because you're still mourning Father, Aliénor?" he asked. "Is that why you've made this decision?"

She pulled away and braced herself to lie. "No, *frai.* I haven't made my decision yet."

"Good." The worry left his face. "This will give Thibaud a chance to talk some sense into you. He won't take well to losing his sword."

She met his gaze. Lying was so much easier than the truth, so much kinder. There must be a way for him to find out about her decision, without ever laying eyes upon her again. Perhaps she could persuade him to join the friary *before* she told everyone. Then it would be too late for him to leave the friary, and he would be far, far away. She would never have to see condemnation or shame in his black, close-set eyes.

She really was a coward.

"Maman is going to the abbey tomorrow," she said. "When are you planning to go to the friary?"

"As soon as I've witnessed the sanctioning of your union with Sir Jehan."

She shook her head. If he waited for that, he'd be waiting until Judgment Day. "You must leave sooner. Whatever I decide, nothing can be done for a while because of Father's death."

"I'm staying. I vowed I would, over a year ago, and a man of God never breaks his vow." He reached out and wiped a tear from her cheek. "You always worried about me too much, *ma sor*. I'm not a boy anymore. I'm a man, and I intend to be the one who gives you away at the church steps." He grinned wickedly. "Even if I have to battle Thibaud for the honor."

Chapter
14

JEHAN COULD STAND IT NO LONGER.

It was the *vendange*. The inhabitants of the village and castle milled around the great hall, enjoying the first taste of the sweet, cool wine pressed from the Tournan grapes. The marauders had stolen last season's casks after the siege of Castelnau, so for many, this was the first time they had tasted the heady liquid from their own vines in a year. They drank the new bounty with utter abandon.

Jehan surreptitiously emptied his cup, for the fourth time, into the rushes. Aliénor had retired early that night, as if she could no longer sit calmly next to him and share his bowl at the feast. He wanted to talk to her, to tell her what he had planned for the evening, but every time he leaned close, someone would appear at his side. Inevitably, the intruder would ask about some trivial matter, such as the order of the next day's hunt or the acquisition of falcons and hounds. Then a page would appear to fill his chalice, or a servant would arrive with the next course. He was never alone in this damned, crowded castle. He was lord here, yet leisure and privacy eluded him like a wily young deer. Each time Aliénor's fingers innocently brushed his during the meal, he wanted to clutch them in his grip, he wanted to sweep her in his arms and claim her as his own.

He could do that now. Aliénor's mother had left that morning for the abbey in Auch. The room that separated his and Aliénor's chambers was now empty. Though the hearth fire in the great hall still burned high and hot, he could wait no longer. He was tired of Thibaud's endless questions about the battle of Poitiers. All he wanted, all he could think of, was the woman he needed in his bed.

He stood up, and his heavy oak chair scraped against the floorboards. He finished the few drops left in his chalice and returned the cup to the stained damask tablecloth. "You may all drink and feast to your hearts' content, but I'm seeking my bed."

"A pity it'll be a cold one, Sir Jehan."

Jehan ignored Thibaud's gravelly laugh and strode out of the room. As far as Thibaud knew, Jehan had refused all offers of womanly comfort since conquering this castle. The aged knight assumed this abstinence was proof that Jehan had asked Aliénor to marry him. For Aliénor's sake, Jehan did not tell him otherwise.

Jehan could understand such foolishness from Laurent, for the boy knew little of the world, but Thibaud, of all knights, should know better. Thibaud knew what it was like to be landless and untitled, to live on the charity of a grudging relative or a demanding lord. When Jehan married, he would not marry a woman as impoverished as Aliénor, he would wed a wealthy wife—a woman with titles and a dowry.

He might take that step sooner than anyone suspected, certainly sooner than Aliénor expected. He hadn't told her the truth. If he had, she might not have agreed to become his mistress, and that was a risk he had not been willing to make. On the fields of Poitiers, the Prince of Wales had promised to offer him a certain wealthy, widowed Englishwoman as a wife as soon as the war with the French was finished. Jehan intended to accept the offer as soon as it was made, for it would double his holdings and secure his future—and the future of Aliénor and their children, for to him, they were all the same.

He wondered what Thibaud would do when he discovered that Aliénor warmed Jehan's bed—willingly, without the benefit of marriage vows. It didn't matter. He would rather lose a hundred such knights than give her up. She was unlike any woman he had ever known. She was brave and defiant, thirsty for life and full of passion, even in her innocence. She was like a bright, blinding light, wrapped up in golden hair and warm, fragrant skin. For so long, he had lived in the dark, ugly world of war. He knew only how to kill and destroy. He had spent the past few days watching her as she worked in and around the castle, rebuilding and nurturing and loving. She was everything soft and gentle and warm and compassionate, and she was his.

He could still hear the muted sound of laughter in the great hall as he climbed the stairs to the upper floor. He passed through the solar, where Aliénor's mother once slept, then reached the aisle between Aliénor's and Laurent's room. The top floor was dark but for a faint, orange glow spilling out from her chamber. He approached and looked in. A small fire burned in the hearth. He noticed that her maid's pallet was empty, as he expected. Esquivat and Margot had disappeared early in the evening. Jehan knew that Esquivat would keep the chambermaid well entertained that night, as he intended to entertain Aliénor.

He walked over the rushes to Aliénor's bed. He pulled the new linen hangings firmly aside.

He took a deep, sharp breath.

She lay propped against the pillows. Her honey-gold hair, burnished to bronze in the flickering light, spread across the white linen, spilled over her shoulders and mingled with the furs. She was naked. Her bare legs lay long and coltish on the rumpled pelts. He stood for a moment, drinking in the sight of her, so desirable, so vulnerable, so unprotected. The blood roared in his ears.

"I hoped you would come to me tonight." Her voice was as husky and dry as fire. "I wondered when you would love me again."

"The pain—"

"There is no more pain." She smiled, then rose to her knees and wrapped her arms around his neck. "There will never be any more pain."

He wound his arms around her; she was so small, so soft, so warm, so passionate. He would never be sated of his need for this woman. It grew, every day, to unbearable proportions, and more so now that he could have her, even if only in darkness and secrecy. She opened her lips and he tasted her, suddenly wanting more than anything to taste all of her. Her fingers struggled with the lacings of his tunic and he helped her, frantically, pulling off the wretched velvet that separated his body from hers, tossing his clothing upon the bed, yanking the linen hangings closed around them so they would be swathed in the soft darkness of secrecy.

He spread her thighs with his hands. He touched her and felt her passion, moist and hot. She gasped aloud, wrapped her arms around his neck, and pulled him close with all her strength. Her breasts softened against his chest. He tasted her desire: It flared as hot as his—it needed to be quenched *now,* or he vowed the world would tremble and collapse around him. He shifted his weight. He plunged into her, all fiery and moist and willing, and he gloried in her sweet cry of pleasure. His head clouded with need as she arched beneath him, driving him deeper, urging their bodies still closer together. He could barely restrain himself, and when she whispered his name, and shuddered like a silk pennon in the wind, he stopped trying. He buried his face in her shoulder and let his own passion explode.

When it was over, he gazed at her flushed features, waiting for those soft, gilded brown eyes to finally blink open. When they did, and he saw the joy and trust filling their depths, he vowed that whatever happened outside these castle walls, he would make sure that Aliénor would never—*ever*—have reason to regret becoming his mistress.

To the delight of every person in the castle, especially Aliénor, Jehan insisted on continual feasting from the *vendange* until the feast of All Saints, skipping a day only when the Church demanded it: on Friday fast days and All Hallows Eve. Aliénor found it hard to believe that she and all who lived in Castelnau were a conquered people. The days were filled with utter revelry. Jehan had invited a band of mummers from Toulouse to stay and regale them with plays, antics, and songs. Each night, the trestle-tables groaned under the weight of countless dishes, and everyone ate and drank his fill in the presence of the new lord.

Jehan claimed the feasts were to celebrate his newly acquired lordship. With unexpected largesse, he presented gifts to his new vassals in anticipation of future service. The castle servants and the villagers received meat, bread, bolts of cloth, wine, and firewood. Thibaud was given another coat of mail and a tunic freshly embroidered with the colors of Tournan. Laurent received a large Bible covered with tooled calfskin, made by the friars of the monastery he planned to enter. Jehan showered Aliénor shamelessly with presents: crimson brocaded silk, the finest linens from Rheims, Brussels longcloth, a gold girdle and circlet, *bishe,* the autumn fur of squirrel, soft leather for shoes—so many and such rich gifts that Laurent raised his brows in mild disapproval.

She accepted them all. It had been a long time since she had felt the smoothness of fine linen against her skin, the weight of a golden girdle around her hips. Nothing, not even the decree of the *Etats* of *Langue d'oc,* which prohibited the wearing of fine garments in order to mourn the capture of the King of France, prevented her from accepting Jehan's gifts. As soon as she had cut and sewn the first new garment, she ceremonially burned the two surcoats she had worn constantly for a year. She wanted to look lovely for Jehan. She wanted to hold his attention, to keep him loving her forever as she sensed he loved her now.

She knew the real reason for the endless feasts. When the trestle-tables overflowed with food and wine, the servants, villagers, and men-at-arms rarely wandered far from the great hall, and they slept early and soundly, in straw pallets along the wall or in the lower floors of the donjon. During the nightly revelry, she had ample opportunity to slip unnoticed through her mother's empty room and climb the stairs to Jehan's chamber on the top floor of the donjon. No one but his squire knew about her movements. Even her chambermaid was still in ignorance, for when Margot wasn't otherwise occupied, Aliénor padded her own bed, then drew the linens closed before slipping out. Margot had not yet caught her returning to her chamber before dawn.

Jehan's continual patience proved one thing beyond doubt: He loved her. She was sure of it, though he never told her. His love showed in actions, not words. He sought her company in the daytime, and as his visits grew in frequency, his reasons for finding her became more creative. Once he even joined her in the kitchens on the pretense of delivering, with his own hands, platters of meat left too long on the trestle-tables after the midday meal. His presence upset the servants so much that one woman nearly caught her apron in the hearth fire. His love showed most intensely at night, when he swept her in his arms, called her his enchantress, then took her, over and over, as if his hunger could never be sated. Aliénor began to wonder if, perhaps, someday— someday soon—she could be more to him than just a mistress.

She sat on her bed and carefully cut the outline of a new surcoat from a piece of shimmering, fawn-colored silk. She knew the ease of their secret relationship would end that night. It was the last of the feasts, the feast of All Saints. No longer would Margot sleep through her nightly roamings, nor would Laurent fall into bed sotted with wine.

Laurent. The dark cloud that hovered in the distant recesses of her mind came, suddenly, to the fore. During the feasts it was so easy not to think about what she had to do. She spent her days planning the meals, decorating the castle with the draperies Jehan had seized during his warring, arranging the upcoming slaughtering, smoking and salting, and preparing for the storage of foodstuffs in the lower rooms of the castle. The chores that filled her days, along with the glorious lovemaking that filled her nights, left little time to ponder the situation. Fortunately, Laurent spent most of his time in the small chapel, praying and preparing for the time when he would join the friary. Except for Mass, she rarely saw him. She could almost pretend that life could continue as it was now—with Jehan's love, and the continuing love of Laurent—and she could live as if she really were Jehan's wife.

"There you are. I thought you'd be in the kitchens watching the servants bake the soul cakes."

She started and twisted on the bed. Laurent stood in the doorway, wearing a fine woolen mantle trimmed with one of Jehan's gifts, lambskin. It was as if her brother had materialized out of her thoughts. "I was," she replied, fingering the fine silk, "but they seemed to be doing well enough without me."

"Sir Jehan sent me to fetch you."

All kinds of possibilities flowed through her mind. Her face flooded with color. "What is it?"

"There's a peddler in the courtyard, and his mule is well laden."

She jumped up, relieved. "Well . . . I hope he has wax candles. I'm tired of smelly tallow sticks."

"Sir Jehan depends heavily on you, *ma sor.*"

"Of course he does." She lifted the skirts of her violet velvet surcoat from the rushes as she walked toward the door. "What would a warring knight know about running a large estate?"

"He knows how to keep the coffers filled." He gestured to the discarded silk on the bed. "Another surcoat?"

"I'm making it for Christmas."

"Soon you shall have one for every day of the year."

Her chest constricted, uncomfortably. She took her scarlet mantle from the peg near the hearth. Wordlessly, she brushed past him and headed down the stairs. *If he thinks I sin by wearing fine clothes,* she thought as she wrapped herself in the thick squirrel fur that lined the cloak, *what will he think when he discovers I strip myself naked, nightly, for Jehan's pleasure?*

The rich, spicy scent of the freshly baked soul cakes

wafted out of the pantry. She passed through the aisle and entered the great hall, which was filled with men pouring freely from the casks of wine that lay tapped at the lower end of the hall. The fire cast a flickering light upon the tapestries that covered the walls. She tightened her mantle around her shoulders as she pushed through the door and braved the cold air. She skimmed down the stairs and passed some children playing a game of hoodman blind. Most of the villagers huddled near the kitchens, where the heat from the three enormous hearths spilled out into the courtyard itself.

She crossed the yard swiftly. Jehan stood near the portal, speaking to a dusty-footed merchant whose wares lay open in a large sack at his feet. When she had last seen her lover—in the faint, predawn light—his hair was amuss, his chin stubbled, his eyes half closed, and his body naked but for a few pelts. Now a thigh-length tunic and fur-lined hose covered his powerful form. His jaw was shaved clean of beard. He turned and looked at her. Absolutely no trace of sleepiness lingered in his eyes.

He walked toward her.

"Good morning, Aliénor." Her blood simmered as he lifted her fingers to his lips. "I trust you slept well?"

"Sleep?" she whispered incredulously. "Did *you* sleep, Sir Jehan?"

"I slept as well as I could," he said, lowering his voice, "with a glorious creature lying warm beside me."

"Last night was All Hallows Eve," she teased. "Perhaps you were plagued with the wandering spirits of the dead."

"This spirit was far from dead. She had very smooth flesh and very hot blood." His gaze slipped from the golden tresses flying out beneath her silken veil to her wide, open bodice. "She kept me . . . up . . . all night."

She tried not to giggle. "I'll have to speak to the women servants."

"This was no servant. She was far, far too demanding."

"Demanding?"

"She has lips of silk, and a body so lithe and agile—"

"You seem to remember the creature well."

"Only by touch. She disappears each morning, before the sun rises."

She heard the gentle rebuke. "You'd best beware." She tried to pull her hand away. "This creature might steal your soul."

"I think my heart is in more danger."

She drew in a deep, soft breath. They were in the middle of the courtyard. He shouldn't say such things to her, not here, not now. She wanted to weave her fingers in his hair and look closely into his eyes. She wanted to kiss him and show him that she had already lost her heart, completely, utterly, irretrievably. His grip softened on her fingers, and her hand fell limply from his. She tried to regain her composure.

"I assume you ordered me away from my fire into the cold for a reason." She tilted her chin toward the portal. "Do you want me to bargain with that peddler?"

"No. I bought a gift for you."

"Another!"

"Are you complaining?"

"Absolutely not."

The dimple deepened on his cheek. He turned and led her to the merchant.

The peddler bowed awkwardly, dust sifting off the top of his hat. "A good day to you, Vicomtesse de Tournan."

"I'm not the Vicomtesse," she said quickly. "I'm the daughter of the late Vicomte de Tournan."

"Begging your pardon, milady, but it's all the same to the common folk." He turned to Jehan and tilted his head toward Aliénor. "She'll look good astride the filly with all that hair. If those thieves hadn't stolen the match from me when I crossed the Garonne river I'd have sold you the pair."

"I've heard that the brigands grow fierce along the roads around Bordeaux."

"They're like the pox, they are! They're behind every tree and under every rock, hiding, waiting to steal a living from honest men—"

"You are safe here," Aliénor interrupted. "But if both of you continue to tease me, I'll water the wine to nothing tonight."

"You see, good man, that she's as fierce as she is lovely." Jehan smiled at her. "You'd best bring out my purchase before the lady challenges me to a joust."

The merchant gestured to someone near the stables. A page emerged a moment later, struggling with a fine, feisty mare.

Aliénor gasped.

"I don't want you riding a stallion anymore," Jehan explained. "I thought you'd want your own horse."

"She's lovely!"

The mare pranced as the page led her out into the open courtyard. Aliénor had not had her own mare since the Prince's men stole every horse in the castle last fall. When her father's six men-at-arms returned in the winter, they brought only their stallions. The poor beasts had since been worked to the bone both in the fields and in the hunt. This was a fine gift, finer than all the others. She approached the horse and ran her hand over the mare's fine blond coat.

"I've never seen a horse such a color."

"As rare as a pig with horns," the peddler said. "The color won't wash off, either, like some other horses whose coats are dyed to please a lady's fancy."

Jehan walked up behind her. She glanced up at him, over her shoulder. His eyes were as bright as the open sky. "If you continue to give me such rich gifts, Jehan, you're going to turn me into a spoiled little wretch."

"I'll test your true gratitude later, *brèisha.*"

"Another gift for my sister?"

She looked in the direction of the voice and saw Laurent approaching from across the courtyard. His leg dragged against the paving stones. "She's lovely, isn't she, Laurent?"

"She's worthy of a vicomtesse, *ma sor,* as were all the other gifts. You've found the way to my sister's heart, Sir Jehan."

"Have I?" He dared to toy with the edge of her veil. "That was my intention."

Laurent stopped in front of the mare. "It's a pity we can't return your generosity."

"Your sister thanks me with the brightness of her smile."

"It's a smile that comes easily these past weeks."

Aliénor tightened her grip on the reins. Over the past two weeks, Laurent had learned to use words like tiny little needles, and she was beginning to feel like a pincushion. "Are you surprised, *frai?* This time last year I was wondering how we would all survive the winter. Now there's food on the table, tapestries on the walls, and furs on the beds."

"Sir Jehan has done us well," he agreed calmly. "Your smile is as bright as the sun, and I wouldn't do anything to dim it."

She felt a flash of guilt.

"I just worry about your future," he continued. "Have you chosen, Sir Jehan, what will be my sister's fate?"

Aliénor started. Not once during the weeks of feasting had Laurent mentioned the question of her choice. He had promised her he would let her mourn, he would let her get used to the foolish, misguided idea of marrying Jehan. He had promised that he wouldn't plague her.

So he has finally thrust the dagger.

"That decision is your sister's," Jehan said.

"You're a patient knight, my lord."

Jehan lifted a brow. "I'm bound by promises made in unusual circumstances."

"Then I shall plead your cause for you."

"You sound more like an older brother," she snapped, "not the boy I used to bathe as a child."

Laurent flushed, a strange sight on a boy who was more man than child. "You cared for me when I was younger, *sor,* but now I'm nearly a man of God."

"And taking your responsibilities seriously, I see."

"The longer you stay in this castle, without planning to marry or join a convent, the more danger there is for sin."

Sin. There was so much glorious sin. She would never again stop sinning, stop celebrating all the wonder and joy of love. A love out of wedlock. An adulterous love. A love that, once admitted to her brother, would tear him from her side forever. The noose tightened around her neck. She felt Jehan's gaze on her. She stared at Laurent's honest, worried face. She should tell him, now, but they stood in the middle of the courtyard and every servant within earshot strained to hear her answer. She couldn't tell him here, not in public. Surely he deserved better than that.

"I was going to buy a stallion like this for you, Laurent," Jehan said, when Aliénor didn't answer. "But he was stolen from this merchant just north of here."

"I couldn't accept such a rich gift."

"He would have been your parting gift." Jehan ran his hand over the mare's blond coat. "It's long past time when you should be in that friary."

"It is long past time for many things."

"Enough, *frai.*"

"Aliénor, you should have been taken care of when Sir Jehan first claimed this castle."

"Aliénor is *châtelaine* here," Jehan argued, "and shall remain *châtelaine* until she chooses her fate."

"That's no position for an unmarried maiden."

"Hush, Laurent!"

Jehan gestured to her. "Does she look as if she is suffering?"

"No. She looks happier and lovelier than she's looked since Father returned from Italy last year."

"Peace, then!"

"It's that unholy joy, Sir Jehan, that I fear above all else."

She started. He stared at her with those dark, all-seeing eyes. *He suspects I've already lain with the knight.* Of course he sensed her sin. He had always sensed her faults. She wondered if the truth were branded on her face.

"The friars in Toulouse are waiting for you, and they have been for several weeks." Jehan dropped his hand from the mare and glared at Laurent. "My generosity wears thin."

"I've promised to stay here until my sister is settled." Laurent tilted his chin. "Not even you, Sir Jehan, can make me leave for the friary a moment before."

She watched the two men, the two men she loved above all others, and her heart sank. They stared at each other in animosity. They both loved her. They both wanted only the best for her, yet their desires for her fate were as far apart as Heaven and Hell. No matter what she chose, a convent or a leman's bed, she would lose one of them. She didn't want to lose either. She gave the reins of the mare to the page and walked to her brother's side. With surprising strength, he shook off her grip.

"Choose, *ma sor.*" He looked suspiciously at Jehan. "Choose before it's too late."

Aliénor slipped noiselessly through her mother's room, clutching the edges of her fur-lined mantle tight around her body. She was exhausted from the All Saints celebration, but not so exhausted that she would give up one moment of a night with Jehan. She could still hear the men in the great hall, discussing in loud voices all the news that Sir Rostanh had brought with him from Bordeaux.

Sir Rostanh was an unexpected guest. He was one of her father's vassals who had been captured at the battle of Poitiers. He had been released by the English after promising he would return the following spring with his ransom. Jehan welcomed him with unusual warmth. He offered to pay his ransom and return his lands if Sir Rostanh swore fealty to him. The knight agreed.

Sir Rostanh then proceeded to regale them with stories of the elaborate feasts held by the Prince of Wales in the King of France's honor. He told him what news he had heard from Paris. Apparently Charles, the eighteen-year-old Regent, was having difficulty with the *Etats,* a body of representatives called to approve taxes to raise his father's ransom. Charles ordered the riotous body to disband after they demanded he dismiss seven of his father's counselors and release the rebellious King of Navarre from prison. The

Etats refused to be dismissed, and the people of Paris were rioting in the streets.

To complicate matters, Rostanh had been told that the King of Navarre's supporters were trying to rally the Parisians to his cause; Navarre claimed he was the rightful heir to the throne of France. All in all, it did not bode well for France when a third of its noblemen were dead on the fields of Poitiers, a third under ransom, and still another third fighting against the Regent. Nor did it bode well to have a king in captivity, an untried young man holding the throne, and a pretender growing more and more powerful. The men discussed the dreary political events all night long, through the feast, through the minstrel's songs, until Aliénor could not stand it a moment longer.

She passed through the narrow hall that connected the castle proper to the ancient donjon. As usual, the floor below Jehan's was bereft of servants. She slipped up the stairs and pushed on the thick oak door. It gave under her hands.

"Jeh—"

He emerged from the shadows and pulled her hard into his embrace. He smothered her lips in a kiss. He tasted of hypocras. He was naked, and she thrilled at the texture of his hot, bare skin against her. He slammed the door shut, then yanked the mantle off her shoulders and tossed it on the floor. She wore nothing but a thin shift beneath it.

"I have been waiting for hours." He lifted her in his arms and brought her to the bed, the bed he had brought up from the solar, only days after *Maman* left for the abbey in Auch.

"Laurent was tossing and turning." She sank into the soft pelts. "I had to make sure he was asleep before I passed his room."

"One more minute and I would have come to get you."

"Don't!" She clutched his hand as he tore heedlessly at her shift. "I could never explain to Margot why my last one was shredded."

He growled angrily as he shifted his weight and pulled the shift up her thighs and over her head. He rolled it into a ball and tossed it toward the discarded mantle. His anger dissipated as soon as his hands touched her bare flesh.

"Brèisha . . ."

She moaned as his fingers traveled familiarly over her eager body. She had dreamed about this from the moment she left his side that morning. Every brush of their bodies, every innocent touch of his fingers, roused her latent passion and reminded her of what waited when the sun set and the feast ended. Now, finally, nothing constrained them anymore—no clothing, no shame, no fear of discovery.

"Sir Rostanh's squire stared at you all night," he murmured as he covered her, fully, the spray of hair on his chest grazing against her taut nipples. "I was ready to kill him."

"He's nothing but a boy."

"He's twenty."

"Hush." She ran her hands over the long length of his well-muscled back. "I am blind to all men but you."

His hands slid over her smooth skin, pausing to curve into her waist, to hug the swell of her hip, to bring her body closer to his. His lips covered hers. She curled both her hands into his thick, black shock of hair and caressed his head as his mouth moved over hers, saying in actions what could not be expressed in words. She kissed him with ardor—she had long learned this silent language of love— and now she told him with every small gesture that she wanted him, she needed him, she loved him.

He combed her tangled hair from her face. He kissed her forehead, her nose, teasingly brushed past her lips to kiss her chin, and lower. He paused at her breasts, and she protested weakly as he left their aching peaks to trail kisses over the flatness of her abdomen. She realized his intent. He listened to none of her feeble protestations. His weight held her legs open, wide, exposed. He clutched her hands as she reached for his shoulders.

"I will have you, Aliénor, in all ways."

She quivered at the first intimate brush of his tongue over the delicate softness of her. Her cheeks flushed as the stroking continued, shamelessly, endlessly. She closed her eyes as the pleasure undulated through her body. Was there no end to this, the joy of his lovemaking? Would he always surprise her? Would he always find a new way to bring her to greater heights, to love her until her heart burst with the feeling? He released her hands. She clawed the pelts by her sides. She moaned and pressed her cheek against the fur. His hands journeyed slowly up her body to caress her breasts. She could not bear it anymore: The ache grew too taut, and she needed him too much. She took his hands from her bosom and lifted them to her mouth. She kissed each callused finger until Jehan stopped his ministrations and pulled his body up until he covered her. She felt him, aroused, against her thigh.

Then she thought of something wicked.

Before he could adjust his weight and take her, she moved away from him. He groaned and tried to draw her back, but she kissed his collarbone and shifted away from his body. Her fingers slid over the ripples of his abdomen, lower, until she found what she sought. He laughed gruffly as her fingers curled around him, but his laugh stopped abruptly as she lifted her face to his and he saw the gleam in her eyes.

"It's your turn."

He sucked in his breath. She bent over and kissed that part of him. His body, the long, strong, muscular body that she had grown to know so well, suddenly shuddered and stiffened. She thrilled at the sense of power, as she tasted the length of him, as she fondled and enticed and experimented with her touch. He jerked with each new embrace, and his toes curled in desire. Finally he reached for her. He pulled her up forcefully, then laid her flat against the bed.

"Witch!"

She giggled, but he stopped her laughter with a kiss. He nudged her thighs apart. He probed for entrance at the heart of her body. Her breath caught in her throat as he thrust in her, tolerating no resistance, no restraint. He took her as he had taken her every night since the first. She tilted her hips and lifted her legs, aching with each driving stroke. He filled her with need and love. Soon his motions grew wilder, more and more uncontrolled. Her body throbbed in rhythm with his, pulsing faster and faster, until that sublime light exploded, until there was nothing else in her world but Jehan, Jehan who held her so close in his arms.

He stayed inside her. They lay entwined for a long time. Her fingers still dug gently into his back, as if fixed there by the force of their loving. Her hair swirled around them like a golden web. As their damp bodies slowly cooled, even his heavy form could not keep her warm. She shivered at the drafts whirling around them. He reluctantly slipped off her, then buried both of them under the mountain of pelts.

She snuggled against him and rubbed her nose between the muscles of his chest. He ran his fingers through her unbound hair, spreading the tresses across the furs. He wiped the perspiration from the nape of her neck, then trailed a finger down the indentation of her spine. Suddenly his arms tightened around her. Hard.

Her voice was muffled in his chest. "I can't breathe, Jehan."

"I don't want you to go."

"I'm not going anywhere." His grip loosened enough so she could look up at him. She thrilled at the possessiveness in his voice. "At least not until morning."

"Stay tomorrow morning. And all day. I want to wake up with you beside me."

"With Thibaud's sword poised over your throat?"

"I have nothing to fear from Thibaud. He already knows."

She gasped. "You told him?"

"When I insisted on leaving the banquet tonight, rather than drinking another tankard of wine with him, he glowered like an angry father."

"Oh." She sighed in relief. "He was just piqued that you preferred bed over his company."

"He knew it was more than sleep I craved." He buried a hand in her hair. "He'll know soon enough, Aliénor, as soon as you decide to tell him, and all the others in this castle."

She bit her lower lip. This afternoon, Laurent had expressed his worry; and tonight, Jehan showed the first open signs of impatience. She was squeezed between two mountains, and they were coming closer and closer, threatening to crush her.

"Two weeks is longer than any man would wait," he argued. "I want to claim you in front of all the world." He slipped his free hand around her waist until it rested on her abdomen. "And I want to claim you before nature no longer allows us to hide."

"There are some women who never grow big with child."

"You will." His fingers splayed over her belly. "I want you to bear my sons."

Her heart fluttered. She wanted his sons, too. She wanted as much of him as she could possess. But the thought of exposing her sin to Laurent, above all others, ripped and clawed at her heart, like a falcon tearing at its prey.

"I'm tired of sneaking around my own castle like a thief in the night. I want you in my bed when I wake in the morning."

"I've thought of a way," she said, hesitantly. "We could make arrangements for me to join a convent. Not real arrangements, just enough to convince Laurent that I'm provided for—"

"I'm not going to deceive your brother into leaving. I'd sooner throw him out."

"No!"

"Shall I allow a beardless boy to dictate how I live in *my* castle?"

"He'll blame you for this."

"Let him blame me—just tell him."

Her throat tightened and parched as tears pricked her lids. She suddenly realized she had spent two weeks hoping for something she did not deserve. She had hoped Jehan would realize that she would be a worthy wife. She had hoped he would make her an offer before she ever told her family the truth of their illicit relationship. She had hoped that somehow, in her arms, he could forget his cold, dark days in the hills of Gascony and, in gratitude, make her his wife.

What a fool she was: a naive, desperate fool.

"Couret . . ." His warm lips pressed against her puckered forehead. "Such dragons roar in your head. Let me slay them for you."

His voice was so soft, so full of concern. She closed her eyes against the tears. He was a good man, a patient man, a rare creature—a strong knight who deferred to the whim of a woman. She knew he would keep their relationship a secret for as long as she wanted, though he chafed at the delay. Perhaps, if she told him the truth, he would find a way to ease her fears.

She ran her fingers over the crisp curls on his chest. "He'll be ashamed of me, Jehan."

"Do you think the Prince of Wales's mistresses are ashamed? Or those of the French bishops? They are honored above some wives. Laurent is young and has much to learn, and the only shame in this, *couret,* is in hiding it."

"For years it was me who protected him. But since Papa left, Laurent has protected me. He takes his duties seriously."

"His duties are now mine. Let me explain that to him—"

"No!"

"You must love him dearly to hide the joy you share, nightly, with me." His arm tightened around her. "I hope, *couret,* that I can someday inspire such love from you."

"I chose you, didn't I?" She met his gaze evenly. "You must know, Jehan, that when I chose you, I chose you above all else. Including my brother. I couldn't bear it if he hated you, or if you hated him. I love you both, more than anything."

His fingers tightened on her hair. His eyes flared. She suddenly realized what she had said.

"Say it again."

She pressed her hand against his heart. "You teased me about losing your heart this afternoon, and I wanted to tell you then: I've already lost mine."

"Say it."

"I love you." Her voice grew husky. "But I love Laurent,

too. I must find a way to tell him that I've done what he always feared."

But Jehan wasn't listening. The arm that wound so tightly around her hardened like a band of iron. He kissed her as if he would merge their bodies into one, as if he could merge their souls by merging their flesh. He released her only so that he could run his hands over her skin, invading her softest, most intimate places with a urgency that left her breathless. Her worries about Laurent scattered away, driven like rabbits before a pack of hounds. It was impossible to think rationally when Jehan touched her like this, when he stroked her and moved his great muscular body until the world faded into the background and all that remained was the smell of him, the taste of his skin, the sound of his heart beating. She no longer wanted to think. She wanted only to feel.

She wanted, only, to love.

Chapter
15

ALIÉNOR WAITED IN THE SHELTER OF THE BOULDERS. THE *AUTAN* wind tugged at the edges of her fur-lined mantle. She glanced up, beyond the bare, twisted branches of an oak tree, and scanned the rolling gray clouds. Any minute, those clouds would burst and she would be caught in a chilling winter storm.

She didn't care. She needed to see Jehan. Four days before, the feasts had ended, and so had the ease of their clandestine relationship. The first night after All Saints, Margot had waited in Aliénor's chamber to help her undress before retiring and then gone to sleep on her own pallet. Aliénor had delayed going to Jehan until well into the morning in order to be sure her chambermaid was asleep. Her caution came to naught, for the servant caught her returning before dawn. Aliénor lied and said she had simply risen early, but she knew Margot did not believe her.

Suddenly she heard the distant sound of hoofbeats. She tightened her grip on the mare's reins and drew her behind the enormous boulder. Above the whistle of the wind and the loud scattering of debris along the forest floor, she couldn't determine the precise direction of the sound, nor the number of riders. Several days before, Sir Rostanh announced that he had seen a group of mounted and well-armed brigands on his way back from Bordeaux, not far north of Castelnau. She wondered if the thieves had wandered down into these lands. Her fingers curled over the hilt of the dagger that hung from her golden girdle.

The clatter of hoofbeats grew louder, and she distinguished the pace of two different horses. She watched with bated breath as the figures rode through the fencing of trees. She recognized the snarling head and the high-stepped stride of Jehan's destrier.

She stepped out into the clearing. Jehan saw her and straightened in his saddle. He pulled his stallion to an abrupt, violent halt. His squire jerked his gelding to a stop behind the larger beast, struggling to prevent a collision. Tersely, Jehan ordered Esquivat to circle the area and search for intruders. Jehan dismounted.

"I ordered everyone to stay in the castle for a reason, Aliénor." Jehan strode across the clearing, then picked her up and crushed her in his embrace. "These forests are dangerous."

"I knew you would come."

"Reckless, stubborn wench."

"It's been three long days."

"Why didn't you come to me last night?"

"Margot is suspicious."

"Tell her, as I've told my squire." His grip tightened. "Damn it, Aliénor, tell everyone! How much longer do you expect me to wait?"

She curled her fingers in the pelt of his hood. She had tried twice over the past three days to explain to Laurent that she was happy with her life, though she never told him exactly what duties, beyond those of a *châtelaine,* she performed. Laurent insisted that her current position was temporary; she must make a choice. Like a true Tournan, he dug his heels deeper and deeper.

"I've tried to persuade him to forget the silly vow he made a year ago, I've tried to persuade him to join the friary, but he won't listen." She rubbed her cheek against the wool of his mantle. He's stubborn beyond belief."

"If you wait any longer," Jehan said, his tone softer, "he'll hear it from the servants."

"I know." She closed her eyes and breathed in Jehan's scent, deeply, hungrily. "I lured you out here so I could tell you my decision. I'd rather face the scorn of a thousand men than live like this any longer. I'm telling Laurent—and the rest of the world—before the sun sets."

Whatever the consequences.

She felt the relief flood through his powerful body. He threaded his fingers through her hair.

"Will you stay with me," she asked, "when I tell him?"

"Yes."

"He'll hate you."

"I'll strangle him if he says anything that hurts you." He wrapped his mantle around her so they were both swathed in its folds. His dark hair, unbound, tossed in the breeze. "Come, let's get out of the wind."

They walked toward the boulders. Jehan sheltered her between his body and a high, smooth rock. Esquivat returned to the clearing and said there was no one in sight. Jehan lifted her chin with one finger. "We should return to the castle, *brèisha.*"

"Let's stay."

"You'll catch your death of cold."

"You can keep me warm."

"If I stay with you, I'll have you out of your clothes."

Her lips curved. "All the better."

Jehan ordered Esquivat to stand guard for a while, somewhere down the path. He forced her against the boulder. "I'm not setting a good example for my squire. I'm putting the virtue of a lot of innocent noblewomen in danger."

"If this is danger, my love, then they will be as grateful as I."

He kissed her. His lips rubbed cold and rough over her own. She wound her arms around his neck and warmed her hands in the fur of his hood. Impatiently, he thrust the edges of her cloak over her shoulders and crushed her between him and the rock. He was dressed in full armor. The links of his haubergeon, exposed beneath the edge of his tunic, nipped at the honey-colored velvet of her surcoat. He dug his fingers into her waist and lifted her high against the boulder.

"*Diou,* I've missed you."

She moaned in agreement. A fine rain fell on her upturned face. She clung to the width of his shoulders. He kissed his way down to her breasts. She could barely feel the heat of his mouth through the layers of linen and velvet. With one hand he impatiently unfastened the tiny silver buttons that ran down the front of the surcoat and yanked the edges aside. He bit gently at her nipple through the linen undertunic—a muffled, hot caress that teased her, that made her ache for the feel of his rough tongue stroking the bare, puckered peak. She wanted him to tear the precious fabric of her clothing into shreds. She wanted to be naked against him, though the wind chilled her skin and the frigid spray felt like tiny icicles on her cheeks.

This was madness. A winter storm groaned and threatened around them. Nothing shielded them from the rage of nature, or the sight of man and God, but a few bare, black boughs. The passion of days of restraint roared in her head. She couldn't halt the inevitable course of their loving any more than she could stop the tempest. Tears of frustration sprang to her eyes as she ran her fingers over his chest and felt nothing but metal plates beneath the cloth. Her hand slipped lower, to the edge of his haubergeon. She lifted the rows of links. Mindlessly, she unlaced the front of his hose, until she found the soft rope-bound edge of his braies. She slipped her hand under the edge. Her nails scraped his bare, flat abdomen.

"*Aliénor.*"

She opened her eyes. His hair was dark and slick with rain. His eyes shone so bright, so blue. Mist played around their bodies as it rose from the ground to greet the rain. He shifted until he held her firm against the rock, solely by the weight of his body. She removed her hand from its position dangerously close to *him* and clutched his shoulders for support. He slipped his hands up her legs, past the hose gartered above her knee, to the bare flesh of her thighs. She surrendered herself to him, without question. He clutched her buttocks, forcing her to lift her thighs and wrap them around his hips. He held her there with one strong arm as he struggled beneath the hem of his haubergeon. Then he lowered her. She gasped as he thrust into her, as hot as a brand.

She no longer felt the hard limestone boulder pressed against her back. He held her hips firm as he moved inside her. His lips slid slickly over the rain-washed length of her neck. She clutched his head and swept his hair away from his face as she kissed his forehead, his temple, as she lost all her senses. His haubergeon tugged at the crumpled skirts bunched between them. She didn't care. Already, at his first stroke, Jehan had brought her to the dizzying heights of love.

The rain pattered on the littered earth as she tried to catch her breath. The swiftness and intensity of the coupling stunned her. She could tell, from the way he still shuddered, that he was as overwhelmed as she. The wet tresses of her hair spread over his shoulders, as tenacious as ivy. Slowly, he unwrapped her legs from around his waist, eased her down, and brushed her skirts over her legs. With his fingers, he combed her rain-darkened hair away from her face.

"One of these days, *brèisha,* I'm going to make long, slow, deliberate love to you."

"Hmm?"

"I'm always ravishing you like a man who hasn't had a woman in years."

"Do you mean," she asked breathlessly, "that it can be better than this?"

"I don't know—I always want you too much to find out. I rode out here, fully intending to strangle you for leaving the castle." He looked down at her. "As soon as I laid eyes on you, standing in this clearing like some sort of fairy, with your hair blowing about in the wind, I could think of nothing else but making love to you."

"And I thought you were worried about my safety."

"Don't run off again, *brèisha,* or I'll lock you in my room."

"What a wonderful thought." She blinked as he wiped a trail of rain from her face. "Of course, if I was your *brèisha,* your witch, I would have called off the storm."

"You didn't create it?"

"*You* are the one who creates storms," she said softly. "You do it every time you touch me."

He kissed her. She heard a single set of slow hoofbeats. She wondered if Esquivat was just returning to the clearing, or if he had witnessed their lovemaking, only moments before, and was making sure he approached loudly so they wouldn't be embarrassed by his sudden presence. She didn't break away from Jehan's sweet kiss until the hoofbeats stopped in the clearing. Jehan stared deep into her eyes as he addressed his squire.

"A few minutes earlier, Esquivat, and I would have had your head for interrupting me."

Aliénor's blood froze as she heard the choked reply.

"It isn't Esquivat."

She started in Jehan's tight embrace, then twisted to face the intruder. Laurent sat high on his gelding with a sword dangling in one hand. "Laurent! What . . . what are you doing here?"

"I came to find you." He stared, stunned, at their intimate embrace. "Thibaud told me you rode out alone. I thought the brigands might have found you."

"Jehan found me," she said, nonsensically.

"Does this mean you'll marry?"

Laurent sat, waiting for an explanation. She looked into Jehan's vivid blue eyes. He spoke volumes of encouragement, though he didn't say a word. She was not ready for this, not now. She would never be ready for this. Jehan stepped away from her, then entwined his fingers with hers. Taking a deep breath, gripping Jehan's hand tightly, she turned to face her brother. "There is something I must tell you, Laurent—"

"By all the saints!"

She followed her brother's shocked gaze and looked down upon herself. Her surcoat gaped open to her waist, exposing the undertunic, and her velvet skirts were crumpled and ragged. Too hastily, and too late, she pulled her mantle around her.

Her brother's incredulous voice filled the clearing: "He has shamed you!"

"He hasn't shamed me!" Her thoughts ran through her head, like rabbits running away from foxes, emerging and disappearing and emerging again in a hurried, tangled chase. "There's no shame in it!"

"You must marry immediately, before the sun sets, before anyone discovers you—"

"There will be no marriage, *frai.*"

"But you can't enter a convent now!"

"I never intended to go to a convent."

"I don't understand. I thought—"

"I know what you thought. You thought I had a choice between a convent and marriage, but you were wrong." The blood rushed out of her head, making her feel dizzy and disoriented. "The choice was between going to a convent and becoming his mistress."

A strange silence echoed through the forest, despite the gusty wind, despite the debris that swirled in confusion around them. The color slowly ebbed out of her brother's face. Laurent looked at Jehan in disbelief.

"You . . . you promised to protect her, to care for her like you cared for the rest of us."

"I *am* caring for her."

"You . . . you raped my sister."

She snapped, "He did no such thing!"

"Your dress speaks for itself—"

"I chose his bed, *frai.* I gave myself to Jehan of my own free will."

"Without the vows of the Church? Without the sanction of God?"

"Yes." She hugged her mantle around her. She looked at her brother for as long as she could, forcing herself to face the sickening, growing horror in his eyes. "There it is, Laurent, what I've been trying to tell you for weeks. Don't hate me for it."

"I don't hate you, *sor*. You are blood of my blood, heart of my heart."

She caught her breath.

"This . . . this isn't your fault." He shook his head stubbornly. "You were innocent before he came. You were grieving over Father's death when he spoke in your ear like the Devil—" He choked on his words. He turned to Jehan, his pale face flushing with sudden anger. "I came here to save her from brigands. Now I see she was taken by the worst brigand of all!"

Aliénor saw Jehan stiffen. Laurent's barb dug deep, far deeper than her brother could know.

"Your sister," Jehan said stiffly, "will be well cared for."

"Well cared for!" Fury exploded in Laurent's eyes. *"As your who—"*

"Don't!" Jehan surged toward him swiftly, gripping the hilt of his sword. "If you say it I'll kill you."

"No!" She clutched Jehan's arm. Tears surged to her eyes, wretched tears, tears of despair as she restrained her lover from hurting her brother. The echo of what Laurent had almost said reverberated through her mind.

Her brother ignored the knight between them, the knight gripping his weighty sword. He leaned over the saddlebow and pleaded with her. "You mustn't do this, Aliénor—"

"I already have, *frai.*"

"You'll burn in Hell."

"If God will punish me for loving him, then I shall be punished."

"Do you realize what you're doing?"

"Yes, yes!" She shook her wind-blown hair out of her face. "I love him. I can't leave him, *frai*, not while I live."

He kicked his horse back, away from her. He looked terribly, fatefully like their father in the deepest of rages, but this was worse, for it was a virgin fury, tainted with betrayal. Esquivat, hearing the commotion, rode into the clearing from the opposite path. Laurent ignored the squire and glared at Jehan.

"You blinded us—all of us! You made us all think you were a chivalrous knight. You promised her protection, then, like the snake in Eden, stole her virtue and her honor."

"Your sister has made her choice," Jehan said. "Nothing you can do or say will change that."

Laurent looked at Aliénor. His voice was deadly calm. "You know what I must do."

Grief surged in her heart, overwhelmed her, stole from her the power of speech. She knew what he must do. He must ignore her existence, never joke with her in the afternoons as they romped through the forests, never break bread together over the same table. He must act as if she were already dead and buried.

"I feared that someday, *ma sor,* I would have to save you from yourself."

He whirled his mount around. Her chest constricted until it was impossible for her to breathe. This was her brother, the child she had drawn out of dark, dirty corners, the child with the large, fearful black eyes, the boy who, in the course of a few moments, had turned into a man. Flesh of her flesh, *heart of my heart.* She cried out his name, desperately, through the rain, through the wind, but it was too late.

Laurent had galloped out of the clearing.

"So that's the way of it, is it?" Thibaud sat by the hearth in the great hall. The fire blazed behind him. He looked from Aliénor's tear-stained face to Jehan's unwavering stare. "I've suspected this for a long time, but I thought you'd marry her before anyone else discovered you."

"Quiet, *oncle.*" She took a dry mantle from a servant's hands and wrapped it around her shoulders. "I've heard enough blame. I don't need anymore from you."

"It's you who should be quiet, woman. Are you shameless? Don't you understand what you've done?"

"Leave her alone," Jehan snapped. "Save your anger for the one who deserves it: me."

"At least you admit it. But I'll not absolve her of guilt, for she said that she came to you willingly——"

"I love him, Thibaud. What would you have me do? Hide myself in a convent? I prefer dishonor to that slow death."

"At least you recognize this for what it is."

"You've suspected for weeks, *oncle,* by your own admission. You could have stopped us, if you wanted to."

"I thought he'd marry you."

"You grow foolish with the years. I have no land, no title, no dowry——"

"Because *he* took them." He peered at her more closely. "Are you carrying his bastard?"

"No." She flushed. "I don't even have that to give him yet."

Thibaud frowned, then fixed his fierce gaze on Jehan. "She's a woman, and thus has all a woman's weaknesses. But I expected more from you."

"Easy, Thibaud. I allowed Laurent to curse my name, but he's not a knight. I'll challenge you to the sword despite your age."

"If I were a younger man, like Laurent, I might snap up that gauntlet."

"Stop, both of you!"

"Quiet, woman." Thibaud stood up. "You have the mark of shame upon you now."

Aliénor gasped as Jehan pulled his sword from his baldric and settled the point in Thibaud's throat.

"Watch how you speak to your *petite nièce,* Sir Thibaud. You will find that I guard her, and her name, as jealously as any wife's."

"For how long?" Thibaud's black eyes blazed fearlessly above the long length of glimmering steel. "Until you find a wife? What then, Sir Jehan? Will you bring your wife in and march her in front of Aliénor? I'll be here, then, watching her die with a broken heart."

"This castle is hers—I have promised her that. She'll never have to leave it and I'll never bring a wife here."

"Your wife may say differently."

"My wife will have castles of her own. She will listen to what I say."

"Stop, stop, stop!" Aliénor cried, sickened to the core with all this talk of wives. "Put your sword away, Jehan, for my sake, and Thibaud—enough! There is nothing you can do. I have made my choice. Don't be such a fool to risk your head for nothing."

Thibaud lifted his empty hands to his hips. "I won't challenge him. I'm not such an old fool that I don't recognize a lost cause when I see one." Jehan withdrew his sword and put it away. "I just hope Laurent has as much sense."

"We must find him."

Thibaud shook his head. "You won't find him. When your brother left this castle to look for you, he was a worried boy. When he came back, he was an angry young man. He won't return."

"But . . ." Aliénor looked imploringly at Jehan. "The forests and roads are swarming with brigands."

"We've sent out a dozen men-at-arms to search for him," Jehan said, "and he has less than an hour's start. We'll find him."

Then, despite the servants that hovered near the buttery, despite the presence of Thibaud, glaring at them, despite the room full of men-at-arms, Jehan took her in his arms. "In the meantime, Aliénor, it is time you took your rightful place by my side."

"Yes, Jehan."

"There will be no more secrecy in this castle."

Jehan woke as the first feeble rays of sunlight seeped through the thin skin covering the window of his chamber. Instinctively, he reached for Aliénor. He pulled her close, seeking warmth from her small, soft body in the frigid chill of the morning. She curled defenselessly within his embrace. He listened to the even sound of her breathing. She lay so peaceful, so still and calm. He was afraid to move. He didn't want to wake her and force her to face the pain that had been a part of her life for two long months.

Laurent was still missing. Jehan had expected to find her brother the same afternoon he raced away. But the rain obscured the boy's path thoroughly, and his men wandered through the hills for hours in vain. As days passed, and Laurent still did not return, Aliénor's despair grew worse. Jehan knew the only thing he could do to comfort her was to find her brother, so he joined the men in the search. Over the weeks that followed, he sought the boy who hated him with all his heart. He asked about Laurent at every bastide from Pavie to Mirande, at every monastery, every village, and every church in between. No one had seen him. The boy had simply disappeared into the hills, leaving no footprints, no sign of fires or hunting, absolutely nothing behind. As November turned to December, Jehan no longer searched for a young man, but for a corpse.

Two weeks before, at the start of the Christmas feasts, Aliénor had finally asked him to halt the search. *He must be hiding from us,* she said. *He must not want to be found.* Jehan realized that her love for her brother was so strong that she was unable to accept the truth: No one could survive two cold winter months in the war-torn hills of Gascony. He feared that love. He feared that someday she would blame him, her lover, for her brother's untimely death.

She shifted against him as if she sensed his restlessness. He kissed the top of her head and traced her bare, narrow back with his fingers. He had never cared for a woman this much. He wanted to ease her pain, a pain she buried deeper and deeper as the months passed. He wanted to make her smile and laugh, without the ever-present shadow of grief. He felt powerless. All his strength, all his power, all his wealth, his connections with the King of England, his prowess in war—they were useless in the face of Aliénor's sorrow.

She stirred anew. Her hair spilled over the pelts like rivers of honey, and he brushed a wayward tress from her face. She opened her eyes and blinked up at him.

"It's morning, *fée.*"

Her lips curled in a smile. "I can't be a fairy, my love. I'm still by your side."

"Good."

"Must we rise?"

"No. There's still time before Mass."

She shifted her position, and he felt the fullness of her breast against his side. He wanted her. He always wanted her in the morning, when she lay pliant against him, when her skin smelled musky and womanly. She had become a part of him so swiftly and so completely that he wondered what he would do when the Prince of Wales called him to fight by his side again. He was not sure he could leave her for a single day.

Her stomach growled. Jehan laughed softly. "Your appetite, my love, is voracious."

"Mmmm."

"How can you be hungry? We feasted well last night, during the Epiphany."

"My stomach knows Lent follows not long after."

"Then I'll have to fill you with almond milk and plump trout once Lent starts if I'm ever to get any sleep."

"I hate fasting. It reminds me of last winter."

"This Lent *won't* remind you of last winter, that I promise you."

She snuggled closer and he watched her lips curve into a seductive smile. "What of the other fasts, Jehan? I understand that a man and woman must abstain from all their hungers during this time of penance."

He tightened his grip around her and drew her up until her face was level with his. "If I must fast during the day, my love, I will surely feast in the evenings."

"And the mornings?"

"Especially the mornings."

Much later, he pulled the furs over her flushed body and

nipped the curve of her shoulder. The morning light was stronger now. He stood up from the bed, tied his braies, and slipped his arms into his shift. His breath formed a mist in the chilly room. Through the thick walls of the donjon, the faint sound of activity rose from within the castle. Soon the churchbell would ring and call the villagers to Mass, and he would escort Aliénor into the small chapel, as he had every day since Laurent disappeared.

Jehan watched as she untangled her limbs from the furs and rose from the bed. The golden glow of morning bathed her skin as she stretched her arms high over her head, unabashed at her glorious nakedness.

"Ride with me today." He had a sudden urge to see her racing over the hills with her blond hair unbound and flying in the wind. "We can bring your new goshawk and train him to the lure."

"Have you forgotten something?" She searched for her shift on the floor. "Today you must mete out petty justice to your vassals."

He groaned. He *had* forgotten. Once a month he was obligated to sit in the carved oak chair in the great hall and listen to his vassals argue about whose chicken belonged to whom and who'd killed someone else's sheep and who had moved the border stones one step deeper into someone else's holding. He hated this part of his new lordship. He was tempted to distribute swords among the garrulous peasants and allow them to settle their differences in blood.

"Have you thought about what you are going to do about the blacksmith's son?"

Jehan remembered the dispute. The servants had talked about little else over the past weeks. In this tiny village, it wasn't often that a young girl became pregnant out of wedlock. "I'm going to make the bastard marry the girl he seduced."

"You mustn't do that!" She slipped her arms through the sleeves of the shift and let the fine linen drift over her curves. "Constance hates Isarn."

"She's going to have his child."

"That doesn't matter," she retorted. "Isarn is a cruel, arrogant boy who should be punished for what he has done—but Constance is innocent in all of this."

Jehan lifted a brow. It was common knowledge that a woman had to enjoy the act of lovemaking in order to conceive a child. That, more than anything Isarn said, condemned the girl and admitted her crime. But he had long learned that his wife was wise in such matters, wiser and more patient than he. He walked up behind her, pulled her against his body, and nuzzled her ear. "I see you've already considered the matter, *couret.*"

"Constance is in love with a boy named Hughes, a boy she has known since childhood." She hugged his arms around her abdomen. "He still wants to marry her, despite the child, despite Isarn."

"But Constance's father is pressing for marriage with Isarn."

"Only because he knows that if it's a forced marriage, he won't have to pay the full bride's price." She tilted her head back and looked up at him, her eyes all golden and warm. "There is a way you can make Constance happy, punish Isarn, and give Constance's father what he wants."

Jehan smiled slowly. He kissed the curve of her cheek. "You are a devious wench."

"Isarn deserves much worse."

"Yes," Jehan mused, "but making him provide for Constance's dowry and pay for the bridal feast will be a fine turn of justice."

Her eyelids fluttered closed as he nuzzled her neck. "How wise a husband I have."

"And I, how cunning a wife."

Her throaty laugh was drowned out by the sound of someone knocking at the door.

"My lord?"

His squire's voice rose high and uncertain. "What is it, Esquivat?"

"I think you'd better come down to the ramparts, my lord. There's a line of armed men marching toward the castle, from the east."

Jehan looked down and met her startled gaze. He released her and reached for his haubergeon. "I'm coming."

Brigands. Questions passed through his mind in rapid succession: How many? How well armed? Who leads them? He pulled on the heavy chain-mail shirt and tied the leather laces, then reached for the overtunic emblazoned with the colors of Tournan. Until now, he had only heard of a few instances where brigands attacked castles. He wondered if they had grown so bold that they would challenge a castle of this size, of this strength, held by a Gascon with English loyalties. If these were the same brigands that scoured the area all winter, the men released from the Prince of Wales's service, then he might even know the leading knights among them.

He glanced at his chausses, then reached for his baldric with its sword and dagger. There would be time enough, after he checked on the men who approached, for his squire to arm him more completely. He approached the door. Aliénor rushed to his side, hastily buttoning a tunic. He handed her a mantle and they left the chamber together.

He heard the cries of the men-at-arms on the ramparts as he descended the stairs to the lower floor. He crossed the empty room and walked out into the cold, early morning air.

Dawn cast a pale gray glow over the barren hills of Gascony. A group of men marched in the valley. It was a small contingent. Half of them were on foot, carrying pikes in their hands. Only a few of the mounted men wore armor bright enough to gleam in the dim light; the others rode helmetless, and their horses were bare of war trappings.

"There's not much to them, is there?" Aliénor commented, watching the sad-looking group. "I wonder what they want."

"They can't possibly hope to seize the castle." Jehan turned when Esquivat appeared at his side. "Has the leader been identified?"

The squire glanced uncertainly at Aliénor.

"She's faced brigands before," Jehan said. "You don't have to hide anything from my lady's ears."

"He's carrying the Tournan standard, my lord."

"*What?*"

"It's blue and green, in quarters, with an eagle in gold."

Aliénor gasped aloud. She pushed by the men and raced to the edge of the ramparts. She leaned over the limestone wall, her unbound hair flying in the breeze. "No, no," she murmured, staring at the line of approaching men. "It can't be . . ."

He walked up behind her and followed her gaze. The leader rode a horse that, even from this distance, looked vaguely familiar.

"My God," she said breathlessly, lifting her hands to her face. "It's my brother, Jehan. It's Laurent."

Chapter

16

ALIÉNOR SQUEEZED HER EYES SHUT. HER BROTHER COULDN'T BE approaching Castelnau now, after two cold winter months alone and unprotected in the ruined, perilous lands of Gascony. The sight was a cruel trick of her mind, an image conjured up from months of worry and anguish and dwindling hope. She blinked her eyes open. The figure was still there, as real as the slap of the icy wind against her face. He's an impostor, she told herself. Laurent rarely rode so swiftly, and he never rode standing up in the saddle. There was no humility in his horse's brisk stride. Then she saw his twisted foot lying at an awkward angle in the horse's left stirrup.

Laurent had returned to Castelnau.

She gripped the edge of the wall. For weeks she had feared he was dead. She waited each day, in dread, for Jehan's scouts to come back with his body. She prayed more fervently than she had ever prayed before, surprising Father Dubosc with her regular attendance at Mass and her frequent trips to the chapel. *Laurent is alive.* He rode toward her, vibrant and unharmed. She bowed her head as relief flooded over her and drained all the strength from her body.

"Are you all right, *couret?*"

She turned and buried her face in Jehan's chest. "I can't believe it."

"Believe it, love. I recognize the stallion."

"These past months, when he didn't return, I thought he was . . ."

"I feared the same."

"He's here now. He's here." She breathed the scent of damp wool emanating from Jehan's mantle. It will all be better now, she thought. There will be no more anger and hatred, no more shame and guilt. Laurent will see how happy she is in Jehan's care. He will see that she is a wife in all but name, that she has more love than any woman could ever hope from a husband. Then she will beg Laurent's forgiveness for not telling him sooner, for delaying the inevitable until he discovered her shame in the most painful fashion. "*Diou!* There's so much I have to say. I don't know where I'll begin. I'll hug him first. I'll hug him so tight that I'll hear his heart beating."

Jehan remained silent for a moment. "You'll have to wait for the reunion, Aliénor. He won't be coming into the castle yet."

She looked up at him. His gaze flickered from her to the approaching riders. She feared, for a brief, stark moment, that he would spurn her brother's apologies. Certainly, that was why her brother returned to Castelnau. He came to apologize for racing away, for saying such ugly things to Jehan that day in the clearing. "Forgive him, Jehan, for my sake."

"Your brother never should have left here without sending word to you of his safety."

"Then forgive him for that," she urged, "as I have. Let him reenter his home."

"A man doesn't approach a fortress with an army when he wants to beg forgiveness, *couret.*"

"Army?" She glanced over her shoulder at the group of men, half on foot, who approached. "That's not an army!"

"Not a strong one, I agree, but it's an army nonetheless. Complete with foot soldiers armed with pikes and a small group of men-at-arms. *English* men-at-arms." His voice lowered. "By the looks of them, brigands."

Her eyes widened in fear. She turned back to the approaching men. "Maybe he is a prisoner."

"A prisoner doesn't ride at the head of an army. And he doesn't bear his own standard."

"But there's no other explanation."

"Yes, there is." Jehan grasped a strand of her hair held aloft by the wind. He wound it around his finger. "Your brother came to fight."

"Laurent loathes fighting!"

"It seems he's overcome that loathing."

Jehan's gaze was steady on hers, blue and bright and determined. She pulled away from him and glanced around the castle. Villagers swarmed in the courtyard, and men-at-arms lined the walls. The portcullis was down and the drawbridge raised. Her blood chilled to ice. "You're preparing for siege!"

"As I would when any strange army rides to the walls of my castle."

"This is no strange army. This is my brother!"

"A brother who hates me for what I've done to you." He took her arm. "Come."

"No." She dug her heels into the cold stones. "I'm staying. I must know why my brother approaches so."

"It'll be halfway to prime before Laurent arrives at the portal. Come with me while I put on my armor."

Giving her no opportunity to argue, he pulled her toward the donjon and called for his squire en route. He led her up the stairs, through the doorway of their chamber, and released her as he closed the door behind them. She stood, motionless, in the middle of the room. She watched Jehan pull his tunic over his head and unlace his haubergeon. When Esquivat arrived and began gathering the pieces of Jehan's armor, she walked to the eastern window. She picked and clawed at an edge of the oiled skin until she peeled a section away, then peered into the valley where the last of the men followed Laurent's standard. When they left her sight she released the oiled skin and leaned back against the wall.

She wondered where Laurent had hidden these past months, why he had never sent word to her of his safety, and, most of all, why he had waited so long to return. She remembered, abruptly, that today was the day after the feast of the Epiphany. It was the end of the truce of God—the ban against private warring during holy days.

Suddenly Laurent's words came back to her.

You know what I must do.

Aliénor shook her head. It was too preposterous to believe, too frightening to consider, but even as she denied the possibility, she realized that it would be just like Laurent to follow the dictates of the Church in war as he did in life.

"He's come for you, Aliénor." Jehan spoke from the chair near the hearth, where Esquivat tightened the supporting laces of his chausses at the knees. "He's come to save you from me."

"No—he must be here to . . . to tell us he's alive." She wound her mantle around her body. "Perhaps he's found a position as a squire in another man's castle."

"Bearing his own standard?"

"He can't be here to save me from this," she said, nodding to the comfortable tangle of their room. There had been so much glory in their couplings, so much love in her life these past months, despite her brother's abrupt departure. Not even the chaplain had murmured a word when her position became known. It seemed that he, like many of the villagers, condemned Jehan, not her, for her fall from grace. As a result, everyone treated her as the new lord's respected wife. "If my brother has come to save me from dishonor, Jehan, it's a tardy, misguided cause."

"It's a cause I intend to see he loses."

She started at the angry tone of his voice. He stood up. His thick black hair curled against his neck. She watched Jehan lift his mighty arms as his squire buckled his coat-of-plates. Jehan pulled his tunic over his head. She approached him as the squire laced the garment up the sides. She did not know what to say. She did not know how to convince Jehan not to harm her brother, the man who now approached this castle with an army.

She stopped in front of him. He waved away his squire.

When the door closed behind the boy, he pulled her into his arms. "I wonder," he said. "Who do you care for more, Aliénor? Me or your brother?"

"How can you ask such a thing?" Her voice was muffled. "I love you both."

"Your brother may ask you to leave me, *courect*. To go with him to a convent."

"I made that choice months ago."

"Then you may lose your brother."

"No! I won't lose him. I'll have you both. You'll reconcile, with time."

"After what I've done to you, I don't think your brother will ever forgive me."

"You've made me happier than any woman in Gascony. Why should Laurent hate you for it?"

"Couret . . ." His hands slid beneath her mantle and moved over her thin silk tunic, warming her back far more effectively than fur or wool. "Your brother is mad if he thinks I'll let you go."

"I'll make him understand."

"No matter what you say to him, he'll always see me as the instrument of your disgrace."

"I've never heard such foolishness. I came to you as willingly as an eagle to its roost."

He clutched her tighter and kissed her hair. "He's a fool to come to this castle like this."

"He's a boy."

"No one who raises an army—even a tattered, weak army—can be called a boy."

She pressed her cheek against his chest. She hated the feel of his armor beneath his tunic. She hated the steel arm plates that pricked her back. She suddenly realized she was pressing her cheek against the eagle of the Tournan heraldry, and she thought, *How ironic it is that the two men I love shall wear the same colors into battle.*

Then, just as quickly, she thought, *There must not be a battle. My brother must not fight my lover.*

She looked up at him. "Tell me you're not going to fight him."

"If your brother attacks like a knight, I must treat him like one."

"You are a knight," she argued, "but he's not. He's only fifteen years old."

"At fifteen, the Prince of Wales was knighted on French soil and soon after fought at Crécy."

"The Prince was raised as a knight! My brother wasn't. If you fight, you'll kill him!"

"I won't kill him—that I swear."

She pushed out of his embrace. "Then promise me you won't fight him at all."

"If Laurent insists on a battle, *couret,* I can't refuse the challenge and still call myself a man."

"I will never understand men!" She turned and paced in front of the hearth. "Such foolishness, such purposeless, angry gestures—"

"Though I don't like the situation, your brother is fighting a just cause."

"But you know he's wrong!"

"It's a worthy gesture, nonetheless, to fight for the honor of his sister. If I were your brother, I would have done the same."

"Which only shows that both of you are as mad as rabid dogs!" She stopped her pacing in front of him. "If you understand him so well, then certainly you can find some way to force Laurent to give himself up, *if* he insists on battle."

"He's as stubborn as you. Perhaps more. There's no way to avoid a fight without giving up honor, as well."

"I don't care a bean for honor!" She stepped closer to him and spread her hands over the blue and green colors of his tunic. "I know you can find another way. You managed to lure my father out of Castelnau last year and seize a fortress that's never before been taken."

"Only because your father was prone to mindless rages."

"And you managed to avoid burning this castle, without risking the anger of the Prince."

"Circumstances, Aliénor."

"Then, last fall, you recaptured this castle from me, as cleverly as a fox." She dug her fingers into the fine gold stitches of the eagle of Tournan. "Certainly you can trick a fifteen-year-old boy into surrendering to you, without a battle."

"You'd rather I trick your brother, than see him fight like a knight?"

"He's no knight. He's a boy who should be in a friary by now, who thinks he's doing the right thing for his sister." She stood on her toes. "Please, Jehan. He's young and brash. Don't make him pay dearly for some misguided cause."

He brushed a strand of hair from her cheek, then tilted her chin. "I can't promise you this, *couret.*" He kissed her softly. "But I will promise to try."

Jehan sat in a large carved wooden chair near the blazing heat of the hearth. The great hall was as silent as a church despite the crowd of men in the room. The chaplain stood in front of him, his robes bespattered with mud. He had just returned from Laurent's camp, on the edge of the open field in front of Castelnau.

"Is that *all* Laurent wants?" Jehan asked. "Just the lands and castle of the Tournan estate, my sword, my spurs, and the release of all I hold prisoner—including his sister, Aliénor de Tournan?"

"That's the sum of it, my lord."

"He is, indeed, his father's son." He rose from the chair. "What of his men?"

"The foot soldiers are nothing more than peasánts," the chaplain explained. "But the mounted men are seasoned fighters. There are a dozen of them. English, by their accents. As I spoke to *Senhor* Laurent, they hovered around us, eager for battle."

"Fool! He's enlisted the help of brigands to take this castle. Has he lost his senses? Doesn't he realize that if, by some miracle, they managed to enter this fortress they'll destroy it?" He looked directly at Aliénor, who stood by the buttery, a bright swath of violet velvet in the shadows. "And what of her? What does he think those brigands would do if they set eyes upon her?"

He ran a hand through his hair. The situation was worse than he expected. Laurent couldn't take this castle by force, not with the size and quality of his ragged army, even with the addition of the brigands; but the presence of those Englishmen made the situation dangerous and difficult. Jehan had originally planned to trick Laurent into entering the castle in peace. Now he knew those plans were impossible. The brigands would never allow Laurent to give up a fight: That would deny them the only chance they had of plunder and pillage. Jehan frowned. He preferred a quick, decisive battle. He knew how easily he would defeat Laurent's pitiful army. The peasants would fall like sheaves of wheat, and he and his vassals could overwhelm the brigands with sheer numbers. The incident would be over before midday and Laurent would be a sullen prisoner in the tower.

Yet he knew he could not attack, at least not yet, at least not until he had used every other nonviolent possibility, for Aliénor's sake. Laurent could easily be wounded, perhaps fatally, during a battle. She would never forgive him if he harmed her brother. He had to persuade him to surrender without bloodshed. At the same time, he had to preserve Laurent's honor if he ever wanted Aliénor's brother to be reconciled with him. It was a tangled web. He didn't know how separate the threads.

"He is very self-possessed, Sir Jehan," the chaplain continued, hesitantly. "I've never seen him like this. He's determined, he is without doubt or fear. He's even somewhat in control of the mounted men who follow him."

"His cause is just, good chaplain." Thibaud's usually booming voice was oddly subdued. "He believes that God is on his side. How else could an impoverished, crippled boy of fifteen gather an army in two months?"

"He lured them with the promise of reward and pillage," Jehan argued. "There's no other way to recruit mercenaries."

"Laurent is as impoverished as any peasant. He would never allow them to destroy his home. He's young, but not a fool."

"He's desperate and has nothing else to offer."

"He can offer them honor. You know that those brigands were probably knights in the Prince of Wales's employ, released after the battle of Poitiers. They have no other way to live but by brigandry. After so many months of pillaging, they might have found some salvation in Laurent's cause."

"You make this sound like a damned crusade."

"To Laurent," Thibaud said, "I expect it is."

Jehan clutched the hilt of his sword. "Then go join your great-nephew, Thibaud. But know this: First you must break your vow of homage to me."

"Fie!" He shook his white mane of hair. "I've seen enough battles to know that the righteousness of the cause bears little effect on the outcome."

"Then make your point."

"I want no war between my lord and my great-nephew."

"I want no less, but *your* great-nephew threw the gauntlet. I'm doing what I can to avoid picking it up." He released the hilt of his sword. "If you know a way, then tell me. Otherwise, hold your peace."

"There is a way."

"Speak!"

"Marry Aliénor."

The words echoed in the hall. Jehan's fingers curled into fists at his sides. He should have been alert to this tactic; he should have been wary of Thibaud. Of course he would suggest such a solution: It was simple and saved family honor and prevented a battle all at the same time. He had walked blindly into his trap. Aliénor stirred near the buttery. He couldn't look at her. He felt an intense flash of fury at Thibaud for suggesting this in her presence.

"Laurent demanded I release his sister, not marry her," he argued. "He also asked for this castle and these lands."

"He's an intelligent boy: He knows to ask for more and settle for less." He tilted his head toward where Aliénor stood in the shadows. "You know, as well as I, that the boy is doing this for her sake."

"Marriage is out of the question."

"Is it, Sir Jehan?"

"You should understand above all others."

"God's bones, I may be a poor vassal in your castle, but I never had a castle of my own!"

"Obviously."

"Is this fine fortress not enough for you?"

Thibaud was like a dog biting into a piece of flesh, stubbornly clamping it between his jaws, holding on until the skin bled and tore away. What enraged Jehan was that the person who would suffer most from Thibaud's persistence was Aliénor. "I will not cut the throat of my prospects."

Thibaud lifted a bushy brow. "So the Prince has already promised you a wife."

"I've served him well."

"Your ambition blinds you."

"Your lack of it blinds *you*. I won't spend my old age impoverished in another man's castle. Nor will I risk the future of my sons—"

"Your *legitimate* sons."

"—to satisfy the misguided whim of a powerless boy." Jehan clutched the back of the carved wooden chair. "I won't toss my future away because a child has thrown a tantrum outside my castle walls."

"If you fight Laurent, you'll lose what you now have."

"If I fight the boy, I'll crush his forces."

"You will lose Aliénor."

"She is *mine.*"

The aged knight looked at him, glanced into the shadows, where Aliénor stood, then shook his shaggy head. "For a knight of your cleverness, you know little about a woman's heart."

"I don't need the tired wisdom of an old man," Jehan said, painfully aware of Aliénor's presence, furious at the aged knight who had pulled words from him that should never have been spoken. "If marriage is the only option you offer to save your great-nephew's life, then guard your tongue." He gestured to the head watchman. "Exactly how many men does Laurent have?"

"Thirty-two, Sir Jehan."

"Provisions?"

"Light. But the Arrats river is high and there will be plenty of fish."

"Are they making preparations for attack?"

"Not yet."

"They will." He glared at Thibaud and the others. "The brigands will grow bored quickly if we forced them into a siege."

"Siege!" Gilles stepped forward. "My lord, if we attacked we could wipe them away like a swarm of flies."

"I won't shed Tournan blood, not if I can help it."

"If it comes to that," Thibaud interrupted, "I'd rather be thrown in the tower for treason than fight my own blood."

Jehan frowned. Several men-at-arms, the late Vicomte's men, nodded behind him. "If those twelve Englishmen manage to enter this castle, not even Laurent in his saintly state will be able to prevent them from pillage," he warned. "You shall guard the ramparts if it comes to open battle."

Thibaud reluctantly nodded.

"This is what we will do: The brigands won't like the lean rations or the cold weather and will probably leave for easier quarry if we refuse to budge from the castle. Once they leave, only pride could keep Laurent here with those peasants. We'll deal with him then."

Gilles shook his head. "I still say we should attack."

"What honor is there in fighting serfs? Or a beardless boy with a misguided sense of justice? I won't fight, not until I have no other choice." He gestured to the chaplain. "Go.

Tell Laurent that I refuse to surrender to his terms. Tell him that there are no prisoners here, and that if he surrenders, he will be welcomed without harm."

"Tell him this, also."

Jehan turned. Aliénor walked into the circle of men. Her gaze settled on the chaplain. She no longer wore the black veil she had worn every day while Laurent was missing. A golden circlet rested on her brow, over a sheer violet silk veil. Despite the change in colors, she looked more in mourning now than she had all winter. Her eyes were red and swollen. His heart lurched. He wanted to ride out and batter her damned stubborn brother for causing her so much grief.

"Tell him that you've heard these words from me," she said to the chaplain. "Perhaps it will make a difference. Tell him that I, his sister, am here of my own free will. I'm not a prisoner. Tell him if he persists he will cause nothing but grief. Tell him . . ." She faltered. "Tell him that I beg his forgiveness, and that I plead with him to disband his men and enter this castle, unarmed, and surrender to the mercy of Sir Jehan."

Thibaud walked to her side. "He's doing this to save to your honor, woman."

"I didn't ask to be saved." She tilted her chin. "Win or lose, when this is all over, I will still be Jehan's mistress."

Three days later, Aliénor paced in her chamber—her old chamber—while Margot folded her tunics and placed them in the chest at the base of her bed. Aliénor wore only a shift as she walked back and forth in front of the hearth. She poured the interlocking links of her gold girdle from one hand to another, worrying with them like rosary beads.

"You should get into bed," Margot admonished hesitantly. "You'll catch your death dressed as you are."

"My brother is camped outside this castle, in the open, far colder than I am."

"He could be here, too, *damaiselo*. If he chose."

"*Diou*, I wish he would choose." For three days the

chaplain had traveled back and forth from Laurent's camp to the great hall. While the chaplain relayed the messages, she hovered nearby, in the shadows at the bottom of the stairs. Each successive missive shocked her more. They insulted Jehan's name, his parentage, his honor, his prowess in battle. She was convinced these messages came from the Englishmen, not her brother, but the chaplain vowed on the name of every saint that he'd received the words directly from Laurent. What madness had struck her brother that made him call for Jehan to fight like a knight? Could this be her gentle sibling, who never used profanity, who begged forgiveness from God at the slightest transgression?

When Jehan finally came to bed last night, she asked permission to ride out and see Laurent. Certainly, he would listen to her, she said, if she pleaded for him to leave. Jehan refused her request flatly. He argued that Laurent had already heard her message, through the chaplain, and had spurned it. Jehan knew that if she rode out to speak to him, Laurent would seize her as his prisoner; then she would be in danger from the English, who were already growing restless outside the walls. Jehan refused to listen to any of her pleading.

She frowned and tossed her girdle to the floor. Jehan hadn't so much as touched her in three days. She wanted things to be as they were before Laurent returned to the castle: She wanted Jehan to rise with her in the morning, to hold her while he slept, to retire with her at night, to treat her as a well-loved wife instead of a mistress whose brother had returned to fight for her honor. Since Laurent arrived, Jehan spent all his time with his men. He hardly spoke to her. He grew more and more impatient as he waited for the English brigands to become bored with the siege and leave. She knew the inactivity went against his nature. He was doing it for her—she was the cause of his restraint—and it was yet another thing that had come between them since Laurent arrived. Tonight, she had moved all her things out of their room. She would return to his bed when the whole situation was over, and she didn't feel like such a . . . such a *mistress*.

There was something else, something she had tried not to think about since Laurent arrived, but it came to her nonetheless, in the darkest, loneliest part of the nights. Three days ago, Thibaud had suggested that if Jehan married her, Laurent would stop his senseless siege. Jehan had refused. She knew all the reasons. Marriage was for wealth and power, not for love. That was the way of things. She suspected that the Prince of Wales had already offered Jehan another woman as a wife—a woman with status and dowry—and it would be foolish for Jehan to forgo such a marriage for her sake.

Yet she could not help thinking that it would be such a perfect solution. Her honor would be saved. Laurent would be satisfied. There would be no battle. Jehan and Laurent would be bound by blood and the Church. She would have a name for her children and Jehan would have a wife. Would he truly be giving up so much? He was the Vicomte de Tournan, with vast lands and a dozen landed vassals, and the estate was firmly in his hands, yet he still could not get the taste and the fear of brigandry out of his mouth. She knew he loved her; he had shown his love in a hundred ways over the past months. Hadn't she run this castle as efficiently as any wife? Hadn't she given herself to him, willingly, in spite of the shame that sometimes lingered when she entered the chapel, or when she walked alone among the villagers? Why, then, was she feeling this overwhelming, crushing sense of worthlessness?

"*Damaiselo,* you are shivering."

She turned to Margot and realized she was still standing, half naked, in front of the fire. She walked to the bed and dragged a fox fur off the pile of pelts. "I'm going to sit by the fire for a while."

"Should I bring you your sewing?"

The pieces of a *mi-parti* surcoat she had been embroidering for Candlemas Day lay upon the chest at the end of the bed. She had abandoned it when Laurent arrived, and now she had lost all taste for it. "No. No sewing tonight. You may go."

Margot headed toward the door. Suddenly she cried out and scurried out of the room.

Aliénor glanced up. Jehan's silhouette filled the portal. His eyes were like hot blue flames.

"Why are you here?"

She tightened her grip on the fur. "I'm sleeping here."

"Your bed, Aliénor, is in the donjon."

He crossed the room. He wrapped one arm around her shoulders, slipped the other beneath her knees, and swept her off her feet. The pelt tumbled out of her stiff fingers and fell to the floor. "What difference does it make where I sleep?" She clutched his shoulders for support. "You haven't warmed my bed for three days."

"Ah, my mistress complains." He carried her bodily out of the bedchamber. "If you wanted me, *bréisha,* you had only to touch me."

"You are always so angry—"

"You look at me as if I'm your brother's executioner."

She gasped as he shifted her higher in his arms. "If I argue with you it's because you won't even let me speak to him."

"I won't put you in danger. And I won't let you go." He carried her through the solar, then through the hallway to the donjon. He started up the stairs. "Your brother curses me to Hell for doing to you what I'm going to do to you right now. Perhaps he's right. Perhaps I'll burn in Hell for taking you like this." His grip tightened as he pushed the ancient oak door open. He deposited her on the bed and covered her body with his own. "I vow it's worth eternal hellfires, *bréisha,* to feel you beneath me like this."

He pulled the shift off her body. His lips and hands and fingers touched her everywhere, everywhere at once. She wove her fingers through his hair. She pressed his head closer to her swelling breast, then to her arched throat, then to her parted lips, as he kissed her with utter abandon. For three days she had ached for his touch. He found all the moist, quivering hollows of her body and plundered them mercilessly. He tore his own clothes off and tossed them to the wooden floorboards. His naked body covered her own. The hair on his legs and his chest brushed against her tender flesh. She felt the heat of him throbbing against her abdomen. His kiss was urgent, feverish, rough, and glorious. She missed him. She loved him. She needed him.

Now.

"Nothing will stand between us, Aliénor. No walls, no clothes, and definitely not your brother." He wrapped his fingers in her hair as he entered her. "You're mine, *bréisha.* Always. Mine."

They awoke to the sound of cries filtering in through the window. Jehan rose quickly, like a warrior, and covered her naked body with pelts before he opened the door and yelled down the stairs for his squire to come help him arm. She watched from the big canopied bed as Jehan stoked the fire until the pale orange light flooded the chilly chamber. He did not meet her eyes.

Esquivat burst in, his hair awry, wearing nothing but his shift and a sagging pair of hose. He skillfully kept his gaze averted from the bed and walked to where Jehan's armor was stored. Jehan pulled on his hose, his braies, and then lifted his shift over his head. The squire handed him the padded undergarments for his armor. Jehan asked, curtly, what all the noise was about.

"The men are riding around the castle, cursing the watchmen on the ramparts."

"They're finally getting bored."

Esquivat laced Jehan's haubergeon, then buckled him into his coat-of-plates. When he'd finished, Jehan stretched into his tunic and laid his swordbelt over the chair. "Go, Esquivat. Wake the rest of the castle and tell them to go to their positions and watch—just watch." He glanced at Aliénor, then just as quickly glanced away. "And get Margot. Tell her to bring hot water for her mistress, enough for a bath."

Esquivat closed the door quietly behind him. Jehan stood by the hearth, one hand placed flat above the fireplace, with his back to her. A draft toyed with the lower edge of his linen tunic. She watched him, waiting, wondering why he was so quiet, especially after the night they had just shared. She flushed at the memory. He had certainly made up for three days of abstinence. Every time she drifted off into a languid sleep, he woke her anew, as feverish with passion as the moment he'd carried her in.

"Did I hurt you last night, *couret?*"

She lifted a brow. So that was the cause of this silent deference. He was rough last night, incensed with desire to the point of madness; but even in the midst of that ravenous passion he had not hurt her. She smiled, slyly. "I don't know if anyone has ever died of pleasure, Jehan."

He turned. He saw the teasing light in her eyes, and all darkness left his face. "*Ai*, Aliénor." He walked to the bed and sat on the edge. "I was afraid I'd find you covered with bruises."

"You can be very inventive in your anger."

"You should never have taken your things out of this chamber."

"If it will lead to more nights like that," she teased, "then maybe I will."

"Don't. This is your bed, this is where you belong."

"I'll tell Margot to return my clothes."

He dragged himself up, over the furs, and pulled her, and a number of pelts, into his embrace. "When I found you gone, I thought you had slipped out to see your brother."

"I've considered it." She nuzzled the curve of his shoulder. "I just want him to understand, and to stop this foolishness, so everything can be normal again."

"If you defy me in this, I shall attack Laurent and his men, for no other reason than to get you back."

"Is that a threat? To keep me here?"

"Yes."

"*Ailas*, Jehan, I never want to leave."

Margot knocked on the door and entered. She turned to leave when she saw Jehan and Aliénor entwined on the bed, but Jehan ordered the chambermaid to come in. She wobbled in under the weight of two pails of steaming water. Aliénor knew immediately that Margot must have planned this bath since last night, when Jehan carried her out of her old chamber, for it took much longer than a few minutes to warm two pails of water. Margot deposited the buckets near the fire. Esquivat followed with an old wooden tub. He set it by the hearth so it stood close to the flames, then he left. Margot poured the water into the bath.

"I have to go and see what your wretched brother is doing." Jehan rose from the bed and brushed his hand against her cheek. "Take your bath, *couret*. I think you'll need it."

She watched him as he buckled on his baldric and left the chamber. Margot left soon after to get more water. Rising naked from the bed, Aliénor tested the water with her toe, then sank into the narrow bath. Margot returned soon after with two more pails of water.

Jehan was right: She did need the soaking. The warmth eased the soreness in her thighs. Humming a song she'd learned from a minstrel during Twelfth Night, she scrubbed her hair, using a precious bar of the herb-scented soap Jehan had given her for Christmas. She felt warm and well-loved, secure again in Jehan's need for her. It was simply a matter of time before he realized that she deserved to be his wife. If she could only speak to Laurent and make him understand. . . .

As the water grew cold, she rinsed herself off, then stood up and dried herself with the large linen Margot handed her. Shivering despite the blazing fire in the hearth, she slipped into a shift while her skin was still damp, then covered it with a rose-colored tunic. A darker, velvet surcoat followed, and then Margot gartered her hose just above her knee. She sat on the stump by the hearth as Margot combed through her soaking hair with a silver comb—another gift from

Jehan. When her hair was nearly dry, she rolled it up into a gilded net, linked her golden girdle around her hips, reached for a fur-lined mantle, and headed out of the chamber.

She descended the stairs. A man-at-arms kneeled by the arrow-slit window, peering out into the dim blue light of dawn. His quiver of arrows lay ready by his side. She frowned, crossed the room, and pushed open the door to the ramparts. The cold January air swept over her, chilling her ears to ice.

Thibaud, suddenly, was beside her. "Why is it, woman, that I always find you on the ramparts before a battle?"

She started. "Battle?"

"There'll be one, if these Englishmen have their way."

She followed Thibaud's gaze. She saw the dark shapes of three horsemen hovering by the corner tower.

"They've been riding like sorcerers since the first light of dawn, calling Sir Jehan a coward and scorning his honor. They want a battle, they do." He clutched the hilt of his sword. "By God, they'll get one if they continue."

She looked at her great-uncle sharply. "Will you raise arms against your own blood?"

"I won't touch Laurent, woman—you should know that." The wind ruffled through his mane of white hair. "But those creatures aren't men. They're animals scenting blood, and your brother can't control them any longer. He's been seen riding among them, trying to talk with them."

"If we fight them, we will have to fight Laurent."

"Sir Jehan has waited longer than any knight should." Thibaud took her by the arm firmly. "Go inside. The things they are yelling are not fit for your ears."

"I'm not an innocent maiden anymore, as you well know." Just then, she heard one man below yell an obscenity up at the southeast tower. She gasped. "How dare they!"

"They've called him worse."

"The swine!"

"Sir Jehan has heard it all, yet he still refuses to fight. He allows these fiends to insult him and curse him, making him look like a coward." Thibaud frowned as he looked at her. "More than I would do for any woman."

She felt a flash of guilt but quickly stifled it. It had to be worth it, to keep Laurent out of the danger of battle. "The taunts of brigands aren't worth Jehan's attention."

The three riders kicked their horses into a gallop and rode the length of the eastern walls. One of them pointed in her direction. Thibaud cursed loudly. He pulled Aliénor away from the edge of the ramparts. It was too late. She heard them distinctly as they yelled up through the thin, misty, early morning air.

"Putain. Putain de St. Simon."

Thibaud shoved her toward the door. "Go, Aliénor. Go before they yell louder and Sir Jehan hears them. His tolerance has worn thin enough."

She was too shocked to move. She stumbled back as she heard their cries grow in volume, as other riders came around the corner of the castle and joined in the refrain. *Whore.* They'd called her a whore. *St. Simon's whore.* These couldn't be Laurent's men. Laurent would never say anything like this, he would never order his men to call her, his only sister, a whore. The wrought-iron strapping on the door dug into her back.

Putain. Putain de St. Simon.

Jehan was there, suddenly, a large looming shape in the bluish light of dawn. He glanced at her, at Thibaud, then he glared over the edge of the ramparts, to the growing group of horsemen. The words turned into a chant, a refrain, that grew louder and louder. She could do nothing but put her hands over her ears and pray that they would stop. She was ashamed to the core, ashamed to hear the word screamed aloud in the virgin light of dawn.

He took her by the arms. "Come, Aliénor."

"They aren't Laurent's men—they can't be."

"Laurent can no longer control them." He pushed her through the oak door. "Get inside."

He closed the door behind them. Even through the thick

walls of the donjon, she could still hear the refrain. Jehan turned to the man-at-arms crouching by the window slit. "Tell my men to prepare to ride."

She gasped. "No, no, no, Jehan! They taunt you like this just to get you to fight. Laurent would never tell them to say such things.—"

"They could insult me until Judgment Day, and I wouldn't fire a single arrow. But they've insulted you and I won't stand for it."

"I don't care what they say about me!"

"I do." He forced her to face him in the shadows of the donjon. His chin was tight, his cheeks lean, and his eyes blazed with a strange, intense emotion. "Listen to me, Aliénor, for I have said this to no woman—nay, never expected to say it to any woman." His grip tightened. "I love you, *bréisha*."

She wondered why he chose to tell her such a wondrous thing now, when so much else was happening. "I know, Jehan."

"You know?"

"Yes. I've known for months." She brushed the mist off the front of his mantle. "You wouldn't treat me so well if you didn't love me."

He shook his head. "I should have known that you would see it more clearly than I."

"What does this have to do with my brother?"

"It has everything to do with your brother." He tightened his grip on her shoulders. "For the love of you, Aliénor, I swear I shall do everything in my power to keep Laurent from harm. But mark me: I can no longer stay inactive and call myself a knight."

She stared at him, mute, as he answered her fearful, unspoken question.

"Yes, Aliénor. I'm going to fight."

Chapter
17

ALIÉNOR STOOD ON THE RAMPARTS. THE FRIGID *AUTAN* WIND
swept open the edges of her mantle, exposing her body to the
bite of the cold. She couldn't feel it, no more than she could
feel the hardness of the wall pressed against her abdomen, or
the icy stones stealing the warmth from the soles of her
slippered feet. All she felt was a looming sense of doom. She
stood frozen like a wooden doll, staring out over the
limestone wall, waiting for fate to unfold before her.

Thibaud paused behind her. He hovered, as if debating
whether to order her to leave the open battlements and go
into the castle, where she would be safe from stray arrows.
He mumbled something under his breath and continued on
his way. She heard the jangle of chain mail, the discordant
clatter of metal against metal, the restless, anxious clicking
of many hooves, all rising from the crowded courtyard
below. She did not turn around. She knew Jehan's men were
now mounted and armed, prepared to ride out to face her
brother's pitiful contingent. There was nothing she could do
to stop them.

She had tried. She had argued with Jehan until her throat
was raw. She insisted that he was falling directly into the
brigands' trap by riding out into open battle. Jehan argued
that he had already delayed more than any knight should,
that he could not allow the brigands to sully her name, that
there was no other possible way to end this standoff. In
truth, she could no longer blame Jehan for attacking. Her

anger and frustration focused on her brother, her stubborn, foolish, reckless brother who now stood only fifty meters in front of the castle.

She stared at the peasants lined up near the edge of the clearing, close to where the muddy earth gave way to craggy limestone and made a precipitous drop to the village below. Had Laurent never learned, during all the battles in Gascony, that the righteousness of a cause rarely had an effect on the outcome? Did he truly think that his pitiful band of commoners armed with rusty scythes and crudely hewn pikes could defeat Jehan's well-trained, well-armed, well-mounted knights? This battle had one possible end: merciless slaughter. She could only hope, and pray, that in the heat of battle none of Jehan's men-at-arms forgot his orders to leave Laurent unharmed.

She wondered, as she thought back to the day when she first made the choice to give herself to Jehan, if this battle weren't inevitable. She sensed the hand of God in the unrolling of time. Both men were driven by forces that surpassed common sense, compassion, and constraint. It was not in the power of a mere woman to stop destiny.

Her heart was empty, numb, and exhausted. She breathed in the winter scent of frosted earth as the watchman in the portal cried that all was clear. She heard the squeak of pulleys as the portcullis rose and the drawbridge lowered. Around her, archers strung their crossbows. Upon Jehan's cry, the strings twanged and a spray of iron-tipped arrows pierced the ground in front of the portal. The archers reloaded as the first riders poured out of the castle, and then they sprayed the open ground again, preventing Laurent's men from approaching.

Her gaze was drawn to Jehan as a traveler is drawn to a distant light. The Tournan colors draped his horse and shone bright and stark in the dawn. Her heart lurched a little, threatening to crack the tough shell she had erected around her. This was the man she loved above all others, the man who, just this morning, told her he loved her. This was the man whose babies she longed to bear, whose love she needed as others needed food and wine. The scene unfolding before her was so unreal, so incredible, that it seemed more like a mummer's play on a grand scale than a battle between the two men she loved above all on Earth.

Such meaningless pageantry. The horses poured out of the castle, forming a graceful line, as the portcullis squealed downward and the drawbridge drew up behind them. She would never understand knights, or war, or their twisted sense of right and wrong, of honor and dishonor. She watched as Laurent's peasants surged forward, clutching boiled, waxed-leather shields. Jehan pulled his sword from his baldric and held it high over his head, a banner for his men to follow into the fray. The two lines crossed the boggy earth, one on foot, one well mounted, until finally they clashed. She didn't wince as she heard the first cries of pain of man and beast. She didn't turn away as she saw a pike pierce the dark flesh of one of the horses, nor did she swoon when a knight sank his sword into a peasant's shoulder and the man fell to the ground like a weight. She listened to the horrifying sound of metal against bone, the grunts of exertion, the neighing of wounded horses and the sucking noise of hooves struggling in the muddy earth. She forced herself to watch every bloody movement, to witness with her own eyes the battle she had done everything in her power to prevent.

She wondered why the brigands didn't join in the fray, but rather stayed back, with Laurent, watching the slaughter. The peasants aimed their weapons not at the knights but at the mounts. She thought, abstractly, *How wise of Laurent, to try to unhorse and exhaust the knights so they would be at greater disadvantage when the brigands attack,* then wondered what madness had struck her brother to make him agree to such a worthless loss of life.

Her gaze unconsciously sought Jehan. An arrow hit him in the shoulder and he jerked back, but the point had not pierced his coat-of-plates, and it hung useless, caught in his tunic. He brushed the arrow away as if brushing away a persistent fly. He stroked and sliced through the battle, clearing the peasants around him who aimed mercilessly for his mount. This was the Jehan she knew so little about: the warrior the Prince of Wales admired, the bachelor knight who'd risen to power by the strength of his sword arm. Could this blood-spattered warrior be the same man who, through the previous night, had made love to her with utter abandon? How could any man give death, and life, with such equal passion?

She shook away the thought, for it cracked her defenses anew. She refused to feel anything—*anything*—until this was all over. If she allowed herself the luxury of feeling, she knew she would crumple into a hurt little ball—or, worse, scream like a madwoman and launch herself into the heart of the fray. She must control herself, for a little longer, until this senseless fighting was over. *It will not be long,* she thought. The greater part of her brother's peasant army already lay dead or wounded and groaning in the mud, slaughtered like pigs in November. Several of Jehan's men-at-arms broke away from the fighting and headed toward Laurent and his brigands. Laurent lifted his sword high in the air and cried out; she could not hear the words across the field. The brigands spurred into action and galloped toward the men-at-arms.

She smelled battle lust. It smelled like warm blood and dying flesh, a thin but tenuous odor on the wind. Battle cries rang in the air as the brigands and Jehan's men finally met, sword to sword. Jehan kicked his horse away from the peasants who plagued him and headed directly for the brigands—for worthier foe. His eagerness to attack the mounted enemy was obvious in every taut, muscled line of his lean, tall body. She watched as he raised his shield and warded off a brigand's blow, then, with lightning swiftness, struck back at the brigand with such force that the tip of his sword pierced his opponent's mail, drawing a stream of blood.

A peasant ran up beside Jehan and struck him in the leg with a dagger. With one sweep of his arm, Jehan knocked the man off his feet and sent him flying several lengths to the ground. Two brigands closed in. One struck Jehan hard on the shoulder with the flat of his sword. Jehan lifted his shield to ward off another blow, then struck swiftly, disabling one of the brigands. Jehan whirled around, keeping both men in his sight, guarding his bruised, numbed, struck side and waving his bloodied sword in his other hand. She watched his lethal, graceful movements as he stood up abruptly and surged to the left, toward one of the brigands, striking him so unexpectedly and so hard on the chest that the Englishman toppled from his horse. Then, without a pause, Jehan surged in the opposite direction and sliced the other brigand's horse on the neck. Jehan backed away and waited, warily, for another man to strike.

She saw Laurent riding on the periphery of the skirmish. She dug her fingers into the grainy surface of the stone wall. She knew what he was doing. She knew as surely as if she and her brother were of one mind, as if he had told her his plans before the battle itself. He sought Jehan in the melee. He sought the one man among thirty who slashed and stroked his way through the brigands as if they were nothing but a thick, tangled forest through which he was determined to cut a wide path. Laurent suddenly stopped. *No,* she thought. *No. Laurent.* He ignored her internal screaming.

Her brother approached her lover from behind.

Blood pounded in her ears and filled her head with pressure. The air thickened around her, making it hard to breath. She watched the last, dying movements of the battle in a sort of wavering haze, as if it were a dream. She sensed she would always remember this moment passing precisely like this, like a *danse macabre,* made up of perfectly repeatable steps. She was frozen in space, forced to watch the terrible display before her, powerless, voiceless, hopeless.

Laurent and Jehan wore the same colors. As her brother moved in behind Jehan, he looked like a distorted mirror image of the larger knight. He stood up in his stirrups, stretched his young body to its full height, and put all the weight of his twisted, crippled form behind the blow. Her brother's sword crashed against Jehan's back, slicing the embroidered neck of his tunic and drawing a thin red line of blood. Jehan jerked forward, then straightened in surprise. He rose to his full, mighty height on the stallion, his bloodstained thighs straining with his weight, just as Laurent had done only moments before. She watched the warrior she loved lift his gleaming, three-foot sword. Reacting by instinct, without looking behind him, he sliced a hissing arc through the air, through the mist, through the man who had struck him.

Laurent clutched his chest as blood, like a great, blossoming rose, spilled out from beneath his hand. Jehan stared at him, then dropped his sword.

Aliénor fell to the ground like a stone.

Jehan sat by an empty hearth in the dark, cold upper room of the donjon. He thrust his bloody hands through his hair, settled his elbows on his thighs, and bowed his head. He heard the thick oak door squeal open.

"Get out."

He spit the words out, bitterly, not moving from his stance. He wanted no help removing his blood-splattered armor, no woman tending his superficial wounds, no squire bringing him food or wine. He wanted to sit in the cold and dark and dirt and blood and stare into the stained emptiness of his soul. He had already thrown out his squire twice. What must he do to let these fools know that he had lost all sense of reason?

Must he kill another man?

He closed his eyes. He remembered every detail of the moment as if it were etched on his mind. The battle had gone well, as he expected. During a brief moment when he wasn't under attack, he saw Laurent staying, wisely, outside the fray, safe on the edge of the clearing. It was almost over. There were few brigands left. He remembered the stench of earth and torn flesh. Blood pumped hard through his body and battle lust raged in his head. He struck at each brigand, thinking all the time of the name they called Aliénor. *Putain. Putain de St. Simon.*

Then someone struck him from behind, hard enough to rattle his chain mail and drive the links into his neck. He thought the Englishman he had just unhorsed must have somehow found his mount. He didn't think for long. He simply reacted, as he always did during battle, rising up on his horse, his sword out and ready. He remembered seeing the faint rays of the sun shining on a cap of honey-blond hair as he twisted. Something tightened inside him, removing the blood-red haze of his battle lust, just for a moment, long enough for him to realize that the man who stood behind him was not a brigand but someone else, someone who had the same fair hair as Aliénor. Long enough to realize what was about to happen but not long enough to deflect his blow or stop the momentum of his heavy sword. He remembered watching in a horrified daze as his sword tore through a single layer of ancient, rusting mail, tore through something else, something soft, before finally he grasped enough control to pull it back, pull it away, to toss it to the ground as he watched Laurent teeter on the saddle, wide-eyed, clutch his chest, and slowly fall to the muddy earth.

"I bring word of Aliénor."

He jerked his head up. Thibaud stood in the portal, his white hair glowing eerily in the dim room. Jehan stared at the aged knight, into the black, Tournan eyes, and realized they were just like Laurent's eyes: the eyes of the boy he had killed on the field of battle this morning, the eyes he had closed in death with his own hands.

"Your squire told me you nearly broke his neck tossing him down the stairs so I thought—"

"Has she awakened?"

Thibaud nodded. "She hasn't said a word, not a single word, though the women wail around her." He shrugged heavily. "The grief will come, in time. She does as well as any woman can, any woman who has just lost her only brother."

Jehan stood up and paced around the room. His *sabatons* clanked against the wooden floorboards. *She hasn't said a word.* Nothing indicated her grief to him more deeply than this ominous silence. He preferred that she weep aloud, that she wail like the other women; or, better, that she find so much hate and anger in her that she would charge to his room with a dagger and try to strike him, the man who killed her brother. Then he was sure she would survive the pain. When a woman as passionate as Aliénor closed up her grief inside, he knew the pain would fester more quickly than any wound of the flesh. The thought of her agony clawed at him. He wanted to storm out of this donjon and wrap his arms around her, force her to express her anguish. For the past two months he had watched her bury that torment deeper and deeper while she waited for word of Laurent's death. Within five days, she discovered that Laurent was alive, that he had raised an army against her lover; and then she saw her brother die by her lover's hands.

"God's bones, it's cold in here."

Jehan stared at the aged knight and blinked away the clinging fog of his thoughts. Thibaud closed the door. He walked toward the hearth and tossed a split log into the dying fire. He lowered his tallow candle and tried to light the dried, ragged bark. Jehan wondered why the knight stayed, why he bothered to bring news of Aliénor, when it was obvious that Jehan was nearly blind with anguish and fury. He peered at him through the gloom. "I killed your great-nephew today."

Thibaud gestured to Jehan's leg. "You should let one of the servants tend that wound in your thigh before it festers."

"Did you hear me?"

The aged knight rose to his feet as the bark sparked and flared. He placed the tallow candle on the mantel. "I know you killed Laurent today."

"Is that all you have to say?"

"God's bones! What do you want me to say?" He eased himself down on the stump near the hearth. "Laurent incited you into battle. You fought. He died." He met

Jehan's gaze evenly. "Then you knighted him on the battle-field."

Jehan made a scornful grunt. "A desperate gesture of guilt."

"There are some knights, Sir Jehan, who would never show such generosity to a vanquished foe."

"I took his *life.*"

"You gave him his manhood."

"The boy deserved to be knighted. He fought a just cause and died for it."

"Ah, then you finally admit it."

Jehan turned away. He remembered the dark blood that poured out and stained the colors of Tournan emblazoned on Laurent's tunic. There had been no doubt as he stared at the rusted links of Laurent's sliced haubergeon: The wound was fatal. Laurent knew it too. Yet he didn't cry for a priest, or confess his sins to the men around him. Instead, he looked up at Jehan, the man who killed him, and spoke of his sister. He begged Jehan to leave her, for the sake of her immortal soul, while his own soul was about to leave his body. Jehan realized then, vividly, how much Laurent loved his sister. The boy had given his life in order to save her honor. The boy made the ultimate sacrifice, and lost.

Jehan never felt so humble, so unworthy, so wretched. He had continued to refuse to marry Aliénor, when that would have saved her from dishonor, yet this boy died for that cause. The world was not as it should be. This boy, who was not even a knight, showed greater chivalry and greater courage than any knight he had ever known. Jehan did the one thing he could think of, the one thing that might expiate from his soul the dark stain of this crime: He knighted the boy on the field of battle.

"My great-nephew became a man today," Thibaud continued. "Though he died in the process, I am proud."

Jehan shook his head swift and hard. "For a man who only days ago was cursing me because I wouldn't marry your great-niece—"

"Faith, I haven't forgiven you for that."

"—you're showing great generosity to the knight who just killed your great-nephew."

"Verily, it's not the same. Aliénor's a woman, prone to a woman's weaknesses, and you have done wrong by her. But you fought Laurent as honor demanded." Thibaud waved to some distant place beyond the chamber walls. "My great-nephew raised an *army*. He convinced brigands who would sooner kill him for his armor to fight on his side. He rode to this castle in the colors of his father and fought for what he believed was right. And in the end, he won his spurs. I could ask no better fate for a crippled boy who was destined to pine his life away in cloisters." The aged knight stared at him steadily, his chin raised beneath the snowy beard. "He chose death over dishonor, Sir Jehan. It was his choice, and he chose it like a man."

"Aliénor won't understand all this talk of honor and chivalry and knighthood," he retorted. "She'll spit at it, and at me."

"Ah, then it is Aliénor who causes your torment."

"I *killed* her brother."

"In the heat of battle. You're a knight, not a sorcerer, Sir Jehan. You couldn't cast a spell around him to keep him safe."

"I made a promise to Aliénor that I wouldn't fight him."

"The boy taunted you for five days."

"Words. *Words!*" He spoke through clenched teeth. "What kind of man, what kind of knight, couldn't withstand a young man's desperate taunts?"

"The English called Aliénor a whore."

Jehan stiffened.

"You see, you still would fight, again, if you faced the situation anew."

Jehan flexed his right hand into a fist. He would give his sword—and his sword arm—for the opportunity to take back that single fatal stroke. "I would *not* commit murder again."

"You didn't murder Laurent. He attacked you from behind. Aliénor knows that, too."

Jehan tilted his head back and closed his eyes. "She watched from the ramparts, didn't she?"

"She'd sooner don chain mail and fight than cower in a corner. She saw everything."

"She should have been spared that."

"Laurent didn't give you any other choice."

Jehan blinked his eyes open, blindly. "Now she'll wish, for the rest of her life, that she had hidden away from me."

"God's bones, she saw exactly what I saw! She knows that you didn't kill him intentionally—"

"What difference does it make? It was my decision to fight that led to his death. Laurent fought for his sister's honor, and *I* fought to keep her in disgrace."

"I thought you gave Aliénor a choice."

"I did: I gave her a choice between a life with me and something she hated more than death." He ran a hand through his tangled, bloody hair. The anguish tore through him, as sharp-edged as a sword, but it let no blood, it did not bring the relief of death. It brought constant desolation, endless misery, the knowledge that he had lost something precious, something absolutely irreplaceable. "I convinced myself it was a choice, because it fit my sense of chivalry to give her one. I knew what she would choose all along—I intended to persuade her to be my mistress even if she chose otherwise. I gave her no choice."

"This admission comes late, Sir Jehan."

"I was blinded by my own love for her."

"Love, is it?" Thibaud placed his hands on his knees and straightened. "If you loved her you should have married her."

"It's too late now for that, isn't it, Thibaud?" He spread his fingers. "Do you think Aliénor will marry her brother's murderer, while his blood still dries upon my hands?"

"I suppose young men never listen to old men's advice." Thibaud pulled a wrought-iron poker from the stand next to the hearth and toyed with the single, low-burning log. "I've watched you over the past months. I've watched you make the same mistakes that I made, twenty-five years ago. It's a painful process, watching another man relive your own errors. I was in love once. Like you, I lost her."

Jehan started. He had not dared to say the words aloud. He hadn't dared to speak his own fears. Hearing them in Thibaud's low voice made them all the more real.

"She was the heiress to a barony. I thought her holdings were too small and King Philip VI could do me better. I wooed the maiden, nonetheless, for she was as fair as a spring flower. I went off to war. When I returned, she was married to another man. She died giving birth to her first child. A stillborn child. *My* child."

Jehan stared at the aged knight, seeing suddenly the sadness behind the dark eyes.

"I never forgave myself." He replaced the poker in the holder and spread his gnarled, scarred hands. "I could have married another but I never allowed myself the comfort. I, too, went through the anguish you are now feeling, the guilt, the knowledge of how much pain, how much death you have caused because of your lapse in honor."

"What are you telling me? That I have nothing to look forward to but a wretched, lonely old age?"

"I'm telling you *not* to make my mistake." He pointed a knurled finger at him. "You may have lost Aliénor's heart, but she's still alive, walking, and breathing."

"Then what I have is worse," he argued. "She'll look at me with hate—she will see me only as the man who murdered her brother. She'll wish me dead."

Thibaud rose from his seat and took the tallow candle in his hand. "I didn't say it would be easy. She may hate you for what's happened. But there may come a day when she understands. It may not be soon. It may not be ever."

"There will be no forgiveness. Not from Aliénor, or from myself."

"If you love her, then you must wait patiently. You must hope. And you must pray."

Vita mutatur, non tollitur.
Life is changed, but not taken away.

Aliénor stood in the silent church, the scent of frankincense swirling thickly around her. She had spent the morning wrapping her brother's body in a perfumed winding sheet, seeing for the last time the pale features of his motionless face. Father Dubosc was wrong: Life *was* taken away. It was snatched from the sweetest of flowers, when the fragrance was strong and fresh and the dew still clung to the petals. Life was changed irrevocably, eternally, and nothing —nothing—would ever be the same.

When the Mass ended, she followed Father Dubosc out of the chapel and into the courtyard. Her father's six old vassals heaved the small casket upon their shoulders and followed the chaplain as he murmured in Latin. Aliénor held the reins of Laurent's riderless horse as she walked numbly behind the pallbearers. The procession passed through the portal, out onto the battlefield where her brother had breathed his last. A new grave gaped wide and open in the blessed ground outside the eastern walls, and as the churchbells chimed to announce the passing of a soul, the men lowered her brother into the cold, frosty earth. She clutched a handful of dirt, dug her fingers into the icy clay, then threw it into the gaping grave. As if to mock her grief, the sun suddenly broke through the clouds.

Goodbye, frai.

She went to her room. She took no comfort from the men who honored her brother, called him a brave young man, and assured her he died with glory. She took no comfort in the knight's trappings that filled his coffin, or the words *Sir Laurent de Tournan* that were carved on a limestone plate embedded in the timber of the church's nave. Her brother was dead, slain in his attempt to save her honor, dead in her name, dead by her lover's hand. He had risked everything. He had fought against what he knew was wrong while she stayed in this castle, a whore of luxury, giving herself shamelessly to a man outside the bonds of wedlock.

There were times when the shame overwhelmed her, suffocated her, reminding her of the time as a girl when she had nearly drowned in the swift-flowing, frigid waters of the

Arrats. The water had washed over her, pulled her along in the strong current, choked her with its ice until she felt the coldness of death tug at her skirts. She felt like that now, but it was shame that was choking her. Shame so deep and so heavy that she swore she would die with it, she would smother in it, and she knew this time that no man or woman could pull her from the abyss.

She remembered a hundred times when her brother scolded her for riding astride with her legs exposed to the thighs, or chiding her for reveling in luxury and riches, in the wealth of summer food. Without a fight, she had surrendered her virtue, despite Laurent's warnings, thinking only of the glory of Jehan's embrace, a glory that should only be shared between a man and his wife. She had more than just fallen from grace—she had leaped off the precipice into sin—and the price she paid was far, far greater, far higher, than she had ever known.

She tried to blame Jehan. She tried to throw the heavy load of her guilt onto his shoulders. She tried to dredge up anger and hatred and spill it upon him in a series of ugly, mindless curses. But every time she pictured his handsome, rugged face in her mind's eye, the anguish surged in her heart anew. She had not only lost a brother, she had lost a lover. Never again would she be able to look upon Jehan without seeing her own shame. They shared the blame for Laurent's untimely death. Jehan may have struck the blow, but it was *her* decision that forced Laurent into the position of her protector. It was *her* choice to follow the sinful urges of her wretched body. Her soul cried out to her brother for forgiveness, but it was as if she were crying to the moon.

A week passed. Daily, Margot brought food and returned hours later to take the untouched plate away. Aliénor was sick not only in soul but in body, for the mere smell of bread made her retch. The nights tormented her. Her dreams tormented her, but most of all, her memories tormented her. She wanted to run far, far away from where she could still see the wooden dolls that her brother had carved for the village children, far away from the walls that seemed, even now, to echo with his voice. There were times when she thought it would be better to be mad than to suffer through such endless pain. She wondered if madness ran in the Tournan blood. She remembered her father's rages, her mother's slow descent into dotage, her brother and his distorted belief that he could save her with nothing but a band of peasants and his belief in righteousness. She prayed for madness. She prayed for some comfort from her tortured thoughts.

Madness never came. Instead, she found herself faced with cold reality. She could no longer live in Jehan's castle. Every day she remained, she mocked Laurent's death and make his swift, senseless demise utterly without meaning. She could join her mother at the abbey in Auch, but she resisted the idea of joining a religious order. How could she, when she had refused the sacrament of communion since the day her brother died, and intended to continue refusing it until she purged her soul of this sin? There had to be another alternative. As the days passed, an idea formed in her mind. It took root and grew until she knew there was no other way. There was no other place she could go where she would never again risk the chance of laying eyes on Jehan.

She vowed her brother's death would not be in vain.

Two weeks after Laurent's funeral Mass, Aliénor ate some of the bread and wine Margot brought for her breakfast. The food gave her strength and helped stave off the endless sickness. When Margot returned to take the plate away, she brightened when she saw that Aliénor had eaten nearly all of it.

"Help me dress," Aliénor said quietly.

"Yes, *damaiselo!*"

"In mourning clothes."

"Of course."

Margot helped her out of bed and fussed around her, slipping a black wool surcoat over Aliénor's pure white tunic. The chambermaid paled noticeably when Aliénor told her to tell Jehan to meet her in the great hall.

"I don't know if I can do that, *damaiselo.*"

"I must speak to him."

"He's . . ." She glanced toward the door, then back to Aliénor. "He's drunk all the time. He's thrown out every man who knocks on his door. He nearly broke Esquivat's neck—"

"Then have Thibaud do it."

Not long after Margot scurried off to do her bidding, Aliénor descended the stairs to the lower floors. The effort of standing up and walking after so many days abed made her dizzy, and she clutched the stone wall for support. She mustered her strength and took deep, long breaths. The servants in the buttery quieted as they saw her pass and Aliénor heard the whispering rise as she entered the hall itself. Several men-at-arms sat near the fire, cleaning and sharpening their weapons. When she entered, Thibaud rose and ushered them out.

She walked across the brittle rushes to a chair by the hearth. She placed both her hands on it and held on, for the dizziness struck her again. She settled in the chair. She heard Thibaud's steps as he returned.

"He's coming?"

"Yes. It'll be the first time he's left the donjon since he returned from the battle." Thibaud paused hesitantly and placed a hand on her shoulder. "He's tormented, Aliénor, as if it were his own brother who died."

"We are both equally to blame."

"Faith, you are kinder to him than I expected."

"What did you expect, *oncle?*" She rubbed her eyes wearily. "I can't blame Jehan for striking out at an attacker during battle. But he, like me, must share the shame of what we've . . . we've done."

"Ailas, Aliénor, if that's what you speak of . . . truly, there's not much shame in that."

"If I had chosen more wisely, my brother would be alive today."

"He would be alive, but unknighted, and praying away in a Franciscan friary."

"Just as he always wanted."

Thibaud removed his hand from her shoulder. She sensed in him an unease, an urge to ask her more questions, but he said nothing. She closed her eyes and willed her strength to return. She had to fight off this sickness. She had to have the strength to face Jehan and do what was right.

Thibaud stopped his restless pacing when Jehan arrived. She leaned her head back on the hard, carved wooden chair and opened her eyes. She stared at the bearded, wild-eyed knight, dressed still in his blood-spattered tunic, carrying a wineskin, as he walked into the great hall. He had lost weight. It showed in the hollows beneath his wide cheek-bones, in the way his baldric hung low on his hips. He stopped abruptly as he saw her in the hearth chair. For a moment, they looked at each other. Aliénor took a deep, ragged breath. She felt as if she were being drawn into the vortex of his own anguish, his own guilt, his own shame. She pulled her gaze away.

His voice was low and gravelly. "They told me you were sick."

"I am sick," she corrected. "It's a sickness of the soul, Jehan. No amount of food or sleep or bleeding can cure it."

"Then I, too, have that sickness." He spread his free hand open, palm up, and looked at it. "Thibaud tells me you haven't attended Mass since the battle."

"I have no right."

"Your brother's blood is on *my* hands, not yours."

She stood up abruptly. She turned and stared into the fire. The dizziness overwhelmed her and she clutched the arm of the wooden chair. She heard his swift footsteps, but she raised her hand to stop him. "No, don't, Jehan." He stopped in his tracks. She took a deep breath and waited for the weakness to pass.

"If I could," he began, his voice quivering with a timbre she had never before heard, "I would give anything—*everything*—to cure your pain."

There was so much conviction, so much agony in his words. "There was a time, once, when you could have stopped the pain," she said, "but the time for such promises is gone."

"Is it, *couret?*"

"Once, you had a chance to save my brother's life." She tightened her grip on the chair and choked out the words. "Instead, you chose not to marry me."

"I was a fool."

"Then we both were fools, for I, too, once had a chance to choose. I chose to be your mistress and left my brother no other choice of his own."

"Then these past months: They mean nothing now?" He stepped closer, willing her to turn and face him. "Would you give them up, *couret?*"

"If it would bring my brother back to life, then *yes,* Jehan. I would give it all up."

She looked at him. Looking into his dark blue eyes was as painful as looking into the still face of her dead brother. It was hard to believe that a man so strong, a warrior, could display so much anguish. She felt the ache in him, the torment, the hurt and self-anger. It took a man this strong to show such weakness. It would be so easy to run to him, to hide her face in his chest, to give and receive comfort in his arms. She remembered, with sudden vividness, the nights they had spent curled against one other in the cold upper room of the donjon. She felt an overwhelming urge to touch him, to feel the strength of his arms around her, to feel the warmth of his lips on her brow.

She crushed the feeling before it blossomed. It was shameful, it was as dangerous as the feelings that had first led her to give herself to him. She knew she could never touch him again. They had sinned, and their sinning had led to her brother's death. There would be no more love, no more comfort, between them.

"Why don't you scream at me?" He pounded his chest with his clenched fist. "Why don't you curse me to Hell for what I've done to your brother, for what I've done to *you!*"

"I wish I could." She felt the prick of tears, the first time she had felt tears in over a week, when she bathed her bedlinens with the sorrow. "I wish I could wash my heart and my soul free of guilt and say 'It was you, Jehan, it was you who did it.' But I knew my brother—I knew he would never stay here and suffer me living with you as we did. I thrust that knowledge out of my mind, for it got in the way of what I wanted. That's why I waited so long to tell him, that's why he caught us the way he did. That's why he attacked the castle."

"You curse yourself for being human, for being a passionate woman—"

"Don't."

"God and man will forgive you for those faults, *couret*, but can you forgive *me* for being a fool?"

"My brother is dead." The tears misted her vision. "When I look at you, I will *always* see him, pleading with me to leave you. I can't forgive myself—don't dare ask me to forgive you, too."

His fingers choked the neck of the wineskin. "I still love you."

She turned away. The anguish squeezed her heart. "It doesn't matter anymore."

She listened to the crackling of the fire and watched the flames consume the wood. The heat warmed the front of her woolen surcoat and dried the single tear that had slipped out of her eye and ran over her cheek. She heard Jehan's halting footsteps as he approached the hearth. He paused on the other side. The golden light flickered over his face, sending strange shadows over his contorted features.

"Your brother lost his life," he murmured, "but verily, he won the war."

She fought desperately to hold back the tears. There was too much to be resolved. Her throat was as parched as the dusty summer soil, but she forced out the words she came down here to say. "I must leave Castelnau."

He nodded in understanding. "I'll send you to your mother at the abbey in Auch."

"No—I must go farther away." *So far away, my dear lost love, that there will be no chance that I will ever see you again.* "I want to go to Paris."

"Paris!" Thibaud, who had stood quietly aside and watched the two of them, suddenly stepped forward. "Of all places, why Paris?"

"I intend to throw myself upon the mercy of my father's lord."

"You can't!" Thibaud exclaimed. "The King of France is a prisoner of the English."

"But his son, Charles, is acting as Regent in his place. I will go to him and present myself as one of his loyal vassal's children, dispossessed because of war."

"He'll just toss you in a convent!"

"A convent is out of the question. I choke on the taste of Communion bread." She knotted her hands in front of her. "The Crown owes this family something. My father died at Poitiers, fighting under the King's banner. I intend to ask the Regent to take me in as his ward until I can decide what to do."

"God's wounds, Aliénor, the boy has enough problems, trying to get his father's ransom money and deal with the unruly Parisians—"

"Which is why I hoped you'd escort me, Thibaud. You once had influence in the French court."

"In the court of the Regent's grandfather! And we'll never make it through the heart of France, not in these times. The roads are thick with brigands."

"It's Jehan's choice." She looked directly at Jehan, who seemed completely absorbed in the flames. "He can grant it, or he can send me to my mother in Auch."

"It's granted," Jehan said quietly, not moving. "I will escort you to Paris myself."

"Are you *mad?*" Thibaud's enormous chest widened. "France and England are at war! You'll be captured and killed the moment you step into French territory!"

Jehan looked directly at her. "I can think of no cause more worth dying for."

Chapter
18

"His Grace the Duke of Normandy."

Aliénor dipped into a deep curtsy as the name of the Regent was announced. When she rose, she looked straight into the chestnut-colored eyes of Charles, the firstborn son of the captured King of France.

She had waited three long weeks for this interview. She had begun to wonder if the lengthy journey through the treacherous, brigand-infested countryside had been in vain. Since she had arrived in Paris, she traveled every morning between the Abbey of St. Martin, where she lodged north of the city, to the royal church, Notre Dame de L'Etoile, in the hopes of speaking to the Regent after the morning Mass. The crush of petitioners was always too great. Thibaud had no more luck in the royal palace after the Duke's midday meal: The number of clergymen, noblemen, and ambassadors who came to speak with the Regent always overflowed the great hall.

She and her great-uncle stood in that great hall now, alone but for the Regent, a few advisors, and a single row of huge stone pillars carved with the likenesses of kings of France. She felt a little dazed by the wide, empty space and the high, wood-vaulted ceiling. She was still not sure who told the Duke of Normandy about her presence in this crowded city, and why the Regent took the time to give her a private audience. She had nearly choked on her repast of bread and wine this morning when she received the summons pressed with the royal seal.

She looked at the man who held her future in his hands. The Regent sat behind a massive black marble table, engulfed in a capacious carved and gilded chair. Lank, reddish-blond hair hung straight to his shoulders. His long, pinched nose and thin, white lips gave him the appearance of utter weariness. It was no wonder, she thought. France was bankrupt, the body of representatives called to approve taxes, the *Etats,* was in revolt, and Englishmen terrorized the countryside. For six months, this nineteen-year-old duke had been forced to try to bring order to his father's disastrous affairs.

"So you are the dispossessed Gascon border heiress."

She started, not only from the sound of the Duke's voice, but also from his gaze. His bright, sharp eyes bore no trace of weariness as they focused on her. She remembered that this young prince had sired at least two bastard children, though he was long married. She wondered if she erred by coming to him dressed in her richest honey-colored silk surcoat, with her hair long and free beneath a sheer veil.

"I've never been described quite that way, Your Grace." She shrugged. "It's true, nonetheless."

"That was how your petitioner described you."

Aliénor started. She glanced at Thibaud, who shrugged his shoulders, and she thought, *For the love of God, this is some terrible mistake.*

"Forgive me, Your Grace, but the only petitioner I have is my great-uncle, Sir Thibaud de Tournan." She gestured to her aged relative as Thibaud bowed. "With the crush of men always about you, he hasn't yet been able to speak to you about my concerns."

"On the contrary, *demoiselle,* you *do* have another petitioner. He left here abruptly yesterday, racing away from a dozen of my guards." The Regent made a tent of his fingers and peered at her over their smooth tips. "You know nothing of Sir Jehan de St. Simon?"

Jehan!

"He claimed he was a Gascon nobleman with French loyalties." The Regent gestured with a beringed hand to one of the four men that stood nearby. "Monsieur de la Forêt, my father's chancellor, recognized him as a St. Simon, but not before Sir Jehan had an opportunity to plead your case eloquently."

Aliénor stood in stunned silence. *I should have known. I should have known all along.* Jehan had risked his freedom and his life for nearly two months during the perilous journey to Paris. Despite her protestations that Thibaud and a score of men-at-arms would suffice, Jehan had insisted on escorting her out of Castelnau. But not only did he lead her through the brigand-infested lands held by the English, but also beyond, deep into French lands. A truce had not yet been negotiated between the two sovereigns, and every moment he spent north of Poitiers he was in dire jeopardy. The single concession he made to his own danger was to avoid large towns and castles. And when, four times between the Loire and the Seine, they were attacked by brigands, he fought like a man possessed. Why, now that he was in the heart of his enemies' lands, did she expect him to act any differently?

"I was surprised to find an English knight in this royal palace, *demoiselle.*"

The Regent waited for an explanation. She tried to regain her composure. "I had no idea that Sir Jehan was pleading my case, Your Grace. He . . . he obviously found a way to speak to you on my behalf, and took advantage of it without my knowledge."

"The knight piqued my curiosity. Yesterday, in this very room, my advisors heard him telling stories about my father and the Prince of Wales in Bordeaux. I called him to me. He told me what he knew, then he told me about you." The Regent leaned forward in his chair. "When the chancellor identified him as a knight of the English Prince, I had to summon you, *demoiselle,* for no other reason than to find out why an English knight pleaded a French noblewoman's cause."

"I appreciate your generosity, Your Grace."

"Sir Jehan suggested the audience be private." The Duke's sharp eyes seemed to pierce her clothing. "How do you know this English knight?"

"He is the knight who escorted me to Paris from my home in Gascony."

The Duke lifted a brow. "He escorted you willingly through French land?"

"Yes, Your Grace."

"He risked much. His reasons must be compelling."

"They are: It is Sir Jehan himself who dispossessed me."

The Regent's brows pressed up against the gold rim of his low crown.

"If you will spare me just a few moments . . ." As quickly and as dispassionately as she could, Allénor recited the events that led up to the loss of her castle, the death of her father at Poitiers, the seizure of the viscounty by the Prince of Wales, and Jehan's swift recapture of the estate. As she reached this part of her tale, she hesitated. It was easy enough to relate the events up to Jehan's arrival as the new Vicomte de Tournan, but soon she would have to tell the Regent about her own disgrace.

The Duke accepted her hesitation as the end of her story. "Unfortunately, *demoiselle,* I have heard many such tales in the past months."

"Ah, but she has not finished the tale, *Monseigneur.*" Thibaud stepped forward and bowed gracefully despite his aged frame. He turned to Aliénor. "Come, woman, you've told the Regent only of French losses, and nothing of French victories!"

"There have been no victories."

"Perhaps not victories of land or castles, but victories of honor, indeed!" Thibaud glanced at the Duke. "You have heard little, I trow, of the prowess of French knights in the past months, since our incomprehensible defeat at Poitiers."

"All I've heard from the *Etats,*" he said, speaking the

name as if it were a curse, "are lectures on the cowardice and greediness of French knights."

"All through France, I have been spit on and cursed by the common people. They blame all French knights for the capture of your father and the devastation of their lands. We, of finer blood, know that treason is not possible in the heart of a French knight. And I know a tale, Your Grace, of a knight whose chivalry shines on all of us, a tale that if the people heard it, they would be humbled."

She stared at Thibaud. She had never seen him act like such a courtier: bowing, obsequious, his lips stretched in a tight smile. She had never heard him speak for so long without cursing.

"Indeed, good knight," the Regent commented, "I have heard little of chivalry."

"Then let me tell you of my great-nephew, and you shall hear of the valor and virtue of a knight born on Gascon soil."

She started. *She* wanted to tell Laurent's story. She couldn't stand by, idly listening, while Thibaud spoke of her disgrace.

"*Ailas,* Aliénor, I know it's still painful for you," Thibaud said as she opened her mouth to protest. He shook his head sadly at the Regent. "She is still deep in mourning, *Monseigneur,* for her brother, Sir Laurent de Tournan, is the man of whom I speak."

"Thibaud, please—"

"Calm yourself, *ma petite nièce.*" He glared at her with a tight smile beneath his beard. "And hearken what I say: I shall spare you as much pain as possible."

Stunned into silence, she listened as Thibaud began his story.

"Laurent de Tournan was the third son of the Vicomte de Tournan. He was born with a grave deformity, a twisted foot, and since his parents were already blessed with two strong, healthy sons, Laurent's life was dedicated to the Church.

"He was a pious young boy, his heart and his mind always turned toward God. When he was still a child, the plague grievously stole the lives of his two older brothers, and, suddenly, he found himself an unlikely heir to great estates. His father . . ." Thibaud paused for only a moment, but long enough for Aliénor to realize that he was searching for a convenient lie. "His father recognized the saintliness in the boy and, rather than tear him away from his calling, decided to make his sister, the young woman who stands before you, heiress to his estates. But when the castle and his sister were captured by the English, Laurent de Tournan found himself with a different sort of calling.

"He was beardless and barely fifteen when he escaped the castle of his boyhood. He intended to raise an army to defeat the English usurper, take back what was his birthright, and restore the rightful order of his and his sister's lives."

Aliénor stood motionless. The shame flooded her body, as fresh and forceful as when Laurent had died on the battlefield, two and a half months before. She waited for Thibaud to utter the painful truth. *He gave his life to save his sister's honor.* But as her great-uncle forged ahead in his tale, she realized exactly how Thibaud had chosen to spare her as much pain as possible.

He said nothing about her shame.

"In a matter of weeks, miraculously, this crippled boy attacked the castle of his youth with his own army," Thibaud continued. "He incited the English into battle. He fought valiantly as if he were a knight of thirty years, not a boy of fifteen, and never have I been so proud to be a Tournan as on the day he battled against Sir Jehan."

The Regent leaned forward in his seat. "A crippled boy battled an English knight?"

"Yes, *Monseigneur.* He lost the battle, but there was no shame in the loss. He fought well and hard. Even Sir Jehan was impressed by the boy's bravery—so impressed that Sir Jehan knighted Laurent on the field of battle, as the boy breathed his last. My great-nephew was buried Sir Laurent de Tournan."

She stared at Thibaud. How could he tell the tale of Laurent's death without exposing the shame of her relationship with Sir Jehan? She realized Thibaud's story was true but for two things: her father's reason for dispossessing her brother, and her brother's motivations for attacking the castle. She had never heard her brother's death related in such glorious terms—she couldn't even speak of it during the long voyage through France. Something stirred inside her, something akin to pride. For the first time since Laurent's untimely death, she felt the heavy curtain of her shame open a fraction and let in a bit of light and air.

"This tale is good." The Regent leaned back in his chair. "It has been long since I have heard of such chivalry. I, myself, will say a prayer for Sir Laurent's soul at vespers."

"I could ask for no greater gift."

"Did you fight on the side of your great-nephew, Sir Thibaud?"

"Non, Monseigneur. I was bound by my lord not to fight. I remained neutral while I watched the attack."

"The threads of these stories grow still more knotted. Who is your lord?"

"Sir Jehan, Your Grace."

"Sir Jehan," the Duke said pointedly, "is a vassal of the Prince of Wales."

"It's the man's only fault, for he's a fine, chivalrous knight. Despite my age, Sir Jehan offered me vassalage where no one else would have me." Thibaud's chest expanded. "In my day, I fought for three French kings, *Monseigneur.* The last of them was King Philip VI, your grandfather. I knew your father, King Jean, when he was but a boy. It pricks my conscience to be vassal of a man who is bound to the English, but when King Jean reached maturity and took the crown, he grievously forgot the pension that his father promised me. The late Vicomte de Tournan, my nephew, took me in, and when the Vicomte died on the fields of Poitiers, Sir Jehan offered to make me his man." Thibaud spread his arms. "These are difficult times. A man of my age has little choice. I refuse to enter thievery like

321

many of my kind. Ah, but for the days of my youth, when a knight was a knight, when honor was so strong that he would never become a brigand, as so many knights have."

"Where did you fight with my grandfather, Sir Thibaud?"

"At Crécy and Calais."

"I know his exploits well."

"I know of some exploits that I wager not even *you* have been told."

The Regent smiled. "You must tell me of those. All I hear in these terrible days are of burning and plundering and brigandry. It would do me good to hear of brighter days."

"I am acting as my great-niece's escort, *Monseigneur*, so I shall be available at your every call."

"Though I am much beleaguered by the *Etats*. I am sure I can reinstate your pension if you stay here, in Paris, as one of my retainers."

Thibaud lifted his bushy brows and bowed low in front of the Regent. "It will be my greatest honor. Though Sir Jehan is a great knight, his liege lord is English and, given the choice, I'd prefer to serve the French." He glanced at Aliénor. "And Sir Jehan left so abruptly yesterday that I can assume he has released me of my services, at least temporarily."

She started out of her stillness. "Jehan left yesterday?"

"He *escaped* yesterday," the Regent corrected. "When we discovered his identity, we pursued him out of this castle and through the streets of Paris. We hoped to hold him prisoner and ransom him as the Prince of Wales has done to so many French knights. Unfortunately, he eluded my men."

"I found him and his men missing last night but thought nothing of it until this morning," Thibaud explained, "when we received your summons. I can only assume that Sir Jehan has left Paris permanently, leaving me without means to support myself, nor a way to return to Gascony." He bowed anew. "I thank you, Your Grace, for your generosity. It is welcome and well timed."

The Regent nodded. He turned and examined Aliénor,

from the circlet that glittered on her brow, down the length of her gold brocaded tunic, to the leather slippers peeking out from the voluminous folds. "You have my deepest sympathy, *demoiselle*. So many of my father's vassals have lost their estates in war." He ran his long fingers over the three stripes of ermine fur on the shoulder of his robe. "Tell me, are you the last of the Tournans?"

"My great-uncle and I are all who remain. My mother has entered a convent."

"Then, if your father lived, you would be the heiress to the lands of Tournan?"

"Yes."

"And these lands, where are they?"

She wondered why the Regent was so concerned about the placement of her lost lands. "The estate is on the border between the English lands of Aquitaine and the French lands of the counts of Toulouse, on a river called the Arrats. They were once borderlands, although with all the warring, I know not how much land the English now control."

"Neither do we. We have been arguing long and hard with the English over the peace treaty." His dark, small eyes rested on her speculatively. "Sir Jehan did not lie. As a dispossessed Gascon border heiress, you may help us in defining those borders."

She knew better than to deny it, though she wondered what in God's name she, a woman, could do to help the Regent of France.

"I shall take you in as my ward, *demoiselle*." He leaned back in his chair. "It is the least I can do to honor your brother's memory, and your father's loyalty to the King. You shall stay with my wife and her ladies. Be prepared to travel, for Paris is no place for ladies, and I intend to leave the city soon—with the Duchess and her court."

She dipped in a grateful curtsy. "You honor me, *Monseigneur,* and I thank you."

The Duke looked away in dismissal. Thibaud bowed and began to leave the great hall.

She rose slowly from her crouched position. She hesitated. The Regent had already agreed to take her in as his ward, and she was grateful for that. But there was one thing he didn't know. One thing that might change his mind about sending her to the ladies of the royal court. She had planned to tell the Duke only after Jehan bid her farewell. Now Jehan was gone, sooner and more suddenly than she expected. There was no longer a reason for secrecy.

Thibaud tugged on her arm. "Come, Aliénor."

"Wait, *oncle.*"

He saw the intent in her eye. "There is no reason to burden the Regent with details, details that will not change anything."

"This is a detail, *oncle,* that you know nothing about."

His weathered skin paled. She turned and met the Regent's bright, sharp gaze.

"I am with child, Your Grace. Jehan de St. Simon's child."

Laurent, *le bâtard de St. Simon,* turned eight months old in June 1358. In her small chamber in an empty wing of a castle just outside the city of Meaux, Aliénor swaddled the babe in a clean set of linens and laughed into his bright blue eyes. The child was the very image of his father, with a thick crop of black hair and the barest beginnings of a dimple on his right cheek. The more malicious women in court whispered that it was part of her penance, as an adulteress, to be forced to stare at the mirror image of her lover, but she found no penance in this. From the moment the child emerged from her body, squalling and blue and covered with the birthing fluids, she loved him more than life itself.

Since she had entered the whirl of the Duchess's court over a year before, she had lived as quietly and as isolated as a woman excommunicated from all Christian society. As an adulteress, she could hardly socialize with the lilies of France while she grew big with the fruit of her sin, an English knight's child. She simply followed wherever the royal court wandered: through the provinces, in and out of a dozen royal castles, back into Paris whenever the Regent was compelled to return. Several months before, the Regent had finally sent the Duchess here, to a castle set securely on an island in the middle of the Marne river, a day's ride from Paris, while he dealt with the rising conflict with the increasingly rebellious *Etats*.

She didn't mind the quiet or the isolation. It gave her ample time to think on all that had happened in Gascony. She lived alone with her disgrace, refusing to attend Mass, feeling the child grow and kick in her belly, the physical evidence of her sin. But something happened on St. Wilfred's Day in 1357. It was as if she had squeezed more than a healthy babe from her pain-wracked body in the dark hours of the night. The child who emerged from her loins bore no mark of sin—in fact, he bore no mark whatsoever: He was as perfect a child as the royal midwife had ever seen. All the shame, all the anguish, all the self-pity that had plagued her since her brother died dissolved upon the sight of this creature, this new life risen from the ashes of death.

She was no longer alone. Her days revolved around the babe's sleeping, his feeding, his changing, his playfulness. At times she stopped and looked down at him—into Jehan's son's face—and thought, *I have no right to be so happy. I have no right to take so much joy and comfort from this babe.* She had received the greatest gift, when she deserved nothing but sorrow.

Soon she stopped questioning. She started to attend Mass. She took Holy Communion. When the Duke of Normandy visited his wife and new daughter, who was born a few weeks before Laurent, Aliénor prevailed upon him to influence the Church on her son's behalf. Within a few weeks, the babe was baptized Laurent Jehan, thus forever linking the two men she had loved and lost.

Jehan was far, far away now, probably in London with the Prince of Wales, negotiating a wealthy marriage. She couldn't tell him about the child last year. She knew he would have done something desperate. He had spent two months after her brother's death seeking a death of his own—fighting without restraint, marching boldly through enemy lands—and her pregnancy would have been a perfect excuse for him to explate his guilt. He would have turned back to Gascony. He would have forced her to live near him, where he could care for her and the child. Perhaps he would have married her if his agony were greater than the ambition that caused them both so much pain. In either case, she couldn't bear the thought of living forever in the misery of their mutual anguish. She could bear it no better then than she could bear it now. It was best this way. Jehan would find solace in a wife. She found solace in her son.

She knotted the sides of Laurent's linen and lifted him high above her head. She rubbed her nose against the soft flesh of his belly, where he smelled so milky, so much like a babe.

"You're coddling him again."

She turned as Blanche d'Athènes walked—or, rather, waddled—into the room. Her round face split into a smile. Blanche was the one woman within the court who had befriended Aliénor despite her disgrace. Blanche, like herself, was forced to prevail on the graciousness of the Regent for shelter and sustenance after the death at Poitiers of her distant nephew, the Duc d'Athènes. The elderly widow felt as displaced in the court as Aliénor did. Aliénor made an eternal friend by asking the lonely woman to be her son's godmother.

Laurent gurgled in recognition.

"Ah!" Blanche pressed her hands to her heart. "He recognizes his godmother already!"

"Of course he does." Blanche spoiled him as if he were her own grandchild. Whenever Aliénor objected, Blanche pulled on her old-fashioned white linen wimple and grew teary-eyed at the thought of all her own lost babies. "My son knows that when you're here, he'll soon have a new gift."

Blanche reached into a pouch that hung around her neck and pulled out a silver ball. It jingled with the sweet sound of brass chimes.

"Blanche!"

"It's the Duchess's daughter's toy—the babe grew tired of it quickly, and the Duchess was about to discard it."

"So you agreed to discard it for her?"

"Either it would be given to your child, Aliénor, or to one of the children of the other ladies. You didn't receive a single piece of cloth for Christmas last year, or for the Easter celebrations—"

"You're incorrigible!"

"—and all because you birthed a boy, and the Duchess, who may someday be Queen of France, birthed a mere daughter." She walked farther into the room and sat on the bed. "Besides, the little Princess's chamber is so full of glitter and cloth that this ball won't be missed."

Aliénor laid Laurent on the bed. Blanche waved the ball over him. He gurgled, entranced, reaching for the object that shone so brightly in the dim, candlelit room. Aliénor left the two of them for a moment while she searched in the small chest at the foot of the bed for the babe's tunic.

"I suppose I'll have to confess to the priest in the morning," Blanche said.

"He'll probably assign you a month of penance."

"He will, the old goat! He scowls at you so much during Mass. And he scowls at my godchild, too."

"If it weren't for the Duke, he would have ordered my excommunication by now."

"He wouldn't dare! Why, the Duke has practically found a husband for you."

"Blanche!"

"It's true!" She rubbed the silver ball on Laurent's bare, rounded belly. "There'll be a fat dispensation fee for the priest, and everyone else, all the way up to the Pope if you're married and the babe legitimized—"

"The priest knows how unlikely that is, which is why he continues to scowl."

"I heard what the Regent told you two weeks ago."

"All he told me is that Guy de Baste arrived in the Regent's court, and the knight mentioned my name."

"The knight did much more than that. I sat beside you when the Regent told you, remember?"

Aliénor sighed, knowing that Blanche would discuss the situation whether she wanted her to or not. It was a distasteful subject, an upsetting subject—something she preferred not to think about.

The Regent arrived in Meaux in May. The visit was a surprise, for the situation in France was becoming critical. Last November, Charles of Navarre escaped from prison and was now scheming to rally the Parisians to his cause—his claim to the French throne. In February, the Regent witnessed the growing rage of the Parisians when they broke into the royal palace and killed two marshals right before his eyes, claiming they were killing traitors to the French throne. The young Duke left Paris soon after and was now fortifying his provincial castles—specifically his castles around Paris—with the intention of taking the rebellious city by storm.

During his stay, Aliénor was forced to join the entire court at mealtimes. She couldn't excuse herself from the feasts, but since she sat far, far below the salt, she hoped she wouldn't be noticed. The Duke sought her out one evening during the dancing. He told her Guy de Baste was in Paris. She was surprised, for she remembered what Jehan had told her about Guy's questionable loyalties. The Regent said there was a possibility Sir Guy would marry her, if the Regent could dower her with some Gascon lands, and if she agreed to certain conditions. She was too shocked to do more than thank the Regent for thinking of her, when there were so many more important things on his mind. Then she realized he probably mentioned it because he was eager to remove an adulteress and her illegitimate son from the court of the future Queen of France.

Still, she couldn't bring herself to show any enthusiasm for Sir Guy's interest. Sir Guy's "certain conditions" frightened her. She knew what they were. No man would tolerate his wife's bastards in his house. She would have to give up Laurent—something she swore she would never, *ever*, do.

"You're crushing that tunic, Aliénor."

She looked down at the crumpled lavender tunic she had embroidered over the winter with dark purple thread. She smoothed it out with her hands. "Why would a vicomte be interested in a penniless adulteress with an illegitimate child?"

"He would if the Regent planned to endow you. It has been known to happen."

"Well, it hasn't happened yet." Aliénor slipped the tunic over Laurent's head. "The Regent has better things to do than worry about one of his wards." *Thank God.*

"That wretched great-uncle of yours hasn't sent word, either?"

She frowned, for Blanche and Thibaud had been at each other's throats the entire time her great-uncle was here in Meaux. "He's busy with the Regent planning the siege of Paris."

"More likely he's spinning fanciful yarns for the Regent's pleasure! Soon I expect him to take the fool Mitton's place in the Duke's affections."

"Now, Blanche—"

"Your great-uncle should think more about you and less about himself! Who will protect you when he's gone? How long does he expect to live?"

"Thibaud will outlive us all." She finished dressing Laurent and summoned the wetnurse. "Come with us. We're going to walk through the fields outside the castle."

Blanche straightened suddenly. "It's far too hot!"

"In Gascony, the heat of the summer is far worse than this."

"Is that why last summer, in the thickness of your pregnancy, you bloomed like some strange, exotic flower while I fell faint with the heat?" She stood up and straightened the wrinkles of her peach and red *mi-parti* surcoat. "Well, I, *mon amie,* am not gifted with your Gascon blood."

"You don't have to come with me." She headed to the door with Laurent in her arms. As Aliénor suspected,

Blanche followed her through the empty hall, huffing to catch up with her. She shifted Laurent into one arm, pulled open a small side door, and stepped out into the bright sunshine.

Blanche followed hard on her heels. "Aliénor, there's something I should tell you."

"Well, come then, and tell me." Aliénor breathed in the fresh, humid air. She was surprised to seen no one strolling about the yard, nor sitting beneath the shade of the elms that grew at even intervals. She headed toward the portal, then stopped short. The iron portcullis was lowered. In rapid succession, she noticed the men-at-arms milling on the ramparts, the piles of stones, and the neat, leaning stacks of arrows arranged at intervals along the battlements.

The castle was prepared for siege.

"I didn't want to tell you, you being a mother and all," Blanche said as Aliénor glared at her. "When my first was born, the sight of a single beggar sent me screaming to the guardhouse of my castle in Champagne to lower the portcullis."

"What has happened?"

"It's that horrid little man, the mayor of Meaux. He's been complaining for weeks that the Regent took control of this castle unjustly. And now he's opened the city of Meaux to thousands of armed peasants, peasants sent here by that demon, Etienne Marcel."

A coldness clutched Aliénor's heart as Blanche spoke the name of the leader of the bourgeois in Paris, the man who'd ordered the killing of two of the Regent's marshals.

"They're not attacking, Aliénor, not yet. They're feasting on meat and wine across the river, in the city."

"You should have told me!"

"I was afraid you'd remember all those stories the Duchesse d'Orleans told us, after she fled from her castle at Beaumont-sur-Oise when it was attacked."

"I remember them, Blanche." She remembered too vividly the tales of roasted men and disemboweled women. "But hiding this from me does no good at all."

Aliénor swept the courtyard with her gaze. A handful of ladies stood by the rear portal of the castle, like a cluster of bright, agitated flowers, speaking with the constable. She wondered where the rest of the ladies were and assumed they were huddled together in the great hall. She scanned the ramparts. When the Regent departed a few weeks before, he left behind only eight knights and their men to garrison this castle—a weak force to protect nearly three hundred women and children. She felt powerless as she glanced around the courtyard. She was used to controlling the defenses of a castle, not sitting quietly aside. Suddenly, she noticed something curious—something very curious. She nudged Blanche and pointed to the battlements, where a small crowd of knights peered over the wall. "Why are all the Regent's knights staring over the ramparts, Blanche, on the Brie side of the castle?"

Blanche looked at her blankly.

"The city of Meaux is on the other side of the river. Why are those men staring off in the opposite direction?"

"I don't know. . . . That does seem odd, doesn't it?"

"Unless the peasants decided to swim the Marne river and attack from the opposite side, then there is something else happening. Look, there's the Duchess of Normandy—go ask her." Aliénor nudged Blanche toward the women. Blanche waddled over as quickly as she could, dressed in a tunic so tight, in the new style, that the laces in the back strained against the restraint. Aliénor held Laurent close to her chest. The news shocked her more than she was willing to tell. She had heard of other peasant uprisings in the past few weeks, but they were distant things, news no greater or lesser than the news of brigand attacks or Charles of Navarre's latest scheme. Suddenly the wolves were at the gates. How could the commoners of Meaux grow so bold to attack a castle that contained the Regent's wife and the ladies and children of the royal court?

She suddenly thought of the land around Castelnau-sur-Arrats after the English attack: the burned windmills, the smoldering cities, the bodies of the murdered and the starving. She thought of the brigands who stole mercilessly from honest pilgrims, who desecrated abbeys and forced nuns to join their camps. She thought of the winter she buried nearly a third of the inhabitants of Castelnau, because *knights* took everything they owned. Then she understood why the people of Meaux attacked. After a generation of war, they were fighting back.

She bit her lower lip and searched for comfort. The castle stood on an island in the middle of the Marne river. She knew the peasants would have to swim the river just to get to the walls. The archers would be able to spear them like so many fish. Still, she could not get an image out of her mind: the image of an army of ants, climbing over their own dead in order to reach their goal.

Blanche returned just as the portcullis rose in the portal on the Brie side of the castle.

"We have nothing to fear, *mon amie*. Chivalry is not dead, despite what your great-uncle thinks." Her wide face broke into a grin. "Across the open fields of Brie rides a troop of knights. They've come to save us."

"Are they the Regent's men?"

"Who cares who they are, as long as they fight against those creatures on the other side of the river!"

The first men galloped in. The Duchess of Normandy and her group of ladies backed far away from the portal as the courtyard filled with knights and their retainers. Pennons of azure and argent glittered in the bright June sunshine, displaying stars and lilies and couchant lions.

"Blanche . . ." Aliénor took a deep breath. "They're Gascon knights."

"Do you know them?"

"I recognize their colors." It had been so long since she'd seen the bright pennons, the brilliant heraldry of her own people. Eagerly, she walked closer to the Duchess of Normandy and her ladies, closer to the leading knights as they dismounted. "The one with the red-gold hair—that's Gaston Phoebus, the Comte de Foix. The man next to him is the Captal de Buch, Gaston's cousin—but he's a vassal of the English!"

"The truce has long been negotiated, Aliénor: English knights can travel freely in France. Is he a brave knight?"

"He's a member of King Edward's Order of the Garter."

"Then praise God he's here." Blanche gestured to another knight. "And who's he? The one with the eagle in gold on his tunic?"

Aliénor tightened her grip on the babe as the world tilted and whirled around her.

It can't be.

She stumbled back against the stocky woman.

"Aliénor? Are you all right?"

She watched as he dismounted, pulled off his basinet, and bowed in front of the Duchess of Normandy. His black hair had grown long, well below his shoulders, and as he rose she saw the glitter of blue eyes in that achingly familiar, sun-bitten face.

Blanche gripped her arm. "Who is he, Aliénor?"

He's the man who killed my brother.

"My God, you're acting like you see the face of the Blessed Mother Mary!"

He's the father of my son.

He must have sensed her shock, for Jehan suddenly looked beyond the Duchess, past the tight gathering of women, to where she leaned breathlessly against Blanche. She stiffened, for she was not prepared for the assault. She was not prepared for the thunder and roar of her heart, or the rush of emotions that pelted her with all the violence of a Gascon hailstorm.

Abruptly, rudely, he pushed past the Duchess and her ladies and headed directly toward her. She waited for the shame and anguish and guilt to overwhelm her, as it had done every time she had looked at him after her brother's death. It didn't come. Questions tumbled in her mind: Why wasn't he with the Prince of Wales in London? What was he doing here, of all places? Here—*here*—in a royal castle?

Here, riding to the rescue of the ladies of the French court, riding to save her? She had come to the court of the Regent of France for one reason: to extricate herself from the web of misery that threatened to choke her to death in Gascony, to run far, far away from Jehan. Yet here Jehan was, by fate rather than design, and Aliénor wondered if God meant to torment her forever for her sin.

This doesn't feel like torment.

No, it didn't feel like torment. Though the courtyard was full of men-at-arms, pawing, restless horses, the cries of welcome of the women who now poured out of the castle, Aliénor heard nothing. Nothing but her own ragged breathing, the breathing of her child—*their child*—and the footsteps of Jehan as he approached her. Her heart thumped and moved and twisted in her chest, as if rising reluctantly from a long, stiff slumber.

He stopped in front of her and hesitated. His hands curled into fists. His gaze roamed over her face, thoroughly, as a blind man might look at his healer after being given sight.

Blanche stepped between them as the silence stretched. "You're frightening the lady, knight!"

He bowed to Aliénor, low, then straightened. His gaze slipped to the moving package in her arms. "I congratulate you on your marriage, Madame. . . ."

"I'm not married."

The moment the words left her lips she realized her mistake. She should not have spoken so quickly. She seemed to have no control over her body, over her mind, or over her tongue. Jehan obviously thought she had married, and the child was the fruit of the union. He could not guess the age of the babe by his size.

"Aliénor."

She tilted the child toward him, so he could see the lock of dark hair peeping out beneath the linen of the swaddling clothes, and the big, blue eyes.

"May I present your son, Jehan." She tilted her chin. "I've named him Laurent."

Chapter
19

JEHAN HOVERED AT THE EDGE OF THE GREAT HALL IN THE CASTLE at Meaux, outside the light of the hundreds of wax candles speared on wrought-iron candelabra that lined the room. A servant skimmed noiselessly past him, spraying the rushes with smoky frankincense until the cloying fragrance hung heavy in the air. He slipped back farther in the shadows. He scanned the crowd of noblewomen in their embroidered silks and jewel-studded, glittering golden girdles. Still no sign of her. Aliénor was not in the hall.

For nearly two months he had waited to talk with her, since the moment he saw her and their son—*their son*—in the courtyard of this castle. Then, they had had only a moment together, for the peasants of Meaux rioted across the Marne river and the constable of the castle urged them to crush the uprising before it raged out of control. Immediately following the battle, a battle that was nothing more than slaughter, Jehan and the other Gascons were called upon to defeat two other peasant uprisings in the area. He chafed at the delay, but honor compelled him to fight with the French against a common enemy, the ferocious "Jacques," the roughly dressed commoners who now took their turn in ravaging through France.

This wait was difficult, for he had forgone so many more critical duties over the past year and a half for Aliénor's sake. Only weeks after Laurent's death, the Prince had invited Jehan to join him in his triumphant voyage to London with the captive King of France, but Jehan declined the invitation, in order to escort Aliénor to Paris. He had promised to join Edward in England as soon as Aliénor was settled, but when the time came, he realized he despised the thought of idling about London, feasting and jousting in tourneys. Fortunately, he met Gaston Phoebus and the Captal de Buch, two southern noblemen on their way to fight the heathens in Prussia, an honorable diversion during the inconvenient period of peace between the English and French. He joined the men. He knew the Prince wouldn't object to his fighting in a holy war. He thought, too, that a crusade against infidels would somehow purge him of guilt, and purge him of the memory of Aliénor.

Nothing had worked. Endless, mindless fighting failed to dim the memory of Aliénor's pained, golden eyes the day she buried her brother, the brother he had killed in battle. It was no wonder. For the sake of his insatiable ambition, he had taken advantage of a woman's desperate situation, and that lapse in his rigid code of honor had cost him the woman he loved and the life of a fifteen-year-old boy.

What a fool he had been. All those months he had taken what he needed from Aliénor, without ever offering her anything in return. She had loved him. She had given him everything. She had run Castelnau so efficiently that he had never noticed the work involved until the death of her brother, when suddenly, without her guiding hand, the smoothness of the daily routine fell apart and the servants wandered aimlessly in the great hall. He hadn't realized until too late that Aliénor would have been the perfect partner in his future. He had been too much a fool to recognize that for a man to have a wife as lovely and as worthy as she, a woman who loved him and whom he loved, was a gift far greater than all the wealth of kings.

He knew it now. He knew, too, that it was his own fault that he lived in misery. It was this hunger in him, this wretched greed, which blinded him to all else. It took the spilled blood of a fifteen-year-old boy to give him sight.

Fighting in a hundred holy wars could not purge him of guilt. Only one thing could: returning to France and amending old wrongs. He knew he had to find Aliénor, face her, and do what he should have done long, long ago.

He had not expected his search to be so easy. It was as if a divine hand arranged the attack at Meaux just as he passed nearby. He took comfort in the sign, for he no longer believed he had the power to win what he now wanted by prowess alone, without the help of a greater power. He also took comfort in the sight of Aliénor, standing straight-backed and lovely, holding their *son* in her arms. The child, too, was a sign. Jehan had come back to fix old wrongs. The presence of their son made the situation very clear and so very, very simple.

Jehan straightened as he saw Thibaud in the crowded hall. The aged knight was easy to find, not only because of his mane of white hair, but also because of his clothing: He was the only knight who wore a long tunic, in the old fashion, rather than the short, tight, scalloped tunics and multicolored hose of the younger knights. Jehan caught his eye and beckoned for him. Immediately, Thibaud disattached himself from a group of ladies and wove his way through the crowd.

"God's bones, I never thought you'd arrive." Thibaud gestured to the women. "I feel like I'm in a flock of hens."

"Where is she?"

"Eyes only for one of the birds, eh? She doesn't usually attend dinner with the court."

"She'd best attend this one, or I'll lay siege to her chamber."

"These women will take great pleasure in that. They've been cackling about this feast for months."

"It's time to check on her." Jehan placed a hand on Thibaud's upraised arm as the aged knight gestured to a page. "I'm not sending a boy to do a man's work."

"What? You'll send me, a knight, to fetch a woman?"

"I'm going myself."

"You don't know where her chamber is!"

"You do."

Thibaud frowned behind his snowy beard. "This feast is in your honor. The Duchess of Normandy is already frantic, waiting for your entrance."

"The Duchess can wait a little while longer."

"It isn't wise to insult the future Queen of France."

"You've turned too much into a courtier, Thibaud. I should have taken you to Prussia. Lead me to Aliénor's room."

"My great-niece will cut me to pieces for this, and so will that wench of hers, that widow who always hovers over her and the child." Thibaud slipped past Jehan into the shadows. "You should have arranged to see her in private."

"And give her time to slip away and hide?"

"When has *ma petite nièce* ever hidden from anything?"

"She hid the child from me."

Thibaud frowned but didn't respond. Jehan followed him down a small aisle, which led to a quiet wing of the castle. Rushlights sputtered at wide intervals and their footsteps echoed in the empty hall.

Thibaud pointed toward an open portal, where a faint light spilled out of a small room. "That's her chamber. Let me go first and prepare her for your arrival."

Jehan heard voices as he approached, then the tinkling, musical sound of laughter. *Aliénor's laughter.* It was a strange sound, a heavenly sound, and he wondered how she found the ability to laugh after all that had happened. Thibaud stopped in the portal. Jehan stayed in the shadows and watched her over Thibaud's shoulder.

Aliénor stood near the hearth. Her golden hair flowed around her, capturing the wavering light of the fire, as she balanced the babe on her hip. He feasted his gaze upon her like a man starved. He noticed the new fullness of her breasts, the rope of pearls wound about her smooth brow, and her soft smile as she gazed upon their son. The babe's tiny fingers clung firmly to a long tress of hair.

Thibaud walked into the room. "Is this what has kept you for so long in this chamber, Aliénor?"

"Oncle!"

"The ladies are calling you a coward already, and here you are, coddling my great-great-nephew, as if the whole royal court wasn't waiting for you!"

An elderly woman abruptly stood up from the bed. She placed her hands on ample hips. "I see you're back from riding to war like an old fool on a young horse, Sir Thibaud."

"Blanche—don't start, not now." Aliénor approached Thibaud and turned her cheek for a kiss, shifting the babe's weight easily on her hip. "You didn't tell me you were coming to Meaux."

"I came with Sir Jehan."

Her smile disappeared. "But I thought you were outside Paris, with the Regent."

"I was. Sir Jehan fought against the Jacques with the Regent."

"Then the siege of Paris is over?"

"There was no siege to speak of. The loyal Parisians killed Etienne Marcel, and then they drove Charles of Navarre's supporters out of the city. When Sir Jehan and I left this morning, the commoners opened the gates of Paris to the Regent."

"I see." She turned to Blanche. "Come, Blanche, help me untangle Laurent's fingers from my hair. Thibaud's right. I intended to make a grand entrance, but we're far too late, and if we wait any longer it'll look as if I'm delaying." She bent her head as Blanche extricated her blond hair from Laurent's hand. "You'll escort me into the hall, won't you, *oncle?"*

"Actually, Aliénor—"

"Don't you dare say no!" Blanche's bright green eyes flashed in anger. "You've stayed away from Meaux long enough. It's the least you can do for her!"

"Have you missed my company so sorely, woman?"

"Hmmph! No more than any kitchen servant."

"So that's what's got you so choleric!" Thibaud placed his hands on his hips. "I'm old, not dead, and until I am, I'm going to pull a finch whenever I can—kitchen servant or not."

"Thibaud!" Aliénor frowned at her great-uncle. "How coarse you are. Apologize to Blanche."

"For what? For telling the truth? Behind that damned wimple is a woman, too, and though she claims she's old, I know better."

"Enough." Aliénor walked across the room and handed the child to a wetnurse who sat by a tiny wooden cradle. "I'm glad you're here, *oncle*. The women have been as gleeful as spectators at a hanging all morning, and I wasn't looking forward to walking into the hall alone."

"I think Sir Jehan would prefer to do the honors."

Thibaud turned and gestured to the portal. Aliénor straightened, suddenly, stiffly. Jehan walked through the shadows into the light, his gaze fixed on her. All the color ebbed from her face. She crushed the folds of her crimson silk skirts in her hands.

"You beast!" Blanche glared at Thibaud. "You led him here, didn't you?"

"Out, Thibaud." Jehan gestured to Blanche. "You, too. Argue outside if you must. I want to speak to Aliénor alone."

"We must go," Aliénor said, "or we'll be late for the feast."

"The feast is in my honor. It won't start without me."

Thibaud wordlessly turned on his heels. Blanche glanced at Aliénor once, worriedly, then followed. Aliénor toyed with the hanging end of her silver girdle. Jehan slowly approached the fire.

His heart moved. She had dressed defiantly for the occasion, in a shimmering length of crimson silk over a pale, cream-colored undertunic. It must have taken hours to wind the rope of precious pearls through her long tresses, which were brushed to a golden sheen. He wanted to reach out, to bury his hands in the curls, to feel them soft and warm around his fingers, to breathe in the scent of her skin. He wanted to pluck the pearls from her hair and watch the neat tresses tumble in confusion; he wanted all this silence and all this apprehension to dissolve away and leave them with nothing but honesty and openness and passion.

She looked at him and tilted her chin. "Are you here to see your son?"

"I am here to see you. Until two months ago I didn't know I had a son." He gestured to the boy, who lay against the wetnurse's breast. "Why didn't you tell me?"

"You left abruptly last year."

"You knew long before I left. Thibaud told me the child was born in October." He watched the muscles of her neck grow taut and rigid. "There have never been lies between us, Aliénor. Let's not start now."

"You should have stayed away." She lowered her lashes. "You didn't have to return to Meaux."

"The Duchess of Normandy insisted on honoring the knights who defended this castle."

"Did you have to insist that I join the celebrations?"

"I wanted to see you."

"Then you should have asked to see me alone. You know it will shame me to sit out there in front of the entire court, with the father of my illegitimate child nearby."

"You'd rather I publicly ignored your presence?" He shook his head slowly. "I won't do that, Aliénor. I won't keep secrets, like you've kept this secret from me. You should have told me long before I left Paris."

She turned away. She motioned for the wetnurse to leave. The woman rose from her seat, with Laurent still attached to her breast, and swiftly left the room.

"If I had told you last year, you would have done something foolish." She clasped her hands against her abdomen. "Just as you did when you escorted me through France."

"I would have done what was right."

"Which is why I held my tongue." Her eyes flashed like golden sparks. "Did you think I could bear the thought of living near you, in Gascony, perhaps married off to some unsuspecting peasant?"

"Married *off?*" He could not hide his incredulity. *"Diou de jou*, Aliénor. *I* would have married you."

She stared at him like a startled doe, then, just as quickly, looked away. She unfolded her hands and smoothed the palms over her stomach. When she spoke again, her voice was breathless, throaty, like the rustling of late autumn leaves.

"You would have given up all your prospects, Jehan? Your future, the promise of a wealthy English bride?"

"I gave them up anyway. I gave them up the moment I chose not to go to London to be with the Prince of Wales."

"Then it's true."

"What?"

"You spent the past year in Prussia with the Comte de Foix and the Captal de Buch, fighting heathens."

"Yes."

"There was a time when your ambition was more important to you than anything. More important than I. More important than the life of my brother. I can't believe you didn't go to the Prince after all that happened."

"My fault was greed, Aliénor, as well as ambition. I thought I could have everything—you and a wealthy bride —without paying the price. I paid the price. After losing you, I wanted no more land, no titles, and no bride." He threaded his fingers through his hair. "Why do you think I fought in Prussia? What other way can a knight atone for his sins but to lend his sword to a holy cause?"

"It's a fine thing you've done."

He released a self-deprecating snort. "Your brother would have approved."

"My brother would have approved of anything that sent you far, far away from me."

He stepped closer to her. He had forgotten how small she was, how delicate the bones of her shoulders, her chest, as they rose and fell beneath the silver, embroidered edge of her surcoat. "Your brother's last wish was for me to leave you." He had spent every day since wondering if he had done the right thing. "Would you have married me last year, *couret*, if I had asked?"

She shook her head, and her hair swung heavily against her waist. "Being married to you would have been like being married to my own sin. I wanted to get away from it, not be bound to it eternally."

"So, instead, you took a position here." He gestured to the small, sparsely furnished chamber. "And was thus labeled an adulteress, with an illegitimate child, ostracized by the French court."

"I'm happy here with my son."

"How can you be happy living like a pariah in the royal court? Your brother *died* trying to save your honor."

"A worthless cause. It was too late to recoup my honor the day I gave myself to you." She closed her eyes and rubbed her temple. "I never wanted to have this conversation, Jehan. That's why I came to Paris. I thought I'd never see you again. What is done, is done, and nothing can change it."

"It can be changed."

"You can't bring my brother back to life."

"I can give his death some meaning."

"Meaning!" She walked to the edge of the cradle and clutched the carved wooden edge. "Thibaud tells the story of my brother as if it were some glorious crusade. I suppose in some strange, twisted way I can barely understand, his death had some meaning, some purpose, a purpose only knights can understand. Last year, I was so crippled with suffering and grief that all I wanted to do was crawl someplace dark and hide. I couldn't bear to look at you."

"And now, Aliénor?" He walked to her side, so close he could smell the faint scent of sweet herbs that clung to her skin. "Can you bear to look at me now?"

It was a mistake to stand near her. He could see each strand of honey-blond hair, the streaks of gold in her soft brown eyes, the sweep of lashes that ended in gold tips, and the fine, pale arch of her brows. Her cheek curved so smoothly. His heart stirred. He realized how much control he would have to maintain if he were ever going to win this woman back. He touched her chin as she tried to turn away. "I should never have left Paris."

"The Regent's men would have caught you and thrown you in the Châtelet," she argued. "And any woman can give you a child. I could give you nothing else. And I knew— painfully well—how important it was for you to make a good marriage."

"Was. It *was* important. I've since discovered that the size of a woman's dowry is no measure of her worth as a wife."

"Why did you come here, Jehan?"

"For you, *brèisha."*

She backed away, into the cradle. "Did you come here to make me your mistress again? After all that has happened?"

"Do you think I've learned nothing from the past?"

"Nothing has changed. I . . . we . . . what we've done . . . It caused my brother's death—"

"Your brother died in glory. We have suffered far too long." He reached for her but dropped his hand when she flinched away. "I treated you—the woman I loved—like a common peasant, when you deserved to be crowned like a queen. I still can't believe you don't hate me for it."

"All you did was take what I freely offered."

"All you did, *couret,* was love a man so deeply that you hid that love from a brother you loved just as deeply."

"What we did was *shameful,"* she retorted. "I vowed on all that's holy it will *not* happen again."

She stood as stiff and unyielding as a sword. He wanted to wrap her in his arms, he wanted to kiss her until she grew soft and pliant in his embrace, until she forgot all this guilt, all this endless torment, all this pain. He wanted to prove to her that the fault was *his,* that she was worthy to be the consort of a far better knight, that he was here to make everything as it was . . . if he could. They once shared a wondrous thing, an unusual love between a man and a woman. He wanted to have that love again. He wanted to love her until all her anguish was gone. He surged forward, but she walked abruptly away from him until she faced the hearth. She stood, arms crossed, with her back to him.

He ran a hand through his hair. Between the two of them, there was such a tangle of guilt and shame that he wondered if he could ever separate the knots. She resisted passion with a will that surprised him, a will far, far stronger than his. It was almost as if she were *afraid* of both him and the passions that still trembled between them. He knew then that he would have to win her with logic and reason. He would have to persuade her to do what he wished now, and later, over the years, he would warm her to a deeper loving—the same tender yet passionate loving they had shared in Gascony.

Slowly, slowly.

He had had ample time over the past two months to learn of the Regent's plans for Aliénor. He would use what he knew to bend her, gently, to his will. If that failed, then he would use his other advantage: his son.

"Thibaud tells me that the Regent is making arrangements for you," he began. "Arrangements to marry Guy de Baste."

"I don't know why Sir Guy would be interested in me when I'm as impoverished as a commoner."

"Sir Guy is playing a game of loyalties, a game that, in the end, will bring him huge tracts of land but will bring no king any guarantee of loyalty."

Her silk tunic rustled as she turned to face him. "What do you mean?"

"Sir Guy spent a winter with the English. He told the Regent he spent his time currying favor with the Prince of Wales. Sir Guy claims that if the Regent asks for certain tracts of conquered Gascon land during the peace negotiations, the English will cede them quickly if they think the lands are going to Sir Guy—a man they erroneously believe is loyal to the English."

"So he's fooling the English, then."

"Only God and Sir Guy know what he told the English. He could have told them to submit to this scheme, calling it a gesture of conciliation to the French, when, in fact, Sir

Guy has promised to become an English vassal as soon as he has the lands."

"Either way," she said softly, "he receives the lands, but no one knows who will receive his loyalty."

"Do you want to marry such a man, Aliénor?"

"I have no intention of marrying Sir Guy."

"What?"

"Sir Guy will insist I give up Laurent." She gestured to the empty cradle. "I won't give up my son, not for anything or anybody."

Hope swelled in his chest. "Even though he's my son?"

"Diou, Jehan! You, above all, should understand. My father is dead; my mother is locked away in a convent of her own volition; my brother is gone. But for Thibaud, this babe is all I have left—all I could ever want."

You're not alone, couret, *not anymore.* "Did you know that the Regent already introduced Sir Guy's requests into the negotiations with the English?"

She looked startled. "I'll have to tell him not to pursue this as soon as I see him."

"Good. When you tell him you won't marry Guy de Baste," he said, "tell him you *will* marry me."

She didn't move, not really. Her eyes froze open. Her arms uncrossed and dropped heavily to her sides. The skirts of her surcoat moved in an invisible draft. The fire behind her snapped and flared as a log fell off the higher level of the andiron and crashed down into the embers.

Jehan surged ahead, afraid of her silence. "I should have asked you last year, Aliénor. I should have asked you the moment I seized Castelnau. I was blinded by greed and ambition." He scanned her face, willing her to answer, willing her to do something other than stare at him, pale-faced, in shock. "You were worthy to be my wife, more worthy than I was to be your husband. I came back from Prussia for one reason: to find you and right old wrongs. Marry me, *couret.*"

"You're doing this for my . . . our son."

"I want our son to have a name, but son or no, I would still have asked you to marry me."

She shook her head, dazed.

"By all the saints, Aliénor, I'm in love with you!"

"Don't." Her gilded brown eyes widened. "Don't say such things. We can't marry."

— "Why not?"

"Sir Guy—"

"I've already spoken to Thibaud about him. Your great-uncle intends to persuade the Regent to marry you to me, the father of your child, rather than to that slippery Frenchman."

"The Regent won't give French lands to a knight with English loyalties."

"I am not asking for a dowry."

"What?"

"I will ask for nothing but your hand." When she still didn't speak, he forged ahead. "Thibaud's going to persuade the Regent to give no French land to an English knight, rather than give large tracts of land to a French knight with questionable loyalties."

"You and my great-uncle have worked this all out, haven't you?"

"I'll give you a choice, Aliénor, if that's what you prefer."

"Your choices are never easy. Just once," she sputtered, "I'd like to hear you say: I'm giving you a choice, Aliénor. Peas or beans."

He smiled. Her spirit was returning. "You'll hear plenty of that, if you agree to marry me."

"And if I don't?"

"Then I'll kidnap you and force you into marriage."

"That's no choice at all."

"I want you to be my wife."

"Have you ever *not* had your way?"

"Yes. When your brother died, I wanted to tear him from the grip of death. And after you told me you wanted to leave, and I realized how blind I'd been, I wanted to turn back time so that I could ask you to marry me the first day I seized Castelnau."

He thought he saw something flicker in her gilded brown eyes, something soft, something warm, something vulnerable. She looked away before he could capture it.

In frustration he asked, "Would you rather the Regent marry you off to Sir Guy and take Laurent away?"

"No!"

"Then, damn it, make a decision."

"For my son's sake, I'd be a fool not to marry you."

"Is that a yes?"

"Yes."

The word rang in his ears. *Yes.* She had agreed to be his wife. *His wife.* He wanted to crush her in his embrace, to kiss her, and taste the sweet wine he had been denied so long. He approached her, fired full of need, but she backed away, suddenly, bumping against the limestone edge of the fireplace.

"Don't, Jehan, don't."

"What is it, *couret?*"

"I've been betrothed four times but never married," she said breathlessly. "I don't want to tempt fate."

"Do you think I've learned nothing from a year and a half of misery?" He pulled her into his arms, despite the fact that she pressed her hands against his chest in resistance. His blood surged in his veins as he felt her small, soft, warm body trembling against his own. "I want you more than I've ever wanted a woman, *brèisha,* but I won't make love to you, not until we are married. I've waited a year and a half—I can wait three or four more weeks."

"Three . . . or four weeks?"

"The marriage can't take place until I receive permission from the Prince of Wales." He buried his face in her hair. "I've already sent the letter to London. I also want banns to be read in the church, as it should have been done over a year ago."

She stood stiffly in his embrace. Her heart beat swift and

hard in her chest, like the heartbeat of a wild creature, captured and frightened. He ran his hands down her back, feeling the heat of her skin through the thin layers of silk and linen, tracing the sweet indentation of her spine. *My wife.* It had been so long since he held her close in his arms. She fit so perfectly against his chest—if she would only wrap her arms around him, if she would only succumb to the inevitable. How long had he envisioned this moment, when he would be alone with her again? How often had he dreamed that she would wrap her arms around him and open herself to him as she used to, long ago, when she was an innocent, drunk on the glory of their lovemaking? *No more guilt. No more anguish, no more torment. It will be like it was in Castelnau.* He brushed her hair and her pearls away from her temple, kissing the throbbing pulse. He waited for her to relax and grow pliant in his embrace, but she only trembled harder. Her back grew more rigid, and her heart threatened to burst out of her chest.

"*Couret,* don't be afraid," he murmured. "This is as it should be."

"Don't force me . . . to feel this way." Her voice was husky and muffled. "It's shameful. I feel weak, so weak. Like before my brother died."

He held her tight. *She's afraid of me. She's afraid of loving.* He hated the rigidness of her spine, the tightness of her body. He wanted to feel her supple against him, giving herself with utter abandon. He suddenly wondered if she would ever love so openly again. He wondered if she would ever trust him enough to give herself freely, without doubt. He kissed her head. It was too soon. He had won one battle: She agreed to be his wife. He asked too much to expect the woman he had grievously wronged to open up to him like a flower, without care, without resentment, without restraint. He had a lifetime to show her that there was no shame in lovemaking. He stepped back and released her.

She lifted her eyes, cloudy with confusion, and stumbled back against the hearth. He fixed the rope of pearls around her brow, straightened a lock of hair, and adjusted her bodice over one shoulder. "Come, my love."

"Come where?"

"We're late for the feast." He crooked his elbow at her. "We'd better tell the Duchess of Normandy the news, before she sends armed guards to this room to fetch us."

Chapter
20

THE NEXT EVENING, ALIÉNOR STOOD, STUNNED, IN THE COURT-
yard of the castle at Meaux, greeting her great-uncle as he
arrived back from Paris with forty royal men-at-arms and a
summons for Aliénor and Jehan to come immediately to the
Louvre, the Regent's fortress outside the Parisian walls, to
start the wedding preparations. Jehan had sent Thibaud off
only that morning to present the offer of marriage to the
Regent. She knew she shouldn't be surprised by the Duke's
enthusiastic response—he would rid himself of a poor,
disgraced noblewoman without parting with a hectare of
French land—but the swiftness of the Duke's answer,
combined with Jehan's eagerness, convinced her beyond
doubt that the marriage would actually take place. She
would soon be the wife of Jehan de St. Simon.

Her insides twisted and wound and contorted like a
laundress's well-wrung linens. She should be dancing with
joy at the prospect of marriage. With his proposal, Jehan
endowed her with respect, so quickly, that the Duchess
seated Aliénor way above the salt at the trestle-tables last
night, near two baronesses of the realm. Marriage to Jehan
guaranteed her a life of luxury and wealth, it titled her a
vicomtesse, it saved her from a life in a convent. There was a
time when all these pretty trappings would have been more
than enough to persuade her to marry any man, but Jehan
was not any man, and if there were nothing else drawing

them together, she would have run far, far away from the prospect of eternal bonds.

But there was something drawing them together, something precious and vulnerable: their son. She could not deny her child what was, by right of birth, his just inheritance. Laurent deserved the viscounty of Tournan, he deserved to grow up with a name and a heritage, unstained by the mark of bastardy. She could give him all that, and she could secure her own right to raise him. All she had to do was marry the man who had stolen her castle, stripped her of lands and dowry, taken her virtue, and killed her beloved brother.

And loved me, loved me beyond words, beyond all imagining.

It was too late. Too much had passed between them, and her memories lingered, tenacious, dusting all hope of a bright future with a dull layer of shame and guilt. She would marry Jehan, not only for her son's sake, but also for the sake of her brother. The illicit relationship he tried to save her from would finally be consecrated by God; and her son, his namesake, would no longer be called a bastard. Her life would be as Laurent willed it, so long before. His soul could rest in peace.

But not hers, never hers. Her torment had only begun. When Jehan had pulled her into his arms last night she had weakened like the darkest of sinners. Her body responded without any caution. It had been so long since she had felt his potent caress. She wanted nothing more than to bury her face in his naked chest, open her lips to his kiss, feel the roughness of his tongue against her own. But these thoughts were *sinful*. These uncontrolled, unbridled emotions had once brought her endless misery. She could not desecrate the memory of her brother by succumbing to them, and making the same dangerous mistake twice.

So her thoughts went around and around, like the blades of a windmill, turning fast and jerking to a stop, then spinning out of control by the force of contrary winds. Since he had sought her out in her room last night, Jehan had spent every spare moment at her side: standing next to her at Mass, sharing her bowl at the midday meal, never leaving her a moment outside his presence to think through the feelings wakened and reborn since his marriage proposal. Even now, in the twilight, he stood close to her and spoke to Thibaud about the details of her great-uncle's discussion with the Regent. She took advantage of his distraction to excuse herself—on the pretext that it would take the entire evening to pack up her belongings in preparation for tomorrow's journey. She felt his intense blue gaze on her until she closed the door of the great hall behind her.

Her mind was no clearer when she prepared to leave the next morning at prime. As she mounted a gray mare that the Duchess of Normandy had given her as a perfunctory betrothal gift, Jehan rode his stallion to her side and greeted her. He was so handsome in the dawn light: his blue eyes bright, his stance straight and bold, his chain mail molding to his strong, tall body. The sight of the wind ruffling his hair brought back a thousand memories, all disturbing, all frightening. She had slept not a moment during the long, restless night. Jehan looked as if he could wrestle an entire army and win. He was as eager for this marriage as she was terrified of it. She was relieved when he finally rode away to lead the contingent of knights out of the castle.

Aliénor thought that the escort of forty royal knights with their blue banners spattered with gold *fleur-de-lis,* combined with Jehan's contingent of twenty men dressed in blue and green heraldry, too large and far too regal for a fallen woman, a bastard child, and a single cart of her personal goods. But as she saw the charred outline of the city of Meaux and the scavengers who still picked among the wreckage, she wondered if the Duke weren't correct in sending so many men.

Her fears grew as the contingent rode along the banks of the river Marne. She noticed carcasses of pigs and sheep scattered on the edge of the rutted road, ill-tended wheat fields, and, in some places, harvests rotting in the fields. She called Thibaud over and asked him about the countryside they were going to ride through: Was it as devastated as the lands around Meaux? He told her the lands closer to Paris were worse. Despite the fact that the Regent had captured Paris, Charles of Navarre had enlisted a number of English knights specifically to raid the villages around the city, and the Jacques still rose sporadically, and unpredictably. All disturbing thoughts of Jehan scattered away in the face of more imminent danger. She rode back to where two horses pulled her cart and took Laurent from the wetnurse's arms. Blanche sat next to the wetnurse, holding a perfumed linen against her nose to filter out the dust raised by the horses' hooves. She argued that the babe would be safer in the cart, but Aliénor was insistent. She needed to have him close to her. If anything happened, she would kill any man, English brigand or dirty Jacque, who dared to touch her child.

She nudged the young gray mare ahead of the cart. The August sun broke through the morning mist, and as the day progressed, it grew hot on her veil. She covered her sleeping babe's face with a linen to guard his skin from the blazing rays of the sun.

Suddenly her mare stumbled. She instinctively clutched Laurent to her breast and tightened her grip on the reins. The mare neighed in pain and limped a few more steps before stopping altogether, tossing her head in an effort to loosen Aliénor's restraint. Aliénor tried to maintain control of the horse. Within minutes she heard a set of approaching hooves. Jehan came to a stop beside her prancing mare.

"What's the matter?" he asked.

"She stumbled. I think she caught something in one of her hooves."

Jehan called for his squire as the contingent of sixty-odd riders slowed to a stop. The mare shifted her weight again, neighing, nervous with the presence of Jehan's stallion and with the pain. Twice, the horse nearly caused Aliénor to slide off her precarious perch side-saddle on her back. She clutched Laurent closer. The linen she placed over his face fluttered to the ground. She glanced around for help in dismounting before the horse bucked her off entirely.

Jehan reached for the mare's reins.

"No!" She held her son out to him. "Here. Take Laurent."

He reached for the child, but she jerked the babe away.

"This isn't a sword or a mace, Jehan! Remove those gauntlets."

He growled at the tone of her voice as he swiftly removed the gauntlets sewn with tinned plates and tucked the leather fingers into his baldric. She teetered on the saddle and thrust the babe into his hands. She slid to the ground abruptly, pulling the length of her moss-green skirts off the horse's back.

Laurent woke up with a squall.

Aliénor ignored Jehan and the crying babe as she tried to calm the young mare. She assumed Jehan would ride back to the cart and give the child to his wetnurse. She looked at her mare's lifted hoof and discovered that the Duchess had not ordered the horse to be shod. Further, the mare's hooves were soft with rot. *It is typical,* she thought, *for the Duchess to give me a gift that goes lame within a few leagues.* The road from Meaux to Paris was rutted and strewn with debris, and it was no surprise that an unshod horse caught the edge of a sharp stone. She saw a sliver of rock lodged deeply in the mare's worn hoof.

She felt a prick of anger. She straightened. Jehan's squire approached, dismounted, examined the mare's hoof, and announced to the company that they would have to halt for a brief time in order to remove the stone. He called for some help in holding the beast still. Aliénor stepped away to let the men do their duty, then walked around the mare. Jehan was still there, sitting on his stallion, holding Laurent.

She stopped and drew in a deep, ragged breath.

Jehan gripped his child in his huge dark hands, holding him stiffly over the saddlebow, staring at the creature, almost helplessly. She realized with a jolt that this was the first time Jehan had held his child in his arms. Jehan's hair shone with chestnut highlights in the bright glare of the sun, thick and glossy compared to the black wisps that clung to Laurent's head. Jehan looked so large, fully armored, sitting high upon his enormous stallion. In comparison, Laurent looked tiny, pale, and utterly defenseless engulfed in hands better trained to wield swords. Laurent's arms had somehow come free of the linen swaddling, and now they waved about in the air. Her son was no longer crying. The child and the man stared at one another, blue eyes staring into identical blue eyes, until Jehan slowly bent his elbows, brought the child closer to him, then lifted him high over his head. Laurent gurgled his pleasure.

Her heart rose to her throat. She swallowed instinctively. She didn't know what to do. She stood dumbly in the middle of the rutted road, staring at her husband-to-be as he held his son for the first time. *Laurent should be crying.* He hadn't been fed since prime. Jehan swung him carefully over his head, back and forth, and a slow, dimpled smile grew on his handsome face.

Something blossomed in her chest, something warm, something tender. She crushed the feeling before it grew too strong for her to control. Marrying Jehan solved all her problems about keeping Laurent, but it gave her a whole new frightening crop of difficulties. Why hadn't the torment and anguish of her brother's death destroyed the fragile fabric of the love she and Jehan once shared? He could still affect her as no man could. She did not want to *feel* as she had felt in Gascony. The kind of love they had shared . . . certainly such ardor did not belong between a man and his wife. She did not want to yearn for something that she could not have. *How handsome he is.* Too handsome. Too dangerously handsome. She felt herself weakening.

Again. It seemed that every moment she spent with him, she weakened. She was in danger of losing her peace of mind, a peace of mind for which she had battled so hard during the past year and a half. Now, as she watched Jehan hesitantly play with his son, she realized she could no longer live quietly in the warm circle of solitude with her child.

Jehan would become part of that circle. How could she resist the man who loved her child so dearly?

Aliénor heard the mare neigh and buck with restraint. She turned and watched as six men tried to hold her still and the squire pulled the sliver of stone from her hoof. When she looked at Jehan again, he was hugging the babe comfortably against his chest and staring down at her from the height of his stallion.

"You've named him well," he said. "He's as brave as your brother. I toss him about and all he does is laugh."

"I'm glad you approve," she said dryly. "I called him Laurent Jehan for a reason: to link the two men who have caused me so much trouble."

"I can think of no name more appropriate for a child born of so much passion, and so much pain."

She flushed. She lifted her hands to her hips. "Do you realize you're coddling him like a mother? In front of all the Regent's men?"

"He is my son. A fine, fat one."

"He's a hungry one as well." She crossed the distance that separated them. "I'll take him to his wetnurse."

"No. I will."

Jehan urged his horse around and walked slowly to the cart, clutching the tiny babe to his chest with one hand. She watched him, puzzled, until the squire tapped her on the arm.

"The mare is too lame to carry you," Esquivat explained. "We'll have to find you another mount."

"There are no other horses but the ones pulling the cart," she said. "They're nothing but nags."

"You could ride in the cart with the other women."

"I'd rather wear a hairshirt in the heat of summer than ride in that contraption!"

Esquivat suppressed a smile. "We could send someone ahead to Neuilly-sur-Marne to bring you back a horse."

"How long would that take?"

"A few hours, at least."

"But we must arrive at the Louvre by twilight."

Jehan, relieved of his tiny burden, rode up beside them. "What's the problem?"

"Demoiselle is without a mount. The mare's too lame to travel."

"I should have thought of laming your horse earlier." He smiled widely. "Now you can ride with me."

"No! It's a long trip." She searched frantically for an excuse. "I don't want to strain your fine stallion."

"My fine stallion has been to Prussia and back, with me in full armor. He can withstand your meager weight for a few hours."

"We don't have a saddle for riding pillion."

"You can ride in front. There's enough room."

She frowned up at him. There was too much between them, too many memories, too much unspoken desire. She couldn't share his horse with him. He would be too close. She would be forced to press back against his strong chest. He would wrap his arms around her waist. How in God's name was she going to resist Jehan once they were together in the marriage bed, if just the thought of riding next to him caused her heart to surge and tumble in her breast?

"What are you afraid of, Aliénor?"

"I'm not afraid of anything."

"Liar. Have you forgotten my promise so quickly?" He gestured to the circle of men-at-arms who waited, chewing on cold meat and hunks of cheese and bread. "Besides, what can I do to you dressed in full armor, atop a horse, with three score men watching me?"

You can touch me, Jehan. That's all it seems to take.

"If you want to be in the Louvre by twilight, then we must leave now."

She considered the idea of riding through the dangerous land after dark, and she realized that though her strength of will would be in dire jeopardy so close to Jehan, she would rather risk an attack from him than an attack of brigands in the woods after dark.

Wouldn't she?

Jehan took her silence for yes and announced loudly that they would all be leaving. The men rewrapped their food. Aliénor hesitated as Jehan leaned over the horse and held out his open hand. Esquivat kneeled to help her mount the stallion. Jehan's fingers curled over her hand and he pulled her up. She eased herself into the angle of his thighs. Her tunic twisted beneath her, restricting her movement. She gasped as he adjusted her position with his bare hands, until his muscled thighs framed her hips and the wide expanse of his chest pressed firmly against her shoulder. She smelled the cleaning oil that clung to his chain mail, the sweet-smelling bits of spruce nestled in the blanket beneath the steel saddle. She stiffened, trying to minimize the places where their bodies touched, but he laughed openly at her efforts and wrapped his arm around her waist.

"If you keep shifting your weight like that, I might have to find a way to get you alone."

She stiffened at his words, afraid to move at all. The bulk of his forearm lay firmly against her midriff. She tried to relax as he kicked the huge horse into a walk and headed down the road with the men. She clutched Jehan's arm as the stallion pranced a little, unnerving her. His muscles were corded and hard beneath the mail. *Just as I remember them.* She shook the thought out of her head. As soon as Jehan reined the stallion back into control, she abruptly released his arm.

They rode in silence. As the miles passed and Jehan made no effort to caress her, she tried to relax on the horse. The base of her back already ached from her stiff stance. It would be hours before they saw the walls of Paris and she knew she could not sit straight-backed for all that time. Jehan said nothing as she leaned her head, hesitantly, into the curve of his neck. She tried not to think about the scent of him rising from the edge of his tunic, the scent that nudged awake so many memories. She tried not to look up into his face, though out of the corner of her eye she saw the dark tresses of his hair moving in the breeze and the shadow of a beard that covered his chin. She knew if she looked at him she would be lost, for she had not been this close to him since . . .

She closed her eyes to try to block out the memories, but it only made them stronger. She was separated from his bare chest by the layers of cloth, padding, and mail, but she could hear his strong heart beating beneath her ear. How many times had she wakened in the mornings in Castelnau, with her ear pressed against his bare chest, listening to the slow, even beat of his heart? She remembered one morning, when she had looked up at him and met his eyes, eyes as dark as twilight. He had smiled at her. He had kissed her. Then he had touched her as only Jehan could touch her, so deep inside her body, and she quivered in desire and need.

She started and her eyes flew open. She watched the passing scenery blindly. It was happening again. Jehan wasn't doing a thing, he wasn't doing anything but holding her tight against him so she wouldn't slide off the saddle. Yet, just his nearness was enough to kindle all those old, dangerous memories. Had she learned nothing over the past years? Hadn't she learned that it was shameful to feel this way, to yearn for a man like a whore on the streets of Paris?

"Easy, *brèisha.*" He tightened his grip and spoke into her veil. "You're as nervous as newly caught falcon."

"You're holding me too tight."

"Is that what it is? Then I'll loosen the jesses."

He loosened his grip around her waist. She looked up at him. It was a mistake. She was caught in his gaze as firmly as a fly might be caught in the sticky strings of a spider web. His smile dimmed, slowly. His eyes darkened from a pale blue to the turbid hue of a dark, raging river. He tightened his grip again, drawing her so close that she grasped his chest with an open hand, while her arm slid around his back. She watched his nostrils flare, she saw every short bristle on his ill-shaven cheek, and she wondered why her lips could not move and form the words of protest, the words screaming in her head.

His lips descended. She closed her eyes, more to block out the sight of her surrender, the sight of her shame, than for any other reason. His rough lips brushed her forehead. Then, before she could act, he loosened his grip and adjusted her position until she was once again pressed against him, with her ear to his chest. She lay there, stunned, listening to the rapid, uneven beating of his heart.

It was Jehan. She knew it without seeing him, for the darkness enveloped them both. The darkness was kind, the darkness was a balm to her, for she knew what they did was wrong. He approached her. She felt his heat as he came closer, and then his arms, and then his lips, moving over her face, moist and hot, until they finally met her own lips, and clung, and clung again. She felt like a woman starved of food, who was suddenly presented with a feast. She wanted all of him. She wanted him to touch her, to kiss her, to soothe her sore, aching heart, to make her feel alive again, but all he did was run his hands over her head and hold her tight against him. . . .

"Wake up, Aliénor."

Aliénor curled her fingers into something warm, hard, and bumpy. Her cheek lay against the same strange surface, and it was damp where it lay. She blinked her eyes open slowly, smelling the odor of sweat and horses and newly cut wheat, hearing the rhythmic click-clack of a multitude of horses, the thin ringing of harnesses. The wisps of her dream clung to her, making her achy and frustrated, and she tried desperately to hold on to the memory. Something wet slid down her nape, past the edge of her surcoat, to soak into her tunic. As her vision cleared, she saw the blue and green colors of Jehan's tunic and realized her cheek was pressed against it. She lifted her head and his tunic clung to her cheek, pulling away from the coat-of-plates beneath. His hand was there, suddenly, smoothing the linen away from her skin, lingering one moment too long on her throat.

"You slept peacefully."

She looked up at him. It was near sunset: She could tell by the orange cast of the light on his face. She flushed as she realized she had fallen asleep in his arms. She lifted her hand to her neck and wiped the perspiration beading on her nape. Her veil was hot to the touch, warmed by the incessant force of the August sun. The stallion still swayed rhythmically beneath her.

"Are we at the Louvre yet?"

He gestured to his left, to the walls of Paris and the spires that soared above the edge. She shifted her aching body against him and tried to rub the sleep from her eyes. Indeed, the walls of Paris lay just beyond them, but they did not head toward them or the clusters of dwellings that huddled near the base. Instead, they cut a path around the city, parallel to the walls.

"We should be at the Louvre in a little while," Jehan explained. "We thought, with a troop so large, that it would be better to circle the city than try to go through it."

Aliénor nodded mutely, remembering how crowded the twisted alleys of Paris were when she was trying to get an audience with the Regent. She and Thibaud had lodged outside the walls. She had dreaded each trip through the narrow, muck-filled streets, dodging the cutpurses and the beggars, the lepers and the peddlers, and the gargantuan signs that stretched over every shop. She couldn't imagine how they would get a contingent of sixty men through the city. "Why did the Regent decide to reside in the Louvre, rather than in his royal palace on the Ile de la Cité? I was told the Louvre is little more than a keep."

"The Louvre is easier to defend."

She glanced up at him, trying not to lose her senses at the heady sight of him, so near. He did not look at her but continued to scan the horizon opposite the walls of Paris. "Is the situation still so bad, then, that the Regent must wall himself within a fortress?"

"Charles of Navarre has played one hand against the other. He made peace with the Regent only weeks ago, and now he's made peace with the English and is trying, once again, to seize the city of Paris."

"You don't sound pleased," she said. "Charles of Navarre fights against the Regent. Don't you want him to be allied with the English?"

"I don't trust any man who shifts loyalties so easily."

"Like Guy de Baste?"

"Yes." He glanced at her. "You should know that he is still at the Regent's court."

"The Regent didn't throw him out after what you've told him?"

Jehan lifted a thick, dark brow. "I haven't told the Regent a word."

"But Sir Guy's a traitor!" She stared at him. "How else did you persuade the Regent to agree to this marriage?"

"According to Thibaud, making a marriage offer without asking for dowry was more than enough to persuade the Regent to give me your hand." Jehan shrugged his mighty shoulders. "As long as Sir Guy doesn't give away any English secrets, which as far as I know he hasn't, then I'll keep quiet, no matter how much I detest the man. Have you forgotten so soon, Aliénor, that my loyalty is to the English, not to the French?"

"What about Laurent?" she asked suddenly. "When he's old enough, will you send him to an *Englishman* for his knight's training?"

"It's not such a hellish fate."

"I remember what the English have done to Gascony. I don't want my son to learn such wretched warring skills."

"We will worry about Laurent when he reaches that age. Who knows? Perhaps he'll spite us both, take after his namesake, and insist on joining a Franciscan monastery."

"But what about our—"

She stopped herself sharply. She heard Jehan's swift intake of breath. She stiffened against him and said a prayer to Saint Jude that Jehan would not guess her intent.

Her prayer was not answered.

"Will there be a second son, *brèisha?*" She felt his lips against her veil. "Will you let me fill your womb with child again?"

Just the thought of it made her melt like butter in the open sun. "Do I have a choice?"

"I will not take an unwilling woman—or an unwilling wife—to my bed."

"Then there'll be no child. Not . . . not if I have to feel that shame again."

"Are you ashamed of Laurent?"

"No!"

"Then how can his conception be shameful, *brèisha?* How can you rue what we shared in Gascony?"

She could not answer, for Jehan's hand had spread over her abdomen and covered the flat surface. She felt the roughness and heat of his fingers through the thin silk of her surcoat and tunic. He gently rubbed her stomach, and it seemed as though he were stirring confusion and passion within her. She closed her eyes as his lips found a bare spot of skin just inside the edge of her veil, at her temple.

"What we shared in Gascony led to our son's life," he murmured against her hair. "Understand that, *couret,* and let me love you again."

Her body ached for him, perhaps more strongly than before, when she was but an innocent wanting something she knew nothing about. Now she knew the glory of mating with this strong knight—and the memories threatened to shatter her resistance. It was sinful. It was weakness. But it had grown stronger than she, and, just like in Gascony, she knew she would have no will to deny it.

Ah, Laurent, my precious frai. *You would be disappointed in me to know that I have grown no stronger in the past year, that my nature is still weak, perhaps weaker than before. You would want me to resist. I know you would. But, oh, Laurent, such glory! What woman could resist such an inexorable need?*

Jehan's touch grew rougher, his lips sought her earlobe, her cheekbone. He pulled her hard against him. He loosened his grip on the reins, and the stallion followed the horses in front of him without guidance. She gripped Jehan's forearm. She leaned her head back against his shoulder as his lips sought her throat, her jaw, growing hungrier as they neared her own lips and she, instinctively, turned to meet them.

This time he did not hesitate. Their lips met. He groaned and dropped the reins on her lap, then wove his hand beneath her veil in the tumbling length of her hair. She twisted and pressed her upper body against his. She wound her arms around his neck. Suddenly nothing mattered. She didn't care that sixty men-at-arms surrounded them, that they sat upon a huge stallion, that the dying rays of the reddish sun bathed their entwined bodies. Her body's aching stiffness disappeared. She was utterly lost. His kiss deepened, his lips opened, and she moaned as she felt his tongue brush her own lips, then invade her mouth. She felt a tremor shiver through his body—his huge, well-armored, muscular, knight's body. She knew she, too, was trembling in his arms.

"God's wounds! The wedding's in a few weeks, Sir Jehan. Can't you keep your sword sheathed until then?"

She started as she heard Thibaud's great, booming voice coming from her left. Jehan loosened his grip and she pulled away from his kiss. She flushed as she met his blue eyes. Shame overwhelmed her as she realized how quickly she had succumbed to him in the broad light of day. She turned to face Thibaud. His long, embroidered tunic was tucked up into his baldric.

"Is there a reason," Jehan said dryly, "why you interrupted us, Sir Thibaud?"

"If you keep pawing her like that I'll be forced to challenge you."

"In a matter of weeks she'll be my wife."

"*Oui,* and eight months later she'll give birth to another son." He gestured to a keep just outside the walls of Paris. "You were too involved to notice that we're at the Louvre. The Regent is a pious man, and it's not wise to ride into the castle with your hand in his ward's surcoat."

"Thibaud!"

"It's good to see both of you shaken out of your self-made miseries," he continued, relentlessly. "I thought, for a while, that things were so awry they'd never be put to rights."

She couldn't meet Jehan's eyes, though his gaze had not once left her face.

"It'll be good to have another great-great-nephew to bounce on my knee by next Michaelmas—"

"Why aren't you back at the cart, tormenting Blanche?" Aliénor asked sharply.

"She'll have none of me. She thinks I'm too old."

"Any man who has a great-great-nephew shouldn't be riding like you." She glared at her uncle, who, despite her words, had the glow of health of a man half his age. "All this traveling is going to kill you, Thibaud."

"Fie!" he exclaimed. "All this traveling has given me life again! I cannot wait until we all return to Gascony."

"Gascony!" she cried.

"Keeping secrets from her, Sir Jehan?"

"We were involved in an interesting discussion before you interrupted, Thibaud."

"So I noticed." He smiled at her widely from beneath his snowy beard. "After the wedding, Jehan is going to take you back to Gascony."

She looked at Jehan, finally. She saw the desire in his eyes, the promise, the need. This time she did not look away. "Are we really going home?"

"If you wish."

"Yes."

"Then it is done."

Home. Home to the hills and valleys of Astarac, home to the sweetest of new white wines, to the squawking of geese in the fall, to the sweet lyrical sound of *Langue d'oc*. She would show Laurent his birthright, and bring him up within the strong, limestone walls of Castelnau-sur-Arrats. Her heart trilled in anticipation, but she and Jehan could speak no more, for the guard at the watchtower in the Louvre hailed them. Thibaud rode forward to announce their arrival.

Jehan kicked his mount after Thibaud, past the forward guards, so that they would be the first to enter the keep. In a few moments, the portcullis was raised and the stallion clambered over the wooden drawbridge into the square courtyard of the Louvre.

The courtyard was filled with men: knights in mock swordplay, courtiers strolling around in the cool twilight, officious-looking religious men walking firmly in and out of the round keep. Jehan rode the stallion straight to the drawbridge of the inner keep and stiffly dismounted. He looked up at her. She placed her hands on his shoulders as he gripped her narrow waist and set her feet down on the paving stones. Her legs were stiff and she stumbled, but Jehan did not release her as he set her down. His fingers burned into her waist.

"You'll be supping with me tonight."

She lifted a brow. "Is that an order?"

"Yes." He released her when he was sure she was balanced and he gestured to a page to take his mount. "If I can't be in your bed, *couret,* then I'm going to spend every other moment in your presence."

She flushed, for the shame still lingered. She gathered the flowing length of her silk skirts and turned away from him. Her entire body ached and she longed for a bath to wash the dust from her face and hands, she longed to be alone with her thoughts.

"Demoiselle Aliénor de Tournan."

She started at the sound of her name. A man with flaming red-gold hair, lit still brighter by the last rays of the sun, stepped onto the bridge and bowed before her. He was dressed in the tightest tunic she had ever seen—surely, he would have to be skinned out of it before he retired. Its scalloped edge rested high on his thighs, showing the full length of his red and blue hose, which ended in a pair of slippers that extended to a long point. It took her a moment to remember where she had last seen a courtier with such a brilliant mop of hair. When she did, she flushed to the roots of her hair. "Sir Guy!"

"You remember me."

"Of course."

"I certainly remember you, *demoiselle.*" His gaze slid from her veil to the leather slippers peeping out from beneath the folds of her skirts. "Your circumstances have improved."

She glanced over her shoulder and caught Jehan's eye. Jehan frowned when she saw who she was with. "I am here with Sir Jehan—"

"—de St. Simon," Guy finished, bowing as Jehan approached and stood behind her. "It has been several years, Sir Jehan."

"Since before Poitiers," he responded dryly. "After you spent the Christmas feasts with the Prince in Bordeaux, and before you came to Paris to fight with the French."

"How well you remember. I understand you are my rival for the affections of this lady."

"She is my betrothed."

"The Regent has agreed already?" Sir Guy's green eyes narrowed. "How did you manage such an unusual feat in a single day?"

"I asked for the lady's hand," Jehan explained, lifting her fingers possessively to his lips, "and the Regent gave her to me."

"I did the same, and the Regent did not so easily capitulate." Guy stroked his short, forked beard. "Come, come. The lady is a lovely prize, and I will know how I lost her."

"Will you?"

"It's such a disadvantageous decision, to give a French woman and French lands to a man loyal to the English." He opened his arms, and his long, tapering sleeves brushed against the paving stones. "Especially when a Frenchman offers to take her hand."

"The Regent is giving up no French land." Jehan buried his fingers in her curls, under her veil. "The only dowry I want from this marriage is the lady herself."

She couldn't help it: Her heart swelled at Jehan's words.

Sir Guy looked, at first, as if Jehan were jesting, but soon his expression turned to disbelief, then to shock. The silence stretched until he finally regained his composure. "I suppose it's an honorable gesture to wed the maiden that you misused so badly."

"I don't think you'd recognize honor if you saw it, Sir Guy."

"A pity, *demoiselle,* that you must marry a man loyal to the English."

"At least," Jehan said darkly, "she knows to whom I owe my loyalty."

Aliénor held her breath, but Sir Guy made no move to pull the sword that hung from his baldric. He simply shrugged at Jehan's insult and hesitated, looking at her in such a way that she felt like a horse being examined at market. Jehan pulled her close to his side and Guy raised a brow. She wondered what she had seen in Sir Guy so long before, when she met him in that bastide in Pavie. She must have been faint with starvation. He was handsome, she supposed, in a bold, colorful way, with his bright hair, fair skin, and extravagant dress. He had been kind to her, making her feel desirable and lovely when she knew she was as filthy as a commoner. Now, of course, she knew the truth of his character.

"I am surprised," Guy continued, "that the Prince of Wales allowed you to make an unsuitable match, Sir Jehan."

Jehan shrugged. "The Prince will understand my reasons as soon as he receives my message."

"I see." Sir Guy's eyes glittered strangely. "Pray don't misunderstand me, but I've heard he wanted you to travel with him to London last year, and you refused."

"It was an offer, not an order, and the Prince knew my reasons for declining."

"He was insulted by your refusal when he discovered it was because of a woman." His cold green gaze slid over her. "This woman."

Aliénor's eyes widened. She wondered if what Guy was saying was true, or whether it was simply the bitter talk of a jilted suitor. She felt Jehan's hand on her shoulder, hard, reassuring.

"You have been jumping the hedges for so long, Sir Guy, that you no longer know which side you are on." He clutched the hilt of his sword. "Do you wish to contest my claim?"

"Such boldness." Sir Guy raised his empty hands and stepped back, away from Jehan's menacing bulk, away from Jehan's challenge. "You've been battling in wars for so long that you misinterpreted my statement. I simply wanted to reassure your betrothed." He bowed to her. "Fear not for your future, *demoiselle*. If the Prince refuses Sir Jehan permission to wed, I shall be waiting."

Chapter
21

ALIÉNOR WALKED AS CALMLY AS SHE COULD UP THE STAIRS THAT led to the Regent's private chamber. Just after the midday meal, while she played with Laurent in the crowded room assigned to the women in the castle, she had received a message from the Regent that her presence was required in his chambers immediately. She scarcely had enough time to change into a surcoat of cerise silk before Blanche rushed her out of the room. Now, as she worried her hands in the silver chain of her girdle, she wondered if the message had finally come.

A month had passed since the day Jehan asked her to marry him. She had just finished embroidering a deep green surcoat with gold and silver threads, which she intended to wear for the wedding ceremony. The banns had been read three Sundays in a row, and the simple betrothal agreement had been completed. If the Regent had had his way, the wedding itself would already have taken place at the church door, but Jehan insisted on waiting for word from the Prince of Wales.

In the meantime, Jehan had sent her a betrothal gift of a girdle made of beaten gold and precious pearls. He followed it daily with something new: perfumed soap from the heathen lands, bolts of silk in the colors of clear, bright jewels, a silvered hand mirror. Blanche had cried out in awe over each new gift, and Aliénor felt her own tangled emotions twisting into larger knots. She and Jehan had little time alone together in the crowded castle, but whenever they captured a moment, Jehan took advantage of it to touch her hair, to caress her, to kiss her lips. The last time it happened, on the open ramparts under the light of the stars, it was Jehan who found the strength to pull away. Her will had weakened beyond hope. Part of her wanted to throw herself into his embrace and surrender to the heat of his kisses, despite the consequences, while part of her still wanted to run away and hide from the pain.

She reached the top of the stairs. The two guards at the portal of the chamber opened the doors for her, and she joined the crush of men within the Regent's chambers. The Regent, propped up against pillows on the large canopied bed, looked pale and tired as he spoke quietly to one of his advisors. His long, reddish-gold hair lay lank against the dull pillow. The chamberlain saw her, approached, then led her directly to the foot of the Regent's bed. She curtsied.

"Ah, yes. *Demoiselle* de Tournan." The Regent ran a thin, bony hand over a clutter of parchment lying beside him. He chose a thick piece from the pile and lifted it up. "The Prince of Wales wrote to us concerning you."

She took a deep, slow breath.

"The Prince was not pleased that Sir Jehan requested to marry one of my subjects."

"Certainly, *Monseigneur,* that is understandable."

"The Prince had already offered Sir Jehan a wealthy English widow. By making this request, Sir Jehan spurned the Prince's offer." The Regent looked at her over the edge of the parchment. "I'm afraid, *demoiselle,* that Prince Edward has denied Sir Jehan permission to marry you."

She stood, speechless. This was not what she'd expected. After Guy de Baste's hateful words the first day they arrived at the Louvre, Jehan had convinced her that the Prince of Wales wouldn't *dare* deny a simple request to a man who had fought so many battles by his side. Jehan had told her that it was a mere formality, that the Prince of Wales would give permission without a murmur, and they would be married before Michaelmas Day. He argued with her until she had laughed at the silliness of it all, laughed at Sir Guy, the jilted suitor whose bitterness ran so deep that he tried to create discord between a man and his betrothed. Yet here she was, standing before the Regent of France, who held a piece of parchment denying Jehan permission to marry her.

"Your Grace . . ." She struggled to find her wits. "Has Sir Jehan been told the news?"

"The knight received a missive along with ours, just after the midday meal. It was also pressed with the Prince's seal." The Regent searched the crowd until he saw someone. He beckoned for him to approach. She saw a flash of red hair as Sir Guy emerged from the crowd. "You needn't worry. You've received another offer. The Vicomte de Baste will find the news pleasing."

Sir Guy bowed to her.

"I believe the arrangement we began before Sir Jehan offered for the lady will be sufficient," the Regent began, "but for a few items. . . ."

Aliénor stood numbly at the foot of the bed while the Regent discussed the arrangements. She knew she was dismissed, but her feet would not move. Certainly there must be some mistake. Jehan was the father of her child. They had made so many decisions about the future. They planned to live in Castelnau and raise Laurent among Gascons. They intended to build a new windmill on the southern slopes. She was going to struggle against Jehan's seductive power, struggle against loving him, until her last, dying breath.

She realized, as she lifted her gaze to Guy de Baste, that she had long lost the struggle. She was in love with Jehan.

All over again.

What bitter irony. Only now did she realize how much she wanted to be Jehan's wife, only now, as the possibility was snatched away from her. She had smothered her feelings, thinking they were sinful and unnatural, and that they shamed her brother's memory. Jehan was right: They had both long paid the painful debt for Laurent's death. She knew, suddenly, that Laurent would not want her to continue suffering on Earth. She wanted to live again, she wanted to love again, and she wanted to do both in Jehan's arms.

She curled her fingernails into her palms. Jehan could not marry her. He would never defy a command from his liege lord. Why must the whims of princes come between them? The Prince of Wales had no right to keep them apart. They belonged together—she knew that now, now that she stood and watched her fragile dreams shatter, as she listened to the Regent planning her future. The Regent had no right to marry her to a man she hated. Her blood ran cold as she stared at Guy de Baste. She couldn't marry him. He was a corrupt, faithless knight. She would never expose her son to such a man. Then the realization struck her: If she could not marry Jehan, the Regent would take her child away from her and she would never see him again.

You will not take Laurent.

Guy argued, subtly, for more lands in Armagnac, lands that might or might not be claimed by the English king. He slyly suggested that the King of England would yield them after his son so boldly denied Sir Jehan the right to marry her.

I will not marry, you, Guy de Baste, and you will never have those lands.

She forced herself to remain calm as she realized she was standing stiffly, scowling at both the men. A dozen plans flew through her mind: *I will escape this castle. I will take Laurent. I will defy the Regent's commands. Jehan can take me out of Paris in disguise. I shall cut my hair, dress as a friar, follow his contingent like a pilgrim through France to Gascony. The Regent will never know where I am, he will never force me to marry Guy de Baste. He will not take my son.*

Suddenly the doors of the Regent's chamber burst open. Guy stopped in midsentence as Jehan stormed into the room. Jehan held a crumpled piece of parchment in his hand. He strode to the bed. The guards scrambled in after him, but the Regent impatiently waved them away.

"You've received the news, Sir Jehan?"

"Oui."

"Your Prince was not pleased."

"He *denied* me the simplest request." He scanned the room, staring at each knight, each foreign ambassador, each advisor. "In all my years of service to my lord, never once have I questioned his command. I have followed him through his rebel lands, I have fought at his side at Poitiers. Now I am forced to do something that goes against all honor, against my vow of fealty, and I am forced to do it in front of the men who are his enemies." He tossed the parchment on the floor. "This is one command, *Monseigneur,* that I will not follow."

Jehan turned and approached her. He clutched her shoulders. She flattened her hands against his chest and stared up at him, not daring to believe what she saw in his eyes.

"Yes, Aliénor. Whatever the consequences, I will have you as my wife." Then, in front of the court of the Regent of France, Jehan said, "This time, my loyalty is only unto you."

"Blanche, this is supposed to be a time of joy."

Blanche sat on a chair near the fire, sobbing, watching a chambermaid brush Aliénor's hair in preparation for Jehan's arrival in the bridal chamber. "I know, *mon amie.* It's just . . . The wedding reminded me of mine, so many years ago."

"Come, Blanche." Aliénor winced as the chambermaid untangled another knot. "Did your jilted suitor leave in a huff, refusing to witness the nuptials? Did your first child cry loudly in the middle of your first wedding?"

"The babe was just frightened when Sir Jehan kissed you so hard." She lifted a sodden piece of linen to her reddening nose. "The knight looked as if he were going to break you in two."

Aliénor smiled secretly.

"And the feast was without compare," Blanche continued. "The Regent spared no expense. He looked healthier and happier today than he has since he was a boy."

"He should look happy. It's the first victory he's had against the Prince of Wales in years."

"Did you know your great-uncle was crying like a babe in the courtyard?"

"Thibaud?"

"He was too proud to admit it when I caught him." Blanche sighed, and her great bosom heaved heavily beneath the silk of her lavender gown. "The old fool has a heart, after all."

Aliénor glanced for the hundredth time toward the high, oak doors. She shivered in her thin, cream silk shift. The Regent had offered her and Jehan this chamber for their wedding night, and though a fire crackled high in the hearth, the room was cold and drafty. She would not be cold for long. Any moment now, Jehan would walk through the portal with a crowd of courtiers. The men would witness them lying together on the blessed, canopied bed, and then they would depart, leaving her alone with her new husband.

This time, my loyalty is only unto you.

She closed her eyes, remembering the moment her whole life had been changed by the uttering of those few precious words. Jehan had defied his liege lord for her sake. He had kissed both her hands in the presence of the Regent. If a crush of men hadn't surrounded them, she knew he would have pulled her into his arms and kissed her as a man kisses a woman. She wanted him to touch her like that—for suddenly, the whole world was right again.

The Regent had given them no time to celebrate their newly rediscovered joy. He arranged for an immediate ceremony. She scarcely had enough time to pin her hair beneath her veil and change into her wedding attire before Thibaud came to lead her to the steps of the chapel. After the ceremony, Jehan crushed her in his embrace, and she pressed against him, telling him without words that she, too, felt his yearning. But still, they did not have a moment alone. A Mass followed the ceremony, and a feast followed the Mass. Too many people crowded around them, congratulating them, forcing them to dance the Almaine, to drink too many cups of honeyed wine. She had slipped away from the festivities as early as possible to prepare for the evening. She longed to be alone with Jehan, to express all the emotions that filled her heart, to abandon herself to his embrace, without any fear or shame.

Suddenly she heard the distant cries of courtiers.

Blanche sat up. "They're coming."

The chambermaid dropped the brush and scampered through the doorway to the maid's room. Aliénor smoothed her hands over her shift and stood up. The chamber door opened abruptly and Jehan slipped in—alone—slamming the door closed behind him. As soon as he shot the iron bolt into its sleeve, the courtiers surged against the door and tried to push it open. Aliénor met Blanche's gaze. The elderly woman smiled tearfully, then waddled toward the maid's room and shut the door behind her.

"I assume this means there'll be no witnesses to our bedding," she said.

Jehan turned around as the courtiers began singing an obscene song behind the heavy oak doors. He still wore his wedding clothes: the lush blue and green velvet tunic with the heavy gold baldric and fine black hose.

"We need no witnesses, *couret*. We already have a child to prove the consummation." His indigo gaze slid over her, slowly, from the crown of her head to her bare feet, peeping out from beneath the hem of the shift. "Besides . . . I don't want another man to lay eyes on you like this. Especially those drunken louts."

Her heart fluttered erratically in her chest. The voices in the hall slowly faded as the courtiers gave up their efforts to enter the chamber and returned to the feast. Her gaze fell upon a flagon of wine on a chest at the end of the bed. She walked to it and held up a jewel-encrusted chalice. "The Regent sent us wine from a new cask."

"It is not wine I need, Aliénor. I have had enough of that tonight. It is you I need, you I want, you I have waited for, for so very long." He crossed the room. The empty chalice slipped through her fingers and clattered to the floor. He stopped in front of her. "Tell me that you'll come to my bed."

"Willingly, Jehan." She moaned as he crushed her in his arms. Her breasts flattened against the lush pelt of his velvet tunic. "So very willingly."

"Then it is true, what I saw in your eyes this afternoon. You've forgiven me."

"There was never anything to forgive. I love you, Jehan, with all my heart."

"Brèisha!" He squeezed her. "Two years I've waited to hear those words again."

"I pray you don't regret what you've done today," she whispered. "You risked so much by defying the Prince's order."

"The Prince can be appeased, but I will not live without you, *couret*. Never again."

She wrapped her arms around his neck. The tarry scent of smoke from the great hall's rush fires clung to the fibers of his tunic. His mouth descended and captured hers. He tasted like spiced wine. She clung to his shoulders, then ran her fingers over the body that she once loved so intimately and now could not wait to feel again. He kissed her with a desperation that she matched, touch for touch, breath for breath, until she gasped for air. He lifted her in his arms and carried her to the bed. He nudged open the heavy blue velvet drapes embroidered in gold with the royal insignia of the *fleur-de-lis*. He spread her over the scented linens and covered her with his body. Impatiently, he reached for the neckline of the silk shift and shredded it with one strong tug.

"Jehan! That was a gift from Blanche."

"Blanche will understand that it did its duty." He buried his head between her breasts, then nipped his way over her soft, perfumed skin to one tightening peak. She wove her fingers in his thick, unbound hair. His rough hand explored the curves of her body, traced the hollows and indentations of her belly, probed her quivering flesh. He touched her skillfully, remembering the most sensitive places, discovering them anew and capturing her gasps of pleasure with kisses. She reached impatiently for the ties of his tunic. She wanted to feel him naked against her. They had been apart too long, and she had no patience for slow lovemaking. Not now. When he reached between her thighs and felt the inviting heat of her, he groaned, then released her long enough to struggle out of his tunic and hose.

She pulled the remnants of her shift over her shoulders and tossed it from the bed. She watched him, *her husband,* emerge from the trappings of velvet and linen. Her gaze fell upon the shiny white scars that stained the rippled flatness of his abdomen, a reminder of her father's past brutality. She saw a few other scars, new scars, and she wondered what torment he had survived in the past year. Then, as he dropped his shift to the floor and stood naked and glorious in front of her, she opened her arms to him. He loomed over her, grasped her bare hips, and pulled her up to the middle of the bed.

"I've wanted you for so long." His voice sounded husky, strained, as he spoke against her hair, as it always sounded when they were deep in their lovemaking. Gently, he parted her thighs. She wrapped her arms around his neck and pressed herself closer to him. He understood her silent plea and needed no more encouragement. He filled her. He moved in her. It was as if they had never been apart, for their bodies merged and separated in a timeless rhythm. She clung to his neck, crying out his name, as she lost all sense of space and time, and all she could feel was him, Jehan, *her husband,* filling her womb.

Jehan encircled Aliénor's waist and lifted her up into the saddle of her gray mare. In the misty light of dawn, her eyes were as soft and dark as the eyes of a doe, yet without innocence; they were sultry and full of knowledge, full of the memory of the nights they had spent together. As she settled on the saddle, he released her, then spread a thick foxfur over her knees. Deliberately, he tucked the edges in around her hips and thighs.

"You're coddling me like an old woman."

"I'm coddling you like *my* woman, Vicomtesse." He brushed his hand over her abdomen. "Like a woman with child."

"How hopeful you are! It's only been a month. It could take a while."

"We'll continue practicing, then, until we succeed." He reached up and wound his hand in a honey-colored tress of hair that had fallen forward, out of the covering of her veil. His voice lowered to a growl. "If last night is any proof of your eagerness, *brèisha,* I'd wager you'll be with child before Christmas."

"If last night is any proof of your prowess, I'd wager it will be much sooner."

He urged her head down for a kiss.

"The men are watching," she whispered.

"Let them watch." He captured her lips, gently, and tasted the morning's wine on her breath. Her hair smelled of the perfumed olive-oil soap he had given her as a wedding present. "If the royal guards weren't so eager to leave this morning, I would have lingered in bed."

"We are shocking the abbot."

"The abbot has housed newly married couples before."

"Yes," she murmured as he kissed her anew, "but I'm sure they've never made love in this courtyard."

"What an interesting proposition."

"The stones would be much too hard on my back."

"Ah, but not on mine."

"By my troth!" Thibaud's loud voice echoed on the walls of the abbey. "Not a moment passes where you two aren't attached by the flesh! Have some decency, will you? We're still in God's house." He walked to their side, his hands on his hips, his feet encased in metal shoes and clinking against the stones. He looked from his great-niece to Jehan. "We should be long on the road rather than lolling about after Mass in the good abbot's house. At this rate your wife will be birthing her second child somewhere in the fields of Poitiers."

"Easy, Thibaud." Jehan reluctantly released Aliénor. "It is not like you to show so much jealousy."

"Jealousy!" He shook his great, shaggy head. "The Regent is in Paris, beseiged on all sides by Charles of Navarre, while a whole contingent of his forces breaks the fast in an abbey in Poitiers, waiting for you young lovers to stop wagging your tongues so they can finish escorting you and return to their posts."

Jehan laughed, squeezed Aliénor's hand, and walked toward his stallion. Esquivat helped him mount, then handed him the leather reins. Thibaud glowered and turned to his men, dressed in the livery of the Regent of France. The men quickly finished their bread and wine and scrambled onto their horses.

Jehan kicked his mount close to Aliénor's and led her out of the abbey into the streets of Poitiers. With the colors of Tournan mixing with those of the Regent of France, the contingent wound its way through the narrow streets until it reached the city gates. The army passed through and veered south over the level fields. As soon as they reached open ground, Jehan slowed his mount so Aliénor could catch up and ride beside him. In the growing light of dawn, her face was flushed and happy. He still could not believe she was *his*—his wife, his woman, in all ways. The weeks that they had spent together had dispersed all lingering doubts that she would never love as openly as she had loved him before the death of her brother. If anything, Aliénor had grown more passionate with the years. She cleaved to him, body and soul.

They rode over the fields south of Poitiers. Jehan pointed out the valley where the battle had taken place, two years earlier. The previous evening, he had shown her where her father was buried, just outside the city walls, and now she listened raptly as Jehan told her about the battle itself. They talked about Castelnau-sur-Arrats and the coming winter. They talked about their son. They talked about the young Regent and how he had grown and matured in the past years, how he used his intellect, as well as military strength, to settle disputes. When they finished talking, they rode in silence, enjoying the warm rays of the October sun as it rose higher in the sky.

The land they rode through was scarred and uncultivated, littered with the debris of years of war, for this was a border zone between the English and the French holdings. It was contested land, and thus dangerous, even more dangerous than the brigand-infested countryside around Paris. Jehan smelled the distinctive odor of burnt wood on the breeze and sent three men ahead to scout for thieves.

Aliénor rode close beside him as they rounded a small hill and saw the charred, blackened outlines of a burned village. "I can't believe we're already in English land."

"The Prince of Wales captured much of France at the battle of Poitiers."

"I wish the royal guard were staying with us longer," she murmured. "It's such a long trip to Castelnau, and so dangerous."

"If Thibaud brings this French army any deeper into English land he'll be risking a rekindling of the war. He has to leave us by midday. Besides," Jehan added, "he's needed in Paris."

"By more than just the Regent," she said, a smile slipping over her lips. "I wondered why Blanche chose to stay in Paris rather than joining me in Castelnau. All those months in Meaux, and I never suspected. Thibaud and Blanche!" Her smile dimmed. "Castelnau won't be the same without *oncle.*"

"We'll bring Laurent to Paris to visit his godparents, whenever a lack of war and brigandage allow us."

"There'll be blue geese in Gascony first."

"Take heart, *couret.* The truce between the English and French ends on St. John's Day next year. Maybe then the brigands will find employ in an army and leave the roads safe for travelers."

Her dusky lashes swept over her cheeks. "And if war

382

begins again, Jehan, between my king and yours? Will the Prince ask you to come and fight by his side?"

"Probably."

"You'll fight with him?"

"He's my liege lord, Aliénor, despite my recent defiance. I'm bound to him still. I'll have to make amends soon for marrying you, a sin that I would commit over and over again."

"You'll have to leave me."

"Never, my love." He pulled his mount to a stop and leaned over to cup her cheek. "I may have to tend to my duties, but I will always come back."

Jehan kissed her, despite the laughter that erupted around them, despite Thibaud's bawdy comments. He slipped his other hand beneath her fur-lined mantle, to the warmth of her strong, young body. Their horses bumped against one another. His blood surged with need, with a need that was never satisfied, and he wondered if he could last until nightfall.

She laughed and struggled out of his grip. "You tease me, my husband. It will be hours before we can be alone."

"I should have heeded the Regent's request and stayed in Paris." He readjusted his seat on the hard steel saddle. "Instead, I chose to start a journey that could take months, and suffer through the rare few evenings we have in the cramped, crowded quarters of abbeys. I could have had feather-filled mattresses and thick, warm pelts, and afternoons lying in the furs, with you beneath me."

She glanced around the open fields. "There's not even a tree in sight, much less a forest we could ride into."

"Conjure one up, then, and let's ride away."

Suddenly Jehan heard a cry coming from the front riders. He saw one of his scouts riding hard toward them over the ridge of the next hill. Jehan kicked his stallion forward. He, Thibaud, and the scout met not far from the front of the contingent.

"What is it?" Jehan asked.

"There's an army ahead."

"Brigands?"

"No, my lord. It's an English army. Flying under banners." The scout tried to catch his breath. Thibaud handed him a wineskin and he lifted it to his lips. The golden liquid spilled over his cheeks and stained the front of his tunic. "The standard I saw . . . It didn't seem possible, but it was the Prince of Wales's standard."

"The Prince is in London," Jehan retorted.

"They're his colors, my lord. The banner is quartered with the arms of France and England, with the white bar for an older son."

Thibaud looked at Jehan. "Would the Prince send a contingent to greet you at the border of English lands?"

"There hasn't been enough time," Jehan said. "The Prince doesn't know about the wedding, or my decision to return to Gascony. It must be a trap. Those men must be English brigands." He kicked his stallion into a canter and rode toward a hill. When he reached the height, he saw the glimmer of armor and shields in the distance. It was a large army, nearly as large as his own. He squinted, trying to distinguish the colors of the heraldry, both on the pennons and on the tunics of the knights. The messenger was right: The colors they flew were the colors of the Prince of Wales. Something was wrong; he felt it in his bones. Thibaud rode up beside him. "Send a man," Jehan ordered. "One of my Gascons, not a Frenchman. Send him to greet this army and see what they want."

Thibaud rode down the slope to do his bidding. Jehan scanned the terrain. He now stood on the highest ground in the area, and nothing blocked retreat, though he had no intention of retreating. If those men were brigands, then he intended to fight. He whirled his horse around and galloped back to the body of his army to discuss strategy with his men. A few minutes later he returned to the top of the ridge. The Englishmen waited in the valley, in formation. Something struck him about the front rider of the opposing army: The silver and blue heraldry on his tunic was vaguely familiar. Suddenly, Jehan remembered. He knew then, beyond doubt, that there would be a battle.

His messenger rode to the top of the hill. "My lord!"

"What does he want?"

"The leader is the Vicomte de Baste, my lord. He says that he was sent by order of the Prince of Wales to fight against you, whom he calls a traitor to the English king."

Jehan heard a gasp. He turned around and saw Aliénor as she reined her mare to a halt. "I feared Sir Guy would do something like this," she said breathlessly. "He left Paris so abruptly after you agreed to marry me."

"He fights falsely under the Prince's banner." Jehan glared at the army. "He hopes I'll capitulate without a fight. But I know there hasn't been time for Edward to give him permission to ride under his colors, and the Prince would never respond so aggressively to my defiance."

"But my lord, the Prince *has* given Sir Guy permission." From a pouch slung around his hips, the messenger took out a faded piece of parchment. "Sir Guy gave me this to support his claim."

Jehan took the parchment and called for his chaplain. He handed it to the man. "Read it to me."

"The letter is dated St. Stephen's Day, my lord. It says that in the event Sir Jehan de St. Simon, Vicomte de Tournan, marries the French wh——" The chaplain hesitated, glanced at Aliénor, and then continued: "If Sir Jehan marries the French woman, then Sir Guy, the Vicomte de Baste and newly made vassal of King Edward III, hereby has permission to raise an army against the traitorous vassal, and if Sir Guy succeeds in defeating the knight, he shall receive all the lands and titles now in the knight's possession." The chaplain looked at Sir Jehan. "It is signed Edward, Prince of Wales."

Jehan's hands tightened over the steel saddlebow. He had risked his life a hundred, a thousand times, at Crécy, in Gascony, at Poitiers, at a dozen skirmishes in between, all for the sake of the Prince. He had never asked for a single coin from the Prince, he had never taken anything that

Edward did not willingly give. He had submitted to the Prince's every command, willingly put his own body in danger for the glory of King Edward III. He had bowed his head and sworn everlasting loyalty to him; yet for a single transgression the Prince had turned on him and showed, truly, the lion of England.

"So that's the way of it." He felt Aliénor's hand on his arm. "My own liege lord has raised arms against me because I married against his will." Jehan looked at her. "He must have suspected I would marry you, my love. The letter to Guy is dated the same day as the letter he sent me, the one I received the day we married. Edward prepared for all circumstances."

"Could it be forged?" she asked. "Certainly the Prince wouldn't raise arms against you."

"It's real. It's written by the Prince himself—not a scribe—and though I can't read it, his scribble is familiar."

"What kind of man is your lord," Thibaud asked, "to fight against a faithful vassal for such a reason?"

Jehan didn't answer, but he wondered himself. He found himself wondering about many things.

"Whatever you choose," Thibaud continued, "my men will fight by your side. Those men are English swine, on contested land." His black eyes narrowed. "And Sir Guy's loyalties shift like mercury across an apothecary's table."

"Jehan, you can't fight against the Prince." Aliénor's voice was soft and full of dread. "You're bound by your oath. You defied him by marrying me, but if you raise arms against him . . . that's *treason.*"

He gestured to the enemy with a toss of his head. "They have already called me a traitor. My oath of fealty to the Prince of Wales means nothing now. I am bound by a stronger oath, *couret.* By the oath I spoke four weeks ago, at the portal of Notre Dame."

"Jehan . . ."

"Do you think I've battled with guilt and honor all these years to have you for a few weeks, and then give you up?" He covered her hand with his own. "I'll never give you up, *brèisha.* Not for anything, and certainly not for the whim of a prince."

Tears filled and clouded her golden eyes.

"Fear not, *couret.*" He squeezed her hand. "Sir Guy is not known for his prowess: I watched him flee from the field at Poitiers. This will all be over before the sun rises to its zenith."

"I love you, Jehan."

He smiled, slowly. "I can think of no sweeter words to hear before going into battle." He leaned over and kissed her. "Go now, my love. Take care of our son. Tell him that victory is ours."

Epilogue

St. John's Day, 1360

ALIÉNOR LIFTED HER FACE TO THE HEAT OF THE SUN. THE LIMPID air whirled heavily around her, like a hot, dry blanket, rich with the scent of drying vegetation and dusty earth. Over the ramparts of Castelnau-sur-Arrats she saw the silent blades of the windmill and the drooping leaves of the oaks that formed the beginning of the forest. A drop of perspiration formed on her throat, then slipped slowly down, below the oval neckline of her tawny surcoat, to trail between her breasts. On any other day, she would have left the courtyard and its hot paving stones for the coolness of the castle. But today was different.

Today, Jehan was returning home.

The babe in her arms moved. She glanced down at the face of her eleven-month-old daughter as the child's vivid blue eyes opened wide. A few wispy locks of pale hair, the color of moonlight, peeped out of the linen swaddling. When Jehan had last seen his daughter, Marguerite, she had been nothing but a small, red-faced, squalling little babe. How proud he will be, Aliénor thought, to see her now, so quiet, so serene, so breathtakingly perfect.

Nine months. It had been nine months since Jehan left Castelnau. When the Regent rejected the terms for peace last year, choosing to go to war rather than capitulate to the crushing English demands, she knew the Regent would summon her husband to fight by his side. He wanted to test Jehan's new vow of fealty to the French, for Jehan had repudiated his vow of homage to the English after defeating Sir Guy outside of Poitiers. Though she rejoiced that she and Jehan now shared the same loyalties, she realized that the Regent, just like the Prince of Wales before him, could summon her husband away at will. It was Jehan's duty to go, but he also had a more personal reason for riding off to fight: Among the lands King Edward III demanded in order to keep the peace were those of the viscounty of Tournan.

Now Jehan was back. Aliénor saw the first flutter of the standards of Tournan rise above the edge of the ridge. The horses appeared to shimmer in the hot air as the contingent surmounted the slope. She spotted Jehan in the center of the crowd. He carried his basinet against his side. The sun gleamed off his black hair and off the smooth surfaces of his armor. The villagers surged around him, nearly dancing in the summer heat. He accepted a bouquet of wildflowers from a peasant's hands and then showered the blossoms over the gathered crowd.

He looked happy, triumphant, and so very, very vibrant. Aliénor closed her eyes and said a brief prayer of thanks for his safe return. He kicked his stallion into a brisk stride as he broke free of the crowds near the portal and cantered over the drawbridge. He emerged in the bright sunshine of the courtyard and reined his horse to a stop as he saw her. Absently, he handed his basinet to the stableboy who ran to take the reins of his horse, then swung his leg over the stallion, slipped down to the ground, and strode to her side. The dust of the ride stained his tunic. Sweat gleamed off his forehead and slipped in rivulets down his throat. He looked at her. His gaze was as palpable and powerful as a physical caress.

"Welcome home, Jehan."

"Couret . . . You are well?"

"Yes." She shifted Marguerite into one arm and grasped his hand. "I'm well, now that you're back."

His warm, callused fingers curled over her hand. "I worried about you. I didn't know what to expect when I rode through the valley."

"There was no trouble. The brigands disappeared at the first rumors of war."

"Faith, I hated leaving you here, alone in this castle but for a dozen knights—"

"Two dozen, my love. More than enough to guard the castle. *You* were the one who went off to war, you were the one in danger." She squeezed his hand. "Did all go well, in Paris?"

"Castelnau is safe—it's ours. The war is over, for now." He looked down at the moving bundle in her arms. "Marguerite?"

"Yes." She pulled her hand from Jehan's grasp and adjusted the linens around the babe's face so he could see her better.

"She has your hair."

"A head full of it. We've named her well. She has *Maman's* coloring."

"She has *your* coloring."

"*Maman* might disagree. She's coming here for the Michaelmas feast. She has improved since last year, when we visited her at the abbey." She felt a tug on her skirts. She looked down at her son's dark head.

Laurent pointed at Jehan. *"Qu'ey paire?"*

"Yes, this is your father, Laurent." Laurent put a mud-smeared finger deep in his mouth. He looked up, up, at the great height of his father, then his gaze wandered to Jehan's sword, which gleamed in the light of the midday sun. He pulled the finger out of his mouth and greedily reached for the weapon. Before Laurent could touch the sharp edge, Jehan bent down and lifted him high in the air. The boy cried out in glee.

"My son!" He tossed him higher, then caught him. "Except for his eyes, he looks more and more like his namesake."

"He might resemble my brother, but he certainly doesn't have his disposition. I found him teetering on the edge of the ramparts a few weeks ago, laughing all the while. And twice this week, I've had to pull him out of the kennels, where he rides the mastiffs as if they were horses."

"We'll have to get him a horse of his own. He's nearly big enough—he's twice as big as when I saw him last."

"It has been a long time."

Jehan's gaze strayed to her abdomen. "Have you nothing else to show me, *couret?* I thought, after the decadent week we spent in bed before my departure, that there might be another child."

"Greedy." She flushed. "You left too soon after the birth of Marguerite."

"I never once let the Regent forget that he summoned me away from my bride of less than a year." He balanced Laurent on his shoulders. "Both he and Thibaud were amused that a man who spent a lifetime at war suddenly wanted nothing but peace."

"How is Thibaud?"

"Married."

"Married?"

"He wanted Blanche to be his mistress, and she refused. I told him to stop being a fool, learn from my experiences, and marry the woman. So he did."

Aliénor laughed. She heard someone call for wine and realized she was neglecting her duties as *châtelaine.* "Come, you must be hungry and dry with thirst. I've ordered a feast prepared for you and your men."

"I'm already feasting, my love. I've been starved nine long months for the sight of you."

"Jehan . . ." She leaned her forehead against his chest, the closest she could come to an embrace, for she didn't want to crush Marguerite against Jehan's armor. He slipped his rough hand beneath her veil and lifted her hair from her nape as he kissed the top of her head. He smelled of heat and dust and sweat. The clatter of armor and harnesses, the snorting of tired horses, and the banter of victorious knights filled the courtyard. They were comforting sounds, the sounds of homecoming.

He tilted her head up and kissed her, lightly, on the lips. Then he draped an arm around her shoulders and turned her toward the castle. They ascended the stairs together, with Marguerite in her arms and Laurent bouncing gleefully on Jehan's shoulders. They entered the coolness of the great hall. Aliénor blinked to adjust her eyes to the dimness. The trestle-tables were laid with pristine white cloth and glittered with silver platters and gold chalices, as she had ordered. The servants waiting by the buttery curtsied as they entered. The wetnurse came to her side. Aliénor kissed Marguerite on the forehead and then settled her daughter in the woman's arms.

Laurent squirmed on his father's shoulders. Jehan lifted him off and set him down. The boy dashed to the laden trestle-tables. Jehan took Aliénor's hand and walked to the hearth. He sat heavily in the chair. For the first time, Aliénor noticed the bluish circles beneath his eyes, the weary lines of his face. She knelt at his feet and began unbuckling the separate pieces of his armor.

"Leave that for Esquivat, *couret.*"

"If Esquivat has ridden as hard as you, Jehan, then the boy will need his rest."

"We rode through the night."

She started as she pulled off one of the metal plates on his knees. "That was dangerous, my love."

"I didn't want to spend a night in an abbey when I knew you were less than a day's ride away."

"That was a foolish—and wonderful—thing to do." She unbuckled the leather straps on his metal shoes. "Tell me about Paris."

"There is little to tell."

"Was there a battle?"

"Not one, not during my entire stay."

"How could that be? We heard rumors about King Edward raiding through Burgundy."

"He raided all through France, from October to April, but the Regent never rode out to meet him. And when Edward attacked Paris in April, the Regent simply closed the gates and waited."

"All those months . . ." She tossed the metal shoe aside. "If you knew how much I worried."

"We all wanted to fight. I more than the others: I wanted to fight and get the battle over with, then return home. But the Regent insisted we stay within the walls of Paris. He was right, I suppose. Edward capitulated in the spring. Just before I left, he signed a peace treaty."

"I've never known peace." She tucked a blond tress behind her ear. "I wonder what it will be like."

"It won't last. Edward insisted on three million gold *écus* as ransom for King Jean."

"Diou de jou!"

"There is more. The Regent was forced to capitulate Calais, all of Guyenne, and many towns, bastides, and castles between here and the Loire. Even the Comte d'Armagnac must pay homage to the English king."

"But Castelnau is safe?"

"These are our lands—French lands—and will stay that way. For us, and for our children." He glanced at Laurent, who had climbed upon a trestle-table and now was racing down its length, tipping over goblets, giggling, running from the servants who tried to drag him off. Aliénor shook her head but made no effort to help the servants, for Jehan seemed to enjoy watching his frolicking son. She removed the last of the armored plates, laid them aside, then rose to her feet. He clutched her arm as she turned toward the tables. "Where are you going?"

"To bring you dinner."

"Stop being my servant, *couret*. Come here and be my wife."

He pulled her closer. She smiled and climbed shamelessly upon his lap. He wound an arm around her back and another around the crook of her knees, drawing her close into his body. She pressed her cheek against his shoulder. He nuzzled her hair, pushing aside the edge of the veil, then kissed her forehead. She sighed, squeezed her eyes shut, and wrapped her arms around his neck. She hugged him tightly. "I missed you so, Jehan."

"I missed you, too, *couret.*"

He kissed her. It was not the kiss of a weary man. His arms tightened around her knees. Suddenly she didn't care that his men were filling the great hall. She didn't care that the dust of his clothing stained her surcoat, that the bristles on his cheek scraped her skin raw. All she cared about was the sharp, longed-for pressure of his lips on her own.

When he finally released her, he drew away only far enough for her to see his half-lidded eyes, eyes full of promise.

"Tell me you won't leave again, Jehan, no matter what happens to the peace."

"Very well. The next time the Regent summons me, I shall break my vow of fealty."

"No . . . no." She sighed. "You mustn't do that. We're running out of kings. But . . . at least don't leave until I've got another child crawling in the rushes, and a fourth, firm in my belly."

His lips spread in a slow, lazy smile. "I can think of no promise that I would rather keep."